MW01244419

IN THE SHADOW OF DANTE

A NOVEL BY

JEROME KOMISAR

IN THE SHADOW OF DANTE
a novel by Jerome Komisar

First Edition, December 2014

Copyright © 2014 by Jerome Komisar

Author Services by Pedernales Publishing LLC
www.pedernalespublishing.com

All rights reserved, including the right to reproduce this book or portions
thereof in any form whatsoever. For information contact:

    Hillel-Tzeporah Press
    Washington, D.C.
    hiltzepress@gmail.com

This book is a work of fiction. Names, characters, places and incidents are
either products of the author's imagination or are used fictitiously. Any
resemblance to actual events, locales or persons, living or dead, is entirely
coincidental.

Library of Congress Control Number: 2014918748

ISBN: 978-0-9858584-2-1

For My Grandchildren
Nicholas Levine, Gabriel Komisar, Miranda Gindling
Noah Levine, Amelia Komisar-Bury, Ryley Komisar-Bury
My Muses

IN THE SHADOW
OF DANTE

CHAPTER ONE

"YOU HAVE TO ADMIT it's more than a little nutty," my mother called from the kitchen. "You got a weirdo who masquerades as Dante, a mysterious multi-millionaire who wants to make your faux-Dante a celebrity artist, and a co-author you've never met with a peculiar first name. What was it, again?"

"Magritt; her name is Magritt." I spelled it out for my mother and bid her imagine an irritated toddler calling to his mother, then gritting his teeth—Mah'grit.

"The whole thing is strange, Larry, not just her name," my mother said as she entered the dining room, her patterned bathrobe tied tightly around her narrow waist, its blend of blue and red and honey adding vibrancy to her light skin, her silver hair, the tender-blue of her eyes. "What I don't understand is why in the world you would want to do it. You should go back to writing plays; you should consider doing more acting."

"It's fifty thousand dollars. Isn't that enough of a reason?"

"Are you going hungry? Are you tired of my cooking? Does the roof over your head leak?"

I had to chuckle. My mother was living in a two-bedroom, two-bath apartment in midtown Manhattan at the time, on one of the higher stories but far from the roof, a location and style of condominium for which people kill. And she didn't cook, at least not anymore. We ate takeout from Angels, or Gorgeous Market, or Hale and Hearty Soups.

"What about Paul? I have put a damper on his lifestyle. I don't understand why he doesn't sleep over. I am an understanding adult," I said earnestly.

"What can I say? He's old-fashioned. But he doesn't seem to mind your living here. He likes you."

"You mean he doesn't complain. I'm sure he minds."

My mother, Janet Sullivan, pulled out a dining room chair and sat next to me, her expression more pensive than sad, her small mouth closed, her eyes brightened by the light from the chandelier.

I continued talking. "Really, Mom, don't you think it's time for me to move out? It's going on four months now. You have to be getting tired of having me underfoot."

"Maybe you're tired of being here? Is that the problem? You've had enough of your mother?"

"If you don't watch out, I'll never move out."

I expected her to laugh, but she didn't. Her expression turned stern. The actress was coming out. "No mother would ever take that as a threat."

"Many would," I said, smiling warmly.

My mother held firm. "Well, I am not one of them," she answered and abruptly got up from her chair and walked toward the kitchen.

"But I'm not moving out, Mom," I said to her back. "I'll only be spending a week or two at Gettysburg now and then. I'll still be your tenant."

I followed her into the bedroom, and watched her swing

a large bathroom towel over her shoulders and tie two ends under her chin. She sat before the mirrors of her antique makeup vanity, the only piece of furniture in the apartment that I remembered from my childhood. As always in my memory, its walnut wood was covered with a miraculous assortment of cosmetics, and containers of brushes, and sponges, and cotton balls. We were living with her mother then, my grandmother, in a small apartment in Greenwich Village, its bathroom far too small for a budding actor, its only bedroom just large enough for two narrow beds, a four-drawer bureau, and the vanity. How many times had I sat beside her, bewitched by the transformational ritual, fascinated by the cleansing cream, the fragrant powder, the tiny eye shadow brush, the round disks of lip gloss? "Tell me a story," my mother would sweetly request, while she cleaned her skin with a white cream, "about a handsome young boy who gets caught in a thunderstorm on his way to school." Or, "Tell me a story about an intelligent young boy whose mother loves him dearly."

Janet coated her fingers with a tinted cream. "So the foundation will be paying you," she said as she coated her forehead with the emulsion.

"The Truth Foundation. It seems to be well endowed. It occupies a magnificent East Side mansion, with thick carpets, attractive secretaries, and a brass plaque on the door that reads 'Truth Foundation: We Seek the Real.' Rather pretentious, I know. Harland Van Ness, its Executive Director, offered me the job. All they expect is a small volume about the artist and his paintings."

"What do you know about painting?"

"That's why I have a coauthor. She's a PhD candidate in art history."

"Why can't she do it by herself?"

"They want a writer, that's why."

"Well, you *are* a good writer, but a playwright," she said crisply.

"I haven't written a script for three years. I don't know if I can still consider myself a playwright."

"Of course you are. You were busy, taking that role in *Celestial City*. You expect too much of yourself."

"And *Celestial* wasn't a triumph, not the writing or the acting."

"Poppycock. You're just fishing for a compliment. It was a great play, and you did a fine job. It's the Broadway producers; they don't have the taste they used to. You'll see. Your next play will run for three years, and in the biggest house in town."

Janet Sullivan enjoyed nothing more than celebrating me. Even a leading role in summer stock or a week with Paul on the Riviera came in a far second. When she realized I was as tall as she was, five feet six, she borrowed money from my grandmother and took me to London. When I hit six feet, now with money of her own, we celebrated in Paris; at six feet one we went to Vienna; at six two we toured Rome, Florence, and Venice. When I topped out at six three, she finagled a way for me to join a touring company she was in that was performing Chekov—in English—at the Bolshoi Theater in Moscow and Pushkin's Theater in St. Petersburg. "Let them see what a budding American playwright looks like," she told me.

But once your voice has changed and you need to shave, a maternal muse is not enough; at least it wasn't for me. I needed someone who could keep me warm at night, who lived for the touch of my hand, who cried when I was sad, and who laughed when I was filled with joy. Someone I could walk down the street with hand in hand.

"It will be good for me to get back to writing—any kind of writing," I said.

"Maybe" was as far as my mother would go. She threw away the cotton ball and picked up another. "Harland Van Ness; it's a familiar name but I can't place it."

"A name like that would be hard to forget."

My mother shrugged her shoulders. "And the artist's name?"

"Elias Miller. All of his paintings were inspired by *The Divine Comedy*. He signs them 'Dante the Painter.'"

"Need I say more?" Janet sniped. She caught me looking at her reflection in the large center mirror and gave me a wry smile.

I hadn't lived with my mother since I was seventeen, ever since I finished high school and moved into a college dorm. Even our summers were spent apart, both of us working in summer stock, but for different companies and usually in different states. She worked as an actor, I as an intern first, and then as an assistant stage manager, and finally acting in supporting roles. Over the years, her stunning prettiness had evolved into a mature sensuality, and her body had grown more graceful, her muscles more defined, her hips more feminine. It didn't just happen. She worked on her figure just as she worked at perfecting her makeup. Morning jogs six days a week, weight lifting on Tuesday and Thursday, a class in modern dance Saturday mornings, and yoga in the privacy of her bedroom every morning. Her acting career demanded it, she would tell me, and perhaps being on a television soap opera did. But I had grown to suspect that the continuing demands she placed on herself to look magnificent were because of Paul and not work. Not that he would disappear if she gained a few pounds or if she allowed her wrinkles to be more obvious. The opposite was true. Being attractive was a gift my mother gave to Paul because she knew that nothing as superficial as her looks would cause him to stop loving her.

"Do you like Harland Van Ness?" she asked.

"He's interesting, but I don't think him likable. You know the type: a sixty-year-old man who looks as if he were born in an Armani suit and a school tie. His accent is Harvard Yard, his cufflinks solid gold. But it was an interesting meeting. He was persuasive.

EARLIER THAT AFTERNOON, I had met with Harland Van Ness in the offices of the Truth Foundation. "It's not a very complicated task," he had told me, "just a short biography of the artist, some comments about *The Divine Comedy* and its place in world literature, and a discussion of fifteen or so paintings. Dante the Painter is a retired professor of philosophy and religion named Elias Miller. He once taught at a small college in Pennsylvania. He's half mystic, half genius, half nut, and half artist. I know that adds up to two. He comes with a wife he calls Beatrice. None of Miller's canvases have reached the open market, but over the last decade a few knowledgeable collectors have acquired his oils. You can find them hanging in Fifth Avenue apartments and summer homes in the Hamptons. A small number have made it over the Atlantic.

"Mrs. Madeline Brewster, a former board member of the Truth Foundation, was his sole backer and his friend. A very generous woman. She didn't keep all of his work for herself, but gave some fine Millers to friends and relatives. After her death, the remaining collection was divided among her husband and her children.

"A member of the board, who wishes to remain anonymous—I call him Patron—wants to honor Madeline Brewster by producing a book about the artist. At least that's the cover story. I think Patron half believes in Dante's description of Heaven and Hell and thinks he can avoid the latter by promoting religious art. That's supposition, I know, but I think I am right. What I am certain of is that Patron is enthralled with *The Divine Comedy's* poetic beauty and philosophical brilliance. He acknowledges that people read little but look more, that we are fixated on the visual. So Patron wants to return to the way biblical tales were told when few were literate—through paintings, a select number of Professor Dante's paintings presented in a book, and later, with popularity assured, a larger volume containing all his work."

Harland leaned forward, his head and upper body towering over his large mahogany desk, his eyes holding fast to mine. "Any interest?" he asked.

"I'm a playwright, not a poet, and all I know of Dante is what I learned in a freshman course in Western Lit. The lecturer must have spent ten minutes on *The Divine Comedy*."

"You exaggerate."

"Not by much. It could have been only three minutes."

Harland gave me a "you-know-that's-not-what-I-mean" look and leaned back in his chair. "Your patron saw your last Off-Broadway play—what was it called?"

"*Celestial City*, but it's about a whorehouse named Celestial City. I wasn't competing with Dante's Paradise."

"Your patron knows that, but he was taken by your willingness to engage people's spiritual feelings, and he liked your use of language. He believes you can write—perhaps not a medieval poem, but modern prose with an edge. You would be working with two other people: the painter, of course, who will tell you his story; and an art historian, Magritt Cline. She's your patron's selection, a doctoral student who has published very little, but has great promise. You'll be working at the Millers' place near Gettysburg. Magritt's boyfriend will be staying with her, at least some of the time, and Elias' wife, of course."

"If it were Florence or Rome, maybe my girlfriend might come along," I lied. My girlfriend, Hilla, had thrown me out four months before, a week or so before the New Year.

"Professor Miller wanted to remain in his rural setting, a tranquil place where the three of you could work undisturbed. And Gettysburg . . . can you think of a better place to think about Heaven and Hell?"

"And Professor Miller taught in Pennsylvania," I pointedly tossed in.

"The college he taught at is not far from Gettysburg and he makes his home nearby," Harland said. His tenor voice filled with unexpected enthusiasm. He, too, is an actor, I thought. "It's a very pleasant property, I hear, with two houses and a small lake. You and Magritt will use the guesthouse. Miller's studio is in the larger building where he and Beatrice live."

MY MOTHER THREW AWAY another cotton ball and began to apply a liquid moisturizer with her fingers. "What does Hilla think of the job?" she asked while looking at her reflection in a magnifying mirror.

"I haven't spoken to Hilla in a couple of weeks. I don't think she would be interested."

"You never know."

"I do know. You just won't accept it. Hilla has had enough of me. That's all there is to it."

"You were so close." My mother's voice moved to the back of her mouth whenever she spoke of Hilla, as if the name demanded a hum.

Hilla and I had lived together for five years. I was twenty-four when I moved in; Hilla was thirty-two. They were good years in the main, years in which three of my plays were produced Off Broadway. One of them even made money. They were good years for Hilla, too. Her jewelry designs attracted critical attention, and her gold and silver earrings and necklaces were displayed in the windows of upscale shops on Madison Avenue, in SoHo, and TriBeCa. The growing demand forced her to hire a few young artisans and establish a small studio a dozen blocks from the Riverside Drive apartment where we were living. Between us, there was more than enough money to maintain the duplex apartment she had moved into when she married, and which she took ownership of when her husband moved on to a third wife.

I had expected more from *Celestial City*—a move to Broadway or a movie deal or a cable television special. It ran for two years, longer than any of my previous works, but I was the only one who cried when it closed. The cast only took a deep breath. No out-of-town company showed an interest; no producer was ready for a road company. I showed my disappointment in the way men do, by taking it out on the people closest to me, by withdrawing into silence, by writing in the daytime and ripping up my work at night.

I tenderly touched my mother's long, thin neck. "You look more beautiful than ever," I said, to shift the subject. "Where are you and Paul going tonight?"

She said something about dinner and the theater, but I only half listened. She had planted Hilla in my mind, and I began to wonder what my former lover would think of my writing a book about art. Not much, I concluded.

"You two were so close," my mother repeated minutes later. "I can't understand what happened."

"She threw me out. Isn't that enough?"

"No, that's not enough, not after five years. And you claim you weren't fooling around."

"Mother, I wasn't fooling around and neither was she. It wasn't that simple. And I don't think fooling around alone would have broken us apart."

"Then explain it to me. Don't you think I can understand?"

We had been over this before, countless times, but nothing I came up with ever satisfied my mother. She could not believe that a sane person would simply stop loving her only child. He was too perfect, too handsome, too decent, and too tall. Some recognizable reason was needed, a momentary failure, an unfortunate flirtation, a temporary addiction. "One of you must have done something wrong," she had insisted early on. I could offer no concrete reason. Hilla had tired of me.

"Hilla is very beautiful. Not in a flashy way, but in a way that lasts," my mother said.

"I know," I answered.

"And nice."

"Very nice."

My mother put the final touches to her eye shadow and then carefully adorned her mouth with pink lipstick and a touch of lip gloss. She looked at herself admiringly, smiled broadly to make certain there was no color on her teeth, and removed the towel from her shoulders.

"I'm being a nudge, aren't I?" she said as she got up from the chair and turned toward me.

"Just a little."

She laughed as she made her way to the walk-in closet. When she came out, she was wearing a thin, black silk dress and matching high-heeled shoes.

"You look as beautiful as a bride," I told her.

"In black?"

"Even in black," I said.

She poured Paul a drink when he arrived to pick her up, and when they prepared to go, she turned her cheek to me. I kissed it lightly.

"Paul doesn't think your writing about art is a crazy idea, but he is not always right," she said.

CHAPTER TWO

Two months later my mother helped me pack for my first trip to Gettysburg, looking at once sad and expectant, happy to get me out of her flat but knowing that the place would feel empty once I had left. She was smiling when we took the elevator to the basement garage; she laughed when she pushed the keys to her Mercedes into my hand. "I hope the food is good," she whispered when I kissed her on the cheek.

Professor Miller had suggested that the first week we spent together be short, so I left on a Wednesday, about 11:00 a.m., a good time to avoid the worst of Manhattan's traffic, I thought. How little I had learned. New York has no easy daytime hour and the drive from my mother's apartment through the Holland tunnel felt eternal. I stuck to major highways, interstates like 78 and 83, for as long as possible, driving fifteen miles above the speed limit and being tempted to go faster. Eventually, I ran out of limited access roads and had to take speed limits more seriously.

Harland's directions had me take a right off Route 15 and onto Gilbert's Pass, a two-lane macadam road that ran by aging gas stations, single-story motels, and used car lots. Three miles later, I made a left turn onto Miller Lane, a pockmarked dirt path just wide enough for a single car.

Fully leafed trees—sycamores, honey locusts, and white oaks—arched over the lane, forming a meandering tunnel of silhouetted shapes and shadows. A couple of deer raised their heads as the car went by. At the top of a knoll, the forest abruptly ended, and I found myself looking over the Millers' compound, two slate-roofed nineteenth century farmhouses. Attached to the larger house was what I assumed was an artist's studio, its roof more glass than stone. Directly in front of the buildings was a long lake, its blue surface shimmering in the afternoon light.

A man in his late sixties waved me to the back of the larger house and signaled that I park.

"A Mercedes," Elias Miller said as he stood before my parked car. He rubbed his full gray beard with his hand and smiled broadly. "I should have expected it."

"It's a very small Mercedes; city-sized."

"There are smaller ones in Europe," he said, still rubbing his beard. "Much smaller," he added, sounding a bit judgmental. "Did the Truth Foundation rent it for you?"

"It's my mother's car. She let me use it."

"Now that's rich," he said, and burst out laughing.

I didn't think anything funny had been said. "I'm Larry Sullivan. I'm sure Harland has told you about me. And you must be Dante Alighieri."

"Elias Miller. My students sometimes called me Dante, although rarely to my face, but never Dante Alighieri. That would have been far too long. I sometimes use Dante as a nickname. Pretentious, I know, but it allows me to speak in an Italian accent that took years to develop. Can I help you with your luggage?"

I used the electronic signal to open the trunk and Dante reached in and grabbed my suitcase, his faded striped overalls looking a size too big, his blue shirt's collar unbuttoned.

"No laptop?" he asked.

"I use a fountain pen."

"I like you already," he said, and walked toward the smaller house.

"Has Magritt Cline arrived?"

"No, but she phoned from the road to ask directions. She was just a short distance away, but suggested that if you arrived before she did, we wait for her before settling on your living accommodations."

I gave out a pregnant, "Oh."

"Two men and one woman working together—she just wanted to set the scale early on," he yelled over his shoulder and then laughed at his own observation.

Before I could think of a comment, a beaten-up Ford station wagon roared off the dirt road and parked next to my Mercedes. The car's rear compartment was stuffed with boxes of books and two suitcases. Magritt rolled down the window and poked her head out. "I could use some help," she declared in a deep voice, the words speeding out of her mouth. "It was a hell of a drive. Where's the bathroom?"

Dante pointed to the smaller house, and Magritt dashed toward the front door, her legs in an extended stride. She was very thin, with muscular calves and a tight ass, her leather sandals almost slipping off as she moved across the grass. Her short, black hair took on a red hue in the afternoon sun. The back of her white polo shirt read, in black, "Scholar at Work."

Dante noticed the laptop sitting on the front passenger seat and shrugged. I didn't admit to using one myself.

"Did you get to the bathroom in time?" Dante chuckled when Magritt reappeared.

"Isn't that a little personal for a first meeting?" she said without a smile.

"I bet you were surprised that we have modern plumbing," Dante continued.

"Oh, I'm not that bad, Professor Miller. I've made a trip or two out of Manhattan."

"Larry writes with a pen, and you have a sense of humor. This will not be too bad," he said, his words skating on an undertone of nervous laughter.

Dante dropped my valise and picked up Magritt's luggage. He walked ahead of us on the narrow stone path that led to the guesthouse, his head down, his back slightly bowed. How anxious he must be, I thought, having two strangers suddenly invade his life, two young people with pen and laptop, with scores of irreverent questions. So much of his home screamed privacy: the distance from town, the long dirt road that snow would make impassable and a heavy rain—by glazing the surface with a thin layer of slippery mud—make dangerous. Only the guesthouse hinted at a willingness to allow others into his seemingly hermetic life. Complicated, I thought.

"Come, let's settle in," the professor said as he climbed the steps to the front porch. "You'll like the house. The people who homesteaded the land built it in the 1820s. They used an outhouse back then."

The freshly painted dwelling carried its age well. The front porch steps squeaked only slightly; the roofline was still parallel to the foundation. Built with the rocks and lumber harvested when the land was first cleared, I imagined, the main section of the guesthouse was typical of its time and place, with small rooms, low ceilings, and little interior light. A plaque on the right of the front door declared that Union officers used it during the Civil War, and that Lincoln rested there after delivering his Gettysburg address. A claim, I mused, most probably perpetrated by dozens of local residences. In the 1950s, Dante told us, a lawyer from Philadelphia and his family had added a wing, a large bedroom and study and a bathroom the size of a Manhattan studio apartment. They secured the indoor plumbing and rewired the house, while preserving as much of the structure as they felt was safe and comfortable. The heavy wooden floors were restored, as were the thick-mortared walls, the small living room windows, and the large stone fireplace.

Dante put Magritt's suitcases down in the middle of the living room floor. "Takes you back, doesn't it?" he said. "It's a piece of history, this old house. I sometimes come here just to imagine what it was to live back then, before roads and refrigerators."

"Is there any truth to the story that Lincoln rested here after he gave the Gettysburg Address, Professor?" Magritt asked in a soft voice.

Dante rubbed his beard and struggled to look serious. "Maybe, but I don't think Mary Todd would have approved. Local lore suggests that the Confederates used this house as a brothel, a place where succulent women from Charleston and Atlanta tended to the army's morale. Some of the women, it is said, stayed on to work for the Union cause, and their progeny still farm the land and give battlefield tours. I think that it's a far more likely story that Lincoln came here to use the outhouse, even if it, too, is suspect."

"I have to remember to tell Eric. He'll enjoy the idea of living in a whorehouse," Magritt said.

"Eric?" Dante asked.

"My boyfriend."

"Of course. I just forgot. I plan to welcome him, too," Dante said, and began to chuckle. "But let me leave the two of you here to make your arrangements." And with that, he moved quickly out of the house and closed the front door behind him.

"He seems sane enough," Magritt observed, "but calling himself Dante the Painter? I wonder what his wife is like. Beatrice. Can you imagine?"

"I called him Dante Alighieri when I arrived. He brushed it off. Dante is his nickname, he told me. As for his wife, Beatrice is a common name. It's probably on her birth certificate. Can you imagine how anxious they must be, having two strangers suddenly descend on them?"

Magritt gave me a warm smile. "I hope they are. I'd hate to be the only person whose angst is in high gear. So, do you want to live upstairs or down?"

I threw the choice back to Magritt, who, as I expected, chose the more modern section of the house. I moved into the upstairs bedroom. Sheets, pillowcases, and a large goose-down comforter lay on the bed.

"You'll appreciate my taking the large bedroom when Eric arrives," Magritt said after coming upstairs to see my digs. "He takes up a lot of room. But this isn't too bad, either," she added as she stood in the smaller of the two upstairs rooms, the one furnished as a study. She ran her hand over the freshly polished rolltop desk.

Before I could comment, we heard a rap on the outside door and found Elias Miller standing there, a bottle of Chianti held protectively against his chest.

We spent the early evening outside the Millers' house, seated on the hard wooden benches of a picnic table, munching on the barbequed pork Beatrice had picked up in Gettysburg and washing it down with Italian wines.

"Beatrice doesn't like to cook," Dante announced.

"I love to cook, and I'm good at it," she corrected him, "but only for special occasions, like Christmas and New Year's and when Dante finishes a painting. But to do it three times a day? Life is far too short. Anybody want something else?"

"I didn't say you weren't a good cook," Dante insisted.

Beatrice laughed much like her husband, full throated and unembarrassed. She must have been pretty at one time, with big brown eyes, a small nose, and exceptionally mobile thick lips. Time had cut deep lines in her face and loosened her skin. Thirty or so extra pounds made her look matronly. Yet, she still projected beauty, her shoulders back, her head high on her long neck, her gray hair short and neat, and her makeup so carefully done that you had to look twice to see if she was wearing any.

"Eric loves to cook," Magritt said after her eyes made contact with Beatrice's. "More enthusiasm than artistry—he thinks salt and pepper are the world's only spices—but he gets the eggs, toast, and coffee to the table at the same time, and all hot."

"One doesn't need more," I said.

Magritt glanced in my direction, "Then you'll be happy he's living with us."

Hungry mosquitoes appeared in increasing numbers, as the air grew progressively chillier and the sun sank below the horizon. Magritt and I returned to the guesthouse to slip into long-sleeved shirts and put on sweaters. By the time we got back, the picnic table had been cleared and the remaining plates moved to the small table on the screened porch. Beatrice brought out a plate of cheese and sliced apples, and a pot of decaffeinated coffee. Dante opened a bottle of dessert wine. We toasted our collaboration, our skins brightened by liters of alcohol, our moods buoyant. There are things the Italians do well, I thought, as I studied the satisfied expressions on my hosts' faces. Wine does make for family.

"What made you become a playwright?" Beatrice asked during a lull in the conversation.

"My mother decided for me. I couldn't have been more than seven. She's an actor, and at the time was playing an ingénue on a daytime soap opera and going out with one of its writers. I didn't fully appreciate the implication of 'going out' at the time. One day she had an epiphany. 'You're going to write serious Broadway dramas,' she told me, 'and explore the dark avenues of life in passionate plays—with lots of parts for women, juicy roles that they can sink their teeth into, real women with ideas.'"

"But you write comedies," Magritt blurted out.

"I didn't know you knew my work."

Magritt blushed. "I checked around, but not very much."

"So," Beatrice said. Her tone carried the message. I began to flesh out the answer to her question.

"My first play was about a green cat that rescued her owners from a forest fire and went on to promote conservation and environmental protection. A little derivative, but the fifth-grade parents applauded loudly and the cast took three bows. My mother had the manuscript bound in leather. A superhero named Subway Sandwich anchored my sixth grade piece, and Martha Washington—played by my first deep crush—is all I remember of ninth grade. When I was a high school senior, the contenders for valedictorian were a set of twin girls with long legs, blonde hair, a shared Saab convertible, and early admission to Yale. The class decided a twenty-minute play was preferable to a valedictory speech. Tolerance, as usual, was the graduation theme of the year, so I wrote a cutting edge drama about two lesbians—blondes, of course—making out in the women's bathroom. Tolerance may have been its theme but it wasn't school policy. After the second rehearsal, the principal asked the twins to flip a coin to decide which of them would give the commencement speech."

"You're teasing," Magritt said, her rapid-fire speech slowed down by wine.

"Only a little," I said.

Dante's interest was genuine. "And your first professional piece—what did you write about?" he asked, his demeanor unaltered by the wine.

"It was a terribly pretentious multi-generational drama, part Chekov, part Arthur Miller. I called it *Teutonic*. It followed the rise and decay of a Russian family eking out a living in Brooklyn, tracing its roots back to the Teutonic knights who were driven out of Russia by Saint Alexander Nevsky in the thirteenth century. The Saint had a minor part in the drama. Alexander Boris, the penultimate male descendent, trades in drugs and stolen artifacts. His son, a male hooker, works in a back room. I didn't censor the male nudity. 'The more things change, the more they remain the same' was the thesis. Hard as it may be to believe, it was a comedy. Paul Herman, a friend of my mother's, invested in the production. He is too gracious a man to remind me of it. It played on weekends for three months in a little Off-Off-Broadway theater. One Saturday night it got applause."

"Alexander Nevsky predated me, Laurence, but not by much; he was from a different place and a different church. I didn't know anything about him until I saw Eisenstein's movie by that name. Prokofiev's score is magnificent."

His phrase "predated me" hung in the evening air. Magritt and I looked at each other but said nothing.

"I'm sure the play did better than that," Dante continued.

"But not by much," I said.

I had gone on too long and would have been content to sip some of the dessert wine, but Beatrice bid me continue. I skipped over my first Equity production, *Alas Poor Adam*, and moved on to *Celestial City*.

"*Celestial City* was my first commercial success. It played for two years, paid back its sponsors, and even provided me with some pocket money. I expected it would go longer, and do better. Hope blinded my judgment."

Dante emptied the bottle into our glasses.

"Do you use drink to lubricate your writing?" he asked me.

"I try not to. I have no spare capacity and need to be as alert as I can be."

"Wine made the *Commedia* possible. Nothing in it was doable without my flask of red spirits; it made my blood flow, my courage fly. Drinking was as natural as breathing. I couldn't conceive of doing one without the other. Visual art is different, isn't it, Magritt? In the morning, writers can erase their errors, but sculptors, they lose fingers and hands. Painters, too, could paint anew, but colors were expensive, and preparing a surface was time consuming. And they had to worry about falling off the scaffolding. My friend Giotto envied my use of wine."

Magritt's eyes widened. "Giotto, the muralist?"

"Yes, I'm sure you know of him. Every art historian must. He's known best for his frescoes, Laurence—the tales of Saint Francis, the stories of Christ and Mary, the work he did in Padua. But he did more than frescoes."

"I didn't know he was a friend," Magritt said, her voice turning from skepticism to humor, as if she had decided that Elias Miller was pulling her leg.

"Of course he was. Florence was a small city. And kindred spirits, they were hard to find. Giotto loved his wine, but he didn't drink while he was working. Only after, when the sun had set, when the time came to chase women, to buy a companion for the night. He halted his art when I began mine. I would write under the smell of melting wax, my goblet holding a mixture of wine and water, and then wine alone. Do you close your eyes, Laurence, and write sentences in your mind, waiting for them to take a dignified shape before writing them down?"

I paused before answering, trying to figure out whom I was speaking to before realizing that it didn't matter. "I'm a very rapid typist. I put down whatever comes to mind and then work it until I get what I want. That's the benefit of word processing, and its burden—a capacity for endless reworking. There are benefits. No crinkled paper on the floor; no need to retype an entire page to change a word."

Dante looked disappointed. "I thought you told me you used a fountain pen. You didn't bring a laptop."

"I use a pen, a fountain pen, to write down notes, and when I have a paragraph that won't come out right. But more and more I rely on a computer. I blame modernity."

Professor Miller was only half listening. Dante wanted to talk. "Parchment was expensive, paper as well. Even ink could set you back. Most of my composing was done in my head, and only when I was close to certain did I write it out. Economics demanded it. It does stretch the mind. I think you lose something when words and thoughts are so easily erased and reframed. They're made cheap. And you, Magritt, do you waste words as well, spilling them onto an electronic screen, hoping that spell-check will make them right?"

Magritt looked confused. She studied Beatrice's expression for a moment, searching, I thought, for some suggestion about how to answer the professor. Beatrice didn't seem to notice that Elias Miller had become 700 years old.

"Has the wine put you to sleep, young lady?" Dante questioned, his voice loud enough to wake a student who had fallen asleep in the rear row.

"Almost," Magritt whispered. Then her voice gained

strength. "I don't agree with you, Professor. I think a greater willingness to throw out paragraphs and pages can only improve writing. Wine may make reading *The Divine Comedy* easier, but writing it? Great poets talk about being drunk, but they write when they are sober."

Dante slapped his knee and gave forth a vigorous laugh. He raised his glass to Magritt and, wearing an enormous smile, toasted her. Then he finished his drink and pushed the cork into the empty bottle.

MAGRITT AND I stumbled back to the guesthouse, our balance unsettled by wine, our vision fading as we moved further away from the Millers' porch light.

"We have to remember to keep some lights on when we go over there, or carry flashlights," Magritt suggested.

I grunted agreement.

"Weird, isn't it, Larry—this shift into the body of Dante Alighieri? Do you think he's serious? If I knew it was a joke, I'd think it was funny. This way, it's just bizarre."

"Didn't Harland warn you about his slipping into the persona of the medieval poet?"

"Not a word. He just talked about some patron financing this job. Do you think it's Alzheimer's?"

"I just don't know. Didn't Beatrice call him Dante when we first got over? Maybe it's a family joke."

"Maybe," Magritt concluded.

Inebriated, my head full, my muscles exhausted, I made it to the upstairs bedroom without undue physical injury, expecting that I would be asleep by the time my shoes hit the floor. But sleep proved elusive. It was too dark, too quiet. Absent were streetlights sneaking around the edges of the window shades, the sound of squealing tires, the horns of irate motorists. I thought about Elias and Beatrice. I wondered if she would make coffee in the morning. I tried to imagine how Eric would look. Skinny, I decided, with pale skin and soft hands, effeminate in an apron and chef's hat. I bet he never shaved.

A soft, almost inaudible knock ended my musings, and beams from a mobile light seeped under the door. I hesitated, waiting to see if the petition was repeated. Again, the back of a hand struck delicately against the wood door.

"Larry," Magritt whispered. "Larry."

"Yes," I said.

"It's Magritt. Have you looked out of your window?"

"Let me throw something on."

When I sleep alone, I sleep in my underwear. A habit from my undergraduate years when an unusually experienced coed told me pajamas weren't cool. With Hilla, I slept nude. It was one of the few things she insisted on. Since I wasn't ready to welcome Magritt in my jockey shorts and undershirt, I slipped into my pants and opened the door.

"Look outside," she said, and quickly brushed by me, her flashlight illuminating the highly polished wooden floor, and raced to the window.

"What?"

"Shush," she answered. "They might hear us."

A small campfire was burning at the water's edge, its flames illuminating the logs that surrounded the fire pit. Small sparks rose quickly and then sailed off into the night. Beatrice and Elias were sitting next to each other on one of the logs.

"What am I looking for?" I asked.

"Shush," Magritt said again.

"They'll see your flashlight long before they'd hear my voice."

"Eerie," Magritt whispered and turned off the light.

"I don't understand. They're just sitting by a fire. It would be a bizarre thing to do in Manhattan, but here, I just feel left out, not creepy."

"Watch," she said. "They're talking to people I can't see."

And so they were. It was an animated conversation. Dante turned to his right, and then his left, gesturing with his hands, his head now nodding agreement and then shaking in dissent. Beatrice joined in with similar hand gestures; her short hair flowed with her movements, firelight breaking through its curls.

Fascinated, we stood in front of the window, our shoulders touching, and watched. When Beatrice turned her head toward the house, we instinctively pulled back, each to our side of the window.

"Weird," Magritt whispered. "First he turns into Dante Alighieri, then he talks to invisible people."

Again, standing so closely together that I could smell her shampooed hair, we watched our hosts.

"My room is lower down and closer to the lake. We could see better," Magritt said as she switched on her flashlight and ran it along the floor.

She held the torch close against her thigh, providing enough light for her to move quickly, but I was periodically in the dark and had to ask her to slow down as we made our way along the carpeted hallway and down the carpeted steps. Beatrice was walking away from the campfire when we cautiously parted the drapes that hung over the windows in Magritt's sprawling bedroom. Beatrice flicked on the exterior lights of their home and glanced at the window from which we were watching. Magritt and I froze. Quickly, Beatrice entered the white frame house.

The waterfront conversation was not slowing down. Dante was listening and then talking, turning this way and that, pointing in one direction then another, waving his hands, shrugging.

"Weird," Magritt repeated.

"Scary."

"Should we go out and see what he's up to?"

"I don't think so," I said.

"Coward."

"Always."

"Fuck," Magritt whispered. "I'm a nervous wreck."

Before I could add to our non-conversation, Beatrice reappeared. We thought we heard her shout, "It's getting late," but we were only guessing. In a few minutes, Dante rose, and reached out in one direction and then another to shake invisible hands. Finally, he turned from the lake and went home.

Magritt let go of the drape and let out a deep breath. "Fuck," she whispered. "Do you think they'll tell us about this in the morning?"

"I don't know, and I don't think we can ask. It would sound like we were spying."

"We were."

"They might have guessed we were watching and just put on a show. I wouldn't put that past them," I suggested.

"Can you make it back to your room without the flashlight?"

"I thought I could stay the night."

It was too dark to see Magritt's face, but whatever she murmured was not pleasant. I left without argument and stumbled up the stairs.

It was 3:00 a.m. I was tempted to turn on my cell phone and call Hilla, but she'd think I was drunk.

CHAPTER THREE

ELIAS MILLER, NOT DANTE ALIGHIERI, showed up for breakfast Thursday morning. He looked younger than he did the night before, freshly showered, his beard recently shampooed and neatly combed, his blue polo shirt stretched across his broad chest, his tan chino shorts loose around his muscular thighs. He was barefoot.

"Forever, it seems, certainly since I was a sophomore in high school," Dante said in answer to Magritt's question. "Then it was *Inferno*, the first section of the poem. I think of the *Commedia* as three poems, each describing a third of Dante the Pilgrim's voyage through the afterworld—his descent into Hell, his rise through Purgatory, and his visit to Heaven. *Inferno* has a special appeal to teenagers. How could it not, with its ghouls and goblins, its fire and ice, its visit with Satan and his minions?"

"Teenage boys, maybe, but we girls prefer more romantic views of the afterworld," Magritt grumbled.

"Teenage boys, then," Professor Miller said, his manner light and friendly.

A daylong summer rain had begun before dawn, but the shower was light and we were able to sit comfortably on the Millers' porch, digesting the Danish pastries and fresh rolls Dante had picked up at a nearby convenience store and drinking cup after cup of the Costa Rican coffee Beatrice had prepared. Magritt had suggested that we begin the day by seeing some of Miller's paintings, but the professor wanted to put his efforts into the context of the *Commedia.* "I don't want you to abruptly come upon them," he said. "I want you to be prepared."

Professor Miller broke a roll in half and covered one side of it with a luscious local butter. He continued the discussion before taking a bite. "Dante became a permanent companion when I was in college and taking my first course in Italian literature. The instructor thought the best part of the *Commedia* was its second section, *Purgatorio.* He convinced me it was, and I still think it is. However, *Paradiso* became an obsession while I was in graduate school. Magritt will understand this. I had become temporarily bored with my dissertation—an attempt to explain why Protestants prefer Milton's *Paradise Lost* to *The Divine Comedy*—and had decided to entertain myself by translating *Paradiso.* Like every PhD student, I felt I was living in Hell and didn't want to dwell on it, and I didn't have the patience to wait in Purgatory for salvation. Translating Heaven seemed a perfect diversion. My Italian was good, and I had taken a workshop or two in poetry. The more I labored, however, the more compelled I felt to strike out on an independent course. I wanted to create a poetry that would speak to the contemporary mind, a paradise accessible to recently cultivated sensibilities."

Professor Miller let out a deep breath and bit into the buttered roll. He followed it with half a cup of coffee. "Should I go on?" he asked Magritt.

"Of course," she said. "This is very helpful."

Miller didn't ask my opinion. He drank a little more coffee before continuing. "I'd sit down at the kitchen table, cigarettes and Italian wine within reach—I was still single and living alone—and work through the night like an insomniac stamp collector. My pen would race ahead of my thinking, filling pages of white paper with the magic of a sublime universe. Freud's unconscious, I decided, the id coming through a drink-weakened ego. It was at once glorious and frightening, but in the morning light, the words tarnished, and my efforts failed my visions.

"I concluded that I was no poet; my pen did not soar. I stayed with academic writing, publishing articles about medieval poetry here and there, putting together an anthology for undergraduates, publishing a treatise on competing visions of Heaven, always a little disappointed in myself. Then, '*I found myself within a forest dark,*' as Dante wrote, and discovered a talent for painting. It did not come easy. Beatrice and I had no children—fate, not choice—and were left with surplus income and excess time. We spent a summer in Paris learning to draw, another in Spain playing with watercolors. Beatrice gave up, but once convinced that I would not embarrass myself, I undertook the Master of Fine Arts program at the college where I was teaching.

"I never finished; too many classmates were much more accomplished, but I became an acceptable amateur. Beatrice thought I was good, but storage became a problem, so over time I discarded most of my early work, down to each sketchpad portrait, and found that the only work I kept tied me to Dante. Like so many artists over the centuries, I struggled to write the *Commedia* in pictures, believing that painting is the only style of speech capable of breaking through the Babel of multiple languages. I was well into *Purgatory* before I made my first sale. I never expected to turn commercial, but a trustee of the college, Madeline Brewster, was visiting my office one day and became attracted to a painting of mine. It was a good work but derivative, much of it resting on the shoulders of a drawing William Blake did in the 1820s. I even used his title, *The Flatterers*—a scene from the Eighth Circle of Hell, where unrepentant seducers, flatterers, robbers, and planters of deceit spend eternity, their naked bodies whipped relentlessly by horned demons. I would point it out to students who came to my office to plead for a higher grade. It never deterred them. I hated to lose the painting, but it was my first sale, and to a woman whose judgment I respected. How could I resist?"

Professor Miller looked at me and then at Magritt, expecting that one of us would answer his question, but we had heard it as a rhetorical flourish and said nothing. He leaned forward and picked up his cup of coffee, turned it in his hand as if it were a wine goblet, and finished the drink.

"And the next purchaser, Professor—do you recall who it was?" Magritt asked. She thrust her head forward as if posture alone propelled her words to its target. She was sitting in an armless wooden chair, a notebook resting first on one knee and then on the other as she crossed and re-crossed her restless legs, the flared bottoms of her green shorts overlapping in imitation of a mini-skirt. That day's polo shirt read Bennington College. Her small breasts pressed hard against the cloth.

"Oh, Madeline purchased the next one as well, and the next and next. She was in her late sixties when she bought the first of my work, about ten years older than I was, but remarkably handsome, her slight figure unchanged, I imagine, since the day she married, her hair a perfectly dyed yellow, her eyes hazel. That was fifteen years ago. I was fifty-four and still teaching classes, but doing little scholarship. She was my sole benefactor. Beatrice was jealous, and, in a way, she should have been. I loved Mrs. Brewster, not just for her mature beauty but for her gentleness, her soft voice, her quick wit, and, of course"—the professor paused dramatically and moved his glance from me to Magritt—"for her majestic artistic taste."

Elias waited for us to laugh, and we obliged.

"She died five years ago, still beautiful, although evidently fragile," Dante continued. "By then, she had distributed many of my paintings as gifts to friends and relatives. I never tried to meet the new owners. I was afraid they might be Philistines. There is no more work to sell. Painting does not come easily to me. I make countless sketches and watercolor drawings, experiments in space and colors, in composition, in facial expressions. At the end, perhaps ten canvases, and not very big ones, are finished a year—maybe as many as twelve. I have finished a little over 120 oils. I have done all I want to on the *Inferno* and *Purgatory*. I decided not to paint any of the scenes of Paradise, for much the same reason I think the poem would have been better done if Dante had written *Paradiso* when he was young. I am too used up to make Heaven sing. I took photographs of all my works before I sold them, but the originals live with people I do not know."

Magritt looked disappointed. "I was hoping you had kept track. It would make the research easier."

"I understand," Dante answered, and gave her a sad look.

I nodded in support of Magritt's disappointment, but I was still thinking about Miller's reference to the writing of *Paradiso*. "I didn't quite follow you, Professor," I said, ". . . the comment about Dante's age and his writing."

Miller leaned his chair against the brick wall of the house, looking confused by my question, but in a moment his expression changed and his eyes began to shine.

"Try to imagine," Professor Miller said in a quieter and more personal voice, "the exiled Dante, under penalty of death by fire if he returns to his beloved Florence. He roams the countryside of Verona, forlorn and discouraged, desperately trying to imagine the remainder of his life, his head bowed, his black medieval frock hanging loosely over his bowed body like a burial shroud. Think of the first line of the *Commedia*: *Midway upon the journey of our life I found myself within a forest dark, for the straightforward pathway had been lost.* I expect that's how the Longfellow translation goes. In the Tuscan dialect of the day, it could not have been more beautiful. If Dante had a chance to write it all over again, I doubt if he would change a syllable in *Inferno*. It is 1300. He is thirty-five years old, experienced enough to understand the evils men commit upon each other. He is sufficiently knowledgeable about human failings and fears to be able to balance sin and punishment. With *Purgatorio*—I think if Dante could do it all again he would have delayed the writing of the middle poem to the very last, to a time when he would know everything he was to learn about human dread and desire, about the substance of repentance. Yes, *Purgatorio* could benefit from a rewrite, but not by much. I have always loved that section of the *Commedia*. However, *Paradiso* is another story. A younger man should have written it, his imagination in full flight, his creative powers exploding and his horizons uninhibited by knowledge. Or, perhaps, it should have been written by a young woman flush with life's dreams, a soft, beautiful woman."

"Is that why Dante chose Beatrice to guide him through Heaven?" I asked.

"Remember, Virgil, his guide through Hell and Purgatory, was a pagan. Paradise was closed to him. So Dante needed another to take him to the Empyrean, the home of God and Christ. Beatrice, his childhood love, was a perfect choice. She is the architect of the story. She sends Virgil to find Dante in the dark forest of middle age; she greets him as he comes out of Purgatory, cleansed of all his sins. But the Beatrice who leads him to Heaven is not the woman he knew when they were both young. The Beatrice of the final poem is born of a middle-aged man's imagination. She is not a first love."

Magritt jumped in. "You're talking about a man's dream of the perfect woman, a creature that never existed—an eternal virgin."

The professor found Magritt's flare-up funny. He inhaled deeply, looked at her intently, and squinted. "Has modernity squeezed all the romance out of you, Magritt?" he asked with a large degree of irony. "Beautiful Beatrice had been married young and to a young man. Not even Dante could imagine her as a virgin. But what makes you think my imagined virgin is any less real than your vision of the modern woman?"

"Because I've never bumped into one," Magritt shot back.

The professor's face broke into a brilliant smile, and he let out a thunderous laugh. "Neither have I," he finally said after he caught his breath. "But it is *Paradiso* that I would most want to write anew. I think I failed to get it right the first time. Heaven must excite the blood; it must ignite our better passions. My *Paradiso* is limp before the challenge, absent adventure, too ethereal to touch or taste or hear."

"I thought it quite beautiful," Magritt confessed.

Professor Miller put his head in his hands for a few seconds. "I've done it again," he said without looking up. "I apologize. I get so carried away; I begin to act as if I am the great poet. Have you ever witnessed such conceit? Old age is my only excuse."

"Very old age," I said. "Seven hundred years, give or take a few.

Just then, a cold wet wind tore through the porch, sending a chill through my body. Magritt's lips turned blue and Dante shivered. We acknowledged our collective discomfort and decided to break for lunch, planning to come back together at 1:30 or so.

MAGRITT STAYED AHEAD of me as we stepped over the puddles that poked the gravel path connecting the two houses, her head down, her arms wrapped tightly across her chest for warmth.

"Have you seen many of his paintings?" she yelled without turning around.

"Absolutely none. Have you?"

"No, and I'm a little worried about my reaction. I'm a spoiled art historian. I've studied masterpieces. I'm not very forgiving of the new or newly popular."

"I'm afraid I won't be of much use. I like or dislike art, but with no esthetic understanding. I just like and dislike or remain unmoved."

I opened the door just as my mother had taught me and waved to Magritt to enter the guesthouse in front of me. She kept talking as her body rubbed past mine. "Most artists start with their work; they flood the curious with their oils and sketches, smother them with acres of images and colors. Instead, Miller talks about himself, about Dante, about becoming an artist. He gives us chapter two first. It makes me worry about chapter one."

"Well, maybe we'll become the first critics to publish a

monograph about a painter without ever seeing one of his works. That would be original."

"That would be. Yet it won't get me a professorship. I'm going in for a short swim, care to join me?"

"It's cold out there, and raining."

"I'll wear a bathing suit."

From my bedroom window, I watched Magritt walk down to the lake, drop her white terrycloth bathrobe on the wooden dock, and dive gracefully in the water. I wanted to see more—her stroke, her breathing, how water ran across her legs—but the distance was too great, the wet fog too impenetrable.

I lay down on the bed, closed my eyes, and used images of Hilla to push Magritt from my thoughts, Hilla with her long hair brushed behind her ears, her harlequin eyes filled with listless amorality. I tried to count all the places where we made love: in the hot tub in the Catskills, beside a small ceramic fireplace in Taos, on a houseboat I rented on Cayuga Lake, in her Riverside Drive apartment. So few locations, I thought, for five years of living together, and wondered if geography offered an insight into our failure. My memories only frustrated me. I turned on my side and slowly drifted into a deep sleep.

An hour and a half had passed by the time I made it back to the Millers' farmhouse, somewhat disoriented and very hungry. Magritt was sharing a cup of coffee with Beatrice.

"Care for some?" Beatrice asked, pointing to the coffee maker.

"Please," I said, and looked around to see if she had something to go with it. My gesture was more obvious than I expected.

"I have a honey cake, Larry, if you'd care for some."

"Toast and cheese would be more appreciated."

Beatrice smiled, the lips of her small mouth parting slightly, their corners rising into deep dimples. She quickly pulled out wedges of Italian salami, some roast turkey slices, and a creamy goat cheese that melted in my mouth. She toasted some multigrain bread and poured me a cup of coffee.

"Magritt?" she said.

"No, I've already eaten. But maybe the honey cake?"

We settled down in the kitchen, around a small table that stood beside the room's only window. Beatrice was clearly pleased by my appetite, but a little put off by Magritt, who cut her cake into small pieces and chewed each piece carefully.

"How was your swim?" I asked.

My question did not speed her chewing. When she finally answered, I had just about forgotten the question.

"Perfect," she said. "You should have joined me."

"Next time."

"In this weather?" Beatrice asked.

"The lake is no wetter than the rain," Magritt answered. "But where is Professor Miller? We were to work this afternoon."

"In his office. He's going over some slides to decide which of his paintings to show you. He doesn't want to overwhelm, so he's looking for one or two that will introduce you to his work."

Magritt winked at me before turning to speak to Beatrice. "We'd learn more from seeing the originals than from photographs. Professor Miller said you were holding on to a few."

"They are much too personal. I'm not prepared to show them, not even for scholarship," Beatrice said, and then blushed.

"I understand," I said.
Magritt frowned.

IT TOOK A MINUTE to adjust to the dark of Dante's study, to make out the small desk, the towering bookcase, and the large mirror that hung opposite the heavily shaded window. Cautiously, Magritt and I felt our way to the end of an oak table, where Dante had set up an ancient Kodak slide projector.

"I want to show you photographs of two of my pieces. I think they'll give you some idea of what I'm about. Call it a prologue. You can look at the other slides on your own. In fact, if you tend to be critical, I'd rather you looked at them without me. I am dreadfully thin-skinned." Dante's chuckle did not mask the truth of his comment.

"I'm certain we'll like them," I said, and then wanted to bite my patronizing tongue. As the professor fussed with the projector, I tried to recall the little Harland Van Ness had told me about Miller's art. "There is nothing modern about him, nothing contemporary, no abstract expressionism. He's a figurative painter, half illustrator, half Renaissance copyist." The memory gave me comfort. At least I would be protected from a third-rate de Kooning or Picasso. I sat in the dark expecting only decorative art, with luck, the work of a good amateur, his perspective almost right, his colors bright and uncomplicated, his figures recognizable but without personality.

I was very mistaken. Appearing on the white wall was a riveting image, reportorial in style, but filled with classic forms and surfaces. Two intertwined bodies float in the air, each facing the viewer. Her naked body presses against his chest, his right arm bends gracefully over her shoulder. He is handsome, his body lean and muscular. A white gossamer shroud flows sensuously over his arm and down her legs. She is thin, with small breasts and large brown eyes. An invisible force propels the couple out of a forbiddingly dark background of gnarled and threatening shapes and thrusts. There is nothing lascivious in their embrace, yet the painting screams passion.

"*Francesca and Paolo*, I call it," Dante said. "They're two of the many people you meet in the *Commedia*. Lovers eternally imprisoned in the Second Circle of Hell, the place for the lustful, ever sailing in the dark mist, their love so lightly on the wind."

"Beautiful," I said, unable to be silent.

Magritt jumped out of her chair and quickly walked over to the projected image. She ran her finger along the contours of the bodies, she leaned her head toward the faces. "How large is the painting?" she asked.

Dante had to think before answering. "About forty-eight by thirty."

"Inches?" she continued.

"Of course, Magritt. Inches are all I can do. I don't have a large enough studio to do more. My work is apartment size . . . large apartments, to be sure. And homes. Homes like mine—not enormous, but comfortable, with lots of interior walls.

"Oil on canvas?" Magritt continued.

"Oil and tempera, often on canvas, but sometimes I choose to work on a more solid surface like fiberboard or Masonite. I spend a great deal of time preparing the surface, no matter what the underlying medium. I've used as many as six coats of gesso, and then I cover the surface with horizontal gray strips, using charcoal and white lead like

Rubens did, and then, working from countless sketches, I draw in pencil or ink, and cover that with a layer of varnish. It's a slightly sticky surface, but I am used to it. My talent is in drawing; I'm barely competent in all other aspects of my art. By using the old methods, gesso and egg tempera rather than oil or acrylic, I can fake being a Renaissance master. If I were younger, I'd become a forger, and 'discover' a lost Raphael or Bellini."

"You'd get away with it," Magritt commented under her breath.

"If you'd attest to it, we could go into business. We could incorporate as Fraud and Connoisseur."

Magritt gave him a tempered smile and turned back to the projected image. "Tell me more about the subject."

"You haven't read your Dante very carefully. It's one of the more memorable portions. Dante and Virgil find themselves among carnal sinners—Cleopatra, Helen, Achilles, Francesca and Paolo. Dante asks the couple to tell their story. Francesca tells him how she fell into an illicit love affair with her brother-in-law, Paolo, while the two were reading about Lancelot and Guinevere. Gianciotto, her husband and Paolo's older brother, eventually discovers them and kills them on the spot."

"I was surprised by Dante's reference to Lancelot and Guinevere. I hadn't expected him to be familiar with that fable," I said, to show off. I couldn't compete with Magritt's knowledge of art, but I had read *The Divine Comedy* intently before driving to Gettysburg.

"Dante was well read, and he did have a sense of humor, although you do have to search for it. As with many tales in the *Commedia*, Francesca and Paolo's affair is based on fact or at least on a story that floated around Florence about a murder that took place in 1285, when Dante was about twenty. The Lancelot and Guinevere bit may be creative privilege. I've romanticized them in the painting. Paolo was much older and far less handsome than my portrait of him. He had been married for sixteen years and had two sons. Francesca's hips were a great deal more ample, her face less symmetrical, her breasts less firm, and she was old enough to have a nine-year-old daughter. But modern times demands modern images of beauty."

"It is hardly my conception of Hell. You've drawn them filled with passion, even love. It doesn't strike me as a bad way to survive eternity," Magritt said, her eyes focused on the projection, her right hand toying with her short hair.

"It is ambiguous. I do sympathize with them, a human if not a divine response. Yet they are being severely punished. They will never make it to Heaven, never sit at Christ's feet, never see the lights of Paradise or hear its music. Isn't that punishment enough?" Dante said.

"Perhaps," I exclaimed, "but I agree with Magritt. They don't seem in pain. Anything but."

Dante let out a bellow. "Heretics, both of you," he concluded as his laughter quieted down. "Remember, it's only the Second Circle of Hell. Far greater calamities face those further down."

"And her husband, the murderer, does he end up in Heaven sitting at Christ's feet?" Magritt asked cynically.

With the press of a button, Dante clicked to another slide. A horrid vision covered the wall. We were in the Ninth Circle of the Hell, the eternal home of traitors, of those who conspired against family, country, and God. The great Roman poet, Virgil, Dante's guide through Hell and Purgatory, stands in the center of a frozen lake. Dante is beside him, kneeling on the ice, and pulling up a disembodied head by its hair.

Around our two poets, dozens of anguished faces protrude through the frozen surface of the lake.

"And what do you call this painting?" Magritt asked.

"*Treachery.*"

"The lowest depth of Hell?" I asked. No one bothered to answer, but I knew it was.

Dante walked toward the image and pointed toward the severed head that the great poet is holding. "A traitor from Dante's extended family, the Guelphs, Bocca degli Abate," the professor announced. "On the battlefield of Monteperti, he betrayed his family by cutting off the arm of its standard-bearer and thus bringing about its disastrous defeat at the hands of the Ghibellines. The battle took place in 1260 or so, a few years before my birth. See the villain's agony. It's fully deserved."

And agony it was, his mouth screaming, his eyes frozen opened and filled with fear.

"I wish the pain had been greater, but there is a limit to my talent," Dante said bitterly, and then took a step closer to the wall and pointed to another face. "Here is Gianciotto, Francesca's husband, the murderer. His eternal life is much harsher than his wife's or her lover's, his body forever frozen in ice, his expression ever pained."

Magritt stood next to Dante, her finger running over the wall as if she thought the figures breathed. "How large is this piece?"

"It's a decent size, thirty-six by forty-eight inches. It took me over three months to get it right, to discover the right faces, to find the forms and colors. I plagiarized the composition from a drawing by Doré finished about a hundred years ago. I'm not very good at composition, so I cheat by finding prior illustrations of the scene I want to interpret. I try not to follow them literally, although this one has few original compositional elements. But I like it."

"Doré, you say?" asked Magritt.

Dante nodded.

"I'd like to see a scene from *Purgatorio*, if you have one on hand," I said, hoping to get a different painting to shine on the wall. I didn't want to spend the entire afternoon looking at the tortured faces of the damned.

"I'm sorry, Laurence. I only prepared these two slides. We can arrange for you to use this room as often as you'd like, and I'm sure Magritt knows how to handle the projector. Every art historian must learn that skill; it's a job requirement. But not today. Two works at a time is enough for me. I get carried away with more and find myself returning to the fourteenth century, full of God's word, but fearful for the world of men."

"I always imagined there was less fear in the Middle Ages, when the Bible was accepted as the word of God; when Christ's blessing ruled people's lives," Magritt said.

"Every day we worried. We worried about disease, about unrest, about battles and blood, knowing that at any moment our inscrutable God could destroy our children. He could make us ugly, or fill us with pain. We know of the Book of Job.

"One religion did not keep us from torturing each other, from pillaging the countryside, from burning down our neighbor's village. Examine the Ninth Circle, and there they are, King Arthur's son, Mordred, whose traitorous intentions forced his father to drive a lance through him; Ganellon, Charlemagne's betrayer; and Tribaldello, the pope's legate to my hometown of Florence, who was beheaded for his villainy. Do they come from a peaceful, content, steadfast world? Did a common worship keep them from reviling each other? Free will . . . it is the curse the Creator put on us, the freedom to end up in Hell. Mix free will with ignorance, and you have the fourteenth century.

"Not everyone thought life eternal, that evil is eventually punished and that good is rewarded by a seat in Heaven. Skeptics, freethinkers, call them what you will, viewed such ideas the way we now see fairy tales—wouldn't it be nice? We like to think people were simpler in earlier ages, that people who could not read could not think. But their brains were the size of ours, their intelligence as great."

"But didn't Dante believe in God?" Magritt asked, her head tilted to one side, her voice filled with suspicion.

The painter looked stunned. He gave out a short laugh, but there was no smile. "Why does it matter? Praying in the same Church did not prevent us from mutilating one another. Would not believing in God make us worse? Or believing in different Gods?"

I needed to know more. "But in the afterlife, Virgil cannot enter paradise because he was born before Christ. He is a heathen and not a Christian. *The Divine Comedy* would have no backbone if you dismiss the belief in God. Your paintings would be fantasies and not moral lessons."

Dante's back stiffened, and even in the shadows I could see him frown. He sat back on his chair and tapped his fingers on his right thigh.

"Having Virgil guide Dante was the poet's most inspired decision: Virgil, the great Roman wordsmith, Dante's competition, wise and noble, a student of human frailties. By locking him out of paradise, Dante gave in to the visions of the times, into the doctrines of the popes and bishops. Would God have kept so beautiful a voice from sitting at his feet? Would Christ deny a mind so brilliant, so kind, so full of empathy, an eternal place in Heaven's light?"

Magritt began to speak, but the sound of Beatrice knocking on the door silenced her.

"Cocktail time," Professor Miller declared, sounding as if he had just received a reprieve.

"Already?" Magritt said.

"Already," I answered, worried that she had pressed our host too far.

Beatrice was not calling us to drinks and canapés; she was delivering a message to Magritt that her "party" had pulled in an hour before, but didn't want to disturb her. He had talked with Beatrice for a short time and then gone for a swim. "He's been swimming for over half an hour. I thought you might like to know," Beatrice said. Then she looked at me shyly, as if her message had somehow done me injury.

CHAPTER FOUR

IF MAGRITT WAS EXCITED by her boyfriend's arrival, she hid it well. "He loves to swim," she said, her tone nonchalant. "A half hour is just a warm-up. He'd prefer my letting him swim for a while before interrupting him. Your husband thought you were reminding us that it was cocktail time. I think that would be great. It's been an intense day, and I could use a drink."

"I can do better than cocktails," Professor Miller said, and disappeared toward the kitchen.

A few minutes later, an exuberant Dante celebrated our reaction to his paintings by opening a bottle of sparkling Italian wine, and we toasted our collaboration by gently clinking elegant wine flutes. "Perfect," Magritt said, but when Dante offered her more, she apologized and told him she had better greet Eric. I made excuses as well. I was too curious about her boyfriend to stay behind, so I planned to give a quick glance in his direction before heading to my room.

A dry breeze from the west had driven away the rain, and the air was filled with the scent of wet grass when Magritt and I walked down the gentle slope to the waterfront. I inspected Eric as he briskly swam out to a pre-selected spot in the middle of the lake, flipped over like an Olympian, and swam back to the dock. He gave Magritt a wide smile and a quick wave, turned head-over-heels, and again swam off.

Magritt increased the pace. "He's a beautiful swimmer," she said over her shoulder.

It was an unnecessary comment. Eric's athleticism was hard to miss. He cut through the blue water in an effortless freestyle, the muscles in his broad back rippling with each extension of his arms, his well-developed legs moving rhythmically, his head turning gracefully to the right with every other stroke.

"If I could swim half as well, I'd go back to get my bathing suit and join him," I said.

"Everything doesn't have to be a competition, Larry—but why bother with a bathing suit?"

Magritt ran a few steps ahead of me and was out of her clothes before I had time to blush. I watched her dive off the dock, admiring her elegant body before it disappeared under the water.

Some things, however, *are* competitions, and swimming nude alongside Magritt, with her Adonis in the water, was not a contest I wanted to enter.

A hot blush warmed my face, and I retreated rapidly to the guesthouse, feeling as embarrassed as a teenage boy whose mother had just caught him ogling an unclad centerfold. I rapidly turned around and jogged up the grassy slope to the guesthouse, wondering just how long it would take Eric to fling his swimsuit on the dock.

I threw open the windows of the parlor and, despite the heat, pushed a crumbled section of *The New York Times* under three logs in the fireplace and lit it with a long wooden match. Fresh country air, filled with the smell of pine needles, rushed into the room as I lay down on the couch.

What would Hilla think of the scene that was taking place a hundred yards away? Would she be jealous? Would it turn her on? Would she want to pull me down to the lakeside and compete? Alas, Hilla was not watching the world from my bedroom window, and no matter how much I wanted her there, she would not appear. Still, I fantasized. "Were we ever as passionate as they are?" I asked her. "Of course we were," she answered, "but not enough. We were never Paolo and Francesca."

Hilla cried when she pushed me out of her life, her face contorted by sorrow, her eyes swollen, at once assuring me that she had loved me and announcing that she couldn't live with me. "I don't expect to find what we once had, but I can't go on this way. We'll end up with bitter and empty lives." She slumped into the crimson chair near the living room window, her hair hanging lifelessly along the sides of her face. "You believe I'm saying these things because I've found someone else. I haven't. I haven't even looked. We're running on empty, Larry, and you don't even know it. I just don't understand you," she mumbled, and then, thinking it would make it easier on me, added, "I just don't understand men."

Damn her, I thought, and cursed Magritt for igniting my glands with her tight peach-shaped ass, for propelling me back to Hilla, back to my once-warm bed.

Hilla did know men. Her husband had taught her—and her lovers. But Hilla didn't know women. Heterosexual women believe they know about women. They don't. They know only what is finely filtered through their habits and their character. Men know women, how their eyes close or shadow or gaze into the dark. How sweat breaks out on their foreheads. How their heads rise out of pillows and soft nervous laughter slips through their lips.

What I don't know are men. My male characters look different from one another, but each is stuffed with my emotions. Lust fills their groins when it fills mine; loneliness drives them to sleepless nights when loneliness drives me. Oh, I know that each man is different, that some men fuck once a month and others twice a day, yet their differences escape my language and my scripts. In my heart, all men are alike. But each new lover instructs me anew that every woman is different.

I fill my plays with women, with mothers, with wives, with concubines, and with prostitutes. None, however, is a whore; I don't believe in whores. "Whore is a word used by men who are frightened by beauty," I have a middle-aged woman say in an unfinished drama. "It is a word created by women to keep their husbands tightly tucked in bed, by uptight girls who vomit at the thought of kissing pubic hair." Hilla didn't like the scene. "Do you actually think any woman would say something like that in this day and age? Haven't you heard of the sexual revolution?"

I closed my eyes and imagined Hilla floating in the Second Circle of the *Inferno*, my arms entwining her, our love compelling my wings to spread and our bodies to soar. Then I pictured myself in the frozen lake, my eyes and nostrils full of ice, my mouth in a petrified smile. Damn, Magritt, her panties lying on the green grass; a swimming lover to surprise.

I struggled off the couch and slowly made my way to the second floor. From the bedroom bureau, I pulled a bottle of Scotch and poured a short drink. Once Hilla was free of me, what happened then? My blood thinned and wearied, my mind froze, my body rebelled against the sexual fantasies of movies, TV shows, and Broadway plays. How can I call myself a writer? Dante knew Heaven and Hell, he climbed

Satan's hairy body to reach the base of Purgatory. Me, I still didn't know the difference between sex and love.

"I mystify my chroniclers, Laurence," Professor Miller had said when he was immersed in the persona of Dante. "They complicate what I have made simple, and simplify what to me was the great mystery. They do not allow my Beatrice to be flesh and blood. She is virtue, they claim, a symbol of the eternal Church. They admit they cannot know my mind and yet go on to insist that she is an allegory for all things worth praising. They forget she is a woman."

"LARRY," MAGRITT YELLED up the stairs. "You let the fire die. Are you all right?"

I had to shake my head before I could speak. "Perfect—just jotting down some ideas from this afternoon, that's all."

"Don't rush. I'll add some wood to the fire—it smells terrific—and Eric and I will shower. He'll cook dinner tonight."

"Eric?" I yelled back, convinced that Magritt was just testing to see if I was listening.

"He usually does. I'll call you when it's ready."

It wasn't a gourmet meal: heated frozen meatballs from some deli in Gettysburg and overcooked spaghetti. The Italian bread was good, and he had selected a nice wine from Piedmont. No one had thought about dessert, so we cut up a couple of apples and took some goat cheese from the refrigerator. In Manhattan, I would have picked up far better food at a little place near 80th Street and Broadway that catered to single women and gay men. Still, Eric's was a better meal than I would have made for myself, and sitting around the table with Magritt and her lover was a step-up from eating alone.

"Did you swim competitively?" I asked Eric after telling him how much I enjoyed the spaghetti and meatballs.

Eric bestowed a "thank you for noticing" smile. "When I was in high school I dreamed of going to the Olympics; but when I swam for Yale I never got above second tier. Now that I don't have to practice, I love swimming; it's sensual as hell."

"We spent the day in Hell, and there was nothing sensual about it, let me tell you," Magritt said.

"The floating couple, they didn't look celibate," I needled.

The wine seemed to benefit Magritt more than Eric, her expression more relaxed, her speech slower, her skin more radiant. Lucky guy, I thought, when I looked at Eric.

"I'm lost," he said to me when he noticed my glance.

Magritt filled him in. "A deceased couple embracing, that's what Larry's referring to. Miller took the painting from the Second Circle of the *Inferno*, an eternal resting place for women who can't keep their legs crossed and men with opened zippers. If the originals are like the slides, he has a way of getting all his figures to move. It's quite an achievement, using short quivering strokes to avoid stasis. I wonder where he got the technique, or if he just developed it. Were you as surprised as I was at how remarkable his paintings are, Larry?"

"I expected a good amateur at best, but nothing like what we saw."

"Slides often make art look better than it is, particularly mediocre pieces. The colors are more vivid, the imperfections hidden. I'll have to see, but I am taken aback."

"And the second piece?" I asked.

"Fascinating, absolutely fascinating," Magritt said. She leaned over the table and transferred thin slices of apple and pieces of cheese from the serving dish to a small white plate. "If the painting looks as good as its photograph, it will be quite something."

"It was a little too grotesque for my tastes. I can't imagine hanging it in my living room," I observed.

Eric gave out a quiet laugh. "I knew I'd like you," he said, and winked at Magritt.

"Philistines, both of you." She laughed.

"I don't get it," I said, feeling parenthesized by a private joke.

"I use the wall-in-the-living-room test as well," Eric said. "If I can't see it hanging over my couch, or bed, or looking at me taped on the refrigerator, I can't think of it as being good—except of course if it's just too big for my place. Magritt tries to convince me that there is more to art than my living room."

"Have you told Eric about last night?" I asked Magritt, for no particular reason except it popped into my mind.

"Oh, it's unimportant, Larry. I didn't mention it."

"What about last night?" Eric asked. Curiosity illuminated his light-blue eyes. He was handsome, not in the bon vivant way of a matinee idol, but like the boy next door who late in the drama seems suddenly mature, available, a noble catch. It was easy to see why Magritt was attracted to him. What woman wouldn't be? If he were a little taller I could cast him as a heavyweight contender, but at five foot ten, baseball would be the better sport for him, or soccer.

Magritt put her fork down and turned her full attention to her boyfriend.

"Larry and I caught the Millers in a private moment, that's all. It would be gossiping to repeat it. So I won't."

"I like gossip," Eric said, his voice all innocence. "But by their age, they should know enough to draw the blinds."

Magritt began to laugh and I joined her. She picked up her fork and poked it into a piece of apple, but stopped before putting anything into her mouth. "It was the faces, Larry, the faces. We have to go back and study them again. Dozens of faces in the ice, with just hints of their frozen bodies, but each face is different, each expression anguished and yet each expression unique. It's as if the professor spent days studying faces in distress, studying bewildered eyes, examining furrowed brows. Mouths opened and closed, handsome and ugly, males and females, young and old— Renaissance painting at its best. I was reminded of faces painted by Rembrandt and Vermeer, but Miller's palette is more seventeenth century Venice, with deep reds and glowing yellows."

"I just didn't look that closely, but I don't think Vermeer had any Asian faces, or black. Dante the Painter is trying to include every racial group, at least the more familiar races. I think he goes beyond Dante the Poet," I contributed.

"You must study them, Larry. Please. You too, Eric; I'd value your opinion even if you are a Philistine. Each face was different, and yet there was a common thread. Some people have unique faces, a one-of-a-kind face that doesn't remind you of anyone you've ever met or bumped into. Other people have faces that are somehow familiar; you look at them and see an old friend, or a neighbor, a cousin. The professor has chosen the features of familiar faces. I recognized people. I've seen them on a bus, in the subway, on a movie screen. Oh, I can't name them, but they were familiar, everyday faces from everywhere I have ever been. I even thought I saw myself."

"In the Ninth Circle of Hell? That doesn't sound very appealing," I said.

The middle digit of her right hand rose slowly. "I'm serious. Let's study it again, and then you can tell me I'm crazy. I think you'll find that I'm right. He consciously chose faces we would recognize."

"So he's truly good," Eric said.

"Yes," I quickly responded.

Magritt's voice turned academic. "We'll have to see the actual work, but the slides hold promise."

"I get the feeling that we're expected to rely on Dante's slides," I said.

"Never," Magritt barked and waved her forefinger at me. "It's impossible. The slides may not be honest representations, and they may not be the best photographs for our manuscript. I won't hear of it."

"Easy," Eric said, and grabbed hold of her gesturing hand. "They'll let you see whatever you want. I'll bet on it."

"They'll have to!" Magritt shouted back.

I was ready to question Eric's certainty, but Magritt continued before I had a chance. "Eric thinks someone is setting the base for a con game; that our manuscript will be used to hype Miller's art and allow our unnamed patron to sell an oil bought for $2,000 for $20,000."

"Or a $20,000 painting for $2 million. If he's as good as you say, and the art market as full of money as *The New York Times* suggests, that's not out of reach," Eric conjectured.

"Tantalizing," I said.

"Crap," Magritt concluded. "The art market may be wine and roses, but you don't grab an unknown artist, and I mean unknown, and make him a star with one 'authorized publication.' If money were what they wanted, they'd take some known artist, a mid-price artist—someone young, with the best years to come—and get us to write about him, or her, or it. An orangutan that splashed pseudo-Pollocks would be a better bet for stardom than a sixty-nine-year-old artist with one fan. Believe me."

Eric, his dark blue muscle shirt strangling his chest, rolled his shoulders forward then back, and showed off his right bicep. "I love swimming in a lake, the water gently running over my flesh, feeling almost weightless, one stroke after another, constructing unthinking motions with no purpose other than to twist back, to roll over, to let the hot sun race across my back. My mind wanders. I think of Magritt. I think of the case I'm working on. I think of Dante Miller, the underpaid humanities professor, no grant from the National Science Foundation, no research fellowship from the National Institutes of Health, no consultancy with the World Bank, finally discovering a way to get his share of the pie, to avenge a lifetime of feeling underpaid and underappreciated. Money, that's what it's all about—manna, not heaven."

Magritt dropped the fork on her plate, but before she could argue, Eric cut her off.

"I know. I'm jaded, too much the cynic, the confidence man who projects his own pathology on everyone else, an eat-or-be-eaten celebrant. I know. But I'm enjoying the mystery of it. My suspicions make a far better story than having an innocent secret patron who has too much money. Conspiracy theories are always the most interesting." Eric moved his chair away from the table and stretched his arms over his head. "I did the cooking. Can I leave the cleanup to you two?"

MAGRITT LEANED OVER the sink as she washed the dishes, her short black hair hanging straight over the water, the clasp of her flesh-colored bra bulging out of the back of her thin white polo shirt.

"Eric's conspiracy theory is almost convincing," I said.

"If you don't insist on any evidence, it's perfect. And it is fun to talk about. However, to take it seriously is a little beyond me. Do you really think Dante is an ingenious fraud, a guy who talks to imaginary beings while toasting marshmallows, who half the time thinks he's Dante the fourteenth century poet? Sometimes the simplest story is the true story: Lee Harvey shot Kennedy, and he did it alone. Eric's tale would make you a better Broadway play, but not much else."

Magritt scraped spaghetti from the edge of a pot then scrubbed it clean. I dried the dishes. When we returned to the living room, Eric was looking out the window into the darkness, an unlit cigar hanging from his mouth.

"I'm going out for a smoke. Anyone care to join me?'

Magritt and I declined, choosing instead to stoke the fire, throw in another log, and rest on the couch.

"I embarrassed you this afternoon, didn't I, pulling off my clothes and jumping into the water? I thought show business people were beyond that, with all the nudity on stage, the studio couch, the out-of-town trials and hotel rooms," Magritt said, her tone almost apologetic, her speech rapid.

"Surprised, not embarrassed," I said, vanity keeping me from telling the truth. "Art historians sit over thick books in huge cathedrals; they don't strip."

"I was undressing, not stripping."

"Is there a difference?"

"Maybe someday I'll show you," Magritt answered, and gave me a small smile. Then she looked as if she were about to blush.

Eric opened a late-bottled vintage Port, which proved too sweet for my taste but seemed pleasing to Magritt and her lover. We finished it in front of the open fire, together yet apart. Eric engrossed himself in the previous weekend's Sunday *Times*; I began to read one of Philip Roth's early novels, *When She Was Good*, which I had found on a bookshelf in the room next to my bedroom, and quickly grew jealous of his talent. Magritt rewrote the notes she had made earlier in the day, every now and then asking me if I remembered this or that, and how I had interpreted Miller's words, his movements, his paintings.

"Damn," she barked after a half hour of appreciated silence. "You have to help me, Larry. I must see the originals. Slides are for students, not for scholars, and we are supposed to be scholars. I can't imagine putting my name on a piece of work without having seen the actual material—unless, of course, they burned in a castle or disappeared into Kazakhstan. But you must insist with me; two voices will be stronger than one."

Eric jumped in. "Are you on that kick again? Don't get worked up over something that will never happen. If they do cut you off from the originals, you'll have time enough to play the violated princess."

"Fuck you," she burst out.

"That's the best idea you've had all night," her lover answered.

"Sweet, isn't he?" Magritt said to me, but it was clear that she would accept his invitation.

We went to bed to the sound of a new storm. Thunder shook the old house and bolts of lightning ignited my window's yellow shade. In one of those half dreams that mix restless thoughts with uncontrolled visions, Hilla came to me in the little black dress we had bought together in a boutique shop on Madison Avenue, a magic dress, at once seductive and spiritual. It slid off her like oil.

I had spent my life around beautiful women—my mother, her friends, the countless actresses who struggled to project the emotions I penned for them. But Hilla's beauty was different. It was confident, and certain, and secure. No doubt prevented her from holding her head high, her neck decorated by a simple gold chain, her long, thick honey-chestnut hair waving free around a perfect face. How mischievous was life, to steal that all away from me.

Outside, claps of mournful thunder followed rapidly upon streaks of lightning. Night's blackness covered the lake, and all that I could see was the bare bulb that lit the Millers' porch. Had Beatrice ever tired of Dante, I asked myself, over their 700 years? Did she share Hilla's love of the physical aspects of love, even now in old age, her skin no longer elastic, her face and body signed by time? Or was timeless love not in the woman, but in the man, in what he permits himself to see, to feel, in what he is privileged to understand?

CHAPTER FIVE

THE RELENTLESS, heavy rain that had begun the night before had given way to a spectacular morning by the time I left the guesthouse early Friday. Sun rays broke from a sapphire sky, igniting the few droplets of water that still hugged the grass. I stood by the open door of the guesthouse, breathing in the cool sumptuous mountain air and smiling at the cacophony of birdcalls that emanated from the surrounding forest. As the door shut behind me, a deer with twin fawns raced into the woods. I sprinted up the steps to the Millers' porch two at a time.

Magritt was in the kitchen buttering a small muffin and chatting with Beatrice. I poured myself a cup of coffee and sat down between them.

"Are the menfolk up?" I asked Beatrice.

"Is that the type of dialogue that's used Off-Off-Broadway?" Magritt said, and stuffed some muffin into her mouth.

"Dante's picking up eggs and the paper. He'll bring the *Times* for you. And Eric, Magritt told me, left for Boston when the thunder ended," Beatrice answered, as if she hadn't heard Magritt's comment.

I teased my coauthor. "Did you throw him out?"

"Business," Magritt answered. "He'll be back on Sunday. And I'll be heading to Manhattan this afternoon."

"Are you and Dante heading out as well?" I asked.

"We're stay-at-home people."

"Good," I said. "I had planned to go back for the weekend, but it's just too beautiful out here. If I can borrow some soap for the washing machine, I'd like to stay."

"I'd rather you just take some," Beatrice said with a smile.

Magritt bit off some more of the muffin.

So began the morning, slow and easy, unhurried by the projects of life, comfortable with time. Country air, I decided. I wondered how farmers had the energy to rise at dawn and milk the cows.

"Tell me a little about Dante's work habits, Beatrice. Does he get going early to catch the morning light? Does he work through the night using electric bulbs or candle light?" I asked over my second cup of coffee.

"He'd burn down the house," Beatrice answered without a smile. When Dante was not around, she became shy and introspective, rarely smiling, almost never a laugh. When they were together, she became his mirror image, laughing spontaneously, her eyes full of mischief. I wondered if it was an act, if the real Beatrice had learned to save herself for her husband. Or did she need him around in order to be whole?

Beatrice rubbed her hands nervously; her wrinkled skin dotted with countless age marks, her knuckles slightly swollen by arthritis.

"He draws all the time, but painting, that's sporadic. Only when he reaches the 'grand design,' as he puts it, does he get out the oils. Then he's ceaseless, day and night, indoors mostly but not always, until he's satisfied. He destroys far more pieces than he finishes, sometimes painting over them, sometimes throwing them into a campfire near the lake. Eventually, the grand design, improved by experiment, emerges.

"He's very good, isn't he? Remember, he took up painting after he turned fifty, and he acts as if he is trying to catch up with the years he spent doing other things. I was jealous at first of all the time he devoted to his art, but it is far preferable to being discarded for a trophy wife."

"He told us he had stopped painting," Magritt said, her squinted eyes peeking over the wire frames of her glasses. For the last few days Magritt had been wearing contacts most of the time, which made her eyes look larger. In glasses, they seemed small and narrow.

Beatrice smiled softly. "I should have used the past tense," she said.

"But why did he stop? He's spry and talented," Magritt pressed.

"There are some things you need to talk to Dante about."

"Does it have something to do with Dante Alighieri?" I asked, trying to seek out, without offending her, if his adoption of Dante's persona was more than a personality tick—if it signaled a deep pathology.

"I don't understand?"

"Well, I'm sure you've noticed that at times he speaks as if he's Dante the poet, not Dante the artist. I was just wondering . . ."

"He's not impaired, Larry," Beatrice answered, her tone hard, as if I had just shouted an insult.

Magritt came to my rescue. "Larry didn't mean that."

I wouldn't let go. "I'm not being judgmental, but you have to admit that it's not an everyday occurrence talking to someone who acts 700 years old."

"Don't be hypnotized by his use of the first person. Listen to him. Don't dissect the man before you know his value," Beatrice shot back. Her back had stiffened and she had stopped rubbing her hands.

"I'm not dissecting him, Beatrice. I just want to know if this is new, or did he always shift personalities? Is this a teaching style or is it a belief?"

"Ask him, Larry, not me. He's never reluctant to talk about himself, although he doesn't like to dwell on the personal."

I was ready to apologize, to say it was wrong for me to ask her questions best answered by her husband, but the sound of Elias Miller's car kicking up gravel in the parking area behind the house rescued me from continuing to say things I had not thought through.

The room was ice when the artist entered, but he acted as if he didn't notice. He handed the *Times* to me and presented the eggs to Beatrice.

"Where's Eric?" he asked.

Dante was in an effusive mood, smiling easily, laughing at his own comments. His skin was ruddy and his short pants revealed solid thighs. His body was younger than his face, a bit overweight but muscular, the physique of a man who had spent his days hiking mountain paths and his evenings with good food and drink. But the lines in his face seemed to have deepened during the night, and the bags under his eyes grown weighty. Magritt and I had disturbed his sleep, I thought, our presence imbuing him with middle-of-the-night questions. It was to be expected.

After two fried eggs, an English muffin, and several cups of coffee, Dante turned to art.

"My den is ready for your use. There are countless slides, more than one for each painting. And there are drawings—

faces, mainly. I love faces. If I had gone into art before I ran into the *Commedia*, I would have become a portraitist, maybe with a camera. I would have liked that, painting beautiful women but taking pictures of all humanity. Beatrice would have been my favorite subject."

"But there would have been others," Beatrice said with laughter in her voice.

"There is much more to your art than portraits. Your shadowed backgrounds are complex, with multiple hues, and the lake—the ice made me feel cold," Magritt said, her head pushed forward, her neck elongated.

"It took a great deal of work."

"I'm certain. It shows. But I'd have to see the originals to understand your technical skills," Magritt continued.

"Of course, Magritt, you must. Can you imagine reading me only in inadequate English translations, never to hear the music of my Italian, to sense the true rhythms of my muse? How distant you would remain from my spirit."

I glanced at Beatrice, but she turned away and acted as if she had not noticed anything unusual.

"Great," Magritt exclaimed. She pushed her body so far forward on the chair that I thought she was going to fall off. "When and how?"

"There's the rub, as they say. Most of them, I believe, are still concentrated in a few hands, but they may have scattered since Madeline's death. I don't know where many of them are, or who owns them. Some may have been lost, or auctioned off at charity dinners, and now lie in steamy attics under piles of old newspapers."

"I doubt it," Beatrice inserted.

Dante smiled luxuriously. His features were designed for celebration: a large mouth, his lips turned up at the corners, his eyes a dazzling blue, his teeth large and white. It was as if the structure of his face was commanded by his personality . . . or could it have been the other way around?

"I don't know how we can go forward with only slides," Magritt continued, emphasizing the "we," to my discomfort.

"No doubt, no doubt. I'm not suggesting you'll have to, but Harland will have to be your guide. He is likely to know where my paintings now hang."

"Was he that close to your patron? What was her name?" inquired Magritt, forever the researcher.

"Madeline Brewster. He was her son-in-law. I guess no one told you that. He has a few of the paintings, but he told me he keeps some of them in a vault. I don't think he likes looking within the *Inferno* when he's relaxing at night. I doubt if he finds *Purgatorio* much more comforting. But do you need to see all my work? You are not preparing a catalog raisonné. All you need to do is select a few images that express what I have been attempting to do. I see two steps: Choose the most intriguing paintings from the slides, and then have Harland guide you to the originals. Don't you think that will work?"

"Possibly," Magritt responded, looking directly into the professor's face and forcing her dark brown eyes to open wide. Then she turned and gave me a positive nod, her expression relaxed. Good for you, Professor Miller, I thought.

No slides were examined on Friday. Magritt left for Manhattan before noon and looking at the slides alone would have been futile. Magritt would not have accepted my evaluations, and I wouldn't have trusted them.

I SPENT THE WEEKEND skimming through the multiple translations of the *Commedia* Dante had stored in the guesthouse, fascinated by the enormous diversity among the English translations, and by the endless footnotes and commentary that swelled many editions. Surprising, too, were the multiple artists affected by Dante's poem, painters as contemporary as Salvador Dali and Robert Rauschenberg, as classic as Delacroix, Botticelli, and Blake.

"You're certainly in good company," I said to Dante. It was Saturday evening. We were sitting on a log facing the lake, digesting the heavy dinner we had taken on the screened porch.

Dante looked out over the darkening lake, and pointed to the ducks swimming near the shore, and then to a distant rowboat that carried a lone fisherman.

"Beautiful, isn't it? I love this time of day, the time between light and dark, when all things seem possible. There is gentleness in the air. You can think the earth holds still for a minute so that day and night can whisper to one another. Great artists are inspired by nature, Laurence, but few have tried to paint this hour of the day."

He paused for a moment, gave out a soft laugh, and picked up a stick from the ground.

"Artists love light," he continued. "Even when they paint night they fill it with moon and stars. But twilight—do you know of any landscapes made mysterious by this hour? Dante has inspired artists I cannot even dream of emulating. How could he not fascinate them? His poetry is full of images: of fear, of punishment, of exile—it brims over with fallen people, whores and popes, scoundrels and emperors. Beautiful people, too, roam my afterworld: Beatrice and Virgil, Thomas Aquinas, Emperor Justinian, King Solomon. How can a draftsman deny Satan and Jesus and God?

"Some artists try to make the poem more accessible, others use the *Commedia* to project their personal artistic visions. I am doing something different, Laurence. I am preparing a new edition of the great poem, not simply translating it. Don't get me wrong; I'm not treating the *Commedia* as an early draft. I worked too hard on its writing. I threw out too many false starts; I burnt too many sheets of mundane poetry. I love the *Commedia*. I am proud of it. Time, however, has taught me things. I have a different vision now. The Church is no longer the only hope for order and decency; religion is not alone in keeping chaos at bay. And knowledge extinguishes the need to block from our minds and history the black side of belief."

Dante paused and waited for me to say something. I couldn't find my words. What do you say to a dead genius? How do you talk to a poet who has been silent for 700 years?

Dante continued. "I knew unchaste popes and evil politicians. I survived traitors and scoundrels. Yet, Laurence, I had not realized—can you believe—that a whole people could mask their evil under noble words, that cultured nations could perpetrate horrors that challenge Satan's villainy. The twentieth century has been a mean and powerful teacher."

"True," was all I said before my companion interrupted me.

"It's getting chilly," he said.

I went inside to say goodnight to Beatrice and slowly wandered back to the guesthouse. "A new edition of my poem," he had said. How was I to explain that to Magritt?

ERIC SURPRISED ME in the morning, standing by the kitchen counter and pouring milk into a bowl of cereal.

"I didn't expect to see you until Monday. When did you get in?"

"Late last night. You must have been fast asleep. It turned out to be a shorter lookout than I expected. I wouldn't have driven all the way to Boston if I knew it was only going to be just a day's work. Would you like some coffee?"

"I'll make it," I suggested. When he didn't resist, I opened a half-full bag of beans and pulled out the electric grinder.

Eric sat down at the kitchen table, his thick, reddish blonde hair in disordered waves.

"What was the job?"

"A cheating wife case—nothing thrilling, no stolen jewels, no dead bodies. But it might make a cute one-act play."

"Did you catch her?"

"It wasn't hard. She drives a 1960s pink Cadillac convertible. Can you think of anything easier to follow? But she wasn't dallying. The three people closest to her, her husband, her recently married son, a daughter in graduate school on the West Coast, each have secret lives. Her husband's work—he's a research chemist—is beyond her understanding. Her children's love lives are private. Only she was without an elusive persona. So she created one, not with boy-toys but with some of her former college roommates who found themselves with similar dilemmas and longed for private lives. They meet for lunch, sometimes for dinner. They go out of town for a night and two. Her husband, who's a good ten years older than she, became suspicious. He concluded that she was jumping some delayed adolescent at a local motel and her girlfriends were covering for her."

"So it wasn't sex."

"In a strange way, it was."

"She fell in love with the other woman," I joked.

"You playwrights think you know sex, but you don't,"

Eric said, unexpectedly argumentative. "You should become a private detective for a while or work in an emergency room. You writers are too caught up in the sensation-of-the-day, gays and lesbians, multiple partners; adultery is too common to bother writing about, pedophilia too risky. When the wife realized her husband's qualms, she also recognized that his suspicions made him randy. Familiarity had produced a commonplace sex life, a once-a-week feel and tuck that Victoria's Secret lingerie couldn't turn around. When he suspected she was straying, he became a lion, night and day, as if he might never have another chance. So she strung out her secret until I came along."

"You exaggerate his prowess."

"Maybe not. After talking to the wife, I talked to the husband. I told him what was going on and recommended he buy Viagra or a vibrator or both."

"It still won't make a one-act play."

"Maybe you'll join me on my next case. It would do you good, Larry. If nothing else, you might pick up a line or two."

I poured him a cup of coffee and sat down next to him. "Is that what you plan to do with your experiences as a detective—write novels or short stories, maybe a play or television script?"

Eric didn't have to think of an answer. He was prepared. "No one takes my career seriously. Not my parents, not Magritt, not you. They think a Yale degree means you have to do something significant—and I put quotes around the word significant. But Larry, I'm not researching life, I'm living it."

"And me? Do you think I'm not living life?"

Eric drew in a deep breath, then his facial muscles relaxed and he threw out a large, appealing smile. "I'm sorry, Larry; I can get very defensive. I wasn't psychoanalyzing you. Yale at least taught me that."

I pushed back from the table, hurt by his allusion to researching life, and tried to think of something to say that would not sound as defensive as he had. No ideas came to me.

"How long have you and Magritt been dating?" I asked, to change the topic.

Eric looked relieved. "Six months, maybe one or two more. Why do you ask?"

"You seem so comfortable together, I thought it was longer."

"We do get along, but it's not because of history. We just don't ask much of each other. Magritt lets me come and go, and I let her. I don't fool around, and I don't think she does. But we both know ours is a temporary mating . . . good this summer but history next."

"That surprises me. I thought you were in love."

Eric avoided looking at me and wiped his perfectly clean face with a paper napkin. "Are you looking for a heavy conversation or wondering if she's available?"

If his biceps weren't twice as large as mine I would have gone with availability. But they were, so I answered, "I'm just being heavy. I recently broke up with someone after five years and I've been thinking about love and commitment."

"Did she put a detective on you?"

"She didn't have to."

"Sex pushes us to fall in love and then forces us out of it. Life's central dilemma, when to push it in and when to take it out," Eric said. Then he laughed at his obvious obscenity. "But you're the playwright. You're supposed to have the answers. I just find out what people do. I don't ask why."

"That I don't believe. Without the 'why' you'd be bored to death."

Eric shrugged his shoulders and let my remark pass. "Did you love her?" he asked.

"Very much," I said without thinking.

"That makes it harder."

"Do you love Magritt?"

Eric smiled and touched my hand. "I won't let myself."

"It was simpler, wasn't it, when getting laid meant getting married or romancing your neighborhood hooker? Biology and obligation went together or you paid cash. Now sex and dating are synonyms. Marriage means less mating, not more. It works against biology," I said, trying to sound sophisticated about life.

"What of love?" Eric asked, suddenly the romantic. He pushed his bowl to the center of the table.

"On every street corner," I answered, sounding more cynical than any of my fictive characters.

Eric let out a loud, comfortable laugh. "You should be the detective, Larry."

I spent the rest of the day reading *Paradiso* and wanting to get laid.

MAGRITT WAS WEARING the tiniest shorts ever manufactured when she arrived Monday afternoon. She waved toward the lake and threw Eric, who was taking his daily laps, a huge smile. I expected her clothes to drop on the grass and her enticing body to jump into the lake, but instead she pulled an overnight bag from the back seat of her car and headed toward the Millers' porch, where Dante and I were treating ourselves to cigars and jealously commenting on Eric's endless energy. "Magritt doesn't give him enough," the professor decided as Eric made his fortieth turn.

"She's been away," I argued.

"Still," he insisted, "if she gave him enough he'd want to save it up for her return."

"Magritt!" Dante yelled out as she approached. His voice filled with mischief. "My, you are looking good."

Magritt tugged at the bottom of her shorts in a vain attempt to lengthen them. "And it's good to see you, too."

She threw the leather satchel on the porch, bent over and kissed Dante on the cheek.

"Don't I get a welcome like that?" I teased.

"Those cigars stink," she said. Whatever had happened over her weekend, our relationship was unchanged.

"I'm excited," she said as she plopped down on a wooden chair near the table, "and hungry. Let me grab something from the refrigerator, and then let's get to work. Time is fleeting."

ELIAS MILLER HAD NOT misinformed us. There were multiple shots of his pieces, differentiated by light, angle, or focus; some clearly the work of an amateur, others—by luck, I decided—looking like the efforts of someone who knew how to use a camera. Each slide contained the name of the painting and the section of the *Commedia* illustrated. We started by sorting the slides in parallel with the poem, beginning with *Inferno I* and running through *Purgatorio XXXIII*. It was a tedious task, but not without fascination. When I turned out the lights in the den and Magritt pulled at her shorts, it was after eight.

Eric and Magritt went into town that evening. I spent the time listening to the silence of the house, feeling lonely rather than alone, and longing for someone to stand with me, to gaze over the long lake, to watch Elias and Beatrice sit by a campfire, their faces pointing out to the water where starlight waltzed. I wanted someone to love.

IN THE MORNING, I awoke to birdcalls and the quacking of a duck. I imagined her chicks following behind in perfect formation.

Magritt was finishing breakfast when I got downstairs, and Eric had left for an assignment in Washington, D.C. I took some coffee, pushed down a banana and—notepaper in hand—walked with Magritt to the Millers' house. On my partner's red polo shirt, spelled out in bright blue letters, was "I Love New York." Curiosity got the best of me. "I thought that on all 'I Love New York' shirts the word love is represented by a heart and not spelled out."

"Well, evidently you're wrong," Magritt answered before picking up a duck plume from the grass. She blew on it softly as if making a wish.

Eric was the one who was wrong. If I had the chance, I'd allow myself to fall in love with a woman like Magritt. It would be worth the heartbreak.

MAGRITT'S WORK HABITS blended comfortably with mine. We breakfasted early each morning and got over to the Millers' house while they were still asleep, about 8:00 a.m. Magritt would run through the notes she had made the day before as introduction to what we were preparing to examine. Then the two of us would review the meticulous comments Dante had written down about each of the compositions we planned to explore, unraveling the canto and lines that inspired his oil. When Dante's notes didn't satisfy and Alighieri's poem continued to perplex, Magritt and I would dip into the extensive annotations that accompanied most of the translations, and we'd debate conflicting poetics and multiple interpretations.

When we broke for lunch, Magritt would don a one-piece black bathing suit and take a long swim before grabbing a cup of coffee and some fruit. I would dine at the Millers, usually with Dante alone. He would elicit the sections of *Commedia* Magritt and I had visited that morning, and—like a respectful colleague who wanted to help but not overrun—offer additional interpretations and analyses.

"Try reading it as memoir," Professor Miller suggested during one of those conversations, "as the experience of a thirty-five-year-old man who has been driven from his home—an alienated and lonely pilgrim seeking meaning in his history; a soul looking for guidance. Beatrice, his long-departed love, reaches out from Heaven to rescue him from a wastrel's life. She arranges for him to travel through Hell and Purgatory with the great Roman poet Virgil, author of the *Aeneid*, and then to journey through Heaven with her. Did Dante actually travel through the worlds that await us after death? Or did he only believe he traveled through them? Or is the *Commedia* a totally imaginative work? Those are questions that none of us can answer. What is important is what we learn from his journey, that we find joy in his language and solace in visions."

"My mind is much too modern for that, Dante, too infused with science. If I were a devout Christian, I might find it easier to conceive of the poet actually thinking he saw the other side. But I don't believe in an afterlife. I have the prejudice of a modern man. I can't believe he explored the afterworld: I can't even imagine that he believed in a life after death. The poetry is too beautiful, his concepts too insightful. I know it's wrong-headed and prejudiced. People of faith can write powerful poems and genuinely understand the human dilemma. But I can't help it, just as I can't believe that the Divine wrote the Bible and that it isn't the scribbling of humankind. Dante wrote a Christian poem because that was what was expected. He took readers to the worlds of the dead to cater to their universal questions about death. He was challenging Virgil for poetry's grand prize. How could he have beaten the *Aeneid* without creating an extraordinary voyage?"

"So you think it is a masterful work by someone who desired a best seller?" Dante said.

"Who wanted to write something that would make him immortal, not immortal in the afterlife, but immortal in this life, among people who breathed, who loved, who bore children. Fame, that's what he was after, and he earned it."

"Is that why you write, for immortality and fame?" the professor asked.

The question took me aback. I fumbled my way to an answer. "I take my writing seriously. Comedy is serious work, and I struggle to make people laugh—isn't that a contribution to human betterment? I think I have something to say. I fill my stage with likeable people who care about each other. That is my message: complicated people, some antisocial and some not, but all with redeeming qualities. I want the audience to remember an enjoyable evening and to leave the theater with a deeper appreciation of our better cherubs."

"Dante had a message, too. No one could labor so assiduously without profoundly valuing what he had to say, without believing he had a message worthy of silver words and golden images."

"And what was it?" I asked irreverently.

"As I would tell my students—that you have to discover on your own, like each of us must discover our own quality and beauty, kindness, and love. He was a Christian, and he was trying to understand Christianity, not simply to instruct others about God and Church, but to show them what kind of journey is necessary—what exile from this world is required—to appreciate life's beauty, to separate light from darkness. If you don't find the answers in the poem, you will find it in my art, Laurence, or I am terribly wrong about you."

"And Magritt . . . will she find it, too?" I asked. It wasn't a serious question, at least to me. To Dante, it required an answer.

"I don't know. She is a scholar and not an artist; she is more rational, more suffused with knowledge."

"I don't know if I should take that as a compliment."

Dante didn't answer; he moved his cup of coffee as if it were a chess piece and he was just beginning the game.

LATER THAT AFTERNOON, I described the conversation to Magritt, but instead of repeating Dante's doubts about her ability to fully appreciate the *Commedia*, I spread his perspective on my potential enlightenment over us both. "I hope he's right," she answered while thumbing through *The New York Times*. "I'd hate to go through all this work and end up in the Ninth Circle with my head frozen in ice and my mind a blank."

CHAPTER SIX

MAGRITT AND I spent the next eight days studying one projected image after another, our eyes strained by the semi-darkness, our backs rebelling against the hard wooden chairs. We looked at each image two or three times, sometimes more, going over it ever more slowly to be certain to see all that was glorious in the geometry, in the bold colors, in the symbols and faces, trying to find the meaning under the image, analyzing the poet and the painter. When our discussions turned quarrelsome we'd break for an hour or two, irritated by each other and frustrated by our slow progress. Magritt would go for a swim; I'd walk along the dirt roads that surrounded the compound, throwing pebbles at imaginary targets and questioning if the task was worth the effort. But finally, visually and intellectually exhausted, we compromised on thirty-six Miller paintings, hoping that scrutinizing the originals would allow us to easily cut back to the fifteen illustrations planned for the published monograph. Miller didn't argue with our selection, although he made it clear that he would have chosen a slightly different set. But we jealously guarded our right to choose, and there was enough overlap between our tastes and his to put the professor at ease.

I emailed Harland Van Ness and described the exacting process Magritt and I had followed to cut Miller's oeuvre down to thirty-six finalists. I added a strongly phrased argument as to why it was imperative for us to see the originals before making our final selections. I listed the thirty-six works by their titles, gave a brief description of each composition, and, to be certain not to mislead, identified their place in the *Commedia.*

After I hit the send button, Magritt and I joined the Millers on their porch and opened the first of the two bottles of sparkling wine Dante had brought up from the cellar.

"To the project," I said, and raised my glass.

"To your mission," Dante answered.

"We're just beginning," Magritt mused, deflating, but only for an instant, the joy of the moment.

Beatrice allowed us a patient and knowing smile. "Well done," she said.

"Is your name really Beatrice, or did you take it up when you discovered your husband's love of the *Commedia?*" I found myself brazenly asking.

Dante let out a booming laugh.

Beatrice's cheeks reddened. "It's my Christian name. I've had it since the day I was born, most probably before. Dante married me because my name was Beatrice. His infatuation with Dante preceded his infatuation with me."

"Because you are everything that Dante saw in Beatrice, by whatever name your parents called you: grace and charity, beauty and wisdom, 'the brightness of everlasting light,' as King Solomon would say," her husband insisted.

"Wow," Magritt commented. "Now that's a heavy burden to carry."

"An impossible burden," Beatrice said.

"But you carry it well," I jumped in.

"Thank you." Beatrice laughed.

Dinner preparation fell to Eric, who had just returned from Washington, D.C. Under Beatrice's scrutiny, he roasted a large, stuffed chicken in the Millers' oven and sautéed freshly picked produce in a cast iron pan Beatrice had pulled up from under the sink. As if to put the lie to Harland's comment about drinking moderately priced Italian wines, Professor Miller brought up a couple bottles of a twelve-year-old Brunello di Montepulciano.

We spent the evening relishing our companionship. Eric talked about his "not very interesting" Washington, D.C., case—following an emergency room physician with a passion for women other than his wife—and Dante and Beatrice told anecdotes drawn from their teaching careers. Beatrice asked if I was working on a new play, if Magritt's dissertation was progressing. She mused about Magritt's future. "College teaching is not a bad way of life, but you might prefer to be a museum curator, or maybe a freelance art critic whose name will appear in national newspapers and magazines, and whose voice will be heard on public broadcasting stations."

"Mankind's burden," Dante pontificated, "endless choices. People often miss that when they read the *Commedia*, that free will is a burden and not a gift, as heavy now as it was in 1300. Knowledge complicates choosing. It makes our decisions less automatic, more reasoned—but not necessarily better. What is so obviously vile is turned heroic by a just cause. Call it a class struggle, or a religious movement, or God's blessing, and you can garner a sympathetic audience. What is evidently good can be turned sour by fear of unintended consequences. Does dropping something into a beggar's cup make me a humanitarian or an enabler? Am I putting bread into someone's stomach or preventing him from finding a higher purpose for life? Am I being worthy by limiting the number of children I bring into this struggling world, or am I committing a profound evil by artificially preventing souls from enjoying God's bounty? When I was a young man, the Church answered all those questions. Even if some bishops were unholy, the Church itself stood for all that was good. It was the bastion against Satan. Now, free will is dizzying. Even if I had the gifts of my youth for pen and paper, I still couldn't conceive of an allegory that would do justice to the contemporary universe of personalities and institutions. Of course, Beatrice would still be there, central for all times, a vision of life's possibilities, the splendor of the light eternal. No, I could not write the *Commedia* today. My poetry required a world made understandable by faith."

Dante filled his glass, and then, as if sensing his self-absorption, offered the bottle to the rest of us.

Magritt motioned for some more wine, her face filling with questions as it so often did when Professor Miller moved into the great poet's character. Beatrice's expression did not change. It remained at once wise and innocent, oblivious to her husband's changing guise. Eric's eyes widened, his shoulders rolled forward, and his spine bowed. I sat still, watching the others watch Dante, his double-size face, his full white beard, his blue eyes full of candor. I could see the scene on stage, four bewildered characters dissecting the fifth. How would I portray Dante Miller? Would he be a jovial eccentric faking 700 years of accumulated understanding, pacing the stage in a white toga, his beard riding on his chest, his hands forever holding a leather-bound book? Or would the play be better served if he were a kindly oddball who unconsciously slipped into the persona of a medieval poet in order to distance himself from the pains of the day? Better yet, at least for ticket sales, I could resurrect Dante Alighieri, his mind inflamed by the twenty-first century, hunkering down in a dark dungeon, writing mystical reports to God about the failings of man. Yes, that would work, off Broadway and on.

"DOES HE DO THAT OFTEN—think he's Dante?" Eric asked after we had settled down in front of the fireplace in the guesthouse, enjoying the smells and warmth of burning logs.

"Only after a glass or two of wine," I said dismissively.

Magritt took the question more seriously. "I find it unsettling. Old age, I tell myself, but he's not that old. At first, I thought he was pulling our legs, talking like Dante to tweak our curiosity. But now, I believe it's some form of pathology. Beatrice seems used to it, but I . . . it gets to me every time."

"Maybe he is losing his faculties. That would explain why he doesn't paint scenes of Heaven, and maybe that's why they want us to finish the project quickly, while he is still well enough to help. He's very likeable, and very talented. I hate to think his best days are over," I said, depressed by my own observation.

Eric continued the conversation. "I wonder if Miller is in on the scheme to pump up the value of his work, and if his Dante act is just a way of getting you more intrigued. I can see him performing his one-man show on television, metamorphosing into Dante right before the viewer's eyes and transforming a staid professor into an instant celebrity. Is he mentally challenged or has Dante Alighieri returned? Just think of what that could do to the price of his paintings."

"You're the one who's beginning to worry me, Eric," Magritt said. "You've been following too many lustful doctors."

"I think both of you are caught up in the machinery of fashion, and you don't know it," Eric surmised.

Magritt and I decided not to argue.

THE LOVERS RETIRED to their bedroom soon after we had finished the delightful Italian dessert wine Dante had gifted us. I tried to catch up with Sunday's *New York Times*, but the first squeak from the couple's double bed drove me upstairs, magazine section in hand but with little enthusiasm for reading. When I opened a window to cool the room, Dante's laughter burst in. Beatrice was sitting on a log, her back curved toward the heat from a fading campfire, her husband standing slightly behind her right side, gesticulating wildly. I thought of rousing Magritt, but Eric's presence dampened the idea, so I stood by the window, a lone voyeur.

Dante helped Beatrice up and the two of them seemed to say goodnight to their invisible company, Dante shaking hands, Beatrice turning her face in one direction and then the other to receive kisses on her cheeks. She left first, walking slowly to their house, her head high, her shoulders squared, a bright flashlight beam illuminating the way. Dante watched her enter their house before throwing wood on the fire. As the flames swelled, he sat down on the ground, resting his back on the log Beatrice had used, his face toward the lake, and his feet close to the rocks that circled the fire pit.

I strained to hear the wood crackle, and I watched the sparks shoot toward the star-filled sky. Incapable of containing my curiosity, I put on a sweater and walked slowly down the sloping lawn to the lake.

"A beautiful night, isn't it?" I said in a soft voice, hoping to avoid startling the painter.

"That it is," he answered as if he had expected to hear my voice, "a most beautiful night, Laurence, full of life's pleasures. Are you alone?"

"I'm afraid so. Magritt and Eric retired early, but I couldn't stay inside."

"Nighttime is made for lovers, although the day isn't bad, either. Here, sit down beside me, let the fire heat your feet. It rushes the blood to the head and helps the complexion."

I emulated my host and sat on the ground, leaning against an adjoining log, my feet stretched toward the fire, my ass cold against the damp dirt, my mind wanting to ask what he and Beatrice were doing when I spied them from the window. But the contentment in his voice and in his posture silenced me.

"'Pure light fills the Empyrean, the light of uncorrupted love, so bright that it is incomprehensible to the mortal mind' . . . or so I wrote. A metaphor for what cannot be known. I could have used night as my metaphor, could I not? A night like this, filled with Heaven's stars, with tranquil air, pure and chaste. But when I wrote, humankind was afraid of the night; it was afraid of what it couldn't see and what it didn't know. The Devil works at night, hidden from God. So I used light, as if seeing lets us know, as if sight cannot deceive. All was illuminated in my Heaven by the power of eternal love."

He took a deep breath and closed his eyes.

I risked a question. "Would you write *Paradiso* differently if you were writing today?"

He didn't hesitate to answer. "Not just *Paradiso*, I would write all of it differently, Laurence. I have changed. I'm older. Experience alone alters the mind. But *Paradiso*, yes, that I would change most of all."

"The poetry is brilliant, among the most moving. And the imagery . . . incredibly inventive: the River of Light from which Pilgrim drinks; the Empyrean's Rose, its countless petals occupied by the blessed, the Virgin Mary seated at its highest point," I said.

"I was very good," Dante said turning his head to me and smiling. "I've always had an enormous ego—which I know is not a medieval concept. Can you imagine a small ego undertaking a journey from Hell to Paradise?"

He paused and turned his bearded face to the lake. The flickering flames played on his features, emphasizing his large nose now, his thick beard a moment later, making him look strangely younger and more relaxed, comfortable living in the mind of someone centuries old, a poet whose intelligence is beyond modern reasoning, a man whose faith was untested by Newton or Darwin or Einstein.

"Remember, Laurence, I was a true and honest writer. *Paradiso* opens with a warning: That which I was about to describe was not what I experienced, but an instructional device designed to help the living understand the world of the worthy dead. The magnificence of Heaven cannot be contained in mere words; it is eternally hidden from mortal imaginings. If I had been entirely honest, I would have left it there. We cannot understand God's mind and the fullness of his creation—period. End of poem. But I didn't. I tried to transcend the battle between revelation and literature like so many poets before and after me. I knew one thing, if the poem was to have the majesty I so sought, the final canticle would have to balance the ones that went before, its structure similar, and its voice even stronger. My solution was imperfect, as all things on Earth are imperfect. I continued the pattern of *Purgatorio* and the *Inferno* and, building on the astronomy of the day, designed a Heaven based on the known planets and theological spheres—the Moon, Mercury, Venus, the Sun, Mars, Jupiter, Saturn, the Fixed Stars, the

Primum Mobile, and finally the Empyrean." Dante stopped, and let out a boisterous laugh. "See, I remember them and in the right order, even after these many years. The Primum Mobile circles the fixed Earth with the speed of light; the other spheres move more slowly, in descending order, the Moon being the slowest. My Heaven had a built-in hierarchy, the closest terrestrial bodies low, the Empyrean—the house of God—the zenith. The major problem, Laurence—if all the blessed live with God, how should the many heavens be populated? Do I rank the blessed starting with those who had just snuck into Heaven and place them on the Moon, the sphere closest to the Earth?"

Dante gave a mournful sound and turned from me to the lake. I waited for him to continue, but he sat silent, recalling, I assumed, some canto from the great poem.

"Your solution has satisfied readers for 700 years. Most writers would be content with that," I commented, expecting the humor in my voice would inspire him to say more.

"I used a hierarchy, but I had Beatrice announce to my readers that the order was meaningless; it was an instructional tool. All in Heaven are content. All live in God's light. How did I make that possible? By suspending all natural law. God does not need physics. He needs no chemistry or biology. He is all-powerful; all-knowing. The blessed are not constrained to a single sphere. Their spirits can be in multiple places at the same time, for time has no meaning, space knows no boundaries, gravity does not exist. Is it true? I ask myself. In the *Inferno* there is truth. The damned deserve to be damned, their punishments are just. Purgatory has veracity. The shades suffer; the shades learn. Sinners are redeemed. I am less certain about Heaven, with God in the Empyrean surrounded by his angels. I miss the God of the Old Testament, the God who walks the Earth, whose voice speaks to Moses. I want

God to walk among us, in love with all his creations, from the blade of grass to the snake that slithers on the lawn."

Dante lifted himself from the ground and stirred the fire with a stick. When its flames reluctantly thickened and stretched, he sat down on the log against which I was leaning, his knee touching my shoulder. "Do you believe in Heaven, Laurence?" he asked quietly.

"I'm a secularist, Dante, not a believer. I think one life is all we get and we have to make the most of it. I don't believe in Divine punishment or reward."

"I believe in Heaven, Laurence, I truly do. But I don't know if it lies in the Heavens. I think it is closer to the ground we are sitting on. If I were to write now, Hell and Purgatory would reside in the inner Earth, and Heaven would be spread across our planet's continents and the oceans."

"Mixing with corrupt humanity, Dante? I don't see how you could convince your readers of that, certainly not for 700 years," I answered.

He let out an unruly laugh and got up from the log. "It is a paradox," he said cryptically, and ended our conversation.

HARLAND'S ANSWER to my email arrived sometime during the night. "Thank you for the update. I agree; you must see the originals to appreciate Miller's work fully. I've already begun to make the necessary arrangements. I'll be in touch."

"Just as I told you," Eric said.

CHAPTER SEVEN

HARLAND WAS AS GOOD as his word. By the end of the following week, he had scheduled a visit for us with Madeline Brewster's widower, Caleb Brewster, and given us alternative dates for visiting with him and his wife Susan— Brewster's daughter—and with Madeline's closest friend, Roberta Whitford. "Son Jonathan has some of Miller's work," Harland emailed, "but I've not been able to arrange a visit. It's not very important. Caleb, Roberta, and I have the bulk of the collection, more than enough to illustrate your monograph even if we decided to triple its size. Call me soon."

On Friday evening, in the second week of July, Magritt and I found ourselves drenched by a warm torrential downpour as we squeezed out of a taxicab on 79th Street and Fifth Avenue. A uniformed doorman peeked out of the windowed entrance to the apartment building, quickly put on his hard-brimmed hat, and slowly opened the heavy door. "Mr. Brewster is expecting you," he said as soon as I gave our names. He waved to us to walk along a thick plastic runner that had been laid down to protect the reception area's plush carpet from rain-soaked footwear—an intrusive bit of practicality in an otherwise glittering entrance hall, its mirrored walls made brilliant by the light from a huge chandelier.

A young woman in a brown short-sleeved blouse rose from the elevator's wooden folding seat, closed the gated door, and pressed the button to the fifteenth floor. "Miserable weather," she said without looking at us. When she pulled the gate back, we were in Caleb Brewster's large foyer. Two handsome young women—identically dressed and with identical Slavic accents—welcomed us. The taller one took my wet umbrella and Magritt's raincoat, gave us a large smile, and asked us to follow her coworker. We followed the shorter woman down a parquet-floored corridor, its right wall lined with art-filled mahogany-and-glass display cases.

Curiosity made it impossible to keep up with the maid as either Magritt or I became fascinated by ancient ceramics, delicate marble carvings, and bronze castings.

"Greek, Greek, Etruscan, Roman," Magritt whispered as she waved her finger at one object and then another. "Chinese, Japanese, I don't know," she continued, her finger running down yet another showcase.

"Hepplewhite," Magritt said when she stopped to peer into the first of the open rooms we were to pass. "Shaker," she whispered after glancing into the second room.

"Move it," I politely suggested.

Brewster was patiently waiting for us at the entrance to the massive drawing room, his hands pressed against the sterling silver handle of his rosewood cane. He was every bit of his eighty-eight years, his hair thin and gray, his back slightly bent, his skin worn pink. Yet there were reminders of a past handsomeness, a long angular face and Roman nose, dark brown eyes, and thin lips. The phrase "classical marble" popped into my mind.

"Miss Cline and Mr. Sullivan, welcome. We've been

looking forward to your visit. Sit and be comfortable," Brewster said in a melodic patrician accent that caught me off guard. He pointed toward the gray couch that faced the fireplace. Magritt and I sank into its thick upholstery. He sat in an orthopedically friendly straight-backed chair and rested the walking stick between his legs.

"We've already eaten, but if you'd like something, it can easily be arranged."

Magritt and I declined.

"Then something to drink—a Bordeaux perhaps, or Scotch? If you would like something sweet, I have some good ports and nice Sauternes, and a long list of non-alcoholic drinks, teas, and coffee."

"Wine would be nice—a dry red, if you have one opened," Magritt said.

"And you, Mr. Sullivan? We usually stay with wine, but if you would like something stronger . . ."

"Wine would be fine," I said, while wondering if Brewster always used the royal "we" or if Magritt and I were being hosted by him and someone else.

"Wine it will be," Brewster concluded.

He lifted his right hand slightly and waved it. The shorter of the maids, the one with dark hair and ample hips, quickly materialized. Just as quickly, she moved away after Brewster quietly spoke to her.

"Harland tells me you're interested in seeing the Miller paintings. I have quite a few, as he must have told you, although a number of them are in Connecticut. My late wife loved his work. The last great crush of her life. Madeline liked artists, male and female, but she had a special place for Elias. 'Dante, my love,' I'd hear her say over the phone, 'how wonderful your last piece is. I wake in the middle of the night and wander off just to gaze at it.' And she did, Miss

Cline, she did. You're the art historian, aren't you . . . Lester's daughter?"

Magritt's eyes widened. "You knew my father?"

"We met when he was a senior in high school. I interviewed him for Stanford, one of the services I perform as a contributing alumnus. I give them money and they allow me to do work for them, a pleasant if unusual relationship. I never regretted recommending him. He is one of the few I sent off who came by to thank me years later. His death was a terrible blow. He was so young and had so much to contribute. And your mother, Sarah, how is she doing?"

"She's fine, thank you; working as hard as ever."

"Good for her," Brewster said, a drop of sadness in his voice. "Do you remember him?" he asked.

"Of course I do," Magritt said, sounding surprised by the question. "I think of him often."

I could feel the sofa's cushion move as Magritt pushed her body deeper into it. I knew her father had died when she was twelve, that her mother had not remarried, that she practiced corporate law, as he had. But I didn't know her father's name was Lester, that her mother was called Sarah. My ignorance embarrassed me. I reached out and tenderly touched Magritt's hand.

"Let's think of happier things," Brewster said. "Do you get passionate about artists the way Madeline did?"

"Only dead ones," Magritt said, without humor.

Brewster's mouth labored to smile. "And you, Mr. Sullivan . . . I have to apologize. I have read some reviews of your work, but have never seen one of your plays. I don't get out very much, and the theater is particularly difficult for me. People complain that I hit them with my cane when I squeeze by to get to my seat. But I'm sure the work is good."

I smiled. What else could I do? And the reviews, he'd most probably had a secretary get them off the Internet.

"Oh," Brewster exclaimed, "I see the wine has come."

The taller, thinner maid, carrying a large tray on a bent arm, slowly walked to the opposite end of the parlor and gracefully placed a wine bottle on top of a pentagonal wooden table. Near the bottle she set an assortment of cheeses, a wicker basket full of crackers, and four glasses.

"Come," Brewster said, and, using his cane for balance, led us to the circle of antique furniture where the refreshments awaited us. "Chippendale," Magritt whispered as we followed our host. "Of course," I responded.

Brewster sat on the edge of a fiddle-back chair and filled our glasses with an opaque red wine, a 1982 St. Julian. "Are you familiar with this painting?" he asked us both, and pointed to the wall closest to the table.

"It is one of the paintings we were looking forward to seeing. A portrait of Virgil and Dante, isn't it?" I said, while realizing what an injustice the image on the slide had done to the original. Dante was depicted in the dark habit of a medieval monk, the hood down upon his back, his head slightly bowed; Virgil's splendid white toga draped around his thin body and his right hand touched his closely cropped gray beard. I could feel the cool touch of the linen, the stiff bristles on Virgil's face.

"Exactly," Brewster said. "You've done your homework. *A Pilgrim Born* is Elias's title. It's from the opening canto of *The Divine Comedy*. Dante awakes to find himself in a dark wood. His progress is blocked by the three threatening beasts you see drawn in the background, three allegorical representations of the multiple sins that block us from making progress in our lives. But you know the story."

"Magnificent," Magritt whispered, absorbed in the painting.

"I like it," Brewster commented, "but I don't find it as powerful as the painting on the opposite wall, *Beatrice and Virgil*. It's from Canto II, a flashback to events that took place before Virgil's appearance in the dark forest. As you may recall, Virgil tells Dante that the Virgin Mary had felt his despair and suffering and asked Saint Lucia to help him. The Saint reached out to Beatrice, Dante's great love, and Beatrice, in turn, traveled down to Hell and entered Limbo, where she asked Virgil to guide Dante the Pilgrim through Hell and Purgatory. The painting depicts Beatrice's entreaty to Virgil. She's beautiful, is she not?"

"An extreme example of delegation," I jested. No one seemed to hear. Beatrice's beauty sealed their ears.

Dante the Painter had fashioned a magnificent image, a slender young woman robed in a flowing purple gown brought alive by threads of gold and silver, its hem and cuffs trimmed in fur. Her skin is fair; her lips are bold and red. Her hair, a deep mahogany, is spun around her head like a halo. Virgil looks different than in the previous portrait—more reverential, his toga not quite as bright, its drape with fewer folds.

Magritt was leaning forward in her seat looking first at the painting and then at Brewster, her eyes in a perpetual squint. When Brewster noticed her intensity, she gave him a half smile, leaned back in her chair, sniffed at her glass, and sipped some wine. "Delicious," she decided after rolling it around her mouth. "It is so much better than Elias Miller's. Don't you think so, Larry?"

"It's very good," I answered in a rather noncommittal voice.

"I'm glad you like it. Sharon's choice, as is the cheese,"

said Brewster. He projected his voice toward the parlor's entryway.

As if on cue, a woman in her early thirties, lithe and long of limb, as they say, glided into the room, her blue silk dress clinging to every curve. "Please excuse; a longer telephone call than I expected," she said with a slight Italian accent.

"No problem, my dear. We were just beginning. Come join us."

She bent over Brewster, kissed him on the forehead, and sat down opposite me. The shimmering dress folded above her knees, exposing delightfully thin thighs when she crossed her legs. I handed her a wine glass after the old man filled it.

"So you are the authors. Caleb has told me so much about you," she said, the fingers of her right hand playing with her long red hair.

"Good things, we hope," I said, then looked over to Magritt. Her eyes were filled with suspicion.

We talked for a few minutes about writing, about art history, about Madeline Brewster's lifetime affair with artistic expression. "She chose each piece in the collection, every one," Brewster said, "and they're still hanging exactly where she had them, very much in order of their appearance in *The Divine Comedy*. It was not her original preference, but hanging the paintings in the same sequence as their subjects appear in the poem made it much easier to explain the work to her guests."

Brewster's facial expression changed, and for a long moment, he seemed to entertain feelings he did not want to share. He lifted his glass and, in the motion of a toast, tilted it toward the painting of Beatrice and Virgil. Then he swallowed a little wine. "I'd like to be able to claim it a Caleb and Madeline Brewster art collection, but it isn't. It was all her. Oh, she had help. Our contributions to the Metropolitan and the Museum of Modern Art gave us access to gifted curators, and there was an endless supply of gallery owners and auction house specialists. But it was Madeline and her tastes alone that got us to purchase what I now display. If it weren't, we'd never have purchased so many of Elias Miller's work."

I looked at Sharon to see how she reacted to mention of the deceased wife. If there were any thoughts, I failed to read them. When she caught my gaze, she uncrossed her legs, then crossed them in the other direction.

"How many Millers do you own?" Magritt asked.

"Madeline bought every one of his paintings, at least all he was willing to part with—over a hundred. She didn't hold on to all of them. She gave some to Susan, our daughter, and some to our son, Jonathan. I don't think they've sold any or given them away. The rest went to other relatives, a few to friends. I didn't keep track. I still have many, perhaps fifty or so. The best, or at least the ones Madeline most wanted to live with, are hanging somewhere in the apartment, but I'm sure you suspect that. Some are in our house in Connecticut; others, a dozen or so, are in storage."

"And you, Sharon, have you continued to collect?" I asked.

"Not at all. I'm content to enjoy the collection as it is. I don't want to disturb a thing."

Magritt cut in. "Could we begin to see Miller's work, Caleb, before I enjoy your wine too much and lose all judgment?"

The four of us finished our drinks and put our empty glasses on the silver tray. By making a sharp right as we left the drawing room, we entered another part of the apartment. Magritt walked ahead with Brewster at her side. Sharon touched my elbow to guide me. I smelled her delicate perfume.

On the right wall of the short corridor was one of Dante's smaller paintings, about sixteen-by-twenty inches, *The Vestibule.* Canto III, Brewster explained, the entryway to the nine circles of Hell, the place where people who never made a choice in life, who ended their lives absent acts of decency or vice are eternally punished. In an enormous dark cave, a dozen or so shades are furiously racing after a crimson banner. Wasps and hornets rip at their flesh.

"It's an incomplete picture of the scene," Brewster said. "In the poem, blood drips from their flesh and feeds maggots and worms that cover the ground. Dante had a genius for matching punishments to sins. If you don't make decisions during your life on earth, you will forever chase a banner that waves this way and that. Perfect, don't you think?"

"I find it an ingenious metaphor, forever chasing a waving banner. It says much about contemporary life. But I can see why you keep it under a dim light," I said.

Sharon let out a mild laugh, and Magritt put her hand behind the small of her back and gave me the finger. Sharon couldn't help but notice.

The master bedroom, a twenty-foot-square room with what Caleb modestly called a dressing room at one end and walk-in closets at the other, was our first stop.

"Are you familiar with that painting?" Brewster asked, pointing to the large painting that was hanging over the king-size bed.

"*Francesca and Paolo*. Dante is particularly proud of it," I answered. "It was the first work he talked to us about, the illicit lovers floating in the Second Circle of the *Inferno*, the place of the unrepentant lustful."

"*Francesca and Paolo*," Brewster echoed. "Have you ever seen two people more intensely in love? Their punishment is to never see the lights of Heaven, I know, or hear angels sing. But when I look at them, I wonder if the artist might not have thought the price was worth the game."

"I asked Elias about that," I continued, "but he just laughed."

"He has a habit of doing that," Brewster commented, "and a tendency to talk as if he were the great poet. At the beginning, I found both habits a bit off-putting. Then, it was just part of the atmosphere, like the Chianti he served."

"Do you have a painting from the First Circle?" Magritt asked while still examining Dante's vision of lust.

"Ah, the locale of virtuous pagans where good people born before the birth of Christ and children who have not experienced baptism's grace spend eternity, physically unharmed but always longing to enter Heaven. Madeline gave our painting of Limbo away. I'm not sure to whom."

"It's one of the paintings we are considering for our monograph. I hope we catch up with it," Magritt added.

"It's a good piece, but even better is the one hanging on the other side of this room, *The Circle of Gluttons*. It depicts the Third Circle of Hell.

Once again, Dante the Painter's gift was on full display. In late Renaissance style—the technique employed in each of the paintings Magritt and I had been shown—Dante had painted the figures of seven gluttonous shades, each immersed in a sea of mud, some to their waists and others up to their armpits. To one side, a monstrous three-headed dog, saliva dripping from his mouths, stands in eternal vigilance, making certain none of the tormented shades escape.

"Does it cause nightmares?" I asked, to lighten the mood.

Sharon giggled.

"It is great art," Brewster insisted. He turned away from me to take Sharon by the elbow, and led us all into an adjoining room, evidently his office. It was an oversized space, almost as large as the master bedroom, furnished in the style of a 1930s' law firm, with high-back leather chairs; a long, dark, leather sofa; and an oversized, leather-inlaid desk. Nothing modern showed—no television, no computer, no printer. Only a large complicated desk phone broke the depression-era atmosphere. This time Brewster pointed with his hand. "Miller's illustration of the Fourth Circle of Hell, from Canto Seven. He called it *The Incontinent*, a name that makes me think of weak bladders and stained pants. It's the torture room for those whose sins were materialistic. As you can see, two groups of shades, the miserly and the extravagant, roll rocks against each other. Was this one of the paintings you wanted to see?"

"It's nice," Magritt said, "but it wasn't on our list."

"Well, I think you should reconsider your decision. Madeline thought it was an appropriate image for my office. She thought me both a miser and a spendthrift; I should have given more to my employees and spent less on myself. I keep it in memory of her."

At least he remembers her, I thought cheekily.

Brewster and Magritt led the way out of the office. Sharon and I walked a few paces behind them.

"Don't you find this—Miller's work—depressing?" I asked the young wife.

"Only if I look at them," she whispered.

We ended up in the room closest to the apartment's entrance, the room Magritt began to refer to as Hepplewhite. Two paintings, *The Wrathful* and *The Boatman of the Styx*, hung on its walls.

Leaning on his cane and facing the three of us, Brewster began his analysis of the first painting, acting much like a docent taking a group of students through a private museum.

"You've made it to the Fifth Circle, halfway down Dante's array of sins and punishments, the home of the unrepentant wrathful and lazy. The painting centers on the River Styx, the second river to run through Hell, a murky quagmire that holds fast to the bodies of the wrathful. The slothful are buried under its muddy crust. You know they are there from the bubbles that reach the river's surface. A horrid fate if ever there was one. Dante clearly did not like sloth.

"The *Boatman of the Styx*," Brewster pointed with his cane, "introduces you to the Sixth Circle. As irritated as the boatman is at finding out that Dante and Virgil are travelers and not damned, he transports them over the river and deposits them on the other side, at the gates of the City of Dis. Miller is very true to Dante's poem. He paints it as a dark and dismal walled medieval city with a huge tower at one side. I find it a remarkable painting. You see only the back of the boatman; his head tilted enough to make out an angry profile. Dante and Virgil grab hold of each other, frightened by the wailing faces protruding from the city's gray stone wall."

Magritt and I stood in partnership before *The Boatman* and then in front of *The Wrathful*, noting the brushstrokes, the ingenious compositions, the choice of colors, both of us moved by the beauty and the horror of the work.

Brewster's voice was sarcastic and cynical when it broke into our musings. "Did *The Boatman* make your list of the eligible?"

Magritt forced herself to smile delicately. "I'm uncertain," she replied.

"Well, all my paintings should," Brewster said. He abruptly turned around and led us to the Shaker room.

"Although I have only one of his paintings from the Seventh Circle hanging in the apartment, *The Land of the*

Suicides, I own many more. If you don't remember, the Seventh Circle is composed of several tiers, each crowded with sinners. The lower you go, the more egregious the sin and cruel the punishment. Imprisoned here are those who committed violence and suicide, and blasphemy, usury, and sodomy. We are again in a dark forest, this one presided over by repulsive harpies—part woman, part beast, with birdlike features. Painful shouts and tortured screams fill the air. After the Last Judgment, suicides will return to earth to claim their bodies but they will never be allowed to wear them. Wrong it is for people to have what once they threw away. A pregnant thought, isn't it? *The Divine Comedy* is full of pregnant thoughts."

"You have mastered Dante," Magritt said, a hint of surprise in her voice.

"Not really, but I've learned to fake it. Over the years, I have explored those sections of the *Comedy* that hang on my walls. I do not understand the poem's finer points, its religious allusions, its ties to Greek and Roman mythology, its references to ancient poets and poetry. Elias tried to instruct me, but I proved a poor student."

"Did Madeline respond to Dante's paintings the same way, by becoming a student of *The Divine Comedy?*" Magritt asked.

Caleb's head shot up. "Elias Miller's paintings. I refuse to give in to Miller's hallucinations." He paused for a moment to give his comment currency. Then he said, "I have other illustrations from the Seventh Circle, and one from the Eighth, paintings of pimps and panderers and seducers, either in Connecticut or in storage. This one is the best."

The Art Nouveau room was our next stop. There was only one painting in it: *Lucifer.*

"Remember," Brewster began, "you are in the bowels

of the earth, in the Ninth Circle, the Devil's home. Dante used a simple architectural structure for the *Inferno*, a spiraling pit that starts barely below the crust of the earth and descends to the planet's core. An inverse hierarchy of sins was fashioned, the least offensive to God were placed closer to earth, the most offensive were punished at the core. Since the harshness of the punishment was correlated to the offensiveness of the sin, the further down you go the more horrific the punishment. Dante left his most horrid punishment for the Ninth Circle. And the worst is before you in all its primal horror," Brewster said, and walked over to a five-by-four-foot portrait of the Devil. "*Lucifer* is Miller's title."

Magritt was already standing in front of the painting, her hands unconsciously gesturing in pace with her quickening thoughts. It was the first painting we had seen that was not imitative of Renaissance art.

"Wow," Magritt said when I stood next to her. "I noticed it from the corner of my eye when we entered the apartment, but I didn't appreciate how truly outrageous it is. Edgar Degas's techniques—the dense red tonality that infuses the entire painting, the broad-brush strokes, the simple way paint is used in some sections of the image and the complex overlay of colors used to create the demon's face. He has mastered Degas's late style. I bet he even used the same preparatory white ground."

I could only half-listen to Magritt talk about technique. Looking at the painting demanded my energy. Elias Miller had outdone himself when he painted Lucifer. Its size alone demanded attention, and its extraordinary ugliness. Lucifer's huge chest towers over the gray frozen lake that encases the lower half of his massive red body. In each of his three hideous mouths, a human form is being chewed.

"The world's three worst sinners spend eternity being chewed upon by the Devil: Judas, Brutus, and Cassius. Their crime: treachery. Can you think of any worse punishment? Clearly, Dante could not," Brewster said, standing behind me. I could feel his breath on my neck.

I did not answer, but a question went through my mind. When Elias Miller put his brush to the canvas, what sinners was he thinking of? Any? All?

"That's about it," Brewster said once we were outside the Art Nouveau room. The apartment tour had been arduous for him. His voice sounded unexpectedly weary and his body leaned more heavily on the cane. "What do you think? Will they make it into your manuscript?"

Magritt responded inelegantly. "Aren't there others? Harland suggested that you had most of the thirty-six paintings we are tracking down."

"Thirty-six?" Sharon said.

"Yes," Magritt said, "thirty-six. Larry and I looked over Elias' slides and selected thirty-six paintings we wanted to examine further. We're going to choose fifteen from the group for the publication."

"When you said thirty-six, I thought you were contemplating including that many in your monograph. That's why I sounded surprised," Sharon said defensively.

Brewster gave her a quick stern look. She put a finger up to her pursed mouth.

"The others must be in Connecticut, or in storage, but trust me, these are the best. They wouldn't be here if they weren't. As to the others, I'm not interested in giving them any publicity. My summerhouse is not as well protected as this apartment. I wouldn't want to attract too much attention," Brewster argued.

"We'd be willing to go out to see them, and we don't intend to say who owns any of the work included in the book—we'll just be discussing their virtues," Magritt argued, her head thrust toward Brewster, her body as rigid as a steel spike.

Brewster's voice turned as frigid as the ice at the bottom of Hell. "You've seen all I planned to show you; you can use them all or not. You needn't see the rest of my collection."

Magritt's mouth opened but nothing came out. I expected the finger to appear. When it didn't, I took up her argument.

"If you'd like to see the work you own represented, the more we see the more likely some will end up in the publication."

"Mr. Sullivan, I have no doubt that the ones I've shown you are among Miller's best. If you end up thinking otherwise, so be it. Only your readers will be cheated."

"I guess there's not much more to say," I concluded.

"Good," he said. He tapped his cane on the floor as if it were a gavel and smiled. "I have a wonderful '83 d'Yquem I'd love you to try."

Magritt refused for both of us. She wasn't going to be bought off with a $600 bottle of wine. I would have accepted Caleb's invitation. I think people should pay for their obnoxiousness.

The maids arrived, the tall one with Magritt's coat, the other with my umbrella. Sharon waited with us for the elevator. She said goodbye to Magritt, and then, to my surprise, slipped a folded piece of paper into my palm when we shook hands.

The paper burned in my jacket pocket as I rode down

the elevator; it burned in my mind as Magritt got into a cab. As soon as I knew she could no longer see me, I opened it under a streetlight. In a simple easy script, Sharon had written out a telephone number. Art was growing more interesting, I thought, as I hurried to my mother's apartment.

CHAPTER EIGHT

I WAITED BEFORE DIALING Sharon's number. The pieces didn't fit together. Nothing memorable had happened between us, no exchange of romantic words, no furtive glances. Her flirtatiousness was so demure that I assumed it was something she did to make her husband's guests feel welcome and attractive. I consider myself good looking, but I don't possess Valentino's profile or Bogart's ruggedness. If I did, I'd have concentrated on my acting. Oh, my company doesn't embarrass beautiful women, but the only ones who fought for my attention were those who thought they could extract something from me—a part in a play, an introduction to a theatrical agent. But I didn't for a minute think of ripping up Sharon's number. Curiosity took hold, and a little adolescence. She was sexy. Give it twelve hours or so, I told myself, so that you don't look as randy as you feel.

Delay was easy. Magritt had invited me to breakfast with her the next morning. We met at a small coffee shop on the corner of Madison Avenue not far from my mother's flat, a place with huge windows, limited table space, and middle-aged waitresses who enjoyed the company of customers. Magritt was still fuming.

"I'm pissed," she said, as if I could have possibly not noticed.

"I can see that."

"Pissed," she repeated, and ordered coffee and a cheese Danish.

"You know, Larry, if we can swing it, I don't think we should use any of Brewster's pieces. That would teach him to be such a controlling prig. And that Tiffany laminated woman—an Olympic trophy if there ever was one. Do you think she's a new Mrs. Brewster? She certainly was acting that way when she wasn't mesmerizing you with her legs. He most probably fucks her with his cane."

"Magritt, can you imagine what your father would say if he heard you speak about a friend that way?"

Magritt glared at me. "Funny, funny," she said with a snarl, "and what nerve, to start out by suggesting that I owe him. 'I recommended your father to Stanford. If it weren't for me you'd be a starving high school dropout.'"

"I don't think he went that far."

"I hate rich people."

Coming from most people, hating rich people is a forgivable prejudice. If you are going to hate people because of their group identification, the rich are as acceptable as any. They can afford your outrage. But from Magritt, with a father whose parents could afford to send him to Stanford and a mother whose name adorned a boutique Manhattan law firm, it was funny.

"Remember you're a scholar, Magritt—truth above all else."

She gave me the finger.

"Anyway," I said, "the important question is not if she's a legal Mrs. Brewster, but is Caleb the person Harland refers to as our patron, the universal benefactor who is paying our way?"

"I don't think that's very important," Magritt said after swallowing some Danish. "I've begun to assume that Patron is a fictional construct. Without him or her, Harland would have to claim we were working for him, a position he doesn't seem to want, or we're working for some group, in which case we might want to meet with its members. An invisible mastermind is a very clever device, if not very original. Particularly if Eric's theory that people are hoping to brand Dante the Painter another Picasso and profit from his celebrity is true. They would want to keep us out of the loop and unquestioning. No one who owns his work wants to be soiled by financing our manuscript. It would label our efforts a paid advertisement for Dante the Painter. They want the cover of independent and scholarly praise. Patron is a rather thin story, but it got us work."

"The thought of our being witless pawns in a capitalistic conspiracy doesn't subtract from my enthusiasm," I said, after finishing my coffee. "I know it should, but it doesn't. I like what we're doing. It could become the plot for my next play."

Magritt laughed. "I've had a similar reaction. Strange as it may seem, the thought of being in the middle of a plot makes me more eager to get on with the work. I don't particularly like Brewster and his leg-crossing companion. Proximity to Dante—poet or painter—hasn't ennobled them. But the paintings, Larry—they are brilliant. To be able to claim we brought Miller to the world's attention, my God, what a high. And if other people make money on his acknowledgment, isn't that one of the prices of fame?"

EXACTLY AT NOON, I dialed the number Sharon had given me. It took six long rings before she answered.

"Busy tonight?" she asked before I could give my name.

"I don't have to be."

"Drinks at the Carlyle about 7:00?" she suggested.

"Perfect," I quickly replied.

Then she hung up. If it wasn't a short-enough conversation to enter the *Guinness World Records*, it came close. Perhaps Brewster was in the room when she took the call, or in the bed. That would explain it, I mused, as a shot of envy ran through me.

SHARON SAT ON THE BAR stool next to mine, a casting director's model of an elegant woman. Her simple, black, scoop-necked dress only hinted at her fine breasts, its asymmetrical ruffled hem resting slightly above her knees. For a touch of spice, she wore a graceful gold necklace and diamond pendant.

Sharon ordered a Meursault and I asked for a Scotch on the rocks, single malt.

"An interesting evening," I commented.

"It was. My husband can be terribly stuffy on occasion, but he was rather pleasant. I think he likes Magritt. He has a soft spot for bright young women," she said, her Italian accent sounding a little deeper than it did the night before.

"I thought he was a little rough on her. I don't understand his reluctance to show us the other pieces. Looking at them won't wear out the paint."

"He's a poor negotiator. He made his mind up before you came and wasn't going to change it. I see his rigidity as a sign of age, but his friends tell me he was always that way."

"He must be difficult to live with."

"Not at all. He doesn't make many demands," Sharon said, and smiled knowingly.

She lifted her wine glass to her mouth and studied herself in the mirror that hung behind the bar. I drank some Scotch.

"I caught your *Celestial City* when it first opened, and I saw *Alas Poor Adam* a while back."

"Not many people have seen either, let alone both. Have you become a fan?"

"I'm a theater junkie, but to be stiflingly honest, I didn't realize you had authored both until Caleb had me search your name on the Internet. I liked *Alas Poor Adam*; it took some funny shots at religion."

"And *Celestial City*?" I asked with some trepidation.

"I have never appreciated the 'good whore' theme. It trivializes prostitution and transforms a trade filled with devastated women into a noble occupation for big hearts with big tits."

"It highlights the humanity that resides in all of us, including the sex worker."

"Sex worker—a scandalous euphemism. It makes it sound like a career you can prepare for at a community college. When Harvard offers a degree in sex working, I'll rethink my prejudice. Until then, the happy, good-natured whore is a very destructive symbol. It's not a trade I'd want for my daughter, or son."

"Wow," I said.

Sharon smiled and touched my hand. "I do get carried away."

"So you have children."

"No, no. Caleb's not up to that, and my first husband didn't want any. You?"

"No, I've never been married and I treat sex cautiously."

"Good," she said, and finished the Meursault.

"Another?" I asked.

She gave me an electric smile. "You have another," she said, and slipped a room key into my hand. "Room 1608. Give me fifteen minutes or so."

She spun around on the stool, gave me a tender look, and walked off without looking back. I ordered a club soda, paid the bill, and went to the men's room thinking, only in America or in the movies.

For no reason other than an inflamed ego, I pictured a hotel suite with champagne cooling in a dark ice container and Sharon lying on a king-size bed with only a long black negligee keeping her warm. Disappointingly, her sense of stagecraft was less advanced than mine. The room was small and overly furnished. The arm of a small couch pressed against its windowed wall, a single upholstered chair next to it. A double bed, its quilt turned down, was parked in front of the darkly stained hutch that held a television set.

Sharon called to me from the bathroom as soon as 1608's door snapped closed. "Give me a couple of minutes more," she said, as if I had a choice.

I stood around wondering if I should take off my sports coat or if I should strip totally and crawl under the blanket to await a personal paradise. Perhaps sitting on the couch would be best, with my legs crossed and a clueless expression on my face. Dante was right—free will can be hell.

Sharon exited the bathroom before I could make a decision. Her high-heeled shoes discarded, but otherwise, fully dressed. She walked directly toward me and kissed me lightly on my lips. Then she turned around. "Would you help me unzip?"

When I woke early the next morning, she was gone.

Silently, she had folded my pants and shirt and placed them neatly over the back of the upholstered chair. On top of them was a neatly scripted note: *"Wonderful! Call me next Tuesday."*

I CALLED MAGRITT from the hotel and she met me for a late breakfast at the coffee shop on Madison Avenue.

"I did the unforgivable, Larry," she said, after ordering a toasted bagel. "I asked my mother to convince Brewster to let us see the other pieces he owns. Can you imagine, a grown woman of twenty-seven—I know I look younger—asking her mother for help? And she hadn't seen Caleb since my father died. The memory of my asking her turns my stomach. Worse, she refused." She sweetened her voice to mimic her mother. "'When Brewster makes up his mind, he makes up his mind.'"

"He seemed to be that type of guy. Let's use what we have, not what we'd like. Otherwise we'll never finish," I said.

"Practical, aren't we?" Magritt snarled. She looked down at the plate in front of her, put a smidgeon of cream cheese on a slice of bagel, and took a small bite. When she finished chewing, she said, "You don't look any better than I feel. Tough night?"

"I didn't think it showed."

"Only around the eyes, the turn of your mouth, the color of your skin. Otherwise, your emotions are completely hidden. Bad sex?"

"I saw an old girlfriend, that's all."

Magritt took off her eyeglasses and cleaned them with a tissue she had taken out of her pocketbook. When she looked at me, her eyes seemed larger without the lenses, and softer. "I've been embarrassed by old boyfriends. It's almost impossible to feel the old attractiveness. Self-protectiveness, in part. You don't want to think highly of the one who got away, or you threw away."

It is the voice and not the words that speak to you. All actors know that. The timbre, the tone, the little laugh in the middle of the sentence, the almost inaudible sigh that punctuates the thought, that is what reveals meaning, that separates pretense from purpose. Magritt's voice was easy and familiar, the voice of a friend, of someone with no interest at the moment other than you. How could I refuse her conversation, however intimate?

I gave out a short, uncomfortable laugh. "A rather blunt question, but no, I was in good shape. I just didn't get the same result. She seems to have outgrown me."

"No orgasm."

"You are getting rather personal."

"I thought you'd want to talk about it."

"Not really. I think sex is private."

"Just for your plays, I guess."

My laughter did not put her off. She continued, "Romance doesn't come easily to me. The lights have to be just right; the music sultry but not obvious; a nice wine, but not too much. More than two glasses drowns my libido." Magritt held her coffee cup in two hands like a chalice and took a long drink.

"And with Eric? Does he bring the right wine?"

"I disappoint him. I know that."

"He doesn't act that way."

"That's because he likes me, but after we've made love he masturbates in the shower."

"How do you know that?" I asked, my voice a mixture of surprise and laughter. She had to be pulling my leg.

"He told me."

How cruel, I thought. I would never tell a lover she didn't satisfy. But I held my tongue. Instead, I offered my second thought, "That may be his problem more than yours. Did you think of that?"

"And you; were you left dissatisfied?"

"If anyone was disappointed it was she."

"Don't be too sure. She may have had the time of her life," Magritt said in a whisper and touched my hand. Her eyes would not let go of my face.

"Maybe," was all I contributed, but I thought Magritt wrong. Sharon had done all the things you would ask of a lover, her hands gentle, her body open and welcoming. Still, I thought her sounds were orchestrated, her eyes purposely closed, her mouth in a rigid grin. No sweat broke out on her forehead; no laughter jumped from her mouth. If it was the best night of her life, she had had a narrow existence, and I couldn't bring myself to believe that.

"Chalk it up to a bad night. Maybe she was preoccupied. Maybe she was getting even for being considered an 'old girlfriend.' You should try again."

"I plan to."

Magritt gave me her most pleasant smile and a very knowing look. "We should talk about our work, don't you think?"

CHAPTER NINE

SHARON ANSWERED AFTER the first ring. It was Tuesday
morning. "How about meeting me at the Frick in front
of Rembrandt's self-portrait?" she said after we had exchanged a few flirtatious pleasantries. "It would be a perfect place to accidentally bump into each other, don't you
think? I'll be there by two-thirty. Don't be late. I hate to
wait."

I was there at two; Sharon, in a stylish tan jacket that
ended at her waist and straight white pants, arrived at three.
Black pearls dropped from her golden earrings.

"Sorry I'm late," she whispered, "but it was unavoidable."

"You look wonderful," I said, and tried to kiss her.

She took a step back. "Not here; it's far too public," she
said, and turned toward Rembrandt's rendering of himself. I
touched her hand, but she pulled it away.

"Magnificent, isn't it? He was fifty-two when he
painted it," Sharon said, "but he looks much older, his skin
riddled with signs of disease. And yet, there is power in his
carriage, and such regal clothes. I think he wanted to hide his
bankruptcy from posterity. What do you think?"

"From his creditors as well."

Sharon smiled at the painting, her arms folded across

her high-necked light blue blouse. A single strand of black pearls hung between her breasts.

I continued. "A good dermatologist would have helped, or a cosmetic foundation."

"Be serious. If he wanted to look healthy, he could have painted himself that way. He wanted us to see his blemished face, to idolize the way he dealt with adversity."

"He could have made himself look like Jude Law," I added.

"I think he looked just the way he looks in the painting. There is too much truth in it. It's one of my favorites."

"I didn't know you had a crush on Rembrandt."

"On the Rembrandt of 52, and on St. Jerome and St. Francis; their portraits are here as well. Do you know the Frick?"

"My mother use to take me here once a year or so when I was in junior high. We'd take the subway from Greenwich Village. That's where I was raised, in a tiny apartment we shared with my grandmother. After her death, there was just the two of us. My mother waited until I left for college before she moved uptown."

"Oh," Sharon said, and took a step back from the Rembrandt. I wondered if she had heard anything I had said.

"I didn't know you were an art enthusiast," I said, to break the silence.

"I love art, but only a little at a time. I have an hour-long attention span when I visit museums. Then my girdle rides up and my feet itch. That's why the Frick is perfect for me. You can get to your favorites in an hour while strolling through a magnificent mansion. Can you imagine how much this would be worth today, the building and the art? It makes Caleb's collection seem puny."

"I don't know if the Millers have a market value, but

thirty people could retire on the value of your apartment itself, and then there are the sculptures and ceramics."

"Not a very happy retirement, Larry."

She turned around and walked quickly away. When I caught up she said, "And the Frick has some artists I wish Madeline had collected, like Bellini, Turner, and El Greco. Don't get me wrong. I like Elias Miller's paintings, and the rest of her collection, but sometimes I need to get away."

"I understand."

"Maybe, but I doubt it. It's bad enough that I have to retrain her old husband, but I have to live with her art as well. Her taste is all over the place. We still use the double bed she died in and the porcelain she bought when they celebrated their fiftieth anniversary."

She pulled down the dark sunglasses she had pushed high up into her red hair and looked like a Broadway ingénue hoping to be recognized. "Come, let's say hello to some of my favorite art."

Her long, well-manicured fingers touched my elbow when she directed me toward the Living Hall, where El Greco's masterpiece of St. Jerome hung over a sealed fireplace. I slipped my arm around her waist. She pushed it away. "Not in public, Larry," she insisted and walked in front of me. I could see her return her sunglasses to her hair and noticed the freckles on her neck.

"The very essence of piety," she said, her tone reverential, her eyes looking up into the saint's face. She seemed prepared to kiss his ring.

"Aren't we all?"

"You are in a silly mood, Mr. Sullivan."

"Unrequited horniness, Mrs. Brewster," I said, but it wasn't what I felt. I was becoming convinced that she was playing a calculated game, her sexy garment to be examined but not touched, her body moving toward me and then jetting away. But knowing she was playing with me only increased her attractiveness. Novelty alone would have kept me flirting with her. Sex made the game irresistible.

"What did you say?" Sharon asked as if she had heard my thoughts.

"Nothing," I answered.

She led me across the oriental rug and around the enormous medieval banqueting table that sat in the center of the room. Once on the other side, she said, "*St. Francis,* by Bellini. Whenever I come here, I try to see something in this painting that I haven't noticed before, an animal or bird, a skull, a sandal, a rock formation. They all have symbolic meanings, I know, but they are beyond me. I am just overwhelmed by how much Bellini was trying to tell, and I wonder if the painter's Renaissance patrons could more accurately read its language, or if they were literate in a way that I am not. Elias Miller's paintings remind me of Bellini. There is more in them than I can understand. Do you feel the same?"

"I try to understand them. I read the poem. I look at the painting. Then I study the painting again, at least its photograph. And if I remain befuddled, I ask Dante."

"Dante?"

"Elias Miller."

"Good. For a moment I thought Elias's disease was contagious and your mind had bent."

"I don't think Dante's mind is as bent as Caleb makes it out to be," I insisted.

Sharon stared at me for a moment and then turned away.

I spoke to her profile. "Other than Miller's work, I don't try to read paintings. Magritt does that. I just try to enjoy them."

Sharon's face lit up. "Then we're the same. We just enjoy. And now to my favorite," she said, her Italian inflections turning sweet.

She moved ahead of me and crossed the museum floor like a self-possessed athlete, her stride long, her shoulders square, her head held high. I imagined that every person in the room was watching her, but I couldn't take my eyes off her long enough to study what the other visitors were doing.

We stopped in front of Edgar Degas' *The Rehearsal*, a small painting, no more than eighteen by twenty-four inches, petite in comparison to the portraits of St. Francis and St. Jerome, but still, its brilliant colors challenged those classics, and its imaginative imagery compelled viewing. I found it wonderfully theatrical and idealistic, perfect human forms with perfect faces, their bodies in perfect arcs. I wondered, in a self-absorbed moment, if an able artist would one day paint a scene from one of my plays.

"I can see you in a Degas painting, Sharon, your long legs resting on a ballet bar, your flawless reflection filling a mirror," I said in a shallow attempt at flattery.

"You read my mind, Larry. No wonder I like you."

She let me hold her hand for a second. When she pulled it away, she glanced at her small gold watch. "Time goes too fast. I have to head back."

"You just got here," I exclaimed.

"It only seems that way. Caleb is expecting some friends over this evening and I have to be off."

"Now that's unfair."

Sharon gave me a sweet smile. "Oh, we'll get some quality time yet."

"Can I at least walk you home?"

"No. Stay here for fifteen minutes before leaving. The expression on your face is telling, you know."

She pulled the sunglasses out of her hair and walked quickly away. I had to cover my mouth not to shout after her, at once aghast at her rapid exit and humiliated by my own hunger. Testosterone, I told myself, simple testosterone.

THE DOOR OF MY MOTHER'S bedroom slammed shut when I entered her apartment. Irate murmurings and the sound of shuffling feet quickly followed.

"I didn't expect you home so soon," Janet said, her tone apologetic, her face flushed, and her yellow dress slightly askew.

"I'm sorry," was all I could think of saying, thoroughly embarrassed for us both.

"Paul took the afternoon off," she explained, her feet bare, her short blonde hair hastily combed.

"I'm sorry," I said once again.

"That it's Paul?" mother said, her gentle voice forgiving me with humor.

"I can leave."

"No. We're glad you're here. It's getting close to dinnertime and we were sorry you weren't joining us."

My mother had mastered the art of little fibs; the welcoming words you know belie the truth but are good to hear. Telling big fictions, that was more difficult for her, except when she talked about my father.

She straightened her dress and walked closer to me. "How about some Scotch?"

"If Paul joins us."

She blushed again.

Janet poured three glasses, two over ice and one neat. Paul loved his Scotch neat, good single malt Scotches that came in fancy bottles and cost as much as orchestra tickets to a popular Broadway play. He'd watch it twirl in his hand, his nose over the rim. He'd close his eyes and take a small expectant sip like a pretentious gourmand. To my mother's horror, his habit popped up in the opening scene of *Celestial City*. Paul enjoyed it.

"What brings you back so soon?" mother asked as she handed the glass to me.

"Something unexpected came up and my date had to leave."

"Oh," my mother said.

It was an invitation to say more. Paul appearance saved me.

"Good to see you, Larry," Paul Herman said in his familiar tenor voice. He walked slowly into the room, looking as if he had come directly from his tailor, his dark pinstriped suit jacket buttoned and his tie perfectly dimpled.

Mother handed her lover his glass and sat down at one end of the richly flowered couch my grandmother had owned. It was Janet's favorite piece of furniture. She had nursed me while sitting on it, and, years later, we had sat together on its soft cushions while she told me stories about my father—his acting, his drinking, his disappearance. Not at once, but over time. "Disappearance" was her word. It became my fantasy. Perhaps the KGB or FBI or some other lettered institution had stolen him away? My mother didn't use the word abandonment until I had begun college. By then, I had figured it out. It made it easier for her to tell the truth.

Paul sat down at the other end of the couch. You would think they were on a first date. "How is the work going, Larry—are you adapting to being a fine arts critic?" Paul asked.

"Oh, I'm far from that. Magritt Cline, my colleague, is the critical voice. I'm just the scribe. But the project is going well. We finally got to see some of Miller's work last week."

"Yes," Paul casually continued, "Caleb told me you were over the other night. He enjoyed meeting you."

My God, I thought, is the world that small? "I didn't know you knew Caleb Brewster," I said, trying to leave the question mark out of my voice.

"We did some business a while back. The call was a surprise. I hadn't heard from him in years."

"And what did he have to say?" I pressed.

"Only that he enjoyed finally meeting you, and he was looking forward to your efforts. He thanked me for suggesting you to Harland and asked about your mother. I asked him what he was up to, but he told me he was just enjoying his money, nothing more."

"Suggesting me to Harland? Now that's news."

Paul looked perplexed and uneasy. "Didn't Harland mention it to you? I thought he had told you that I suggested you for the job. I'm sorry, Larry. I wasn't keeping anything from you."

I contained my irritation. Paul was too important to me. "So you know Harland, too?"

"Slightly. He asked me to join the board of the Truth Foundation when it was first being structured. I would have, but I was already overcommitted and had to turn him down."

"Oh," I said, hoping the expression would be pregnant enough to force him to continue.

Instead, Paul took a long drink to ease his discomfort.

Ease up, I told myself. Circle back to Harland later. "Did Brewster complain to you about my behavior? The evening didn't end very well. My coauthor was particularly out-of-joint. Brewster limited our access to his collection, although I don't know why, and he turned mulish when we complained. If it weren't for his wife, I would have found the evening terribly boorish."

Paul looked blank. "Are you certain there is a wife?"

"Sharon. She's a young and very attractive woman."

Paul put his glass to his lips, leaned back, and finished drinking the seventeen-year-old Scotch from Islay. "I haven't seen Caleb since Madeline's funeral. He and I were business colleagues, not personal friends. Madeline was the Brewster I liked. But remarried? . . . He isn't a kid."

"She's about thirty; a good half-century younger was my guess. If you had met her, you'd remember."

"Arm candy," mother commented, scorn coating her tongue.

"It surprises me, Larry. Brewster never struck me as someone who would buy himself anything, let alone an expensive wife. Madeline was the only one in the family who spent money. Caleb invested. She got away with buying art by convincing Caleb that every one of her purchases would appreciate—even their bedroom set. 'Better than the stock market,' she would tell him. Even Miller's art, she convinced him, would multiply his dollars."

"She's most probably turning over in her grave," my mother concluded.

"Do you know Miller's work, Paul?"

My mother answered. "Paul has a couple of his paintings. They're in his study. I can't believe I didn't mention them to you when you told me about your Gettysburg gig. But we didn't talk much about the job; and I know the artist as Dante the Painter, not Elias Miller. I can't believe you haven't seen them. You've been over to Paul's."

"It has been a while. I remember his collection of books, not his collection of art."

Paul got up from the couch and walked toward the bar, his back straight, his gray hair exceptionally thick for a man in his sixties. An amateur actor who made his money buying and selling Manhattan real estate, he met my mother when she came backstage to applaud him one night for his performance in a production of *All My Sons*. When I went off to college, he filled her suddenly vacant hours. He made my absence less painful for her and materially easier for me. Eleven years ago, I counted. It seemed like yesterday.

"Madeline was very proud of her Miller discoveries," Paul said after filling his glass. "The first painting of his I came by was a Christmas present from her, an image of Dante and Virgil, an army of dead souls shuffling in front of them. Miller called it *Limbo*. I was embarrassed to take it; Madeline and I weren't that close and I had nothing with which to reciprocate. I told her so, but she brushed me off. 'You will appreciate the art,' she told me, 'and that is reason enough.' After her death, I learned that she had bequeathed me another Miller, *Pope Simony*. 'For your decency,' she wrote. I don't know why she was so generous."

"She was secretly in love with you, or wanted to convert you, or both," Janet said. "Or is there something you refuse to tell me?" The laughter in my mother's voice gave her away. This wasn't the first time they had had this conversation.

"Your mother has been teasing me about this for years," Paul happily said.

"I can understand why. But the second painting—what is it?" I asked.

"It is a smaller piece and quite good. *Pope Simony*, it's called, after the sin of exploiting your position for unwholesome reasons. In medieval times, it referred to the ecclesiastical crime of selling positions in the hierarchy of the Church. Dante comes upon Pope Nicholas III entombed upside down, the soles of his feet on fire. They are all in the Eighth Circle of Hell, if I remember right. Nicholas predicts the damnation of Pope Boniface VIII, Dante's real-life enemy, and Pope Clement V, Boniface's successor.

"I was fascinated by the concept of simony, the misuse of power. There was something going on in the country at the time, or in the city, some move by the president or mayor that had me riled up. Maybe it was an act of a president of a major corporation, or a Hollywood star giving unlearned lip to a political cause? I don't remember, and it's unimportant. I find cases of simony every time I open a newspaper, people in authority misusing their positions."

"Is that how I ended up working on the project, your relationship with Caleb Brewster?"

My mother looked away and Paul looked at his highly polished shoes. A full thirty seconds must have passed before he answered.

"You don't owe anything to Caleb Brewster. I mentioned you to Harland Van Ness at the Truth Foundation. He knew I owned a couple Millers—he is Caleb and Madeline's son-in-law, as I'm sure you know—and saw her giving me *Limbo*. He wanted to see if I was interested in putting some money into a monograph on Elias Miller. I told him I might be if it truly honored Madeline."

"So he hired me to persuade you?"

"Simony," Paul said. "I was ready to put money into the publication, Larry, but not because he hired you. Madeline deserves recognition, as does Miller. Harland never got back to me. He must have raised all the money needed somewhere else." Paul paused and looked at me, his expression thoughtful. "I think it will be a good and important book. Dante the Painter deserves a larger audience."

"Harland didn't include you among the people who

owned some of the work we wanted to see, and *Limbo* is on our list. I wonder why."

Paul sipped some Scotch before he answered. "For that you'll have to ask Harland, but I will be happy to show you the paintings. I'm proud of them."

"Interesting," I said.

AFTER PAUL LEFT, I telephoned Magritt to tell her about his collection, his invitation, and his relationship to Caleb and Harland. She wasn't home. I called Elias Miller to fill him in on what Magritt and I were up to, but he was sitting by the lake and Beatrice didn't want to disturb him. "Is it important?" she asked. I had to admit that it wasn't.

Finally, with no one at home, I looked in a mirror and complained about Paul to my reflection.

CHAPTER TEN

EARLY SATURDAY, MY MOTHER woke me to take a call from Magritt.

"You tried to reach me yesterday. I'm sorry, but I just picked up my messages this morning. Was it anything important?"

"No," I said while trying to remember why I had called. To complain about Paul, I realized, and felt a bit foolish. "Nothing important, Magritt, I was just regressing back in time and was having a teenage fit over my mother's boyfriend. I was looking for a supportive friend."

"I'm sorry I wasn't in—I've never seen you in a temper tantrum."

"It wasn't that bad, but it wasn't pretty. What is that I'm hearing in the background? It sounds like you're surfing."

"Not quite. Eric rented a place on Fire Island. I'm sitting on the screened porch watching waves break against the shore, the water green, the sunlight streaking across the ocean's surface. There is almost no one around at this hour of the morning. All I hear are ocean and gulls. You'd like it here—its restless beauty, the absence of unnatural sounds," Magritt said, her voice meditative.

"It sounds ideal."

Magritt took a deep breath, then her voice deepened. "Oh, it is—the place at least. Still, it's frustrating. We've been snapping at each other. Oh, it's okay to be crabby when it's gray and raining, but when it's this brilliant out—what a waste. I seem to have exasperated Eric. He thinks I'm too preoccupied with the book and Dante to pay attention to him; he says my body is at the shore but my mind is in Gettysburg."

"I'm sorry, Magritt. But the weekend is just beginning. He'll cheer up."

"Maybe, but I'm not certain if I will. He's off for a long swim; if he comes back in the same mood it's going to be a long three days."

"If a salt-water swim doesn't transform Eric, you can always grab the car keys and come home. I'm available for dinner," I said, only half-jokingly.

Magritt's voice filled with smiles. "It is very tempting, Larry," she giggled. "But speaking of dinner, I talked to Harland's wife, Susan." Her tone became all business. "I set up an appointment for Monday evening, two weeks from now. I hope that's convenient for you. All their paintings illustrate sections of *Purgatorio*. You might want to go over the notes you jotted down after talking to Dante about that section. Remember? I was picking up things in town with Beatrice, so I missed the conversation. You had some questions about Giotto when I got back."

"I remember the conversation very well. The way he was talking to me, I thought he believed I was the fourteenth century artist reincarnate."

"You never know, Larry. Reincarnation as a playwright—why not? By the way, have you been able to reach Brewster's son and Roberta Whitford?"

I gulped. "I haven't tried."

"Well, get off the stick, Mr. Sullivan," she said, her voice once again cheerful.

"I'll get on it today. Don't worry."

"Good. Listen, I have to run," she said in a rushed voice. "Eric's coming out of the water and will want company when he's making breakfast."

"Call me if you get too much sand, salt, and sun. It's a deadly combination. I'm much safer."

"Well, I'm not quite sure of that," she said, and then began to laugh, a contagious laugh that triggered my own. When we hung up, I wondered what Eric would think if he had heard her laughter.

I grabbed a cup of coffee and sank into the living room's upholstered chair, sensing how much wishful thinking there was in my teasing Magritt about dinner. I had no plans for the weekend, no tickets to a play, no rendezvous at a mid-town bar, no lover to tease into bed. Society demands more than that on Saturday nights, it demands energy and experimentation, companionship and romance. I saw nothing in front of me but an empty evening, a night of feeling sorry for myself. Damn it, I said to myself, and pushed my body deeper into the chair. A testosterone-driven picture of Magritt lying on a half-buried blanket invaded my mind, her fingers trying to wipe away the sand that was scratching her skin at the edges of a bikini. But Sharon refused to allow Magritt a monopoly on my imagination and voluptuous images of her stormed my thoughts, pictures of her in our hotel room, pictures of her walking toward me in the Frick. Then I switched to Magritt, then back to Sharon, then to Magritt. Even Hilla showed up, young and magnificent. If I were sixteen it would have been fun, but for a man of twenty-nine, the hormonal output demanded by three women was exhausting. I finished the coffee, took a cold shower, and lay down on a cold bed.

Finally, I forced myself to relive the conversation I had had with Elias Miller about the writing of *Purgatorio*.

We were sitting on the screened porch of his house, sipping an Italian red wine and waiting for the sun to finally dip below the horizon. Dante was in a particularly cheerful mood and, after his third glass of the grape, became totally immersed in the persona of the great Poet.

"*Purgatorio* presented a host of writing problems. I wanted to make it more complex than the *Inferno*, for its role in the drama of the afterlife is more complicated. Hell is the eternal resting place of unrepentant sinners, but in Purgatory, sin is forgiven and redemption is promised. All the shades will someday enjoy eternity with Christ. As a fellow writer, Laurence, you can appreciate the difficulty of adding redemption to sin and punishment. Picturing *Purgatorio* as a mountain was my idea. Giotto suggested that I make it an island. 'You don't want your readers to think they can walk there, do you?' he quarreled. Giotto loved to squabble, even when he was sober. 'And an island will give you mystery, an island with a single mountain, difficult to climb at the beginning, easier as you reach the sky.' I debated his vision. 'Mountains are easier to climb at the base, not the top.' 'You are the creator, Dante. You can make the mountain any way you like.'"

Dante the Painter reached for the bottle and filled my glass. For the moment, he forgot about his. "Where was I?" he asked, his face in a puzzled frown.

"You were in the middle of a conversation with your friend Giotto."

"Yes, of course, in the public house in Padua. Giotto was working on his frescos for the Scrovegni Chapel. Magnificent frescoes, his people more alive than any depicted by other artists, their emotions touching the viewer. His brush foretelling the great Italian art of the Renaissance. I was scratching away on the *Commedia* and was speculating on how best to separate *Purgatorio* from the *Inferno*. 'Alter your poetic style,' Giotto suggested. 'Not a great change, but distinct enough to have your readers realize that they are in a different realm. And your sinners, unlike the prisoners in Hell—your readers must see them as worthy of redemption. Aren't we all sinners? Don't we all want to get to Heaven? And you must do more than tie the punishment to the sin; you must show the conduct that is expected of us, something tangible, a distinct model of virtuous behavior. For those who are being punished for the sin of Pride, you need an example of humility, like King David dancing barefoot before his God. I would balance the sin of Avarice with the virtuous poverty of Mary, the Mother of God.'

"I took Giotto's advice, as I did so often. Purgatory is a mountain of seven terraces, one for each of the seven fatal sins, but I needed an anti-purgatory, a place for me to gather those who made God wait—the indolent, the excommunicated, the multitudes who delay repenting until the last moments of their life. I located anti-Purgatory in the mountain's base."

Dante poured some wine for himself, took a drink, and let out a boisterous laugh. "I do miss Giotto. He was a virtuous braggart, a divine combination of artistic genius and self-promotion. He didn't allow politics to interfere with his artistry and ended up a very rich man. I could have learned more from him."

THAT AFTERNOON, I fulfilled my pledge to Magritt and called Brewster's son, Jonathan, and Madeline's long-time friend, Roberta Whitford.

Jonathan Brewster's voice grew cold and distant when he realized why I was calling. "I know the Truth Foundation, and my sister has told me about your monograph. I'm just not interested, Mr. Sullivan. Perhaps in five or ten years, if my mother is no longer as strong a presence in my life. They were gifts from her, private treasures that she wanted to share with me. I don't want photographs of them stuck into a paperback that will end up on remainder tables."

"It may become a best-seller," I argued, riled by his ridicule.

"I'm not interested, Mr. Sullivan. I can't make it any plainer than that."

No, he couldn't have made it any clearer. I hung up quickly, not wanting to dig myself in any deeper. A female voice might get a more amiable reception, I thought, and decided to have Magritt try to arrange an appointment when she got back to Manhattan.

An hour later, after two bottles of beer, I worked up the nerve to call Roberta Whitford. She welcomed my call. A deep-throated laugh erupted when I said I was calling on behalf of the Truth Foundation. A jovial invitation was offered when I asked for an appointment to see her collection of Miller's work.

"Bless you," she said. "I love showing them off. Anytime you wish to make it. Today? Tomorrow? You better drive. You could take a train up to Armonk, but it's a long cab ride from there, if you can find a cab that will take you. And bring your bathing suit."

"There will be two of us. Magritt Cline will be coming with me."

"Well, if you think you need a chaperone, bring her along . . . and the bathing suits."

CHAPTER ELEVEN

ERIC AND MAGRITT were leaning against the brick exterior of her apartment house when I arrived on Wednesday morning, she in a short, ice-blue silk jacket and matching T-shirt that glorified her narrow waist, with bell-bottomed, dark-gray slacks that made her legs appear longer. Eric's outfit was less formal, and, to me, far less appealing. His brown shorts hugged his bulging thighs; his sleeveless shirt exhibited muscular arms and shoulders. Apollo at the beach, I thought. It was impossible not to dislike him.

"Are you coming with us?" I hesitantly asked Eric after we had shaken hands and exchanged some affable words.

He gave me an unexpectedly nervous smile and the answer I wanted. "You're on your own, Larry. I'm just having a last look at Magritt."

When he kissed Magritt lightly on the lips and gave her a long goodbye hug, the color drained from her face.

"Did the weekend improve?" I asked, after Eric got into the cab he had waved down.

"I survived," she said, and watched the taxi slowly move down the street. "And the weekend ended. Otherwise . . ." She stopped herself and looked as if something new and unexpected had occurred to her. "Someday I'd like to talk to you about it."

Two cups of coffee and three tollbooths later, I located the intercom attached to the gated entrance to Roberta Whitford's estate. An English-accented butler pronounced Sullivan in the clipped style of his homeland when he answered. "Welcome to Eagle Rock," he said, as an electronic signal opened the gate. I waved at the camera attached to a wrought-iron post, climbed back into the Mercedes, drove around the oval, and parked in front of the red brick mansion. "I'm Mr. Weathering," the butler said with great formality. He marched us across the marble floor of the first level of the enormous house, out through some French doors, and across a lush lawn. He left us at the edge of an Olympic-sized swimming pool.

Ms. Whitford climbed up a ladder that was close to where we were standing and, dripping wet, greeted us. "What a beautiful day," she exclaimed, her voice loud enough to break eggs. "I did tell you to bring your suits, didn't I? I love to swim." Then she stuck out her wet hand. "Call me Robby. I prefer it to Ms. Whitford. That makes me feel so old."

Everything about her was large. Her breasts swelled against the black, single-piece bathing suit, and her ample stomach stretched its elastic material. Magritt came up to her shoulder. Yet, for an overweight woman of seventy or thereabout, she was surprisingly attractive, her large brown eyes soft and alert, her lips plump and expressive. A full mouth of large, bright teeth showed when she smiled.

"Tall, isn't she?" Magritt said as we walked over to a small bathhouse to change into our swimsuits.

Magritt beat me out of the bathhouse, her red bikini looking smaller than it had ever looked before, and she more beautiful.

"Join me!" Robby yelled, and jumped into the pool.

My skin had shriveled by the time I climbed out of the water. A pot of tea and a tray of sandwiches had appeared on a glass-topped table, and white cotton bathrobes and towels hung on three folding chairs. To my delight, Magritt settled on being warmed by the sun and didn't touch her robe. When she noticed the obvious pleasure I took in looking at her, I blushed, embarrassed at revealing how fascinating I found her.

Robby began the conversation. "Harland told you to call me, did he? I'm sure it didn't come easily. We don't have a good relationship. He wanted me to join the Truth Foundation's board, but I thought he should go out and get a real job. I always thought the Brewsters—Madeline, that is—created the Foundation just to give him something honorable to do. Madeline told me he was doing some good work, but she has been gone for years. I always liked his wife, Susan, Madeline's daughter. If she can live with him, he must have something."

"I didn't realize it was a family foundation," I said with surprise.

"They don't announce it. Caleb thought there would be a run on his wealth if the world knew he had a foundation. Few people know how much he is worth. He has an army of employees who look after his investments. Like all classic capitalists, he always wants more. Marx would have understood him. But I'm an old gossip with a cynical streak. I never warmed to him, but Madeline loved him. What can I say? But this project you're on—I don't understand it."

With her normal intensity and a great deal of charm, Magritt explained why we were there, talked a little about Elias Miller's art, and listed the paintings we were interested in and thought Robby owned. Robby studied my face while Magritt talked, trying, it seemed, to discover in my expression those points with which I disagreed. Finding none, she stretched her arms palms forward, her fingers interlocked.

"You know this is not an innocent venture," Robby said in a deep contralto. "Clearly, Caleb and Harland have a personal agenda. They're not the type of men who would finance a publication to pay homage to Madeline, however deserving she might be. And they don't give a hoot about art—Miller's or anyone else's. For the right price, Caleb would auction his mother's grave."

"You sound like my boyfriend," Magritt chimed. "He thinks it's a money-making scheme."

"Isn't it always? They'll use your writings to make a market for Miller's work, and then they'll begin to sell. How much are they paying you?"

I hesitated for a moment. I had always considered earnings as personal, perhaps because I earned so little. But I found it impossible to refuse Robby's frankness. "Fifty thousand dollars to each of us. Miller isn't on the payroll, as far as I know," I answered.

"He may be in on it. Can you truly trust anyone who would sign his work Dante the Painter? I'm sure he has some canvases hidden in the attic. Now they're almost worthless, but if the scheme works, who knows?"

I felt the need to defend the professor. "He's not the type. Half the time he thinks he is Dante the Poet; the other half he's Dante the Painter. There is no in between, no swindler, no budding capitalist."

Robby's roar of laughter almost caused waves in the pool. Elias Miller would like her, I supposed.

Magritt leapt into the conversation. "If they are up to mischief, why would they suggest we see the work you own? Wouldn't our inclusion of one or more of your pieces lower the price of their holdings by making them appear less scarce?"

"It's not baffling," Robby said, iron in her voice. "I'm a rich lady. I can afford to hang a Picasso and a Matisse, a Lucian Freud, a Bellows, a Hopper. I have paintings by them all. I love them, but I treasure my Millers. They hang in a special place . . . you'll see. If I think enough of Dante the Painter to extol his work, can't you hear the cash registers ring? The rich are like any other pack; they follow each other."

As we walked away from the pool, Robby said, "You do have a remarkable figure, Magritt. I've been tempted to wear a bikini . . . then I mix a martini and come to my senses."

DANTE THE PAINTER'S compositions were hung on the third floor of her mansion, in a vast rectangular space where her mother once threw costume parties in her honor. After her parents' deaths she had left the room closed. "Bad memories," she said, "of my parents' unrelenting attempts to marry me off. They never understood I enjoyed being single. I opened the room after Madeline died—I wanted a special place in which to hang her splendid gifts."

Light burst into the vast space through an expansive skylight and the twenty windows that surrounded the room, six on each of the longer walls, four on the shorter. Five Miller paintings hung along the northern wall, tastefully placed between the draped windows. The impact was immediate.

Magritt, her mouth partially opened, looked like a child at a candy store. "Did you hang them yourself?" she asked in a reverent whisper, as if it were the installation that fascinated her.

"I called on a friend who had worked on some exhibits

at the Smithsonian when her husband was in Congress. She is a talent. She liked the paintings, but not the themes. She was interested in Heaven, not Hell or Purgatory. I preferred Purgatory myself. I live in hope that God will give me a chance to repent for all the things I've enjoyed in this life and wasn't supposed to."

"I see," Magritt said, and giggled in the way you do when you want someone to know you like them.

Robby let out a sharp cackle. "You've seen his work before, haven't you?"

"Many," I answered. "Why do you ask?"

"You both look so surprised. Are these that much different than the others?"

Magritt answered. "These are the first we've seen in natural light; the others were illuminated by standard light bulbs. Daylight multiplies the richness of his vision. You'd think he painted them outdoors. It's stunning."

"Their language changes with the weather," Robby said. "You should visit me when snow covers the skylight or clouds filter the sun. The images look different, the shadows deeper, the colors toned by the climate's mood. I could never bring myself to sell them. They are as much a part of me as my legs."

"So you think that's what Harland and Caleb are up to?" I said, not yet absorbed in the moment. "If our manuscript makes a splash, they'll sell their Millers?"

"And they know I won't. They think it's because of my devotion to Madeline, but that's only the half of it. I've fallen in love with them, and you don't sell your old lovers. It would be like giving up happy memories and living only with your regrets."

Magritt was in a trance, scrutinizing each piece, first from a distance, then with her nose three inches away, then at a distance again, overwhelmed by a passion I could not feel, as if the images raced through her blood and overwhelmed her mind. It reminded me of Hilla's passion for opera, her eyes glued to the stage, her emotions enflamed by the orchestra and voices. I liked art. I enjoyed music. But the transcendent appreciation that overran Magritt's face, that would grip Hilla as we held hands during a final act, merely lurked at the edges of my imagination. An errant question ran through my mind: Is that why my work plays at the theater's fringe, why I am always a mile from Broadway? I shook my head to free me from my thinking.

"*Two Suns*—how could it look so feeble in the slide and so powerful in the original?" Magritt said to no one in particular. "It is larger than I expected—twenty by thirty, Robby, would that be right?"

"Larger, around three feet in length and two feet high, if I remember right. A wonderful architectural rendering of an imagined ancient Rome: the Coliseum, the Pantheon, the Mausoleum of Augustus—as they were before the birth of Christ—the bronze statue of Augustus still on top of the cylindrical structure. A church now rests on that site, Magritt, doesn't it?"

"Yes, I think so," Magritt answered, but it was clear that she was too involved with the architectural rendering to think about the question. "You can almost feel the strength of the load-bearing columns and the permanence of the streets and bridges. And the two suns, they feel hot."

"I thought I was the only one kinky enough to feel them," Robby said, and clapped her hands. "Rome at its height when two suns illuminated her, one shone on the roads of this world, the other lighted the path to God. But now—remember Dante was writing about his own time—the sword is fused with the scepter, or something like that, and combined they misrule Italy because neither fears the other. We Americans like to think that we invented the separation of church and state. But it was a revered belief long before Columbus or our constitution. Dante knew the importance of protecting the church from the corrupting influences of the state. Now we think of it the other way, the state must be protected from the church, but either way the significance is the divide. Dante dates the belief even further back. In the same canto, he refers to the Levites' protection of the ancient Temple in Jerusalem. It was illegal for the sons of the tribe of Levi to inherit wealth, for things of this world corrupt, and those called upon to protect the holy shrine must be incorruptible. Interesting theme, isn't it?

"And speaking of the Temple, it's the center of the next painting," Robby continued while walking over to the painting Dante called *Protecting the Temple*.

Like *Two Suns*, it is an architectural image, full of stone walls and grand structures. King Solomon's temple occupies most of the painting, Phoenician in design, much like the temples unearthed in Egypt, and rendered as if it had been constructed of huge blocks of red and white limestone. The temple appears to be twice as wide as it is high. Ten steep steps rise to the front portico, and two bronze pillars stand as sentries to its massive wooden door. A dozen temple guards, in short togas, sit on the steps in animated groups of three or four.

I turned to ask Magritt to learn her thoughts, but she had quietly moved away from my side and was standing a few feet away, a finger against her lips, her glasses pulled high on her small nose, examining the first two paintings toward my left.

"Robby, I don't recall this scene," she said as if disappointed in herself.

"All of my paintings depict scenes from Canto XVI of *Purgatorio*, a remarkable number considering there are a hundred cantos in the *Commedia*. If Miller had devoted the same number to the entire work, he would have produced five hundred oils. The Canto has a special resonance, resting as it does in the middle of *Purgatorio* and therefore in the middle of the entire poem. It grapples with the eternal questions of free will and the tensions between church and state—the privileges of this world and the next. Miller's *Pilgrim and the Poet* is what you're looking at. Dante and Virgil are on the Third Terrace of the Island of Purgatory, the place where the sin of wrath is absolved. As you can see, they are shrouded in dense clouds of stinging smoke. Dante's eyes are shut and his head leans on Virgil's shoulder. It's consistent with the poem, Magritt. Dante closes his eyes to protect them against the stinging smoke, and Virgil offers his shoulder to help guide the temporarily blinded pilgrim. I find it very poignant. In the background of the painting, further up the island, a gathering of shades sings a hymn. Dante wrote that the communal singing of sacred music helped the dead atone for their sins, a process of salvation he repeats often in *Purgatorio*. There is music in Heaven, as well."

"But none in Hell," I said. "There you hear only the sounds of pain and suffering."

Dante the Painter adopted a contemporary style when he painted *Pilgrim and the Poet*, employing swirls of paint to build lusciously colored ridges and valleys, sculpting expressionistic images, with faces and bodies defined by the flow of his brush and not by the precision of his lines.

"How does he manage to get that effect?" I asked Magritt.

"He must have mixed the colors in a slow-drying

medium. That would have allowed him to sculpt the paint and blend the edges of different colors into each other. De Kooning employed that approach in some of his most famous pieces."

It was not the technique that intrigued me, but the extraordinary tenderness of the composition. Dante cradled against Virgil's shoulder, the older poet offering his strength to the younger. It was Virgil as teacher—accepting, supportive, even protective of his middle-aged protégé. And Dante, the frightened pupil, still trying to fashion his voice and to understand the purpose of his labors. I felt myself sink into the composition and wanted to reach out and touch Virgil's gown.

By the time I had pulled myself away from *Pilgrim and the Poet*, Magritt was examining the next painting on the wall, *Discussing Evil*. Again, Dante employed a contemporary, expressionistic style, but this painting was more intellectual and far less emotional than *Pilgrim and the Poet*. The poets are on the Third Terrace of Purgatory and Dante is conversing with the spirit of Marco the Lombard, questioning him about the source of evil. The color of Pilgrim's frock is no longer the deep black used in the paintings of the *Inferno*, but a lighter color, almost a gray, to demonstrate that even Dante's black cloak and hood is made less heavy by the absolution of sins. The world is destitute, declares the *Commedia*, but what is the cause? Does a predestined plan control us all? Or is it in the acts of man? The heavens frame our tendencies, Marco answers, but all are given the power of knowing right from wrong. If we had no choice there would be no free will, and we know that free will is a gift from God.

"Is free will a gift or a burden?" I asked as I translated the painting for myself.

"Now that's a heavy question, Larry," Robby laughed. "If you were planning to spend a weekend with me we might begin to explore it."

"I was just thinking out loud," I pleaded. "I wasn't asking a question."

"Good," Robby continued. "I don't usually think about free will. I'd rather blame Freud."

Magritt let out a laugh.

The last of Miller's paintings in Robby's collection is titled *Hope*. Dante and Virgil are walking away from the viewer, their bodies silhouetted against the rays of light that break through the dark smoke of the Third Terrace.

"Hmm," Magritt said, "it reminds me of the first painting on the wall, *Pilgrim and the Poet*. Two people walking into the unknown together, their bodies so coupled that they seem to be walking to the same beat, almost dancing. It's full of promise, don't you think?"

After Robby and I indicated agreement, we stood silently listening to the art.

"THANK YOU," I said to Robby as we sat around the pool sipping soft drinks. "It is an impressive group of paintings."

"What would you think of using *The Levites Guarding the Temple* for the cover?" Magritt asked, addressing the question to both of us.

Robby answered. "I would be quite proud. I'd be proud to have any one of them on the cover, but Harland might be a little upset. He'd want one of his, and Caleb would argue for one of his."

"It's our choice," Magritt insisted.

"It's too Jewish a theme for the cover of a work on

Dante, even if it's Dante the Painter. I'd prefer using the *Two Suns*," I said.

"That's much too secular," Magritt argued, leaning forward in her chair and wearing the intense, nervous expression that had become so familiar.

"Let's not quarrel," Robby said. "You certainly have time to choose. I'd prefer you went with *Hope*. It may not be the best painting I own, but isn't that what *The Divine Comedy* is about? With a little repentance and the opportunity to cleanse our souls in Purgatory, we can all get to Heaven. But you might decide that an illustration from the *Inferno* would sell more copies, say, a portrait of the Devil. Hell has a far greater audience than Heaven. Just think of all the crime shows on television."

Magritt touched Robby's robust forearm and asked where the nearest lady's room was.

As soon as she was out of earshot, Robby leaned toward me. "Do you think Dante believed in God?" she asked earnestly, her voice just above a whisper, as if the question itself was a sacrilege.

"I've always assumed so."

"We all do. It's our common wisdom about the Middle Ages. Everyone is devout. But why would he talk about the importance of keeping the princes of the church in their place if he believed in their message? He may have believed in God, but he was too smart to believe in all the trappings of religion, in the existence of an afterlife, of eternal punishment and reward. No, he was too immersed in the here and now, too concerned about greed and corruption to be a mystic. 'Tell me the truth,' he says to Marco in the poem, 'so I may announce it to the world: Are our sins made in Heaven, or are they made in us?' *The Divine Comedy* is not a poem about the afterlife; it is a poem about Florence and Rome, pope and emperor," Robby said.

"But it has a deeply religious foundation. I don't think you can avoid that."

"That it does," Robby said, and let out a contagious laugh. She took my hand and said, "This has been a very good day."

THE WESTERN SKY was ablaze with the multiple colors of sunset when Magritt and I left for Manhattan. It filled the car with a luminous, caressing light. Magritt's skin glowed and her hair came alive. I had to struggle to keep my eyes on the road.

"How did your weekend work out?" I asked, to keep the testosterone down.

"We've broken up. What you witnessed this morning was a goodbye."

It was an unexpected reply and it took a moment for her comment to sink in. "I'm sorry—and surprised," was all I could think of saying. Then, belatedly, I added, "You didn't look as if you were coming apart when I picked you up this morning."

"There's no reason to be sorry. We were good friends, but ordinary lovers."

"He looks like a stallion," I said, and quickly realized how unsympathetic that must have sounded.

"He is, but I'm not a filly."

"Did he give you reason?"

"You mean was he sleeping around? Maybe I was the one sleeping around. Why is the man always blamed?"

"I wish you would talk to my mother. She blames me

for my breakup. 'You must have done something wrong,' she keeps saying."

"Well, did you?"

I emitted some ugly sound as a way of answer.

"You've thrown a flirtatious line at me now and then, but you've never seriously tried to get into my pants. I'm just curious. Do I turn you off? Do you prefer other stallions?"

"I'm boringly heterosexual, Magritt. There are still some straight writers in the theater."

"You know that isn't what I meant."

"I am twenty-nine years old, Magritt. Young when it comes to a love life, old if you are still living with your mother. My lover of five years threw me out. My main romantic goal is not to be heartbroken. I can avoid that by sleeping around, or by being celibate. With Eric around, pulling at your pants for a quick one didn't seem like an alternative."

"And now?" she asked.

Her voice was devoid of signals. I couldn't tell if she was serious, or searching for a compliment. "Do you really want to get this heavy, Magritt?" I asked.

"I'm just fishing, Larry. Breaking up with Eric isn't easy, even if it is my doing. Suddenly, I feel unattractive and bereft. I thought a proposition from you—one I would have turned down—would lift my spirits."

"We could pull into a motel," I flippantly suggested.

"It's a bit too late," she said.

"I found it easy to attract women who wanted to exercise their limbs, who thought sex with a budding playwright would open a stage door, or who just wanted to pass some time or chase away the blues. I liked the sexual tension, the thrill of a new conquest, the sense of dominance. But the morning after became a growing problem. I'd wake worrying about the rest of my life. Where am I going? What am I doing? How should I live my life? Dante's questions, Magritt. I could no longer shake them loose. Then I met someone and fell in love. At least it felt like love. I lived with her for five years."

I looked to Magritt to catch her eye, but she was looking out the side window, her hands in her lap. "I've come to like you," I continued, to bring her back to me. "I look forward to spending time with you, to working together. I don't want to put that at risk."

I could sense her head turning toward me. "If I was repulsive you'd try to screw the hell out of me. Is that what you're saying?"

I was relieved to have a reason to laugh. Magritt didn't join me, so I went on, "I stopped my gratuitous flirting with you for the same reason you've stopped giving me the finger. We see each other as people, not cardboard cutouts. Simple gestures are no longer enough. I couldn't make love to you without worrying about how you would feel the morning after—and how I would."

Magritt turned to the passenger's window to watch the brilliant horizon welcome the close of day. I kept my eyes on the road, thinking of how little Sharon meant to me, how lacking our chemistry. I hadn't gone forward after Hilla threw me out. I had gone backward. "It's your turn to say something revealing or to argue with me," I said to Magritt.

She didn't hesitate. "Fear of the future caused me to break up with Eric. I worried that I would push myself into unreal feelings; that I would translate sex into love, that I would twist my fondness for him into something it is not. I don't want to worry about how my actions affect him; I don't want to be in a place where he can hurt me. It makes no sense; I know. Love is much different than sex. It is a burden.

It transforms thrills into obligations. And I don't want to be obligated to him."

"Yes," I said, although I wasn't certain what I was agreeing with.

"Who was the exception, the one person you took to bed whom you cared about?"

"I thought I had snuck that line by you."

"I have a good memory," Magritt announced.

"So I notice. Five years; we lived together for five years. I can hardly believe it."

"You must have cared a great deal about each other. What got you to break off?"

"She threw me out."

"You must have given her good reason."

"I don't believe I did," I blurted out.

"Oh," Magritt said, filling the vowel with disappointment, as if she had predicted what I would say and had been wrong.

"The fact that I hadn't given her a good reason doesn't mean Hilla didn't have one. She has outgrown me. It is that simple. She is where she wants to be in her life, a recognized jewelry designer who is sought after and prosperous, at home with people who thrive in a competitive world, buyers from Tiffany and Cartier, European designers, Asian craftsmen. She thought I had become all that I would ever be and it was not enough."

"But she was wrong."

"And how do you know?"

Magritt chuckled. "If a 700-year-old poet can transform himself into a first-rate painter, life gives us more than one chance to catch the gold ring."

"He is an inspiration, even if he's only seventy. Hilla never realized how competitive I am; how much I want to be a personage."

"A personage?" Magritt said, as if on cue.

"A good comedic word, in sound and image."

Magritt laughed sweetly.

I leaned over and turned the radio on, pressing the search button to find something we would like. Magritt gently moved my hand and took over the hunt. The softness of her touch ran up my arm. Finally, she settled on a string quartet.

"Is this all right?" she asked.

"Perfect."

She leaned back and took a deep breath. "I love twilight," she said.

We drove for a while without speaking, but I found the silence uncomfortable. "If Eric were a Wall Street tycoon, would you feel the same way?" I finally asked her.

"That's not me, Larry. I couldn't care less and, anyway, I have a large enough trust to support two. You're giving up a great deal by not bedding me, you know." She reached over and squeezed my knee, and then she laughed. "I'm only kidding. I feel like you do. I like you, and if we made love, that would be changed. I wish that was the reason I left Eric, because of his job, because he follows philandering husbands and testifies at divorces. It would be far easier than being afraid I'd talk myself into loving him." She paused again and sighed. Then she added, her voice an octave lower than normal, "We do create our own hells, don't we?"

I opened the door for Magritt after I pulled in front of her mother's apartment building, and gave her a long hug. She kissed me on the lips. "I hope we remain friends for a long time," she said.

I drove slowly to the garage where my mother kept the car, alternatively proud that I didn't try to get into Magritt's clothes and depressed by not having tried to make love to her. She had just broken up with Eric. How would I have felt in the morning knowing that? But being friends? My body rebelled at the thought.

CHAPTER TWELVE

WE SET OUT AFTER DINNER. It was Dante's idea. "I've eaten far too much," he claimed, although he had not had more to eat or drink than usual. "A walk around the lake would do us both good."

I didn't disagree.

Magritt was off with her mother for the weekend, attending the wedding of a first cousin on her father's side. "He's my favorite cousin," she said excitedly, "a thoracic surgeon who teaches at Georgetown."

"And his bride?" I asked innocently.

"His husband. I don't know what he does."

"Oh?" I responded.

"It's legal in Washington, D.C.," she announced dramatically.

I had planned to spend the weekend in the City. Lunching with my mother; visiting the Metropolitan Museum to see the recently renovated European Galleries, and ending the day with a half-price ticket to a Broadway show at the end of its run. It didn't matter much what show, as long as I hadn't seen it more than twice. Theaters are my cathedrals, performances my scriptures. But the weather was too perfect to stay indoors: warm and clear, the humidity low, a light breeze refreshing the air. Gettysburg called.

Dante was swimming when I got to the lake, and Beatrice was sitting under a shade tree, whiffing from mosquito repellent. She was reading the all-too-popular erotic romance novel, *Fifty Shades of Gray*.

"Really?" I asked.

Beatrice laughed.

"Is it any good?" I continued.

"In its way," she replied, "but Dante insists that we are too old to experiment."

I slipped into a pair of black swimming trunks and joined Dante in the lake.

In the late afternoon we shared a thick steak that Dante grilled on an open fire and a couple of potatoes that had been roasted at the side of the fire pit. We washed the food down with a good Italian red wine. Beatrice went back to her book; Dante and I put on long pants and long-sleeved shirts, smeared our exposed anatomies with bug repellent and headed off into the woods.

"Is Virgil going to join us and show us the way?" I teased the old professor.

"Don't you know he refuses to cross the pond and remains in Rome? I keep inviting him, but to no avail. Even Beatrice has not been able to entice him. Giotto, however, visits almost every year, but not in the summer. He hates the humidity," Dante answered without a hint of insincerity.

"A pity. I would have enjoyed meeting them," I said, to go along with his gag—if it was a gag.

Dante led the way as we hiked the trail around the lake, brushing aside the recent growth that overhung the rocky footpath and taking care to prevent branches from snapping back and hitting me in the face. A rare wood turtle cut across the path on its way to the lake, and we stopped to watch a large snapping turtle basking on a rock, its thick, threatening head thrust into the air to catch the remaining sunlight. Three young deer came to rigid attention when they caught sight of us.

"Have you considered writing a play about me?" Dante asked as we rested on a fallen log. We had made it more than halfway around the lake and were going back to the Millers' compound.

Dante didn't wait for an answer. "I loved acting, Laurence, not as much as I loved Beatrice, or as much as I loved writing, but very close. Rain or shine, in the bright light of noontime or the dusk of sundown, I'd costume myself in a dark brown tunic, adorn my head with a matching cowl, and stand by the Fontana di Madonna in the Piazza delle Erbe—then and now the most beautiful square in all of Italy—and recite my tales of Hell and Purgatory. Juliet's home was nearby, its famous balcony facing away from the square."

"Verona, then?" I asked to make sure I was on Dante's wavelength.

"Verona, of course. I was living under the protection of the Scaligeri family, rulers of Verona. Most of the *Commedia* was written while I was in refuge there. Cantos from my poem enchanted the throngs that gathered to hear my words."

"How large was a throng in fourteenth century Verona?" I asked, unwilling to let Elias Miller wander into wonderland without knowing he had a critical audience.

"Perhaps throng is too powerful a word," my companion laughed. "Twenty, sometimes less—peasants mostly, all unlettered except for students visiting from Padua who showed up now and again. And few women, but there were some. The size of the audience didn't matter, although I preferred more to less, Laurence, just like you.

"I was a masterful entertainer, my sweet baritone filled with quiet sounds of love when I talked of Paolo and Francesca, full of intemperate loathing when I spoke of the foul deeds of the princes of the Church, trembling with fear as I climbed lower and lower into the Inferno."

"I never pictured you as a street performer, Dante. I always pictured you as a scholar, a quill in hand, an ink stain on your nose."

"I had to make a living. Oh, Cangrande Scaligeri took good care of me, as he took care of Petrarch and Giotto, but I wanted a little pocket change. You look puzzled, Laurence. Are you that suspicious of what I am telling you? I recited my poetry, much like Homer did centuries before. I didn't sing or dance."

"It's hard to imagine peasants flipping florins into your hat."

"A gold florin, never; even silver florin rarely landed at my feet. I had to be satisfied with bronze coins. You have to remember the time, Laurence: There was no printing press, no radio, no daily newspaper. Few people, even among the clergy, could read and write. If my words were going to be heard, they had to shouted from street corners, from village squares, from church pews. They had to be performed. And besides, Laurence, I liked the clapping, like all thespians. Vanity is universal and timeless. Cangrande was very good to me, but the applause of many outweighs the applause of one. All playwrights know that."

"And what did Cangrande think of your outings? Wasn't it pushing the boundaries of his hospitality, a guest of the ruler of Verona begging for coins?"

"I was entertaining, not begging. And Cangrande was a true noble, a man of the arts, and a great warrior. Alas, he was poisoned to death, Laurence—did you know? An overdose of digitalis. Foxglove grows everywhere."

"A warrior and lord and poisoned to death. Now that would be worth exploring for a play."

Dante shrugged his shoulders and dismissed my comment. "The people identified with *Purgatorio*. They were taught that they were sinners, born with the stigma of Adam and Eve, they knew they had to be cleansed to bath eternally in God's light. But it was the *Inferno* that they wanted to hear. There, and only there, was where evil was fully punished, where society's privileged were caged and tortured—the clergy, the nobles, the landowners who thrived on the toil of the peasants, who satiated themselves with luxuries while others starved. They shouted for more when I told of popes eternally locked in Hades, upside down, their heads in the ground, their burning feet in the air. They shouted halleluiah when I told of the punishments awaiting hypocrites and thieves, blasphemers and traitors. They cried with thankfulness when I slowly described Satan sunken in a frozen landscape, each of his three mouths stuffed with a traitor—Judas, Brutus, and Cassius."

"Did they believe?" I asked, unable to visualize his audience, to understand what they understood, to know what they knew.

Dante looked down at his feet and picked up a white stone. He tossed it into the darkening forest before answering. There was sorrow in his voice. "It is 1320. The great plagues of medieval times are still to come, but the fear of death is growing, for new miseries have fallen on Europe and death comes more frequently. The climate itself has turned against life, the air colder, the snows deeper, the growing season shorter. The abundant harvests of the previous century have ended. The fields grow less fertile, the pigs have fewer offspring, the cows produce less milk, the vineyards less wine. Even the nobles and the Church have to sacrifice, but the privileged remain privileged while the destitute grow in number.

"Belief is all the people have, Laurence—the belief that God is good, that life is eternal, that Christ awaits them after death. They believe without questioning, for questioning is expensive. They are too poor to pay the price of doubt. Without faith, they have nothing. God, the Son, and the Holy Ghost sustain the universe. What is questioned is not Christianity, but Christianity's Church. Christianity is God's voice; the Church is man's creation. The Church is gluttonous and hypocritical, its leaders concerned with their own well-being, with their gold and silver, with their paramours. They preach Christ's word but do not practice Christ's teachings."

Dante picked up another stone and threw it into the forest. He turned to look at me. "The Pope lived in Avignon during most of my years in Verona, but it didn't matter to me. Rome still dominated my world. The Catholic Church was the only church, and it was corrupt."

I was caught up with his 700-year-old persona. I found it irresistible. "But did your audience believe that you had traveled through the afterworld and returned?"

Dante laughed. "I hope not, but I'm sure there were some who did. Aren't there always? Sanity demanded that they trust in God, that they believe in an afterlife, that they are certain that justice will prevail, if not here on earth then in Hell, and Purgatory, and Heaven. So my stories gave them comfort, my poetry gifted them with laughter and tears. I was great theater."

"Did you read Dante to your students?" I asked, attempting to bring back the here and now.

"Of course, but as Professor Miller. I haven't played the pilgrim for 700 years."

"And whom should I write my play about, Dante Alighieri or Elias Miller?"

Dante got up from the log and brushed the seat of his pants. "About Beatrice," he said, and began the walk back to his cabin.

CHAPTER THIRTEEN

THE CAFÉ OF THE RITZ HOTEL was only half filled when I got there on Tuesday morning, a half-hour early for my breakfast with Magritt. A pale young man with blonde hair, a Nordic face, and a ski resort body offered to seat me, but I was concerned that Magritt would not find me if I was located at some remote table. I chose to wait quietly by the restaurant's entry and play the game my mother would often instigate when we'd sit together on a park bench or ride the subway. We'd guess the ages and occupations of the passing humanity. We'd identify the tourists. We'd separate the happy from the sad. "Are you certain?" my mother would ask. The stubborn child in me would answer, "Yes," even knowing what came next. "I, too, used to be certain," she'd say, as if certainty was an illness that only experience could cure.

How right she was, I mused, as I stood to the side of the restaurant's entrance and studied the people going by. How could I possibly know what passions pulsed through these strangers' veins? I could only manufacture their emotions. I filtered their sounds through my prejudices. That was my job, to fill stages with names and faces, with designer people who led joyous or horrid lives, who radiated humor, who succumbed to pain. But my creations always failed. They didn't have the multiple depths of the living. Real people shift from mood to mood, from sensation to sensation. They know happiness and misery simultaneously. My plays' inhabitants showed only one face at a time. Businesspeople had sad lives because I didn't believe that making money could bring contentment. Houseparents were driven to erotic desires because I couldn't believe in the consuming enjoyment of raising children. Teachers and plumbers, carpenters and accountants, indeed all my characters who were doing the expected and ordinary things of life, were never depicted as content and never shown as satisfied. I saved eloquent lives for the perceptive neurotics I wrote about, for artists, for actors, for disbarred lawyers and imprisoned doctors, for my prostitutes and bartenders, for fictional characters written to appeal to people who drifted into small theaters because the seats were cheap, because they were curious, because they had no better place to be.

Leaning against that wall in the Ritz Hotel, I realized once again how much I craved a different audience. An audience filled with successful people, with powerful people, with people who had consequential lives—people whose actions had significance, people who would be influenced by my thoughts and give them relevance, an audience that could transform my words into something more permanent than sound. I wanted to play Broadway; I wanted to write an Academy Award-winning script; I wanted the television credit for a successful prime time show about things that mattered—an oxymoron, perhaps, but no less of a dream. Most of all, I wanted to write a divine comedy.

I hit the side of my head with my hand, stunned by the direction of my thinking, pained by the knowledge that I was fanaticizing about the improbable. Where was Magritt? I looked at my watch. It was still early. I asked to be shown to a table to stop my thoughts from darkening the day, but before my Nordic host could move from behind his standup desk, I caught sight of Magritt pushing the revolving door like a hassled teenager, her blouse a washed-out red, her sneakers a pedestrian blue. Her short black hair was still damp when I put my hand to her head and kissed her cheek, my mouth in full smile, my heart lightened by her presence.

"Damn," she said. "I got up late but raced over here to beat you. But here you are. Why so early?"

"Why did you want to get here first?"

"To show you I'm considerate. And I'm underdressed as well," she added, after eyeing my neatly pressed pants and blue blazer.

"I didn't want to be outdone once again. You looked so glamorous the other day, and I was pretty scruffy."

"So today I'm not glamorous?" she said with good cheer.

I asked the Nordic host to seat us toward the rear of the restaurant, where most of the tables were empty.

"The last thing Robby said to me was, 'It's been a very nice day,' or something similar to that sentiment. And it was a very nice day," I said.

Magritt smiled and lifted the menu. It didn't take her long to order a short stack of pancakes and bacon. The host had already filled our coffee cups. I ordered French toast. No meat.

"Expensive place," Magritt said. "Why not our usual spot?"

"You're supposed to call Jonathan Brewster. If you used your cell phone, it would be difficult for me to listen in. Here there are good old-fashioned telephone booths. It would be a tight fit, but nice."

"You are devious, aren't you?" Magritt chuckled.

"I'm not devious. I'm calculating. I think ahead, Magritt. There is a difference."

"Well, thinking ahead, we need a place to work. My mother is in and out, but her apartment is large and she has a luxurious den, the size of most studio apartments. It even has its own bathroom. You will be able to listen to my every word. Did you think I was going to offer my body to Jonathan in exchange for seeing his etchings?"

"Something like that."

"Humph," she said, and didn't smile.

Our order came quickly, but we ate slowly, talking about Robby's collection, about her home, about the project.

"I'm beginning to think Eric and Robby are right, that we're working on a commercial project, not a philanthropic leap into art history," Magritt said after the plates had been cleared and we were working on our third cups of coffee. "If we convince people that Dante is truly a first-rate artist, we'll create a market for his work. The boom in the stock market is infecting everything, not just real estate prices. The art market is hot. Galleries are scratching around for quality pieces. They want to pull in their share of the money that's flooding Manhattan."

"What if we are involved in a commercial venture? Do we drop what we're doing because someone is going to make money? That would be un-American if nothing else. His art is good, Magritt. Turning Elias Miller into a household name would be a good deed, not a reprehensible act, and retelling *The Divine Comedy* will do no existential harm."

"I just hate being used," Magritt snarled. "Please keep telling me we are doing a favor to the world by introducing Dante the Painter. Eventually I might believe it."

"If nothing else, Magritt, we're meeting people we might never have gotten to know."

"Characters for a future play?" she asked ironically.

"You never know, do you?"

Magritt gave out a familiar chuckle and drained her cup. "Are you working on something I should know about?"

"A few random thoughts, but I'm not seriously working on a play. I haven't worked on a script for a while, even before our project came along."

"Don't you miss it?"

"Do you miss writing your dissertation?"

"I kick myself for not working on it. It's guilt, not sorrow. But I'm still searching for a topic. If I had one, I doubt if I'd want to work on anything else. It's different for you. You're a successful playwright. Your scripts have been produced. It's a lot to put aside."

I waved to our waitress and motioned to our coffee cups. She smiled as she refilled them. When she turned away, I asked, "Have you ever seen one of my plays?"

My coauthor averted her eyes and blushed. "My head has been stuck in art books. I don't often get to the theater."

"You haven't missed much."

She gave me a quizzical look. "I doubt that," she said.

"That's nice of you to say, but why do you think so?"

"Because you're curious, and intelligent, and observant. And you write well."

"You mean I'm likeable. That doesn't make an artist."

"Oh, that's part of it. But I think you're being much too humble," Magritt said as she studied my face.

"It's easy to be humble. Not one of my plays has had a second production. Did you know that?"

"But you're young."

"Not that young. I'm not thirty-five, midway through the journey, but I'm close to thirty. I like to think I'm at a turning point, but I have no reason to believe it. I don't see any intrinsic value in my work. If I had been reaching for a grand vision and now was adding depth and wisdom to my imagination, I would feel differently. But all I can think of are similar plays, built around similar characters."

Magritt put down her cup, took off her glasses, and studied my face in a new focus. "You can't be serious. I bet your audience leaves the theater happier than when they entered. That's a gift. It's something to be proud of."

I smiled and forced a laugh. "Just a morning gloom, that's all. I'll shake it loose before noon. Then I'll think I'm the most authentic playwright in the contemporary theater. I have a big ego."

She looked disappointed, sensing, I believed, that I regretted revealing so much of myself. She looked down at the table for a moment to keep from pressuring me to tell her more. When she looked at me again, her expression had softened. "How about trying a play about a wannabe art historian who can't find a topic for her dissertation? It should be good enough for one act and plenty of laughs."

"Who meets a wannabe playwright and they help solve each other's problems."

"Now you've gotten it to two acts. You're not a wannabe, Larry. You are a writer."

"After reading Dante, I wonder, Magritt. He says so much."

"Well, now at least you know the god you're meant to chase."

I tried to lampoon her comment by filling my voice with sarcasm. But I failed. When I said, "Thank you," it was very sincere.

ON THE WALK to her mother's apartment, I was filled with romantic notions, and wondered if Magritt had thought ahead, that we would enter an empty flat, her bed covered with fresh sheets. But my thinking began to disturb me as we ambled down the crowded streets, and by the time we reached her building I was kicking myself for being a compulsive lecher, for translating all signs of collegiality into come-ons. Still, when we got into the elevator I waited for Magritt to push her body against mine, but she leaned into a corner, her arms across her chest. Her mother opened the apartment door.

"Did you forget your keys?" she asked, before realizing that Magritt was not alone.

THE TELEPHONE RANG five times before Jonathan Brewster answered Magritt's call. I pushed my ear close to her face so we could both hear, enjoying the feel of her cheek, the smell of her delicate perfume.

"What if we promise not to use them, but just study them so that we can better understand Miller's contributions? I'm sure your mother would want that," Magritt argued.

"Don't be so sure," he said in the overbearing tone of his father. "My mother wasn't vain. She didn't buy art in order to get her name on a plaque and her picture in a vanity publication. She bought what thrilled her, what gave depth to her life. She gave pieces to people she believed would appreciate them. She wasn't interested in twenty-second glances at the Metropolitan, where throngs of tourists push you along, where earplugs play the supercilious voice of an art expert." He spat out "expert" like a bitter seed. "A photographic essay—my God, how far from the original can you get?"

"They'd be very good representations," I heard Magritt argue, her finger up in the air.

"In size? In pigment?"

"They'd be far better than nothing. Would you rather people never know of Elias Miller's creations?"

Jonathan Brewster let out a long exasperated moan. "Let me think it over," he said, to conclude the conversation.

We knew that he wouldn't.

I called Caleb for help.

"My son is stubborn. He calls it having a mind of his own. If I thought I could help, I would, believe me."

"He has a number of paintings we're interested in. Some of the best," I argued.

"They're all right. What can I say? I have enough of my own to fill your book. Just relax and use the pieces that are available to you."

My next call found Harland in his office.

"Jonathan is a good man, but he marches to his own drummer. Even my wife, his sister, who loves him deeply, can't persuade him to do anything after he's made up his mind."

"Shit," I said.

Magritt shrugged her shoulders and frowned. I would have preferred her giving me the finger. It would have been a far more optimistic statement.

Defeat accompanied me as I left Magritt's apartment.

"I'll call him again," Magritt said.

"It won't help."

"You never know," she said, and tried to push some cheer into her voice. She failed.

"MAKING PROGRESS?" Sharon asked while opening a bottle of chilled champagne. "Are you getting closer to deciding on what paintings to use?"

Sharon and I were in a small, almost unknown Manhattan hotel, a meeting we'd arranged days before the trip to Robby Whitford's estate. I was keen at the time we planned the tryst, but after the trip with Magritt, it seemed wrong, almost unfaithful. Yet, what really had happened with Magritt? Certainly not enough to get me to cancel my rendezvous with Mrs. Brewster.

"Brewster's son is proving a hard-ass. We've given up on seeing his collection. A pity. If Harland is right, he has some good illustrations of the *Inferno.*"

"Madeline gave most of the paintings of Hell to men, although Jonathan might be the exception. She saved Purgatory for her daughter and some of her female friends. A psychological hiccup, I imagine. Madeline's was a solid marriage, although a rather sexless one. Solid is what Caleb is all about—solid investments, solid art, and solid friendships. He doesn't aspire to passion. They balanced each other. Caleb doesn't think Madeline ever liked men, and he didn't need sex."

"An arrangement made in Heaven. She did like Miller, I gather."

"An artist—they're different."

I gave out a pregnant, "Oh."

"Madeline, not me. I know you're a man," she said with seductive power, and handed me a filled glass. The bubbles tickled my nose. "Jonathan will turn around. Just give me a chance to talk to him. He has a couple of pieces I think you'll want to consider. They're not quite as good as Caleb's, but good."

"So you've seen them."

She avoided an answer. "I like Jonathan and his husband. Just let me know the two or three pieces you're most interested in."

"So Jonathan is gay," I said, not wanting to misinterpret her saying "husband."

"Always has been—and very reclusive. He doesn't appreciate company. I think that's the reason he turned you down. He does love to talk about art, but not with people he doesn't know, I guess."

"And his husband?" I asked.

"He's gay as well," she said through a wry smile, her Italian accent made thick.

"I don't know Manny very well," she added, before walking slowly to the side table, where a champagne bottle protruded from a shiny bucket. Her naked body was wrapped in a pink blanket pulled from the hotel's bed. Its color fought against the color of her hair. We had made love twice before opening the bottle and congratulating each other. I wasn't sure about what. Fucking, I imagine, although Sharon gave no sign of climaxing.

"So Jonathan has some work you think should be included in the monograph?" I asked.

She stood over me and waved her glass. "Oh, I don't know if any of them should be used to illustrate Miller's talent, but you might want to refer to them in the text, or in the index."

"Even if they're not for sale?"

Sharon's back stiffened and her facial muscles tightened. "What does sale have to do with anything? None of the work is up for sale, as far as I know."

"I wonder," I said. "Do you invest this much interest in an illustrated pamphlet without an overriding belief that it will pay for itself?"

"It's more than a pamphlet, Larry. At least Caleb expects it will be. He truly wants to celebrate Madeline. They were married for fifty years."

"So Caleb's behind all this," I proclaimed.

Sharon took a deep breath and her expression softened. "And others. I don't know them all. The monograph is your work, not mine. I have other things in mind."

She slipped onto the couch, leaned her body against mine, and let the blanket open.

"Do you sleep with Magritt?" she asked, as if none of the previous conversation had taken place.

It was obvious that she was again taking charge, but I didn't want to argue. Why ruin what was left of the afternoon? "No," I laughed, "what made you think that?"

Her accent grew deeper. "You're a man and she's a woman. You work closely together. Isn't that enough?"

"If I slept with all the women I worked with, I would have driven myself into an early grave. Do you sleep with all the men you work with?"

"I don't work."

"And if you did?"

Like a young actor experimenting with her craft, Sharon filled her voice with sincerity. "I take sex very seriously, Larry. I know you do not think so, the easy way I gave my number to you. The first time I have ever done that. Nervy, wasn't it? I found you terribly attractive and I knew you were too much of a gentleman to take the first step—Brewster and all. So you are very special."

How remarkable, I thought, that she expected me to believe her, her eyes all-innocent, her mouth in a shy smile. And, yet, her brazen lie had an aphrodisiac affect. Logic is no match for testosterone. I blew her a kiss, took her hand, and pushed far back in my mind any question of her motives. Sharon's freckles disappeared and her features turned shadowy as she sat on top of me, her body in an erotic dance. She shifted forward and back, up and down, her pace increasing, then slowing down, then increasing again, her cries growing ever less timid. As her lips tightened into a closed smile, and I felt sweat form at the base of her spine, I exploded into her. Then, as if on cue, her face contorted, her body quivered, and she gave out a deep exhalation.

"Terrific," she said. "Terrific."

Sharon rolled off me and lay on her back, inches away. I reached over, took her head in my arm, and rested it on my chest. She stirred for a moment, but her eyes quickly closed and she drifted away.

I did think it terrific. I smiled broadly, proud of my bedroom performance, almost embarrassed by how shamelessly I applauded my prowess.

My smile did not last. With lust and vanity satisfied, a feeling of emptiness overwhelmed me, a painful void that I could feel and touch. I placed Sharon's head on the pillow and turned on my side, full of uncomfortable thoughts and yearning for an emotional tie that was stronger than the sex.

Where in Purgatory was I, among the lustful, suffering the flames of the Seventh Terrace? No, I felt no heat, only an enduring barrenness—the futility of the gluttonous, of those who wantonly consume. Would it be any different with Magritt? Would she have enough words, enough laughter, enough half-expressed sighs, to make me happy? Could she play Virgil and lead me to a worldly paradise? The outrageousness of the thought made me laugh.

"What's so funny?" Sharon asked dreamily.

"Nothing," I said, and closed my eyes.

CHAPTER FOURTEEN

I PEERED THROUGH the hotel room's window and watched Sharon cross the street, her red hair aflame in the late afternoon sun, her thin body exceptionally graceful as she sprinted in front of an oncoming car. After a few waves of her hand, a cab pulled to the curb. She looked toward the hotel, seeming to search for me before sliding into the car's back seat.

It was after five and the shadows of the surrounding skyscrapers patterned the sidewalk with overlapping polygons and ellipses, a geometric complex as complicated as the questions that teased me. Why the note with her number? Why the come-on at the Frick? Why the sexual charade?

I meandered back to my mother's, surrounded by countless people pushing their way toward a subway entrance or, if they were lucky, hurrying to join a lover for a drink. Their pace forced me to quicken my steps, but their striving and determination only darkened my mood. I was sorry to be alone. I was sorry I didn't feel free to tell Magritt about Sharon, about how ultimately joyless the sex, how trivial the feelings. Poor Magritt, how little would she think of me if she knew the truth?

JANET AND PAUL were sitting quietly in the living room when I unlocked the apartment door, she on the loveseat, he in the high-backed leather chair he had brought over from his apartment years before. "To have a comfortable place to sit," he once told me, but I always considered it a sign of his claim on my mother's life, no less obvious than a gold miner's stake atop a treasured piece of land.

"You just missed a call, someone named Sharon," my mother announced. "She left a message. I wrote it down in the kitchen—an address in Washington, D.C., that has some art you are interested in, and a telephone number. It's Jonathan Brewster's, she told me."

"Did she say anything else?" I asked, thoroughly amazed by how rapidly Sharon had fulfilled her promise.

"No. Were you expecting more?"

"No. No. I already have his number, but not his address. It's a sign that he is amenable to a visit. Jonathan has some pieces Magritt and I want to see. Their transparencies were enticing."

"A drink?" Paul Herman asked, pointing to the glass on the coffee table. "Your mother and I are having gin and tonic. It goes with the warm weather."

Drink relaxes me. Just the act of holding a glass calms me. A learned behavior, I realize, gained from watching the quieting effect of a dry martini on my mother when I was young. The very shape of her body would change as she watched ice cubes drift around the glass, her muscles relaxed, her smile turned spontaneous and real, and her eyes filled with tenderness. That is how she looked that night with Paul in his chair and her son sitting next to her on the loveseat, content with her life, satisfied, at home.

Hilla would look that way. When the writing was not going well, I'd talk her into a drink or two and ask her to tell me about her day, about the designs she was showing, about the married marketing men who had asked for her number or hinted at their availability, men closer to her age who were seeking more from success than a house in the Hamptons. Hilla would sit in a thin blue bathrobe, her long legs crossed, a glass of wine in her hand, her smile always ready to comfort me. At home in the world, I would think, jealous that her sketches came more easily than my manuscripts, that she didn't punish herself after a bad day or after following a stream of thoughts that ended nowhere, that she was more secure than I was. But then I'd lapse into her mood, enthralled by her joy of life. Lucky Paul, I thought, imagining him absorbed in my mother's love of life.

"Was Ms. Whitford's collection as good as you expected?" Janet asked.

"Better. All her work came from a single Canto, but Miller used different styles to tell the tale—Renaissance, Impressionist, Cubist. I had noticed the variety in the slides, and yet, the impact was unexpected."

"It must be from an important segment of the poem," Paul surmised, a touch of surprise in his voice.

"Clearly Dante the Painter thought so—questions of free will and church versus state," I said.

"My Millers are about torture and revenge; they're rather harsh. But, come, let's walk over to my place to see them. You, too, Janet."

My mother refused. "It would be good for you two to talk," she said to me when Paul was standing too far away to hear.

"Talk about what?" I asked, with a bit of foreboding.

"Whatever," was her answer.

IT WAS DRIZZLING when we got outside the apartment house, so we hurried along the five city blocks that separated my mother from her lover. Paul turned up the collar of his sport coat, and I did the same with the collar of my short-sleeved summer shirt, although it offered little protection. Paul undid the two locks on his apartment door and flicked on a light.

"You haven't been up here in a while."

"Has it changed?"

"Not in the least. Janet made me put up a few more bookcases, but you'd hardly notice. They were filled the day they arrived and books are still piled in every available corner."

"So you're still collecting."

"Have you ever met a collector who stopped—outside of bankruptcy or death?"

He turned on the overhead lights in the foyer, the table lights in the living room, and the large crystal chandelier in the dining room. I followed as he went into the kitchen and watched him struggle to unglue cubes of ice from a tray, dropping two in my glass, none in his.

He turned on three table lamps in his den, and we sat in leather high-back chairs just like the one he had brought to my mother's, surrounded by a thousand books, many carefully arranged in rosewood cases, but others strewn on his desk and surrounding chairs, or haphazardly piled against a wall in a corner of the room.

"Are they all first editions?"

"I wish. Some of them have value, but most wouldn't get more than a few dollars from a dealer. Books are a blessing and a curse, you know. I love each and every one, but they do crowd the place. I keep wondering if your mother would finally marry me if I got rid of them. I've proposed to her every New Year's Day for the last decade. It's become a ritual, like exchanging presents. All I get is, 'Wait a while.' 'What are we waiting for, my ninetieth birthday?' I ask her."

"I think my mother's the greatest woman on earth, but giving up your collection, I'm not sure she is worth all that."

"I do."

"I'll put in a good word for you," I said, with a smile on my face.

"Like I did for you when Harland asked if I knew a writer. I hope you have forgiven me for that. It was an awkward moment."

"It's a paying job."

"I was hoping it was more."

"I like writing plays. That's what I do; that's what I want to do."

Paul fidgeted with his drink and looked down at his shoes. "It wasn't a criticism of your plays, Larry. You're talented. The theater is where you belong. I wouldn't have mentioned you if I thought you'd take it to mean you should stop writing plays."

"Or if you thought it might lead to my continuing to live with my mother."

Paul let out a charming laugh, the kind friends exchange not because anything is particularly funny, but because something had inadvertently irritated their friendship and they were searching for a way to put it aside. His laughter made me feel closer to him.

"I do appreciate your giving Harland my name. I'm enjoying the work, thoroughly. I like my co-author and have fallen in love with Elias and his wife. It's good to know that eccentrics exist outside the world of theater."

"There are a lot of them."

"Ms. Whitford told me that the Truth Foundation was a

family venture, an organization created to give Harland a job. I hadn't known that."

"That's surprising. Harland might not have told you, but I expected that Caleb would have filled you in. He likes announcing who is on his payroll. Madeline had Caleb create the Foundation in order to give Harland a prestigious job. Caleb must have taken a great deal of convincing. He thinks his fortune is due to his hard work and extraordinary judgment. Madeline knew that every fortune is ninety percent luck."

Paul shifted the Scotch to his other hand, raised it to his mouth, and then brought it down without taking a drink. "Harland's not a bad guy, Larry; he just expects more of himself than he can achieve. You've met the type. Goes to Harvard on a football scholarship only to discover there are better ballplayers. Gets a Harvard degree but knows he doesn't have an exciting or adroit mind. Instead of accepting undeserved good fortune, he tries to prove he's worthy. He gets a little pompous; he constantly competes. Underneath, he's angered by this constant need to test himself. A tough way to live, I think. I doubt if the idea of making Dante the Painter into a celebrated artist was his, but, then again, I often underestimate him and Caleb."

"You haven't met Caleb's new wife. A trophy wife if there ever was one," I said as an aside. Sharon was not far from the surface of my mind.

"That just proves how little I know about him. Caleb never struck me as a man who would use Viagra."

"Given her looks, he might not need a pharmaceutical aid."

Paul gave up a short laugh, his mind unchanged.

I emptied my glass and rolled the shrunken ice cubes with my finger.

"A refill?"

"No, the paintings."

"Of course," he said, "I almost forgot why I got you up here."

Limbo and *Pope Simony* were hanging on opposite walls of his den, each surrounded by rosewood bookcases that ran from the floor to the ceiling. If it were not for the encased scroll fragments Paul had sitting on top of a standup desk, the room would have looked like the private preserve of a Medici.

"When did you get these?" I asked, and pointed to the large acrylic display case that protected pages of Hebrew lettering.

"Beautiful, aren't they? I was told they came from a wooden synagogue destroyed by the Nazis, but who knows? They could have spent their lives in Brooklyn. A friend of mine who collects Judaica thinks one is from mid-eighteenth century Poland, the other from early nineteenth century Lithuania or Byelorussia. They're Torah fragments, small portions of a destroyed Book of Moses. Orthodox believers would have buried them and said prayers over their grave, but I treat them as works of art. I cannot even conceive of destroying them. Too much has already been lost," Paul said. His voice was filled with a quiet passion.

He took a long drink and came up next to me, our shoulders touching, and together we examined the remarkable calligraphy, the graceful swirls of ink, the bold letters, the mysterious words.

"Beautiful," I said. "To the illiterate, it's a form of Expressionist art, isn't it?

"Beautiful," Paul repeated. He put his hand on the walnut wood of the standup desk, leaned over the case, and smiled. "I found them in a used book shop that carries old

Yiddish novels and Hebrew prayer books. It's in Brooklyn, not far from where I was raised. I had just wandered in out of curiosity and left without purchasing anything. But when I got back here, the apartment felt empty, as if its heart was missing. I have all these books, Laurence, all in English—hundreds of books, maybe thousands. Not one of them could be read by my grandfather the tailor, not one. Could any collection be more barren of history? I called your mother to ask what I should do, and then I ran to the bookstore. It was closed, but the owner lived upstairs. I rang the store's bell until his wife came down and unlocked the door. Janet is still uncomfortable that I keep the scrolls in the same room as *Limbo* and *Pope Simony*. She imagines that the scribe who carefully inked these words of God would be distressed by the Christian imagery, but we live in different times, and I believe there is a common human need to find a deity."

"You never cease to surprise me," I blurted out.

"I hope you mean something good," Paul said with laughter.

"And what deity have you found?"

"Your mother, who else?" he answered with a smile. "Come, the paintings are calling to us."

Limbo was the larger piece. The interior chambers of a five-story sanctuary are exposed to the viewer. Most rooms are filled with writing tables and overflowing bookcases, others with long, wooden dining tables and chairs; a few hold four-poster beds. The shades are dressed in the finery of ancient Greece and noble Rome. A few are conversing. Most are deep in solitary study. The colors are rich, the style Renaissance. There is no blood or gore, no punishment, and yet, somehow Dante the Painter projects a deeply solemn mood.

I spoke first. "I can see why Madeline thought you'd appreciate it. The quantity of books alone would call out your name."

"It goes with my collection, there's no doubt of that," Paul responded.

"The eternal home of deserving pagans," I said. "It doesn't look like the worst way to spend eternity."

"But they will never get to Heaven," Paul said wistfully. "To Dante, that was punishment enough. I often ask myself how a modern should interpret it, someone who has no belief in the afterlife."

"And your answer?"

"It's a sterile place. There is no passion, no sex, and no frivolity. It's a very contemporary Hell: living together in a large structure, but in isolation; talking to your neighbor, but never truly visiting. Half the people in New York would recognize the place. I've made it even more punishing by hanging *Pope Simony* on the other side of the room. When the occupants of *Limbo* look out of their painting, they must confront a metaphor of greed. *Simony* could well be a metaphor for Wall Street."

Pope Simony, too, is painted in the Renaissance style of Venice and Florence. A pope's naked legs protrude from the stone-gray sarcophagus that entombs him. Pope Boniface VIII, Dante's enemy, according to Miller's notes, but it could just as well be Clement V, who also abides in the Eighth Circle of Hell. Only the punishments in the Ninth Circle, Satan's home, are more depraved. The pope's feet are on fire. They will burn through all eternity—a just punishment, Dante felt, for sacrificing the purity of the Bishop of Rome for individual gain, for corrupting the Church for gold and silver.

"Not a very comforting image," Paul said.

I didn't need to answer.

"I'm not pushing for you to include these paintings in your monograph, Laurence. Madeline had far better Millers. I just thought you might be interested."

"They are good, Paul. Magritt will want to see them. Can I have her call to set up some time to come over?"

"I'd be delighted. I haven't seen her in years," he said innocently.

Once again, I stood in front of my mother's boyfriend, my face filled with surprise. "I didn't know you knew Magritt."

"Her mother, really. She did some fundraising for Clinton, both campaigns. So I had dinner over at her place a couple of times." Paul paused, and looked slightly embarrassed. "Other people were there, Laurence, although I don't remember your mother accompanying me. Magritt was introduced at one of the dinners. She was quite young. Her father, I believe, was still alive. I wouldn't recognize her if she sat next to me on the subway. You look surprised."

"I'm always surprised by how tight the circles are in New York City. I never fully realized how small that world is."

"Money sticks to money. I slip in at the far end, a very far end. I contribute to Lincoln Center and the Metropolitan, just enough to get me invited to good places. I like taking your mother to them. My bank account may not compete, but my companion outshines the others."

"WHY DON'T YOU marry Paul?" I asked my mother at breakfast the next morning. The question surprised her, as I knew it would.

"That question is a little too personal, Mr. Sullivan, even for a son—particularly for a son."

"I'm not a little boy."

"Why are you asking? Are you afraid you'll have to take care of me in my old age?"

"Exactly."

"Humph," she answered, and turned back to preparing eggs.

"I'm serious, Mom. What is it that's preventing you from making a commitment?"

"I am committed to Paul, as committed as any wife could possibly be. And he is committed to me. I know that. But living in two separate places, I like that too, and I like saying I'm single; it sounds young and adventurous."

"I'm serious, and you keep pulling my leg."

My mother put half of the omelet on my plate and took the rest. The toast on the table had already turned cold. Before sitting down, she filled our coffee cups, her face in a perpetual frown. The bags under her eyes seemed to grow heavier, and, absent makeup, slight wrinkles could be seen on her once-perfect skin. I felt sorry to have raised the subject.

"Fear," she said once she was firmly on the chair. "I'm afraid that if I ask for more, what I have will disappear. Some peasant psychology I inherited from an unknown ancestor. There is only so much good in the world, and if you believe you have more than your share, remain silent and don't ask for any more. I have more than my share. I have you, and I have Paul—even if he lives a few steps away. I don't want the gods to envy my blessings. I have much more to lose than to gain. If something should happen to Paul, I would move in and tend to his every wound. He would do that for me. When we are older, perhaps one apartment will be enough. By then the gods won't frown. I know it sounds silly, gods and all, but fear isn't an intellectual exercise, just as love isn't."

She smiled with an almost imperceptible movement of her lips. It was not a mirthful smile. It was an expression of hope, hope that the son she loved would understand her.

I leaned over and silently touched her hand.

BEATRICE ANSWERED THE PHONE when I called Elias later that morning. "It's about time we heard from you," she chuckled. "We thought you and Magritt had run off to Scotland."

"Why Scotland?"

"We didn't want you to be able to enjoy the climate."

A full minute went by before Dante got on the phone. "I'm calling from Scotland," I said, but he didn't get the joke. I quickly moved on and asked him about the paintings Paul had shown me.

"I don't know a Paul Herman."

"Madeline gave him the paintings."

"Oh, that's surprising. I was certain Madeline found them interesting. I never thought she would unload them."

"Paul was a friend. She wouldn't have given them to him if she didn't think they were good."

"A nice try, Laurence, but not totally convincing," Dante said, and let out a boisterous laugh. "Have you fallen in love with my paintings?" he asked as he tried to catch his breath.

"We have, Dante, we have."

"And when will you come down to finish the selection?"

"We're planning to see a couple more collections, Harland's and the one owned by Madeline's son Jonathan. With a little help from Caleb's wife, we were finally able to persuade him to see us. Do you know Jonathan?"

"We never met. I never met any of Madeline's children, but if he's like her, you'll enjoy the visit."

"I have the feeling that he's not."

"Bring him a good bottle of wine. It never fails."

CHAPTER FIFTEEN

WE TOOK DANTE'S ADVICE and dropped by Sherry-Lehman on Madison Avenue before leaving Manhattan. A dapper salesman in a camel-colored sports jacket recommended a "good" Amarone.

"That's reasonable," Magritt said when the price came up on the computer screen.

"We have different definitions of reasonable," I murmured before handing over my credit card.

The clerk frowned.

ALL THE DYSPEPTIC VISIONS Magritt and I had formed about Jonathan Brewster disappeared as soon as he opened the front door, grayish-blonde hair falling over his forehead, and a welcoming twinkle in his light-blue eyes. At six feet six, he towered over Magritt when he gave her an unexpected hug, his muscular forearms wrapped around her slender back. Fifty years of successful workouts, I decided when I gingerly shook his hand and noticed his muscles ripple under a short-sleeved white polo shirt.

"Welcome, welcome, to Washington, D.C. It's a normal

August day in your nation's capital, hot and hideously muggy, so join me and enjoy the air conditioner. It's working today," Jonathan said crisply.

In a single step, we were through the entryway and into the living room of the small Dupont Circle townhouse. A triptych by Elias Miller hung on the wall in front of us, its colors and composition brilliant and compelling. I forced myself to look away so I could listen to Jonathan.

"How was the drive? Tedious, I expect, but you made it, and that's what's important. You must be exhausted and thirsty. I bet you could use a cold drink—ice tea, soda, or beer? Yes, yes, a beer would be perfect. I'd like that. Would it be good for you?" When we didn't protest, he turned toward the dining room and yelled out, "Manny, they made it in one piece—beers all around." Then he returned to Magritt and me. "Guinness, Beck's, or Samuel Adams? We're low on variety, I'm afraid."

Jonathan's rapid speech unsettled Magritt. At first, she looked as if she didn't understand the question. Finally, she said softly, "Sam Adams."

"A Guinness for me," I added.

"Did you get that?" Jonathan yelled toward the dining room.

"In a minute," returned a deep bass voice.

"Come, sit down. It's a small parlor but there is enough room for us all. So tell me a little about yourselves."

"Let me look at the painting for a minute or two," Magritt said. "It takes my breath away. Larry and I have seen photographs of it, but they only hinted at its power. The size alone is overwhelming."

The Gates of Purgatory, a triptych of the type I would have expected to find in the Uffizi Gallery in Florence or a grand church in Venice, hung behind a long, gray couch. The central board was three feet square; the two side panels were the same height but a foot narrower. In all, the construction was over five feet in length and three feet high—by far the largest Miller piece we had seen. The technique was pre-Renaissance in composition and colors, with multiple figures and structures, the paint dark and heavy, the faces flat and emotionless. The narrative, taken directly from the *Commedia*, was Dante the Pilgrim's entrance into Purgatory. Sharon's generalization that Madeline gave men only paintings from *Inferno* had no foundation.

"It's an ancient technique," Dante the Painter had told Magritt and me when we discussed a slide of the triptych weeks before, "having multiple images of the same character share the same time and space. Giotto used it, although not very often. I needed to do something dramatic to distinguish the paintings of Purgatory from those of Hell. Purgatory is the most appealing section of the *Commedia*. We all hope to be able to wash away our sins."

"Triptychs were normally employed to communicate biblical events. Do you think the *Commedia* deserves that degree of homage?" I had asked.

Elias Miller had scowled, I remembered, as I stood before the painting, making me feel like a favorite student who had cruelly disappointed his teacher. When he answered, he was Dante the Poet. "The Bible stands alone. My poem cannot stand without the Bible. Biblical allusions, biblical characters, biblical beliefs run through every canto, fill every line. I don't compete with the Bible; I reinforce its teaching. My poem describes the outcomes of sin and reinforces virtue. Like the Bible, it is a blueprint for living. My poem is a bible, Laurence, but it is not The Bible. It's not the word of God but the word of God's loyal follower."

"It's from Canto IX of Purgatory," I heard Jonathan

say. "Dante dreams that he is being carried into a wall of flames by a giant eagle, its talons hooked around his body. When he awakes, he is frightened and confused. Virgil tells him that while he was asleep a woman named Lucia carried him in her arms to the gates of Purgatory. That's depicted in the first section of the triptych: Dante is in the arms of a beautiful woman; in the background, an eagle flies away. As you can see, the middle composition shows Pilgrim and Virgil standing on top of the three steps that lead to Purgatory's silver gateway, and an angel holding a naked sword is carving the letter P into Dante's forehead. In the poem, seven P's are carved. The angel tells him that these wounds must be healed by his experiences in Purgatory if he is to enter Paradise. In the final panel, Dante and Virgil observe a guardian angel unlock the gates to Purgatory. The angel must use the two keys entrusted to him by St. Peter. One key is made of silver, one of gold."

"The seven P's represent the seven major sins that are purged in Purgatory and correspond to the seven terraces he will travel through," Manny added as he entered the room, bottles of beer hanging from his fingers. "Pride, envy, wrath, sloth, avarice, gluttony, and lust. I think I have the order right. I use my own mnemonic, pewsagl."

"Very good," Jonathan said.

"Do your guests ever rebel at being greeted by the Gates of Purgatory when they arrive at your home?" Magritt teased.

"Most of them are taken aback," Manny said as he held out a bottle of Sam Adams. I've gotten used to it. You will notice, I'm sure, that Jon takes the best wall spots for Dante the Painter; he lets me hang my stuff in the bathrooms."

"Untrue," Jonathan yelled out, "a slander. Manny's paintings are all over the house, and his sculptures fill the patio. You'll see. But Dante the Painter, how could I hide such passion, such frightful beauty?"

"See," Manny said, "just listen at how breathless he becomes when he speaks of Dante. You'd think he had just seen Paradise."

"So you're an artist," I blurted out.

"And successful," Jonathan added.

"But no Dante," Manny inserted without conviction, his face in a bogus frown, his thin, wiry body in a delicate bow, his skin a deep mahogany. He was considerably shorter than Jonathan, perhaps five foot seven in his white socks. A red T-shirt and tan slacks completed the outfit. Under his chin was a black goatee cut in the style seen on ancient Egyptian monuments. The rest of his head was shaven clean. "My work is complete—it stands alone. I paint geometric forms in multiple colors, allowing the tints and shapes to stimulate your emotions, to fill you with glee or sadness, to cause amusement. Dante is an intellectual painter. His scenes drive you to read the poetry of his namesake. He whets your appetite and pushes you to explore an artistic work other than his own. I'm independent of others."

Magritt leaned forward in her chair; the bottle of Sam Adams resting on her black slacks. "He does whet the appetite," she said, her eyes glued on Manny. "But I don't think you have to read the *Commedia* to appreciate his work, all you need is to have heard of it to be grabbed by his art. Maybe not even that. Just the titles tell you he's painting scenes of Hell and Purgatory. Your imagination is ignited by that alone."

"But you need a story. My paintings don't need a narrative," Manny argued.

"I've been driven to read *The Divine Comedy*," Jonathan asserted, "some parts quickly, but multiple translations of those sections illustrated by the paintings we own. I've also explored countless commentaries. How could I deny the paintings? They possess me. You live with them; you sleep with them; they become your confidants. Manny's paintings, too, enthrall me, but in a different way. Manny's are very personal. They pull at your senses, as does Dante, but without a plot line. Dante's illustrations tell a story. They resonate differently with each of us, but the story is similar. It adds a communal elegance to the work."

"Jonathan is a romantic, if you haven't noticed," Manny commented, lifted his bottle, and chucked down a good three ounces.

"Have you read Dante?" I asked Manny.

Manny wiped his goatee with the edge of the bottle. "I have, but a long time ago, even before I met Jonathan. I was teaching a class on Salvador Dali and the Surrealists for the Corcoran. In the early 1950s, Dali did 101 watercolor illustrations for an edition of *The Divine Comedy*. I had always been fascinated by Dali's art. Curiosity alone got me to dip into the poem. A difficult but fascinating read."

"And Miller's paintings—have they pushed you to learn more?" I pressed.

Manny gave me a shy smile. "I let Jonathan tell me about them. He doesn't mind."

Jonathan let out a comfortable laugh. "That's what you're here for, isn't it, to hear me talk about the Dante paintings? Let's pull out some cold bottles, and go on to the dining room where *Paradise Regained* hangs. It illustrates the upper Terrace of Purgatory—the Garden of Eden."

Before he could move, Magritt jumped out of her seat and startled Jonathan and his companion by squeezing between them, her knees on the couch, her face jutting over its upholstered back, her nose almost touching the *Gates of*

Purgatory. Its closeness forced her to move in one direction and then the other to take in the entire painting. Then she slid off the couch, stepped back, and slowly absorbed the painting from the other side of the living room.

"It's done on wood, isn't it?"

"Yes," Manny said.

"He has gone a long way to imitate early Italian art. It's remarkable," said Magritt.

"It's even more remarkable when you compare it to the painting in the dining room," Manny added. "Dante the Painter jumped over six centuries of artistic change when he drafted *Paradise Regained*. He becomes an Impressionist, painting in the style of Monet. It shows a remarkable versatility, if nothing else. What amazes me most is that he has mastered both styles—the range of colors, the draftsmanship, the type of brush and brushstroke. He's both an artist and a scholar, a true polymath."

Jonathan let out a light laugh.

"You're an art historian, like I am," Manny said to Magritt. "Are you also an artist?"

"I tried, desperately, but finally realized that I enjoyed other people's work more than my own. Someday, I tell myself, I will try again. Larry is the creative artist," she said as she approached the painting once again.

We remained in the living room for an additional few minutes, not wanting to cause Magritt to end her scrutiny prematurely. When she was satisfied with her thoughts, she led the way into the dining room, and positioned herself only inches from *Paradise Regained*. A minute later, she walked to the other side of the dining table to see the canvas from a distance, only to approach it yet again. "I can see why you think of Monet, the forest and garden, the river blocking Pilgrim's way, but the style is clearly Degas, the draftsmanship, applying his oils directly onto an unprepared canvas to give the painting texture, the figures composed of layers of paint. Degas, yes, you can see it throughout."

"Degas, maybe, but Monet, certainly," Manny argued. There was no humor in his voice.

"Humph," Magritt answered.

I stood back, watching my coauthor scrutinize the painting, enjoying her professional tone, chuckling at the certainty. An extraordinary tenderness overcame me as I watched and listened to her, and a strange sense of pride, as if somehow Magritt's intrepid curiosity and nervous intelligence projected on me, that having her in my company bestowed honor on me. How easy it would be to fall in love with her, I said to myself, then staggered at the thought, quickly thankful that there were other people in the room to occupy my interests.

I turned my eyes from her and examined the painting, and took refuge in Dante's image of beauty and bliss, of Garden and woman. Pilgrim is in a beautiful forest, its floor covered with wildflowers and jade-colored shrubs, its trees filled with emerald-colored leaves. His path is blocked by a sparkling stream that separates him from the woman on the other side of the gently flowing water. His garments and her simple diaphanous dress wave in a mild breeze. In the poem, the woman informs Pilgrim that he is in the Garden of Eden, the place where life began and humankind was created; that the soft wind they feel spreads the seeds that are born in this earthly paradise all over the world.

Two rivers run though the Garden. One washes away memories of sin. The other river enhances remembrance of good deeds. Each penitent has to drink from both streams in order to enter Heaven and in a particular order. First from the river that erases memories of transgression, then from the river that enriches memories of virtue.

How complete the cleansing, I had thought when I first read the end of *Purgatorio*. Not only is Pilgrim required to be purged of sin before he can enter Heaven, he must be purged of all memory of sin. But don't you need a vision of Hell to fully appreciate Heaven? And how can you cherish the Garden of Eden if you have no memory of the mundane? I had asked those questions of Miller. His answer had not satisfied.

"REMEMBER MY THINKING when I wrote the *Commedia*. God was perfect goodness and could only be pleased by perfection," Dante the Painter had told me late one night, an empty bottle of wine from Carmignano on the table. "If a soul is to find eternal life in Heaven, it must be restored to the purity that existed at creation—it must return to God as pure as Adam and Eve before the apple. To even recall sin is an imperfection, a blemish that cannot leave Purgatory."

"But how could a soul know that it is in Heaven if it has no knowledge of anything but goodness?" I had asked.

"It doesn't know it's in Heaven. It knows only pure love—love of God." Dante had lifted the wine bottle to study how much was left. He'd shrugged his shoulders in disappointment before going on. "I struggled to envision the sublime when I wrote *Paradiso*. But mortal imagination cannot conceive paradise. Try as I might, I knew too much of life. I couldn't chase away my knowledge of sin; I couldn't recall only goodness. Commentators have proclaimed *Paradiso* as the most medieval section of the poem. They are wrong. It is no more modern or medieval than the rest, no more understood then than now. If I were to rewrite the *Commedia* today, I'm not certain how I would treat the final third. Differently, I am certain."

"Is that why you've stayed away from illustrating Paradise?" I had asked.

Dante had waved his empty glass. "Maybe," he had said with a laugh.

"YOU LOOK MESMERIZED by the painting," Manny said to me, his shoulder just inches from mine. "It is a very romantic painting; Dante looking younger than he does in any of our other paintings, his eyes hooked on the beautiful young woman. You can almost feel the sexual tension."

"In the Garden of Eden?" Jonathan interrupted. "Blasphemy."

"As you've noticed, he enjoys disagreeing with me. It's his law degree, I think," Manny said, his voice particularly deep and resonant.

Jonathan let out a howl. "Come," he said. "At this pace we won't see all of the paintings until Halloween."

Reluctantly, we moved out of the dining room. Two of Elias Miller's pieces hung—one under the other—halfway up the staircase, four others in the two second-floor bedrooms. All were smaller than the ones on the first floor, portraying scenes from *Purgatorio* and from the *Inferno*, some in the timeless style of the Renaissance, others with a more contemporary flair.

One was strikingly different than the others, part Realist, part Cubist. In the foreground, painted in the realistic style used in the 1930s by American artists like Reginald Marsh and John Sloan, Dante and Virgil struggle to make their way through the weeping, prostrate shades that cover the bare ground. Behind them, in cubist style, is a portion of the Mountain of Purgatory, formed by variously colored geometric shapes.

Jonathan noticed my interest. "From the terrace where the sin of avarice is cleansed," he said. "On earth, the shades turned their backs on Heaven and sought only worldly goods. In Purgatory, they are condemned to continuously stare at the ground. It is titled *The Terrace of the Avaricious*, as you might expect. I don't see it as being very good, but you have to salute Dante's experimentation—to use such different styles in a single painting takes guts."

"But why Cubism?" I asked.

Manny offered the answer. "Remember, while Dante is on the Fifth Terrace, the entire mountain shakes. Dante the Painter must have felt that Cubist constructs suggest motion. I think it succeeds."

Jonathan picked up where Manny left off. "The Terrace of the Avaricious is where Dante the Pilgrim learns that Purgatory does not experience the natural physical forces you find on earth. There is no rain, no lightning. Every time a soul is purified and rises to heaven, the mountain shakes. It's a remarkable way to applaud salvation, don't you think?"

"I don't find it a satisfying work," Magritt said. "Perhaps it would be a good illustration if it were bound within the poem, but it's not as effective as most of Dante's efforts. All you know is what you see. It requires too much prior knowledge."

"Perhaps," said Jonathan, clearly unconvinced.

In the second bedroom, another "Degas," as Magritt proclaimed it—*Lust*. I found it a painful, horrific scene, saturated in red, and marked with streaks of white and blue. Dante and Virgil are driven to the edge of a cliff by a wall of raging flames. Within the flames, tortured shades hold fast to one another, their mouths strangely opened in song and not in pain.

"What do you think?" Jonathan asked Magritt.

"I think I should reconsider chastity," she answered.

"Horrific," I said. "Dante couldn't have had that much against sex."

"It's a very even-handed disgust," Manny said. "In the poem he cleanses both heterosexual and homosexual sinners on the same terrace. That wasn't bad for his time."

"Even for ours," Magritt added, and then blushed.

WE COMPLETED OUR TOUR of Jonathan's collection before settling down in the small, immaculate patio behind the townhouse, where we were shaded from the late-afternoon sun by the large leaves of overarching trees. A soothing breeze kissed our skins. Manny brought out some cold beers, and Jonathan delivered a wooden tray covered with taco chips and a bowl of hot mango salsa. Time flowed gracefully as we drank and nibbled and talked about the politics of Hell and the art of Heaven. Before we realized it, evening had come and we were hungry. Manny brought out a pile of menus from the kitchen and asked Magritt to choose the "cuisine-of-the-night."

"Magritt and I would be happy to take you to dinner. We owe you that at least," I said, but Jonathan insisted that we would become better acquainted if we ate on the patio. Magritt chose the menu from a local Thai restaurant, Manny called in our orders and Jonathan lit four candles to frustrate the hovering mosquitoes. The food arrived in half an hour.

Manny poured white wine—"it goes well with spicy foods"—and Jonathan prepared hot tea.

"I understand you're a lawyer," I said to Jonathan.

"By education, but I don't practice. My mother not only left me art, she left me money. I do the cooking, and Manny goes out to work."

"That's why we had dinner delivered," Manny added without expression. In a vaudeville show, he would have made a perfect straight man, I thought, and then realized how "straight" could be misconstrued. I kept silent.

"Manny and I are writing a book together on homosexuality in art. Not about gays who painted, but the pictorial representation of homosexuals from early religious paintings on. We're exploring eastern and western cultures, the prejudice, and the acceptance."

"And lesbians?" Magritt asked.

"Of course," Jonathan said in an irritated tone, and acted as if Magritt should have taken that for granted.

"We've been working on it for three years. Someday it will be done," Manny added.

"It would be an important contribution," Magritt added. Her voice and posture conveyed her enthusiasm.

"To art history, certainly," Manny said. "But we are after a wider audience. Academe is so narrow and isolated. We'd like it to be reviewed by *The New York Times* and the *Washington Post* and read on the subway."

"That's not easy to accomplish," I said.

"Indeed," Jonathan answered. "And for dessert, should we try the Amarone you brought? It is one of my favorite wines."

"See?" Magritt whispered to me.

"I'T'S MUCH TOO LATE for you to drive back to New York tonight," Jonathan said when the Amarone was finished. "I apologize for keeping you so long, but I can never stop talking about Dante. We have a comfortable bedroom in the basement, with a private bathroom, clean towels, and unused toothbrushes. We'd be happy if you spent the night and promise to get you out early in the morning, with or without breakfast."

His assumption about Magritt and my relationship tickled me, but I quickly tried to think of a way to deny the invitation yet still maintain the fantasy. Fortunately, before I could say anything, Magritt answered.

"That is very kind of you. Are you sure we won't be putting you out?" she said in her most modest voice. She leaned back in the chair, her face tinted by the wine, and winked at me.

"Now how do we do this?" I asked her after Jonathan had shown us to the downstairs room, converted the studio couch into a double bed, and worked with us to put on clean linens. He threw us a warm, knowing smile when he left.

She sat down at the edge of the bed and ran her hand over the blue cotton blanket. "You sleep on the left and I'll sleep on the right. We turn out the lights and nod off. It's not very difficult. Or we make love. That's if you have the strength," she said matter-of-factly before abruptly standing up and dancing to the bathroom.

I listened to Magritt turn on the shower, my mind racing to catch up with what was happening. It was all wrong. I had sent no flowers. There was no quiet dinner in a small out-of-way restaurant, no candles on the table, no piano music in the background. We hadn't shared an apple pie or chocolate mousse. We hadn't taken a long taxicab ride home, my hand rubbing her knee, her head on my shoulder, our breathing harmonized. I rebelled at the thought of a one-night stand, not with Magritt. I wanted a port. I wanted a harbor. I wanted to sink into her body, passionate and vulnerable, safe and adventurous. I wanted my Helen of Troy. I wanted Dante's Beatrice. But what did Magritt want? Was she looking for her Dante, or did she want another Eric, or a gallant Giotto who could award her with her portrait when they parted?

The shower stopped abruptly and Magritt came out of the bathroom. Not a stitch of clothing had been removed. She sat on the bed next to me.

"I thought you were going to shower."

"I just turned it on so you wouldn't hear me pee," she answered without a hint of laughter. "I don't know what got into me, Larry. Too much beer and wine, I think. I just didn't want to embarrass Jonathan. I didn't want him to know he had misjudged us. If you want to go, we can sneak out when they're asleep."

"Or just go upstairs and tell them the truth," I suggested.

"Or that."

"Or we could spend the night. You can sleep on the floor. It's a thick carpet."

"I deserve that," she whispered.

I took hold of her hand. It was surprisingly cold. "No you don't. Never. You deserve dozens of roses and ice-cold champagne, a room with a patio that overlooks the Mediterranean, and a canopy bed with satin sheets and a silk coverlet."

She smiled as if for the first time. "And you? What do you deserve?"

"I want you to let me love you, not just make love to you. Are you strong enough for that?"

She broke from my hand, and again I listened to the shower.

Her hair was wet when we made love, and still moist when we made love the second time. When I woke her in the middle of the night to make love again, she asked me to turn on the lights. "I want you to see me. I'm afraid you might be thinking I'm someone else."

I knew I was making love to Magritt, skinny, intense, shapely Magritt, her small breasts pushing into my chest, her thin, muscular thighs hugging my waist. She began to move in rhythmic waves, her arms firm against my back, her fingers pressing into my flesh. She stiffened and arched away from me, a momentary flash of bewilderment racing across her deep brown eyes. Then she relaxed, her head again on the pillow, her eyes open. I kissed her on the neck and mumbled that I loved her in too quiet a voice for her to hear.

When I rolled to my side, I kept my head above her so I could continue to look into her face.

Within a few seconds, a more familiar Magritt returned. "Yay, me," she exclaimed, and thrust her right arm in salute.

"'Yay me'?"

"That intensity doesn't happen very often. Sometimes I would fear I'd never experience it again."

"Should I be proud?"

She chuckled and pulled me down against her chest.

"Don't turn off the light," she said after I had rolled over onto my back. "I want to talk for a while. Do you mind?"

"No, I'm fully awake. I'll most probably doze off on the drive home."

"I'd rather you didn't."

She sat up and pulled the blanket over her breasts. "I wish I still smoked. I would know what to do. I would light up and inhale, go to the bathroom, and then to sleep. Now I just want to talk to you."

"About what?"

"About anything. It's unimportant. It's the talking that matters."

I turned on my side and kissed her fingers.

"Why in this house, at this time?" she asked. "My inhibitions gone, my glands pumping like crazy, I have the type of orgasm I dream of. You'd think I would have saved it for a rendezvous in Paris, or a honeymoon on Fiji. But in a basement bedroom in Washington, D.C.—that's where you plot a revolution, not where you make love."

I kissed her fingers again, and then placed my head on her lap. "Love and revolution go together. They've never been in conflict. Anyway, Washington is far from revolutionary. Art is sexy, Magritt. It makes one real and whole. It demands our deeper selves. Then there is Jonathan and Manny. They project love."

"You are a romantic, Larry."

"Jonathan's a totally different person than the man we met over the phone. It's difficult to reconcile his initial resistance to our visit and his overarching hospitality now."

"Maybe his stepmother has special persuasive talents," Magritt joked.

"You have a dirty mind."

"Guilty," Magritt said.

"We are in his home, though. That may explain it. People are different in their homes, more secure, more able to hang loose and give. And Manny is here. They seem to lean on each other."

Magritt lowered her voice as if to make certain she wasn't overheard. "I like them. I like them a lot. Do you think Jonathan might have AIDS?"

"What makes you think that?" I asked, bewildered by her thought.

"Just fear. I'm always afraid people I like will disappear.

It's my major neurosis. Disappear like my father disappeared," Magritt whispered.

"I don't disappear, Magritt. I plant deep roots."

She kissed me on the cheek.

Magritt was fast asleep when I slipped out of bed in the morning and ambled to the bathroom, a little unbalanced, my head still fogged with sleep, my thoughts beginning to swell with undefined doubts and a fear that she would only half-remember the night. I came back to the room and watched her lying on her side in the middle of the bed, her knees raised toward her chest, her short black hair in disarray. Bare feet poked out from under the light blue sheet that wrapped around her. I reached out and gently touched her toes, overwhelmed by a rush of tender feelings.

ON THE TRIP BACK from Washington, romance got the better of us, and Magritt and I decided to spend a few more days together visiting with Beatrice and Dante. Harland's collection of paintings could wait.

We called Dante when we got to Magritt's early Friday afternoon.

"It's about time," he said when we asked if we could drive down on Monday to talk about the monograph.

CHAPTER SIXTEEN

SHARON CALLED FROM HER GYM. I was at my mother's apartment. It was early Saturday morning.

"Jonathan says it was a great visit and that you and Magritt stayed overnight. I didn't know you were that tight with her."

I squirmed. "We're not tight."

"I know I'm in a relationship, but it's rather sexless. I was hoping I had exclusive rights to you."

"You do," I said, in unthinking reaction. I should have immediately canceled the lie. Instead, I dug it deeper. "We used the same bed, fully clothed. I was too tired to drive home. Jonathan just jumped to conclusions."

"It shook me up, I have to admit. I felt run over. Is she younger than I am?" Sharon said, her voice angry and abrupt.

"Sharon, she's skinny, with small breasts and bad breath. She's no match for you," I argued, and felt like a piece of shit. Why was I doing this? To not hurt Sharon's feelings or to keep my options open?

"Upsetting, Larry, it's upsetting." There was a long pause, and I thought I heard her choking down her emotions. "Caleb thinks I'm flying up to Syracuse on Tuesday to see my sister and coming back on Wednesday. We would have an entire night. You could explain yourself and make amends."

"I'm going to be spending the week with Dante working on the monograph."

"So soon? I thought it would take longer. Don't you have to see Harland's collection first?"

"That's set for later in the week. But I thought I could get a few things finished before then," I said, trying to sound casual.

"Perhaps you could find a place near Gettysburg for Tuesday night. I'd figure out how to get there."

"It would be a little risky, Sharon. It's not a town in which you can hide."

"And Magritt will be there?"

I thought of repeating myself and declaring once again that Magritt meant nothing. But the lie was eating at me. "Yes, Magritt will be there," I said, my voice strong and clear.

"So there," she said, as if the phrase had deep philosophical meaning. "Call Caleb when you get back. He'll want to know what's going on," she said officiously, and hung up.

MAGRITT AND I dined on Saturday night at a little French restaurant that specialized in candled atmosphere and thousand-calorie desserts. Sunday found us walking through Central Park and along Broadway, holding hands as we crossed the street, feasting on street corner hotdogs and enchiladas, making offbeat comments about window displays and struggling to identify the rich variety of languages that flooded Manhattan's streets. We spent our nights alone.

Magritt slept at her home. I retreated to my mother's, my hormones remembering Washington, my brain dominated by images of Magritt.

Strangely, Sharon's call had lifted a cloud. I felt free of her, free of trying to build something between us that was more than liquid and muscle. But her irritation was unexpected, her flaring jealousy a surprise. I tried to write it off as sexual covetousness, and yet, did our coupling mean more to her than to me? Was she an honest if ineffectual lover, and I the only fraud? If I failed to understand Sharon, was I also misjudging Magritt? Was I just a temporary stand-in for Eric, and Eric a replacement for someone named Harry, and Harry for John? No, I told myself, no.

"Let's not rush things," Magritt said, after I suggested a hotel room.

"Are you sorry about Washington?" I asked, puzzled by her reticence.

"Never," she said with a tremor in her voice, but she didn't change her mind.

On Monday, Magritt and I drove down to Gettysburg in my mother's Mercedes, the sunroof rolled back. I rubbed Magritt's knee when we stopped for a red light, and she played with my right hand as we went south on the New Jersey Turnpike.

Beatrice met us on the front porch, looking astonished to discover that we had driven together. For an uncomfortably long moment, she searched Magritt's face to see if there was something new. When she turned to give me a kiss, I knew she understood more than I had planned to tell her.

"You two look wonderful. How long has it been since I've seen you together, two months, three?" Beatrice asked, her round face tanned, her blue eyes glistening.

"Six weeks," I answered.

"It seems so much longer. But much can change in six weeks."

I waited for Beatrice to wink. She contained herself.

Magritt and I had plotted to use the rooms we had used before, me on the second floor, her on the first. With one wise grin, Beatrice wiped away our planned subterfuge, so we moved into my room, the smaller and less comfortable of the two, to avoid Eric's specter.

The Millers had set their porch table for four. Beatrice took a huge salad from the refrigerator and Dante brought out a woven straw basket full of bread. With a gallant display of skill, he opened one of the bottles of Chianti that Magritt and I had brought from Manhattan.

"Do you think I can fill a book?" Dante asked Magritt, his voice gravelly.

Magritt leaned forward in her chair, surprised that Dante would question the basic assumption of our work—that he was worth study. "Of course," she said in a voice as serious as his was. "A very good book."

"You honestly think so?" Dante continued.

"You're a very good artist, Professor Miller, you know that," Magritt said, her eyes peering over the thin frames of her glasses.

"On Mondays and Wednesdays, but I have my doubts the rest of the week. You have a trained eye, Magritt. You know Raphael and Titian, Manet and Picasso—how can my work possibly compare? The transparencies are one thing; the originals much different. So I fret."

Beatrice banged her hand on the table. "I told you she would like your work. He's been playing the neurotic artist far too long, worried that you'd discover every flaw in his talent. I told him you'd become rabid fans, but he brushed me off."

"I doubt that he brushed you off," I said.

"Thank you," Dante said, "I would never brush off what Beatrice says."

Magritt came to Beatrice's defense, "Your wife was right, as usual. You've been married long enough to know that."

Dante shook his huge head and ran his fingers through his white mane. "So you're not displeased?"

Magritt had had enough. "For God's sake, stop being the fragile artist. I might change my mind about your work."

Dante leaned back and burst into laughter. "Giotto stalked the streets of Florence to find a woman like you."

"Giotto stalked anything that breathed, goats and sheep included," Beatrice said. She turned toward her husband to make certain he saw her frown.

"Slander," Dante said, the word almost smothered by his laughter.

WE WORKED THROUGH the next few days, going over my early draft and deciding how best to describe the paintings Magritt and I were certain belonged in the final work. I was fully prepared to accept Dante's analysis of the *Commedia*, given his unique claim to the original voice. In fact, I looked forward to bowing to his authority. How often can you settle matters of interpretation with such precision? But it was not always that simple. Elias Miller, ever the professor, would insist on entering the discussion, taking, as he had through generations of students, great pleasure in offering multiple interpretations of the complex verses of the *Commedia*.

"It's a complex work," he said. "How else could it have lasted over the centuries if it were not thick with meaning?"

We spent much of Wednesday afternoon—once Magritt

had finished a swim and the rest of us a long nap—drinking a sparkling wine from Veneto and examining the transparency of *The Gates of Purgatory*, Jonathan Brewster's living room painting. I was fixated on the three stone steps Pilgrim and Virgil must climb to reach the locked entrance to the world between Heaven and Hell, and asked about their meaning.

"Most scholars say the steps symbolize the three elements of the Sacrament of Penance," Miller said in full professorial mode, "the white marble step standing for the mirror of self-awareness and confession, the ink-black crumbling step symbolizing true contrition, and the third flaming red stone signifying atonement. I have my doubts. If Dante had the Sacrament of Penance in mind, why did he deviate from the Church's prescribed order: contrition, then confession, and finally satisfaction? Because he wanted his readers to think, that's why, you can say. Of course, the steps might symbolize something else entirely, perhaps the spiritual history of the human race, for example, purity, sin, and redemption—or the purity of the Garden of Eden, humankind's fall from Grace, and finally, purification in the name of Christ."

Dante picked up his glass and took a long drink. "Don't we have any doughnuts to go with this?"

"He doesn't really want a doughnut; certainly not with wine. His request is just a dramatic pause," Beatrice assured us.

Dante gave out a monstrous laugh. His beard quivered. "We've been married too long," he said after he caught his breath.

"What were you thinking of when you painted those steps?" Magritt asked. "Were you following the dictates of the poem?"

"I was thinking about me, Magritt, that's what I was

thinking, about Dante the Painter, and Beatrice his wife, and the elements of our lives. The white marble represents the purity of childhood. The crumbling, dark second step, the turmoil of early middle age when dreams disappear and optimism falters. The final step, it represents maturity, when the love of life burns hot red. But it is not just a painting of mine; it is an illustration of Dante's *Commedia*. It follows his colors, his vision. Was he thinking of the Sacrament of Penance, was he thinking of the history of humanity, or was he thinking of the life of Dante the involuntary pilgrim, forced out of his beloved Florence, longing intently for the life he had been denied? I imagine it was all three. Why do we demand a single interpretation? Isn't that the problem, an addiction to one-dimensional explanations: one divinity, one Church, one common prayer?"

THAT NIGHT WE WENT OUT for supper. Beatrice chose a large diner on the outskirts of Gettysburg, a friendly, unsophisticated restaurant known for its "basic food," as Beatrice put it, where you could order a juicy pot roast with mashed potatoes or fill your need for teenage fare with a thick burger and French fries. The only possible embarrassment was eating too little.

"Giotto would have loved this place," Elias-turned-Dante said, as we listened to a crowded neighboring table burst into laughter, "the tourists, the overweight waitresses, the racket. He loved noise, particularly the wine-fueled clatter of a tavern. And sex, of course—he loved sex. As homely as he was, women found him irresistible. They saw his art and not him, his soul and not his skin."

"And he was rich," Beatrice threw in.

"He saved his pennies; he didn't throw them at women. No, they wanted his sketches, the little portraits he would draw of pretty women sitting in church pews or talking to him from below the scaffolding on which he was resting. A promise to put a woman's profile in a fresco would bring forth more than a blush. 'Dante,' he would instruct me, 'promise a girl that you will put her name into a poem and she will do anything you want.'"

"And did they?" Beatrice asked without humor.

"I was not like Giotto, part ram, part bull. You were always more than enough to gratify my spirit."

"So it's your low testosterone level that cements your fidelity," Beatrice continued.

Dante's burst of laughter frightened the twins sleeping in a double stroller not far from our table. One of them began to cry and then the other. Dante mouthed the words "I'm sorry" in the direction of the parents, and covered his mouth.

"And you, Mr. Larry, do you promise women that you will insert their name into a play?" Beatrice asked.

Magritt answered for me. "They're more interested in getting a part."

"I see," Beatrice concluded. "And are you holding any auditions?"

"Are you interested?" I asked.

"You never know."

"A good day's work," Dante commented after we had toasted our efforts with a middling Valpolicella, "but I am concerned about the introduction. You give too much space to my academic career. I think you need to turn more quickly to the art. My college career can be in a footnote. I began to paint seriously when I turned fifty, putting on canvas my lifelong interest in the writings of Dante Alighieri, and my interest in the universal quest for a transcendental meaning to life. That is enough. Then go to the section you and Magritt have done on earlier Dante illustrators. It's perfect, not too much and not too laudatory." He let out a light laugh and reached for his drink, but began to talk before putting wine to his lips. "And it would be nice if you could add more about my Beatrice and about Giotto. Say more than she is my wife and he was my friend, something substantive, something about how they led me to a better understanding of Heaven and Earth, how they challenged me to ever-higher heights."

"I, too, can fit in a footnote," Beatrice said. "I haven't eaten that much."

MAGRITT WAS THE ONLY ONE of us sober enough to drive when we left the restaurant, so I threw her the keys and sat in the back of the Mercedes with Dante on the way back to the lake.

"I can't believe that this is finally happening," Dante said, "that my work will be presented to a larger world. I have never been in a group show; never had a solo exhibit. This is it, a beginning. I am insanely exhilarated, Laurence, yet naked and anxious, afraid that critical eyes will find me wanting, that my work will prove a fleeting memory. Giotto never worried. He took his money and saved it. He was always certain he was worth it. He was. What magnificent work."

Dante poked his head over the right edge of Magritt's seat. "Have you been to Padua?" He didn't wait for an answer. "Of course you have. No art historian dares stay away. And Giotto's frescoes, have you ever seen anything more beautiful? Did you know that Raphael went to Padua to be inspired by Giotto, and so did da Vinci and Michelangelo?

A hundred years before their visits, Giotto knew they would come, that they would travel to Padua to pay homage to his talents. He knew that the world's greatest painters would go to Rome and Florence and Assisi just to stare upon his handiwork. What certainty, what self-assurance. Not arrogance, no, don't mistake it for arrogance, just the profound knowledge that God had blessed him. 'Do not fret, my friend, the world will sing your songs. If they don't sing them today, they will tomorrow,' he would assure me. 'Remember that, Dante. There is a future to your words, a time when your name will be synonymous with beauty and meaning and mystery. The secret is not to write about today for the sake of tomorrow, but to write for the centuries about those things that have everlasting meaning: God and Heaven, sin and vengeance, reward and punishment, the Garden of Eden.' What an inspiration he was, the perfect muse. How fortunate to have both him and Beatrice, no other poet was as fortunate. Remember, though, it did not all go the same way. I, too, played muse." Dante brushed his bearded face against Magritt's shoulder to make certain she was listening.

"Remember his fresco of the Last Judgment, Magritt, the devil's mouth full of sinners? That was my idea. But Giotto's brilliance, his tenderness, his beauty, that was all him, all him—oh, if I could only paint a third as well."

"You paint well enough," Beatrice said.

"Very well indeed," added Magritt.

Dante leaned back against the Mercedes' leather seat and sighed. Then he closed his eyes.

"Come," Dante said, when we pulled into the driveway at the back of his house. "Join us down at the waterfront. I'll light a fire and we can sit around and listen to the night. It is much too rare an evening to spend inside."

"They're younger than we are and may need their sleep," Beatrice said to erase any pressure we might feel to join them. Magritt turned to me and gently nodded approval.

"Give us a few minutes to change into warmer clothes and we'll be down," I said.

Inside our bedroom, Magritt gave me a deep kiss and began to unbutton my short-sleeved shirt.

"We don't have time for this," I said.

"I'm just helping you get into warmer clothes," she answered, and rubbed her pelvis against my thigh.

"That's a shame."

DANTE AND BEATRICE WERE SITTING on a thick log, watching red-blue flames shoot into the moonless night by the time Magritt and I made it down to the lake. Lights from Gettysburg spiked upwards on the other side of the opaque water, and every so often, the roar of an automobile horn or a truck's backfire shattered the silence. As Magritt and I began to sit down on an adjoining log, an unnerving blast burst from the surrounding forest, its sharp discord declining in volume as it echoed from tree to tree.

"Firecrackers," Dante announced, and shrugged his shoulders in acceptance. "There is no way to avoid modernity, but after the children are put to bed, Heaven will dominate. Even now, if you listen carefully, you can hear the night. Concentrate and you can hear your heart and the flow of your blood."

"I think you're overreaching," I said before emitting a skeptical hum.

"Shush. Delight your ears by listening to silence," Dante insisted.

Magritt slid along the rough log until our hips touched. Her breasts pushed forward as she swelled her lungs with a deep breath, held it for twenty seconds, and slowly exhaled. "The air is so clean, Larry, I can taste its sweetness," she whispered.

"Listen," Dante insisted gently, "listen. What a cacophony: the frogs, the crickets, a quintet of birds, and in the distance an owl playing its solo melody. Can you hear the water move; the fish swim?"

He closed his eyes for a long moment to make certain no one was foolish enough to think his question called for an answer. I watched as the light from the campfire played flickering games with our images. Magritt looked young and innocent, her small hands delicate. Beatrice looked as blissful as a novice, and Dante, his back straight, his thick beard colored by the fire, looked like an Old Testament prophet. I gave him a smile.

"I want to tell you a story," Dante began, "a campfire story, you know the kind, with goblins and ghosts and unexplainable visitations. Do you think you are up for that?"

Magritt answered for both of us with a light laugh.

"Beatrice and I moved here in late June, thirty-five years ago. The house we are now living in had suffered at the hands of its previous owner and needed a great deal of work to make it habitable. We did much of it ourselves, patching interior walls, painting the exterior, installing a wooden floor here and a carpet there. We hired professionals to cement the earthen basement and renovate the plumbing, to insulate the attic and secure the tiled roof. While the work was being done, unwelcome odors filled the house and its interior was fouled with grime and dust. So we spent the summer in an old Coleman tent we had put up alongside the lake and slept in a double sleeping bag we had purchased in Europe on our honeymoon. It was very romantic, the wood fires, the open skies, the pitch-black nights. We found it so enjoyable that the next summer, after the house was complete, we continued the routine. We did so for a number of summers. But after we fixed up the house you are using and began renting it to students during the academic year and to tourists during the summer, sleeping under the stars became a rare activity.

"We did continue to light a fire at night when the weather allowed, and invited our summer renters to join us for the quiet and beauty, but we slept indoors. Over a quarter century we sat on the shores of the lake without anything more unusual happening than the sighting of a black bear scavenging with her cubs. Oh, every so often we would have a guest with a lively imagination. 'Do you ever see ghosts?' an elderly man from Brooklyn once asked. 'What made you think of that?' I said. 'I thought I saw some soldiers in blue wandering the shore last night.' I treated his comment seriously, but laughed about it when I repeated his words to Beatrice. An early sign of dementia, we decided. Another time a young woman from New Jersey said that she would be afraid to live so close to Gettysburg. 'There must be so many unhappy spirits living here, their lives on earth cut brutally short.' 'We don't believe in spirits,' Beatrice told her. 'Then you are misled,' she said sweetly.

"Don't get me wrong; Beatrice and I don't believe in ghosts and spirits. But the human imagination is less civilized than the instructed mind. It can drive you to places where the intellect dare not go. I had spent the afternoon working outside, a large straw hat shading my eyes, and had just completed an image of the River Styx, the shades of the wrathful mired in its mud. It was just about dusk. I had put away the paints and folded my chair, and was ready to take the canvas from the easel when I heard a young man's voice say, 'That doesn't look at all like the lake.' 'I'm not painting the lake,' I answered before turning around. I found myself looking at a fair-complexioned boy, perhaps sixteen or seventeen years old, his thick blonde hair protruding from under a black, large-brimmed cavalry hat. His high-necked dark-blue jacket was unbuttoned, its yellow tape trim waved at me as we talked. At first, I thought him a Civil War reenactor, the type you see around town dressed in recently purchased replicas of Union uniforms. I learned differently. Beatrice came to tell me supper was ready but quickly forgot her message when she saw me talking to myself. She wondered if I had flipped out. It was July, and almost 130 years since the battle.

"That's how it began. Since then, I have met many soldiers who died at Gettysburg, many. Most of them unbearably young, just like the dead in most wars. All of them cheated."

The campfire had lost most of its heat so I got up and threw on a couple more logs. Dante thanked me, his tone solemn. Beatrice nodded in his direction, her face made red by the revitalized flames. Magritt was staring at the artist.

When Magritt spoke, I could tell that she was struggling to erase skepticism from her voice. "Do they rise from their graves on the anniversary of the battle?"

"No," Dante chuckled, "I don't believe they rise from their graves or from where they fell. They go back to where life was good, to the places of their childhood, to the familiar mountains and valleys of their brief lives. But they wander through this countryside, perhaps on the anniversary of their death, not to see the place or relive the horror, but to spend time with their comrades, to once again be in the company of others so terribly misused. Some, however, whose farms are now buried under urban centers, or have been broken apart by twentieth century suburbs, come to these forests for eternal peace, expecting that somehow this land will defy modernity."

"How many have you talked to?" I asked, hesitantly.

Dante wet his lips as if he were enjoying an ice cream cone, and then gave me a broad smile. "I haven't kept track, Laurence, but over the years I have met many who died during the war, Confederate and Union, from Maine and New York, from Alabama and Virginia, infantry and cavalry, volunteers and conscripts. I have talked to a large number, but only a few more than once."

"Many," Beatrice echoed.

What do you say when people you care for drift into the fantastic? Do you shake them by the shoulders and shout them into reality? Do you laugh? Do you say something scornful, full of biased certainty, dismissive of all knowledge but your own? Or do you listen and wonder why two compassionate people, two intelligent minds, require metaphysical visions to make their lives whole? I found myself feeling sorry for Dante and his wife, and at the same time, I brimmed with affection.

"And what do they think of your paintings of Hell?" I continued, trying to eliminate from my voice all sounds of incredulity.

"Not much, I'm afraid. Oh, they admire my skill, but if I wanted to witness Hell, they tell me, I should have experienced Pickett's Charge, or have fought in the Peach Orchard, or cowered and wheezed in the thunder and smoke of the Wheat Field. 'Gettysburg was Hell,' a boy no older than sixteen told me as we both looked across this sylvan lake. 'That's what I learned—that in a war any place can be made into Hell.'"

"They didn't validate Dante's travels into the other world, his concept of Hell or Purgatory?" Magritt questioned, her voice academic, her face filled with interest.

"I didn't expect them to. Would you have expected them to?" Dante answered.

"I wouldn't expect to see spirits at all," she answered and then bit her upper lip. "But if I were going to invite poltergeists to judge my paintings, I'd at least make certain they had only good things to say."

Dante gave out a vibrant laugh. "I didn't anticipate meeting spirits, Magritt. That was the last thing I expected. If Beatrice hadn't accepted what was happening that first day, I would have thought I had had too much sun and given up my wine. And if I couldn't control the spirits' arrival, how could I possibly control what they thought?"

"So you see them, too," I said to Beatrice.

"Not the way Dante does. I feel a presence. I know that I am not alone. But not the way Dante does." She gave her husband a soulful look and then turned to me. "We've never told a soul about our ghosts, never. We realized how ridiculous it would sound."

"Then why tell us? Didn't you think we'd find it ridiculous?" Magritt asked.

In the flickering firelight, I watched Beatrice's face turn shy. "Oh, we were convinced you'd find it preposterous, at least at first. There was no doubt in our minds. But we expected that you would try to protect our egos and give our apparitions a little thought. We know you have seen us down here talking to the invisible, and yet you never pressed us for an explanation. That means a great deal, that you accept us for who we are. We knew you'd be curious and we thought you deserved an explanation, even if it were one you'd find absurd."

"But if you want ghosts to analyze your paintings, why not conjure up Giotto or Monet?" I asked Dante.

"Oh, I ask them, too. What would Titian think about this scene? I ask myself, or Raphael, or Degas. I don't ask too many artists; their opinions would just conflict and I'd be left with more questions than answers. It's a good habit, to ask giants from the past about the present, to try to twist your mind into theirs and view the world from their unique angle. It adds doubt to your belief—a virtue that Dante failed to write about—doubt about your certainties. It doesn't necessarily change your mind, but it does force you to remember that there exist ways different from your own to understand the world. Doubt permits tolerance to breathe; it is as important a virtue as prudence or justice. Doubt can be, should be, a habit of mind.

"Conjuring up Giotto is far different than being visited by souls who once walked this land, who bled into this earth. I do not conjure up my soldiers. They appear without a dinner bell. They bring unpredictable stories. They answer questions I am not wise enough to ask."

Magritt's voice filled with fascination. "Do they tell you about their lives?"

"So you believe me?" Dante said. His eyes reflected the fire, his beard glowed red by the radiance of its flames.

"I want to know," Magritt said, avoiding any greater commitment.

Dante cocked his head slightly and offered a small, knowing smile. "My soldiers are different than the shades in the *Commedia*. They talk much less about themselves and want to talk more about the present. Not about our cars and planes, computers and televisions—they see those as modern toys, no more important to the essence of life than printed books and daily newspapers. They have great difficulty coming to grips with a land where most people do not farm, where children are few, where someone you do not know builds your house, grows your food, cares for your sick, or buries your dead. They fumble at the thought that people can feel at one with the world when the output of their work has no physical dimension. These things are difficult for them to grasp.

"I defend today. I tell them people live longer, that the old joys of love and tenderness, of exploration and learning, are richer than ever. We dance and sing; we have sex; we laugh. I argue that we don't sacrifice lives as easily as their lives were sacrificed. They ask for proof I do not have. They think we destroy more efficiently but no less. Still, we enjoy the conversation. They shrug their shoulders and fill their voices with doubt, but not with bile. I grimace with frustration when they do not understand me; they make a funny face when they think me ridiculous. Still, we enjoy each other's company. People have an infinite capacity to enjoy one another."

"And to hate," Magritt added.

"And to hate. That is my point. That is the point of the *Commedia*. We have an infinite capacity for love and hate, and the free will to choose. How must we live our lives so that we end up with the good and not the evil? It sounds banal when put that simply, but isn't that the only question? Wasn't that the question when my soldiers were sacrificed in the Wheat Field, when I was driven out of my beloved Florence? The question is not how to live to get to Heaven, but how to construct Eden, not one garden but many. Paradise on earth, that's what I was writing about."

"So why did you fill your poem with Heaven, Purgatory, and Hell?" I asked.

"Because I wanted it to be read, that's why. The poem is

an allegory, an allegory about life on earth," Dante said with a tinge of annoyance in his voice. "I ask my soldiers about the afterlife. They tell me it is a fable."

"But aren't they testament to the next world?" I argued. Dante just laughed.

I was not prepared to let him off. "Laughter is not an answer, Dante. What do they tell you about the next world?"

"What they tell me doesn't matter. What matters is the here and now. Do you design your life for some hidden future, or do you mold it for the present, for the terrestrial? If being decent doesn't get you to Heaven, what will—supplication? Suffering? My God is more beneficent than that."

Beatrice used Dante's shoulder to help her get up from the log. He rose after her. "Why don't the two of you stay awhile?" he said. "Just make sure the fire is out before you come in. There is a shovel behind one of the logs if you need to cover the wood with dirt."

Magritt and I watched them disappear into the dark only to see them again silhouetted against the light emanating from their house. They climbed onto the porch without looking back.

"You like them, don't you?" Magritt softly asked.

"More than I can understand," I answered and squeezed her hand.

CHAPTER SEVENTEEN

MAGRITT AND I STAYED in Gettysburg through the weekend, not willing to give up the delights of company and countryside. And on Monday, we extended the duration of our trip back to Manhattan by taking a late lunch at the Dobbin House Tavern in Gettysburg, with Dante and Beatrice, and a leisurely Italian dinner at Michelangelo's Restaurante— how could we resist?—in Binghamton. Eventually, though, I couldn't avoid letting Magritt off at the entrance to her apartment building and watching her disappear through the front door.

I returned to my mother's apartment wearing a long face and unfocused eyes, projecting—as teenagers of every age have a talent to do—the infallible signs of terminal sorrow. It was more than my mother could endure. Two days later she moved in with Paul. "It's just a temporary arrangement," she said, but I caught her singing to herself as she packed her clothes, and she gave Paul a prolonged kiss when he came over to help her move. Paul was overjoyed. Magritt was hesitant.

"It's only a temporary arrangement," I said, planning to add, "we should begin to search for an apartment of our own," but before I could finish my thought, Magritt muttered,

"I know." Afraid to press her further than she wanted to go, I shrugged my shoulders and said nothing.

Magritt placed her toothbrush next to mine, and put just a few pieces of clothing into the dresser drawer I had emptied for her. More of her belongings came a week later, and even more a week after that. Eventually, I gladly gave up sole possession of my closet and dresser and squeezed my clothes around hers.

Magritt filled the apartment. The bathroom smelled of her soap, my bedroom of her perfume. She kicked her shoes off in the entryway. She filled the refrigerator with whitefish salad and orange juice, the freezer with ice cream and éclairs. A freshly baked baguette arrived at the end of her morning run, and soft cheeses I had never tasted turned up on the breakfast table. I would watch her shake water from her hair after a shower; I would watch her press her fingers against her lips when she curled up in Paul's leather chair in the evening, an open book on her lap. She threw a pillow at the TV screen when a DVD froze in the middle of a romantic scene. She wept while listening to Sondheim's *Passion*. Late at night, we submerged into each other's arms and metamorphosed into something new.

A week after our return from Gettysburg, we forced ourselves to focus on the monograph with a visit to the Van Ness/Brewster apartment on East 86th Street. Harland Van Ness waved to us when we got off the elevator on the fifteenth floor, his blue blazer unbuttoned, as was the top of his shirt. A bow to informality, I mused, and felt a bit overdressed in my jacket and tie. "I hope you had no difficulty finding the place," he said, ushering us into the apartment.

Susan Brewster, Harland's wife and Madeline Brewster's daughter, was sitting in the den when Harland introduced Magritt and me, an open newspaper on her lap and the evening news playing on a large television screen. She rose quickly, vigorously shook our hands, and walked us into the parlor. Magritt and Susan selected a white Burgundy; Harland and I took some Scotch.

"My brother, Jonathan, was taken with both of you," Susan said, her voice surprisingly granular. "He sounded remarkably happy when he called to tell me about your visit. For a while I thought he was drunk."

"We brought him a bottle of Amarone," I said.

"I don't think that alone would have done it," Susan said sweetly. A handsome woman of about forty-five, she complemented her husband, balancing his perfected pomposity with a leisurely informality, her blue jeans well worn, a rumpled gray sweatshirt flattening her chest, her body pushed back comfortably into the thickly upholstered armchair.

Magritt didn't join me on the couch. Instead, she remained standing and examined the two large oils that hung on the wall in front of her. "They are magnificent," she said.

Susan spoke, her voice unique, deep and quiet, with an unexpected timbre that hinted at some childhood disease or an adult vocal cord problem. "They're from the opening cantos of the *Purgatorio*. The others in the room and the two in the dining room are from *Purgatorio* as well, but from later sections of the poem."

Harland got out of his chair and walked to the wall. "This is my favorite," he said pointing to the painting on his right. "It is called *Cato*, a portrait of the ancient Roman Dante and Virgil came upon when they were leaving Hell."

"Stunning," Magritt said while slowly approaching the painting. I thought I saw her nose quiver. "Dante is very good with faces," she continued before taking a few steps back. "This one, however, it's brilliant: his use of light, the varnish undercoat, the subtle almost unnoticed use of white, and the effect of egg tempera rather than ordinary oils. See how powerful and distinct his image of Cato is against his ethereal depiction of Dante and Virgil."

"My mother liked it enormously," Susan jumped in, smiling broadly, "particularly the mixture of shock and fear you see on Cato's face. He believes Dante and Virgil are fugitives from Hell—a place from which he believed no shade could escape. They appear to him as harbingers of a failing God, a God who could no longer hold together the construct of the afterworld. A frightening thought. It's a sort of God-is-dead theme long before that thesis entered the modern vocabulary."

A powerful painting, I silently mused, in the style of the early Renaissance, before painters fully developed perspective and mastered composition. Cato is full-faced to the viewer. The tresses of his long flowing gray beard are streaked with white, his body, thin and erect, and his eyes aflame. The four stars in the horizon symbolize the four cardinal virtues—Justice, Prudence, Temperance, and Fortitude—the Southern Hemisphere stars that shone over the Garden of Eden and were unseen by man after Adam and Eve were driven from Earth's paradise.

"Remind me about Cato," I said.

Magritt shrugged her shoulders and Harland looked to his wife.

"Dante referred to the younger Cato, known as Cato of Utica, a first century B.C. Roman and not his great-grandfather, the Roman orator and writer. I don't fully remember the story, but Cato, having been born before Christ, was a pagan. He was also a suicide. Still, Dante placed him in *Purgatorio* and not in *Inferno*, arguing that after his death the Holy Spirit led him to seek Christ's absolution. Dante's reasoning is unclear, at least to me. Cato was virtuous, it seems, and the poet regarded that as implying faith. Dante even placed Jews in *Paradiso*. I don't think that was universally applauded."

"Perhaps Dante was closer to the meaning of Christ than his contemporaries," I said, my eyes still on the painting. Cato's elongated face was riveting. His firm jaw and tight lips projected strength, but his eyes burst with horror, the blue of the irises paled by fear. It is an all-too-modern expression, the face of a war orphan or a widow, of a devastated parent, a defeated soldier. An eternal image of suffering, when faith disappears and only chaos remains.

"The painting has affected you, hasn't it? My mother would be very pleased. But what are you thinking?" Susan asked.

I surprised myself and my audience by saying, "Dolly the sheep." An image of the first cloned mammal had popped into my mind only after Susan asked the question.

Magritt repeated my words but added a question mark, her eyes in a squint. "Dolly the sheep?"

Harland and his wife looked at me. He wore a frown, she, a smile that conveyed curiosity.

"Strange, I know, but when Cato saw Virgil and Dante coming up from the *Inferno*, he thought all his beliefs about God were wrong. God wasn't omnipotent. God wasn't eternal. When Dolly hit the front page of *The New York Times*, I was too young to appreciate how momentous an event it was, but eventually I felt much like Cato, that the boundaries of knowledge are permeable, that mankind is on a road that has no signs, that the universe of my birth would not be the universe of my life." I chuckled nervously before I continued. "That's how I felt when Cato's eyes looked at me, at one with him, threatened by what I did not understand. I'm being a little too dramatic, aren't I?"

"More than a little," Harland said cheerfully.

"I like the thought," Susan commented.

Magritt gave me a knowing nod, as if to say, good for you, Larry, you surprised me, and I like that.

"*The Valley of the Princes*," Harland said, and pointed to the painting that hung next to *Cato*.

I was half-smashed when I'd first encountered *The Valley of the Princes*. Magritt and I had dined with the Millers on bread and cheese and three bottles of an excellent Brunello, a present from the Truth Foundation. The Millers went outside to prepare a campfire while Magritt and I continued to sip wine. A clever punishment, I decided, forcing negligent rulers to suffer each other's arrogant and overbearing personalities, compelled to exist in a realm without subjects, without servants and sycophants. I pondered writing a play about leadership by subjecting the five most recent presidents of the United States to each other's claimed authority. I still like the idea.

Susan Brewster rose gracefully from the green upholstered chair and walked to the opposite side of the room, where three paintings hung. We followed closely behind. "*Pride and Humility*, one of my favorites," she said.

Bent shades of the proud are walking on a gray ledge, bowed by the weight of the huge slabs of stone they carry on their backs. Carved into the background are scenes of humility, pride's antithesis—a humble Virgin Mary being informed of her destiny by the angel Gabriel; King David dancing barefoot in God's praise as his wife, Michal, reproaches him for his humble demonstration of joy.

"Giotto's advice," I mumbled under my breath.

Susan picked up the name. "Giotto?" she said.

"Elias once told me—after he had wrapped himself in the persona of Dante—that Giotto suggested he should describe both the sin and its opposite and not just the sin alone when writing about Purgatory. Dante followed the idea. So does Elias."

Susan let out a comfortable chuckle. "My mother often described Elias wearing the mantel of Dante. She would joke about it, but underneath, I think she half-believed he was the poet."

"Madeline was a romantic," Harland broke in.

"Half the time I think he is 700 years old," I said. "But I, too, am a romantic."

"It's patently ludicrous, Larry," Harland said. "Elias has spent his life stuck in medieval literature. He's become a celebrant of a vanished age. Sometimes I think he's just a fraud."

"That's much too harsh," Magritt argued. "He simply follows a different rhythm of life."

"And celebrant? I don't see that," I added.

"We could argue about this all night," Susan interceded, her craggy voice in high pitch.

We went on to explore paintings hung in the dining room and those in an interior hallway, traveling through the Fourth Terrace of Purgatory, where slothfulness is purged; the Fifth, where avarice is avenged; the Sixth, where the gluttonous are taught the value of abstinence; and finally the Seventh terrace, where lust is contrasted with chastity.

We ended our journey in their master bedroom, where *O Bride of Lebanon*, from Canto XXX of Purgatorio, greeted us.

Beatrice enters the Garden of Eden to greet the poet who has traveled through Hell and Purgatory. With his sins expunged, Dante is ready to enter Paradise. His guide Virgil, being a pagan, cannot escort him into the heavenly realm. Beatrice, Dante's childhood love, takes Virgil's place. A grand procession of elders of the Church, ladies in waiting, and an array of metaphysical creatures accompany Beatrice in the poem and the painting, her chariot drawn by a griffin whose lion's body and eagle's head symbolize wisdom and courage. Beatrice appears to Dante through a shower of flowers, a stern expression on her face, her index finger in a pointed reprimand. Pilgrim is bowing humbly to his love, but her body is as unbending as ivory.

"It must have been rough on poor old Dante to have traveled so far only to be scolded by Beatrice for being unfaithful to her memory by committing sin," Harland said.

"And for betraying his God-given poetic talent, Harland," I added. "A far better finish for *Purgatorio*, I think, than a Hollywood ending with lovers rushing into each other's arms. It confirms that Beatrice cared enough to watch over him from Heaven; that the way he lived had meaning to her. Dante might have found her outburst comforting. In its own way, it's very romantic."

"Well, we each do have our own definitions of romantic," Harland argued. "I think Dante would have felt misused, to have taken so harsh a journey only to be subjected to his love's displeasure."

Magritt gave out an impenetrable hum.

Susan served decaffeinated coffee and Harland talked on and on about the quality of his collection. "You won't find better examples of Miller's work. Mine should have a place in your book."

CHAPTER EIGHTEEN

SOMEHOW, EVEN WITH all the distractions of a flourishing romance, the writing flowed gracefully. In three weeks we pieced together sixty fluid pages. We would call Dante and Beatrice every other night to seek their advice, making certain the hour was late enough to catch Dante submerged in Alighieri's persona. We used a speakerphone and insisted that the Millers get one, too.

Early on, Dante insisted that we include three paintings by other artists. Giotto's *Madonna and Child* was to have a prominent place. He expected that the National Gallery in Washington would permit its use. "A tribute to my old friend," Dante said as I talked to him on the phone, Magritt's head on my lap. Giotto's masterpiece was to be followed by two nineteenth century illustrations of the *Commedia*: *Virgil and Dante*, by the French artist Eugene Delacroix, which hangs in the Louvre; and a watercolor, *Dante in the Empyrean, Drinking at the River of Light*, by the English artist, William Blake, from the Tate Museum's collection in London. Dante was adamant. "Let the readers see what real artists did with my poem."

Magritt and I insisted that the monograph include a photograph of Dante and Beatrice on the shore of their lake, the sun setting over the still water. Beatrice agreed, but only if we included a photograph of Dante alone, his huge beard in disarray, and the wooden handle of a paintbrush touching his lips.

When it came to selecting which of his paintings would appear in the monograph, Elias Miller proved dreadfully taxing. The paintings were his children, and choosing one over another left him emotionally drained. He regressed to an earlier stage in our work and suggested paintings that Magritt and I had never planned to see. He argued that we use fifty images, not fifteen. When I explained that was not the deal with the Truth Foundation, he upped the ante and insisted that we include one image from each of the thirty-four cantos of the *Inferno* and the thirty-three cantos of *Purgatorio*. Beatrice often ended up playing therapist to all of us, reminding us that it was only a book and not a constitution, that choice means sacrifice. I became the spokesperson for potential readers, saying things like: "The theme of that painting is too erudite, Dante. If I were standing in Barnes and Noble and thumbing through the book, that painting would not convince me to buy it."

"Are you a pimp or an artist?" Dante would shout.

"Do you want people to learn about your art?" I would shout back.

Magritt, with her knowledge of art and art history, became the final arbiter. She exercised her authority gently, letting us argue until we were exhausted and thankful for a referee. We fought ourselves down to seventeen works, and avoided the need to cut further by using one painting for the front cover and one for the back. *Francesca and Paolo* went on the front. "A romantic cover will sell," I argued. Magritt agreed. Beatrice, wanting to begin at the beginning of the poem, voted for *A Pilgrim Born*, which depicts Dante lost in the forest of middle age and threatened by three beasts. Dante suggested flipping a coin. "Ha," Beatrice concluded dismissively. For the back cover we all agreed on *Two Suns* from Robby Whitford's collection.

"*Two Suns* speaks to a contemporary issue, the place of God in government," Beatrice said. "The painting itself doesn't tell the tale, but it will trigger the curiosity of potential purchasers and get them to open the book and be enthralled."

"I like the word 'enthralled,'" I said.

I expected my comment would trigger Dante's laughter, but he was much too focused on the painting. "I originally thought of setting the two suns over Washington, D.C., with the Capitol's dome lit brilliantly by both stars, the White House off to the right, the Lincoln Memorial on the left, and images of the Vietnam Memorial and Arlington Cemetery floating above the city. I did a number of sketches, but Beatrice suggested I find a comprehensive metaphor. So I went back to ancient Rome. Using Washington would have made me feel better, but it would have let too many countries off the hook. I may have written an Italian poem, but it is now universal. Beatrice was right. She didn't want me to go backward."

Magritt smiled like a curious student, her head tilted to one side, the speaker- phone resting on her lap. "Did you think of that often, using contemporary images?" she asked. "More often than I like to recall," he answered, a bit of self-deprecating laughter in his voice. "When I painted the two lovers Paolo and Francesca, I modeled them after Elizabeth Taylor and Richard Burton, but Beatrice said half my audience—if I ever had one—wouldn't know who they were. I argued that therefore it didn't matter. 'But half of the viewers *would* know,' said Beatrice, 'and it would subtract from the poem's meaning.' I bowed to her wisdom. I even considered using images of current politicians when I painted the Ninth Circle of the *Inferno*, the eternal resting place of those who perpetrated meaningless splits in the body politic. Politics does that to me; I grow angry and impatient for intelligent contemplation."

"Don't you think intelligent discussions can divide us with as much ease as shallow debates?" I questioned.

"Not in the same way," Dante answered. "I'm an old-fashioned dreamer. I think intelligence can unite us the way religion can, but it has far less power to divide. Metaphysics is boundless. Even second-rate minds can create fables and myths, unyielding gods and vengeful spirits. But intelligent political debate has to be tied to reality; it needs a concrete foundation. Slogans and denunciations are not enough. Slurs and calumny may win votes, but they don't win debates. But I quickly realized that my desire to use contemporary figures in my paintings was due more to prejudice than thought. I found myself behaving as I did when I wrote the *Commedia*, using my art to beat up on people who looked at the world far differently than I. Not that they didn't deserve my outrage. But I wanted to rise above myself in the paintings."

Dante paused for a moment, and I imagined him taking a drink of wine, the telephone on the front porch table. Then he broke into rowdy laughter. "I sound so damn egotistical," he wheezed.

"Like an artist," Magritt said, and poked her elbow into my ribs.

HARLAND WAS DRESSED to the hilt when Magritt and I entered his office. A bold yellow tie enriched the color of his navy-blue serge suit, and a matching handkerchief draped from the jacket's breast pocket. Coffee in china cups, and a silver tray covered with seductive handmade chocolate candies, sat at the edge of his desk, directly in front of the chairs that had been sited for our use.

"Do you mind if I skim through it while you're here?" Harland said, after we had exchanged the usual pleasantries.

He didn't wait for an answer, but quickly pulled the manuscript from the red envelope I had used to protect it. He flipped rapidly through the first chapter, in which Elias Miller and his painting style were introduced, spent somewhat more time on the chapter that cursorily summarized *The Divine Comedy* and its influence, and chuckled when he came to the chapter on previous illustrators of the poem.

"Praise by comparison—good. I wouldn't have thought of it, but it works, comparing him to Botticelli and Blake and Delacroix. Very good indeed. Do you think art critics will agree or just argue?"

"Not all of them," Magritt said.

Harland slowed down when he read through our interpretations of the paintings from the *Inferno*; then our analyses of the illustrations of *Purgatorio*. Finally, he flipped rapidly through the concluding chapter on painting techniques and styles, and the artists Dante emulated, in one painting, Titian, in the next, Degas.

"Do you think it necessary to say so much about the artists he copies? It seems to detract from his genius," Harland wondered.

Magritt argued. "If we don't point it out, the critics will. Better we spin the truth than someone who wants to downplay Dante's success."

Harland paused for a moment and seemed to turn the idea around in his mind. "Maybe," he finally said.

"And what is this?" he asked as he examined the spreadsheet we had placed at the end of the manuscript.

I answered. "It's not part of the publication. We prepared a list of the paintings we selected, who owns them and where they are located. We'll need to hire a professional, someone who has experience dealing with works of art, to prepare the pictures for the monograph. There are numerous photographers here in New York that museums and art galleries employ."

"Yes. Yes. I'm familiar with a number."

Magritt and I sat silently, watching him thumb through the pages again, studying the chapters on *Purgatorio* and the *Inferno*, thinking, I imagined, of the paintings he owned that didn't make the manuscript and were mentioned only in the footnotes or in the list of Miller's work we had placed in an appendix. I expected him to argue for their inclusion, but he didn't.

"The museums that hold the works by Giotto, Delacroix, and Blake we want included will most probably have their own impressions. Our photographer won't have to travel."

My comment got no reaction.

"Good," Harland announced as he returned the manuscript to its folder.

"Have you begun looking for a publisher?" I asked.

"Oh, that's taken care off. We have two on the line, both well known for their fine art publications."

"Even before the photographs are taken? That's surprising," I said.

"The Foundation has many friends."

"Which publishers?" Magritt asked innocently.

Harland pushed back in his chair and threw out a polite smile. "You don't have to trouble yourself with that. The Truth Foundation will handle the business details. I promise you it will be a well-crafted book and very well promoted. Your patron would insist on it if I didn't."

"And the galleys—when should we expect to see them?" I said, suddenly suspicious. Magritt shifted to the edge of her leather chair.

"I expect in a month or two. But the Foundation has many good proofreaders. You needn't be burdened with clerical work."

"It's often not just clerical, Harland," I said. "You often discover an infelicitous word or phrase, or discover an uncovered point. Only Magritt and I could do that."

"You're talking about expensive changes. You should have taken care of those issues in the manuscript."

"There may be changes you or your board want, or Patron. Are you going to leave us out of that process as well?" I continued.

Harland leaned over his desk, his expression stern, but he paused before saying anything. Once again, he pushed back into the dark leather chair. "If you'd like," he began, "I'd be happy to continue to use your services. But you have fulfilled your contracts by delivering the manuscript and I'm ready to have your checks issued. I'd need permission from the Board to extend your work for us."

"We'd like our checks, sooner rather than later, but there is no reason to pay us more to see the manuscript to publication. We expected to do that. Right, Magritt?"

Magritt was still poised on the edge of her chair and looked ready to pounce. She turned her head to look at me and nodded.

"See," I continued, "we both assumed that choosing the right photographs was integral to our efforts, and Dante wants to make certain his works are properly represented. He doesn't want half-assed images of his art."

"No one does, let me assure you," Harland said. He straightened his tie and brought the coffee cup to his mouth, trying, I had the feeling, to distract us from his facial expression. He needn't have bothered. He was inscrutable.

Magritt lowered the register of her voice and tried to sound matter-of-fact. "Then we will get to interview potential photographers?"

"Patron will decide on the photographer, but whomever that turns out to be, I'll insist that there be multiple shots of each piece for your consideration, and if none of them pan out . . . we'll decide what to do next. Hire someone else or ask for alternative photographs. Okay? And once the galleys come in, in a month or two, should I send them to Magritt?"

"That would be fine," I answered.

"Good," Harland responded. "I imagine Elias Miller will not be interested in proofreading, but I can understand his wanting some say over the images of the paintings we publish. That is to be expected. Perhaps the three of you could do that together. It would take less time."

"I'm sure that's the way it will work out," Magritt said. "Thank you for understanding."

Harland smiled. "You've done good work. The checks will go out tomorrow if not later this afternoon, and I'll be in touch with Magritt when the photographs and galleys come in."

He rose from his chair, brushed off the front of his trousers as if they were covered with cookie crumbs, and buttoned his single-breasted jacket. He strolled leisurely around his desk, shook my hand and kissed Magritt on the cheek. "This has been fun," he said as he led us to the door. "And what will you be doing now?" he asked me. "Another play?"

"Yes, I'm looking forward to it. Is the Truth Foundation interested in investing in the performing arts?"

"You never know," he answered, and managed to look serious. "And you, Magritt, any definite plans?"

"Thanks for asking, but I'll go back to what I was doing before, teaching in some college's evening session and hunting for a dissertation topic."

"Well, when you come up with one, and I'm certain it will be quite original—let me know. You can never predict what will interest the Truth Foundation."

A GRAY SEPTEMBER afternoon greeted us when we stepped through the front door of the Truth Foundation, the city's air crisp and clean; the afternoon's light a warm amber. I held Magritt's hand as we walked the long blocks between Manhattan's famous avenues—Park and Madison, 5th and Broadway—silently at first, each absorbed in our own concerns, unwilling to share our thoughts for fear that saying them out loud would guarantee their truth.

Magritt broke the silence. "Why do I feel like a lovesick teenager, just returned from summer camp, her head stuffed with promises she knows will not be kept, and certain that she will never be as happy as she had been?"

"I'm too old to be a summer romance. You have to lift weights and jog for that type of job," I said in a misguided attempt to lighten the moment.

"Not you, at least not just you. I was thinking of the whole thing: living in Gettysburg, talking to a 700-year-old poet, getting to know you. It's been good, Larry, and I feel it's ended."

"There's still much we have to do."

"You don't actually think Harland's going to be in touch, do you? We'll get our checks, but that's it. I doubt if our names will even appear on the cover. Somewhere it will say something like, prepared for the Truth Foundation by Larry and Magritt, beneficiaries of a summer romance."

A $20,000 CHECK was delivered to my mother's apartment the next morning. "The final payment," read the attached note. "Added to the $30,000 you have already received, your contract is fulfilled. Thank you." Harland Van Ness, Executive Director, signed it on the behalf of the Truth Foundation.

"See, I'm right. We won't hear from Harland again," Magritt said in a breathless voice after she closed the door behind the Federal Express man.

"Magritt, we'll see, but let's celebrate our new-found wealth with a good dinner—champagne, wine, and a make-you-feel-guilty dessert. I'm sure your check is at your mother's place."

"I'm sure it's there as well, but I just don't feel like celebrating."

"Then let's make love."

"I don't want to do that, either," Magritt said, suddenly angry, and turned her back toward me.

MAGRITT SPENT HER DAYS at Columbia University's library, catching up on recent publications in art history and hoping that some article would inspire a quest worthy of a doctoral dissertation. I began to sketch out a new play about a young writer hired to ghostwrite the autobiography of a minor American politician, a congressman from a large unnamed city whose legislative history was dictated by the generosity of lobbyists. My writer was to be a naïve patriot suddenly mired in the flesh and blood of late twentieth-century Washington. But early on I ran into difficulties. The comedy was too facile, the drama too sparse. Unanswerable questions bubbled up when I least expected them: Was my congressman a disease or was he merely proof of the impossibility of a world ordered by justice? Was my writer's naivety a sign of inadequacy, or was it an appropriate adaptation to a world that daily grows more impossible to understand? Was laughter an appropriate vehicle for understanding the complexities of today, or would a sordid romance offer more authority . . . or an old fashioned murder mystery in which the congressman is done in by faithful constituents who finally recognize his deceitfulness?

Damn Dante, I raged. Doubt may be a virtue, but it is not an answer. Humans need certainties. I needed certainty. Knowledge was the virtue.

"How are you progressing?" I asked Magritt, who was sitting at the kitchen table, scrutinizing a facsimile of a medieval tome. "I'm not doing too well."

"I'm ready for a drink," she answered.

I struggled with my ghostwriter and congressman for over a week before putting my pen away and dropping the manuscript into a bottom drawer. All good wine needs to age, I told myself.

The next day I returned to my Dante project and called Jonathan Brewster, hoping to find out if he knew what was going on.

A skeptical voice filled me in. "A photographer came over last weekend. I asked about you and Magritt, and he told me you were waiting to see his proofs."

"Did you catch his name?"

"I wrote it down somewhere, Larry. I can look for it."

"Please," I said, and waited for Jonathan to return to the phone, my anger quietly percolating.

"You're in luck. Robert . . . Robert DeCamp, from a gallery in Manhattan. I didn't bother to ask him the name. He acted as if you were lifelong friends. Are you sure you don't know him? A handsome man, around thirty, with a 1960s' pitch-black ponytail."

"I'm afraid not, Jonathan. Magritt and I seem to have been cut out of the final stages."

"Oh, I'm sorry to hear that," he said, surprised. "When Sharon called to arrange for DeCamp's visit, I asked about you and Magritt. She said you were both fine and busy."

"Sharon Brewster?"

Jonathan laughed. "She's close to my father, but I don't think it has gone quite that far. She hasn't asked me to call her Mom."

"I could swear that she once referred to you as her son-in-law."

"You've got my curiosity up, Larry, but if my father had remarried he would have told me and my sister. I'm not close to him, but we're not that far apart. Besides, I can't believe there's a sexual relationship between them, can you? She'd wear him to death."

Thoroughly puzzled, I hung onto the conversation for another minute or two, my mind racing backwards, recalling how orchestrated the evening at Caleb's apartment had been and how carefully timed the comment Sharon made about sleeping in Madeline's bed.

"And the photographer mentioned you and Magritt," I heard Jonathan say.

"I'm certain he did, Jonathan. Did you at least think he did a good job?"

"He was very professional. Manny thought so, too."

"Good," I said. "At least that."

When we hung up, I could feel sweat on my neck and under my arms.

I rang Robby Whitford. "A young hippie," she told me, "with a red rubber band around his short, black ponytail. He reminded me of my flower child days."

"I didn't know you were a flower child."

"There's a lot about me you don't know. You should spend more time with me, you and Magritt. I was far from a child during my flower days. Still, no one complained. We were all pretty mellow in that short-lived paradise."

"Did he seem to be a competent photographer?"

"Oh, I'm not wise enough to judge how good a technician he is. He mentioned you and Magritt, but I got the feeling he didn't know you and wasn't sent by you. He struck me as much too commercial. I told him it was a waste of time to photograph my collection of Millers, since I didn't plan to sell any. He suggested that once I learned of the prices they could get, I would be more than happy to put them on the market. He left me with the feeling that he was an art dealer and that his photographs were an initial step in the marketing process. Does that make sense to you?"

"It makes as much sense as anything else. Magritt and I have been cut out of the final stages, although I think we could be of great help."

"Just sit back and enjoy the movie. There is not much

else you can do. But if you do boil, you can come and visit me and cool down in the pool."

To my relief, Magritt volunteered to call Harland and Caleb. I don't like to argue with people who hold all the cards.

CHAPTER NINETEEN

"CHOOSE YOUR WORD, LARRY," Paul exclaimed over his cell phone. "Serendipity, kismet, luck, fate . . . any one of them is fitting. I just picked up a copy of *The Times* from the floor of the cab I'm riding in, the English *Times*—we are stuck in a traffic jam—and lo and behold, an article on Elias Miller. Well, calling it an article is an overstatement, more of a filler or reference. But can you imagine, *The Times*, of all places."

"*The London Times*?" I echoed, with a question mark in my voice. "You're pulling my leg."

"Want me to read it to you?"

"Absolutely!"

New York's art scene has a new hero, according to a press release that has just landed on my desk, an artist who has the impudence to sign his paintings "Dante the Painter." "Only in America" is an appropriate reaction. We are told that he is being collected by people with knowledge and taste, the very same art aficionados who amass 19th-century French impressionists, Pre-Raphaelites, and modern masters like Lucian Freud and David Hockney. We will not have to wait long to discover the reason for their fascination. A study of his work is to be published early this winter by the Truth Foundation of New York City, a name just as audacious as Dante the Painter. Time of course will judge his substance, but for the moment, I expect that more than a few collectors have their curiosity piqued.

"Is that it?"

"That's it," Paul said.

"I wonder if the Foundation put out the press release. I can't think of any other source. Is there a byline?"

"Leslie Aberdeen. Maybe Magritt will recognize the name. I can't even identify the sex," Paul said, a lilt in his voice.

"Well, at least we know the monograph is going to be published, and soon. But the authors aren't mentioned."

"Not at all."

"But why London?"

"You may have to call Caleb to figure that one out."

I talked to Magritt rather than Caleb. She didn't know a Leslie Aberdeen, but she did know the critic from *The New York Times* whose article on Elias appeared two days later, and she had read reviews by the reporter at the *Chicago Tribune,* whose column about the newly discovered artist appeared the following week. Longer commentaries appeared in *The Village Voice* and *The Washington Post,* but none were as complete as an illustrated essay by Gabriel Dyson carried by *The New Yorker* magazine in late October.

Elias Miller is unfamiliar to most who spend their days writing about the art world. A devoted student of the classics, he spent his academic career teaching literature and philosophy in a rural Pennsylvania college. Two decades ago, Miller turned his talent and knowledge to painting. He has attracted only a handful of purchasers, but it is a sophisticated group, connoisseurs all, with addresses in Manhattan, the Hamptons, and Martha's Vineyard. A few of his works have found their way to London.

Elias Miller's anonymity is about to end. This November, The DeCamp-Firenzie Gallery on East 79th Street will exhibit fifty of

Miller's oil paintings, all of them illustrations of Dante's Divine
Comedy, *the medieval poem that has long fascinated painters. Dante
the Artist is the signature Miller applies to his canvases, an incredible
arrogance, you might think, but not after you have seen his work. The
quality of Miller's art may not match the sublime grace of Alighieri's
masterpiece, but his images come close.*

The review went on to exalt Dante the Painter's
skills ("a Renaissance virtuoso, an Impressionist master"),
his compositional visions ("he reminds this reviewer of
Tintoretto and Caravaggio"), and his creative imagination
("emulates his idol Dante Alighieri"). Two photographic
images accompanied the review: one of the lovers *Francesca
and Paolo* and the other a painting from Caleb Brewster's
collection that Magritt and I did not include in our manuscript,
Virgil and Medusa. "The aggressive imagery of *Virgil and
Medusa* reminded me of the best of German Expressionism,"
Dyson continued, "even if his method is totally Renaissance.
Francesca and Paolo could pass as a painting by Raphael."

Remarkable, I thought, to compare Dante to Raphael
and simultaneously connect him to "the best of German
Expressionism." Dyson had succumbed fully to the
promoters of Dante the Painter, I thought, until I read the
final paragraph.

*Art gallery exhibits normally open to a small gathering of the
faithful. Though running shoes are left at home, the dress is informal
and the crowds familiar. Wednesday's opening at The DeCamp-Firenzie
Gallery on East 79th in Manhattan will be different. It promises to be
a gala black-tie event, the women decked out in couturier's dresses with
pearl and diamond necklaces; the men costumed in tailor-made tuxes,
their limousines waiting quietly on Manhattan's side streets. The wine
will come from Tuscany and Piedmont, the canapés from Giorgione
Restorante. A strong representation of Italian art collectors and critics*

*is expected, as well as art experts whose columns run in the major
newspapers of New York, Paris, and London. There might even be a
television camera or two. The presence of dozens of multimillionaires is
guaranteed. If your chauffeur knows the way, you might want to attend.
If not, I would wait for a week or two. The exhibition will run until
the New Year.*

"They don't teach about the art market in graduate
school," Magritt said after putting down the magazine. "Some
first-rate publicist must be involved, and a number of people
with incredible connections to the media. I'd be surprised if
we don't hear about Dante on the evening news. And a solo
exhibit—I had wondered if that was in the works."

"So now we know," I spat out acerbically. "There will be
an opening exhibit, and it's five days away. At The DeCamp-
Firenzie Gallery—have you ever heard of it?"

"No, I've never heard of it, but I don't know many art
galleries, at least not commercial ones."

"Shit!" I shouted. I tried to think of something clever
to say, but all I could do was reveal my intense irritation.
"How much time do you need to get something into *The New
Yorker*?" I asked rhetorically. "A month at least, I'd expect?
Two or three, perhaps? It's not a newspaper. It doesn't
come together at an evening editorial board meeting. The
article must have been planned before we completed the
manuscript."

"Don't get paranoid on me, Larry. An article on the
current art market was most probably planned for long ago,
but written? I expect it was hammered out last week. Even
New Yorker reviews have to be timely."

"I am naïve about such things. I write my plays before
I try to get them produced. I wonder if Gabriel Dyson was
even shown a copy of our work."

Magritt placed her hand on my forearm and squeezed. "If I had given it any thought, I would have expected Harland to plan his publicity campaign even before he hired us. So would you. There must be a lot of money betting on Dante's manufactured celebrity. We were just hired help. We were only told what we had to know."

"And where is our invitation to the opening? Is it lost somewhere in Harland's desk?" I said, my voice heated.

Magritt raised a glass of bubbly water to her mouth before flashing a smile. "You only invite the servants to the ball if they're going to pick up the dishes or play in the band." Her eyes sparkled at me as she drank.

"And the book—will it ever be published, or has it ended up in a wastepaper basket?" I said, pushing my chair from the table and banging my fork against a plate.

Magritt drew back her shoulders and her eyes widened. Then she took a deep breath and gently smiled. "You're showing your age. They now use paper shredders, Larry."

If Hilla had said that, or my mother, or any of the women I had ever known, an expletive would have exploded from my mouth. If it had been Magritt three months before, I would have accused her of humoring me, of trying to parry my feelings with meaningless wit. Now, things were different. I could feel my eyes soften and my chest grow light. A good sex life allows you to bear the outrages of every day, I thought. But I knew it was more than a good sex life.

"You just won't let me go paranoid, will you?" I finally said.

"Not before we know all the facts. I don't want you to play with only half a deck."

I let out a cackle. "Half a deck, so that's what I'm playing with. Well, if I needed a reason to keep you around, keeping me from playing with half a deck would serve the purpose."

"'Keep me around.' What an expression," she said, and gave me a sour face.

I had to laugh.

"I am outraged, Larry, at not getting an invitation," Magritt continued. "That's the least they could do for us. I would have loved to get dressed up and see you in a tux. Maybe we should just crash the party. They're too sophisticated to throw us out."

"I don't like tuxes, and I don't want to be party to Dante's coming out extravaganza. He's too good an artist for that. His work is all that's necessary for celebrity."

"For a life-long New Yorker—and in show business, no less—you can be so naïve. Do you think Warhol would be Warhol without self-advertisement? Do you think Truman Capote would be half the giant he is without his self-promotion?"

"He was very short, and he's dead. So is Warhol."

"Larry," she said, her hand again on my arm, "it used to be ten percent talent and ninety percent work. Now it's five percent talent, forty percent work, and fifty percent advertisement."

"You lost five percent."

"That's for luck."

"I worry, Magritt. I don't know if Dante is ready to become a pop idol to the wealthy. I don't think he'll appreciate commercialization. He's very private."

"He is also resilient. You don't last for 700 years without having something."

We were in my mother's kitchen, finishing off the poached salmon and boiled potatoes I had brought from a local deli that specialized in take-out food for educated palates. I was dressed in my working uniform, ivory chinos and a gray sweatshirt, my large toe poking through a white cotton sock. Magritt had spent the afternoon interviewing for a part-time teaching position and was still wearing a dark blue skirt and an expensive linen blouse. A luxurious string of white pearls hung around her neck. When she had put it on earlier in the day, I had helped her with its clasp, wishing that the pearls had been a gift from me.

I pushed away from the table and began to get up.

"I'll do the dishes, and you call Dante," Magritt instructed in a firm and controlled voice. "I wonder if he's been invited."

I called my mother instead, but only Paul was at home.

"You didn't get an invitation?" he said, evidently surprised. "It's just a mistake, I'm sure. Why don't you come with Janet and me? We've been thinking of double-dating with you and Magritt. You might have a chance to sign copies of your book."

"I doubt they even published it," I snapped.

"What are you talking about, Larry? It will be available at the opening. Harland mentioned that to me when he called to invite me."

"Are you sure?"

"Harland wouldn't have lied about that. You really have been left out, haven't you?"

Just the mention of the monograph lifted my spirits. "By miles and miles," I said, but my voice had no stridency. "So we were published. Maybe I should rent a tux?"

I told Paul I would extend his invitation to Magritt, and we'd get back to him. Then I called Dante.

Beatrice answered. "Did you see the piece in *The New Yorker*?" she said excitedly. "What a wonderful review. I didn't expect anyone would be writing about the exhibit, but to have such a review—in *The New Yorker*, of all places—come out before it opens . . . it's wondrous. My heart is swelling."

Shit, I thought, what do I say now? Piss on her pleasure by telling her the article was part of a sophisticated advertising scheme, no more meaningful than a thirty-second television commercial and far less expensive? Should I tell her it was making a sham of Dante's work, that it did nothing but make him a toy for the privileged? How could I say that to Beatrice? "It's a nice piece," I ended up saying, lamely.

"Nice? It's wonderful. I couldn't have written a more glowing article—and every bit is deserved."

"It is a great review, and Dante deserves the recognition," I said, but I suspected that my voice was giving me away. "So you know about the opening?"

Beatrice paused before answering. "Of course we do. Harland Van Ness called last week to invite us. He even offered to send a limousine to Gettysburg for us, and we'll have its use in Manhattan. You and Magritt will be there, won't you?"

"We haven't been invited, Beatrice. We didn't even know of the exhibit until a few minutes ago when we read about it in *The New Yorker*."

"I should have called you," Beatrice said. "But I just assumed. There must have been a mix-up or an oversight. How could you not be invited?"

I wanted to caution her, to warn her that the gallery's ends were not necessarily hers, that the rich would fill Dante the Painter's pockets with the false gold of momentary fame. And once they had had their fun, and Caleb had made his money, they would drop Dante the Painter into second-rate auction houses.

An old thought caused me to bite my tongue: the abysmal knowledge that in modern society, commercialization might be the highest achievement, that providing the wealthy yet another opportunity to enrich themselves was the contemporary purpose of art, all of art—theater and movies, novels and poetry, painting and architecture. "The graduates of Harvard and Yale work for the upper class," an older playwright once told me after she'd had too many drinks and too many failures, "and the graduates of Williams and Hamilton work for them. And the graduates of the State University of New York and City University work for the graduates of Williams and Hamilton."

"And who do we work for?" I asked her, "we artists who pen characters late at night, who compose music, who draft paintings, who write essays for *The New Yorker*?"

She answered, "We convince ourselves that we work for ourselves, that we are driven by candor and beauty, when in truth it is only naked ambition. Our work only becomes known if someone can make money, if theater tickets can be sold, if our canvasses demand ever higher prices, if our books sell in vast multiples, if we can entertain the Pope and the Medici. Isn't that what satisfies our egos—money, commercialization? Haven't we become the people we poke fun at, the people we drag onto the stage to laugh at, the people who are driven by manna and not God?" With that, she took another drink.

"Are you still there?" I heard Beatrice say loudly over the phone.

"I'm sorry. Some random thoughts were just running through my mind. That's exactly what Magritt and I have been talking about," I continued, repeating in part what Beatrice had just said. "How could we not have been invited? But we weren't."

"You are now," she said proudly. "Harland told Dante that we could bring guests. In fact, he made a point of it when he spoke to me. 'It should be a fun evening for you and Elias,' he said. 'Bring some friends, a half-dozen, if you'd like—even more, if you want.' You and Magritt are the only people we are looking forward to seeing. We were certain you'd be there."

I resisted the offer. "We'd feel like party crashers, Beatrice."

"You'd be the opposite. There would not be a party without you. Dante will insist you come."

"I'll talk to Magritt."

"There's nothing to talk about. We'll have the driver go by your place, and we'll all arrive at the gallery together. If it weren't for you, none of this would be happening."

It took Magritt only a minute to get me to accept Beatrice's invitation. "They don't know the New York crowd," she argued. "Having friends by their side will make things easier and much more comfortable."

"They're more sophisticated than that," I suggested, sounding more like Magritt than myself.

"And with the possibility of reporters being around, and unexpected questions, we could be of use," my lover added.

Harland called the next day and apologized for getting to us so late. "Of course you're invited," he said. "What in the world would make you think otherwise?"

"Good," I said, wondering who had gotten to him.

CHAPTER TWENTY

A COLD FRONT broke over the city the night before the exhibit, and a driving rain gripped Manhattan throughout the day of the opening. Signal lights were disabled and traffic crawled. By the time the long, glimmering limousine arrived to pick us up, Beatrice and Elias were nervously playing with the buttons on their coats. They mustered as much good cheer as they could when Magritt slid into the back seat next to Beatrice and I said hello to the chauffeur before sitting next to him. I twisted my body toward the rear now and again and tried to put my hosts at ease by describing how bad things would be if it were snow and not rain. My impact was marginal. They were excited but weary, exalted yet nervous. Dante's laugh was subdued; Beatrice's smile restrained. Eventually, I turned toward the windshield and Magritt took over the conversation, telling them about the neighborhoods they were driving through, about the stores the car was crawling past. I sunk into my thoughts as I watched pedestrians struggle against the wind, their collars rolled up and their heads down. I was feeling less and less prepared for the exhibition. Dante was to be the star. I felt good about that. But didn't Magritt and I deserve better parts than that of belatedly invited guests and unnecessary spectators?

Weren't we the librettists and the impresarios, deserving of a little recognition and celebrity? When the limousine doors opened to let us out, I struggled to restrain such negative thoughts. I tucked my hand under Magritt's upper arm and pushed it against her breast. It made her laugh.

THE DECAMP-FIRENZIE GALLERY was carved into the first floor of a multi-storied brick-and-mortar townhouse, the latest link in a chain of occupiers who had repurposed the once-elegant Victorian home to their own uses. Plaster walls with narrow, painted moldings, all in antique white, had replaced the original wood-paneled interiors; the sensuous gas lamps that fought the darkness on the first floor of the mansion when it was built had been replaced by track lighting; the parquet floor once covered with oriental rugs was now hidden under an inch of wall-to-wall muted-color carpeting. Yet despite all the redesign and repurposing, the building was elegant. The graceful flow of rooms, the massive windows, and the height of the ceilings projected an enduring dignity. I will not succumb to fashion and caprice, the structure whispered.

The scent of wet wool hung lightly in the large foyer, where Dante and Beatrice received a numbered card from the young woman who had taken their coats. Magritt and I gave her our umbrella and outer garments. Dante clutched Beatrice's forearm. I took Magritt's elbow. We marched into the gallery's front room together.

"Do I look like an artist?" Dante asked Magritt.

"Better than Warhol," she answered.

"But not as good as Rembrandt?" he responded.

"You will be the most handsome man in the room,"

Beatrice told him, and tenderly covered the hand on her arm with her own.

He was not the best-dressed man. Scattered throughout the crowded and noisy room were handsome, middle-aged men who lifted weights and had first-rate tailors, who had their graying hair styled by artists of the comb and brush. The women wore dresses cut to their figures, their bodies lean and graceful, their shoes and evening bags complementing their outfits. A crumpled suit, an out-of-shape body, or a tasteless outfit was visible here and there, but they were the exceptions and only highlighted the exacting adornment of the others.

Dante looked uncomfortable in his tuxedo, a rather ancient garment with large lapels and an old-fashioned black cummerbund. His white shirt was turning golden. Beatrice, however, seemed perfectly at ease in a black dress that hung loosely on her matronly figure, a simple gold chain around her neck. The handsome tuxedo I had rented made me look sleek and athletic, but it was still inferior to my companion's outfit. Magritt had retrieved a custom-made dark blue satin sheath from her mother's apartment. As she weaved her way through the throng, its skirt clung to her shapely legs and emphasized her narrow hips; its shimmering bodice flattered her breasts. No one in the room was more attractive. She made me feel rich, even important. Silly, I told myself—but it wasn't.

Caleb and Sharon were nowhere to be seen, and neither were Jonathan Brewster or Roberta Whitford, but I hadn't expected them to attend. I spotted my mother and Paul examining one of the paintings at the far side of the room, their heads almost touching. Before I could squeeze through the crowd to reach them, Harland appeared in the doorway to the second parlor, waving an empty wine glass and looking around anxiously. When he finally spotted Dante, he broke into a smile and looked relieved.

"There you are!" he shouted over the clamor and rushed toward the artist. "I was worried that the traffic was going to hold you up. Everything is going magnificently. Many more people than we had hoped for, and all with a deep interest in your art. Just look around. See how they stand in front of your work; how they point to something and tell the person next to them. It's sensational. There are a few reporters in the back room ready to interview you, but look around first to see the installation. It's a first-rate job." Harland hesitated for a moment, and let out a light laugh. "But first I must introduce you. Everyone has been waiting. Let's go into the next room. There is more space there."

Harland wrestled Dante away from Beatrice, wrapped his arm around the painter's shoulders, and pushed him toward the inner parlor. Magritt and I followed closely behind. Once in what had at one time been the home's formal reception room, Harland picked up a fork from a canapé-laden table and clicked it against his wine glass. A neighboring couple followed suit, and before long, the discordant sounds of a dozen ringing glasses permeated the room. A handsome young couple who seemed to be chatting themselves up were the last to fall silent.

"Thank you," Harland began. "Thank you for coming tonight, for spending a few hours with us to see and appreciate the great work of Elias Miller, known to those of us who have long admired him as Dante the Painter. I am Harland Van Ness, the Executive Director of the Truth Foundation, and it is my honor to introduce you to him.

"Elias, the crowd is yours."

Dante didn't miss a beat. A shy smile appeared as he looked over the applauding crowd, and he began to nod in one direction and then the other as if acknowledging familiar faces. "Thank you for coming," I heard Dante say. "Thank you very much. It is humbling to have so many of you here."

"He looks like a politician," I said to Magritt, who was standing beside me and chewing on a large succulent shrimp.

She answered with a full mouth. "More like a professor. You look like you seriously regret the last thing you ate. Would it cost you something to smile?"

"I'm just worried, that's all."

Magritt began to choke on the shrimp. Her face turned pink as she struggled to cough up the stubborn crustacean.

Dante paused and looked in her direction. "Are you all right?" he called over, as people began to turn toward the commotion.

At that moment, her throat cleared and she spat the shrimp into a napkin. Still, I answered for her.

"You took her breath away, but she's recovering," I shouted.

Dante let out a boisterous laugh and waved at me. "Let me introduce my dearest friends: Magritt Cline, the cougher, and Laurence Sullivan, the humorist. They have spent the last few months working on a book about my work. It's a very good book, and if it weren't for modesty, I'd suggest you buy a copy. And let me introduce you to the person that has made all this possible, my wife Beatrice, who is the foundation of my work . . . except, of course, for Dante Alighieri."

Beatrice raised her hand like an obedient student and the crowd gave a round of applause.

"Let me talk a little about Dante Alighieri, the great medieval poet and arguably the most important literary giant of Western Civilization."

Harland moved quickly. "Much as I hate to interrupt

our guest of honor," he began, before turning toward Dante, "we are planning to invite you to talk in a short while, after people have had a chance to appreciate your art. We will be doing it in the next room. It will give the press some time to ask you questions. Is that all right with you?"

Dante was taken aback—the professor surprised to be silenced in front of his class—but then his face lit up and he said, "That would be perfect."

Magritt rose on her toes and spoke into my ear. "Now we know who's in charge, but Dante looks as if he is having a great time, Larry. I feel happy for him."

When Harland moved aside, Dante was besieged by a dozen flattering guests, smiles on their faces and adulation in their eyes, their mouths full of great praise. It reminded me of theater opening parties, the cast and sponsors cheering the author's late entrance, their eyes on him, their faces broad with merriment. I was becoming jealous, I realized, like a teenager whose girlfriend had just discovered his best friend. I wanted to share Dante's glory, to win recognition if only for holding his coattails. I deserved part of the evening. Weren't Magritt and I there first? Didn't we recognize his talent while the entire world was ignorant?

Magritt drove her elbow into my ribs to break me from my private thoughts, and together we walked Beatrice around the crowd that encircled Dante and made our way to the largest of the three gallery spaces. A long, highly polished walnut table was positioned three feet from the right wall. Numerous copies of *Dante the Painter* were stacked on top. Forgetting all sense of decorum, I quickly elbowed between the people in front of me, unexpectedly thrilled by the book's appearance. But before I could seize a copy, Sharon's voice rang out, Italian accent on full display. "Larry, I've been looking for you. When did you arrive?"

I looked up, annoyed at being delayed but surprisingly delighted to hear her cheerful voice.

"And Magritt—is she here as well?" Sharon continued, before I could say a word.

"She's somewhere in the room."

"Of course, I should have expected that. Let me introduce you to Robert DeCamp," she said, turning toward a clean-shaven man about my age. He was dressed like an ad in *Fashions of the Times*, a velvet-collared, tan tuxedo draped over his thin frame, the top button of his black shirt unbuttoned. A heavy gold chain hung around his neck, matching the cufflinks that glistened below the open jacket's sleeves.

Robert's braided black ponytail hardly moved when he lifted his head to study my face. He flashed a broad smile.

"You took the photographs for the book, didn't you?" I asked.

"Yes. It was a pleasant task. I hope you think I did credit to Dante's art."

"I haven't seen them. I was just going to pick up a copy of the book when Sharon called my name."

"Oh," Sharon said. She sounded surprised. "I thought you had been sent a copy."

"I didn't even get an invitation for this evening," I grumbled.

"Oh," she said, again using "oh" as a symbol of surprise. She was a better actor than I had thought.

"And the gallery, is it yours?" I asked Robert.

"And Sharon's."

"Sharon's?"

Sharon smiled demurely. "DeCamp-Firenzie," she whispered. "I'm the Firenzie."

My head shot back and I could feel my face flush. "Your maiden name?" I blurted out.

"My only name," she answered, with a hint of laughter.

"What happened to Mrs. Brewster?"

Robert sucked in his cheeks to keep from laughing.

Sharon looked over my shoulder and into the room. "It's getting crowded," she whispered. "Let's get together soon. It would be nice to have a chance to talk. In the meantime, enjoy the book."

Before I could say anything, she walked behind the table, picked up a copy of the book and handed it to me. "I think you will like it," she continued.

We briefly made eye contact and exchanged our mutual irritation.

"So there it is. Wow, I can't believe it." Magritt said, coming up behind me. "And Sharon—hello. I almost didn't notice you. I was so fixated on the book."

"I think you'll like it," Sharon said. She turned to find another guest.

Magritt took the volume from my hand and walked over to a corner of the room.

"She's dressed down for the evening—that simple dress; little jewelry. I thought she'd be dressed to kill," Magritt said as I joined her.

"She owns the place," I said, still flabbergasted.

Magritt looked at me suspiciously and began to giggle. "You're not serious, are you?"

"She's the Firenzie in DeCamp-Firenzie. And that was Robert DeCamp with her—the other half, and the person who took the photographs."

"And I imagine this place is another of Caleb's investments? He really is out to make money. He sells Madeline's collection and gets the gallery commission as well." Magritt examined the book's cover. No paper cover protected the classy hardback printing. Instead, the publisher had chosen a simple-but-elegant textured gray binding, relying on the embossed gold lettering of the title—on the front and the spine—to attract potential readers. *Dante the Painter*, it read, in an elegant script.

"So much for our cover suggestions," I said to Magritt.

"Shush," she responded, and turned to the title page.

Dante the Painter

The Art and Heart of Elias Miller

Preface by
Harland Van Ness

Introduction by
Sharon Firenzie

Text by
Magritt Cline and Laurence Sullivan

Hillel-Zaporah Press of New York and London, in association with
The DeCamp-Firenzie Gallery of Manhattan

"They at least spelled your name with au and not aw," Magritt commented.

"Turn the page," I insisted.

Van Ness's preface was a straightforward description of the Truth Foundation and a eulogy to Madeline Brewster. It told of her introduction to Elias Miller's paintings while she was a trustee of the college where he taught, and concluded with a touching personal description of Madeline as person, mother-in-law, and grandmother.

But whereas Van Ness's commentary was a pleasant

addition to the volume, Sharon's was competitive, and only narrowly avoided being an act of outright plagiarism by the clever use of paraphrasing and quotations. Drawing upon observations made by Magritt and me, as well as some quotations attributed to Elias Miller, she wrote about the previous illustrators of the *Commedia*, Miller's reasons for adding to the enormous catalog of existing graphics, and his personal addiction to the poetry of Dante Alighieri. Illustrating her remarks were the paintings Elias had selected to represent his predecessors, Eugene Delacroix's *Virgil and Dante* and William Blake's *Dante in the Empyrean, Drinking at the River of Light*.

Much of *Dante the Painter* was as Magritt and I had submitted it, our ideas untouched, our words unaltered, but there was one significant change. In our manuscript, an illustration of the painting being analyzed appeared on the preceding or subsequent page. In the published version, a final section of "plates" concluded the volume—fifty-five in total. After a quick glance, I knew that all of the paintings on our original list of thirty-six had found their way into the publication, and nineteen more. All were prominently displayed on the walls of The DeCamp-Firenzie Gallery. Even the paintings owned by Jonathan Brewster and Robby Whitford were exhibited, but with small not-for-sale signs appended.

"Fuck it," I said to Magritt. "No one will read the text. They'll just race to the last section and look over the paintings. That was just what we were trying to avoid."

"We structured our manuscript so readers would trip over our text as they ran to the illustrations. We couldn't guarantee it would be read," my lover said.

"Magritt, why are you defending them? Look at this shit. Sharon's introduction is redundant. It's nothing but an ego trip. She took our work and twisted it into a marketing pamphlet. How can you not be angry?"

My voice had risen loud enough to attract the people around us. "Shush," Magritt said. "If you want to fight let's at least do it in private. This is Dante's night."

"Don't shush me," I said, and grabbed the book out of her hand. The adolescent in me was prepared to smash it on the floor, but the deep disappointment in Magritt's eyes paralyzed me. I pushed the book back into her hands and quickly walked away, righteous indignation fueling my march through the crowded rooms and out the front door. Fuck it, I said to myself, and held my head up to feel the cold rain against my face.

My escape was incomplete. A young couple was sitting on the cement steps of the townhouse, finishing an argument that most probably had started hours before. He held an umbrella over her head, protecting her glistening hair and slender shoulders. His jacket was wet. I could only guess at their frustrations. Did she have a husband at home? Was she pregnant? Had he just taken a job in California, and was she reluctant to move? The young man finally noticed my presence, took his companion's hand and helped her up. Slowly, arm in arm, they began to walk down the dark street. As I watched them, pangs of jealousy added to my sense of injustice. I wanted Magritt to hold an umbrella over my head. I wanted her to take hold of my hand and help me carry my turmoil. I needed her unconditional love. I needed it to wash over me like the rain.

CHAPTER TWENTY-ONE

WHEN I FINALLY pulled myself together, my jacket damp and hair soaked, and returned to the exhibit, Dante was seated behind the wooden table signing copy after copy of *Dante the Artist*. He chatted briefly with each person who wanted to exchange a word or appeal for a personalized inscription. He laughed at passing comments, his skin vibrant, his eyes alive. "For my granddaughter," I heard a gray haired man say. "Her birthday is coming soon."

"Would you like me to include the date?" Dante responded. I imagined him writing, "Have a Joyous Birthday," on the title page.

Magritt and Beatrice were standing at the edge of the room, talking quietly to one another, their faces flushed by the uncomfortable warmth of the crowded gallery. From the distance, I mused about how similar they looked, how Beatrice's bright gray hair might once have been dark brunette, how her younger skin would have been colored like Magritt's, how the way she stood and held her head, her hands on her hips, her shoulders squared, mirrored Magritt, how their ankles enjoyed a shared, appealing shape. I felt lucky and proud. Perhaps we too would last for 700 years.

Out of the corner of her eye, Magritt noticed me

watching them and threw a broad welcome-back smile in my direction. Beatrice raised her arm far above the crowd and waved for me to come over. As I made my way toward them, profusely apologizing after stepping on an open-toed shoe, Sharon began to tap on a wine glass to quiet the crowd.

"I'm Sharon Firenzie, half of The DeCamp-Firenzie Gallery. The other half is Robert DeCamp," she said, and pointed over her shoulder to the man facing the wall behind her. Robert snapped his head around so quickly that his ponytail struck his ear. He threw a twenty-tooth smile to the congregation.

"I'm so pleased that all of you could get here this evening and share these wonderful hours with us. Until this evening, Elias Miller was known to only a handful of aficionados, and his work was seen only by people lucky enough to be invited into the homes and hearts of these virtuoso collectors. Tonight is his birthday as a public artist. I hope you have come to appreciate his art as much as I do, that you have been moved by his vision." Sharon paused long enough to let out a charming, light laugh. "But you don't want to hear from me; you want to hear from him. Let me introduce the artist to you, the painter who signs his work Dante the Painter—Professor Elias Miller."

The crowd, enthused by wine and art and camaraderie, mixed their lengthy applause with sounds of gaiety. Here and there, a few people moved toward the table while taking small notebooks and pens out of breast pockets and evening bags.

Dante's fingers crawled through his beard. He recognized the crowd's eagerness with a shy smile.

"I'm thrilled by your presence and your warm welcome. This is the first time my art has appeared in public, and I was afraid that you would look at it for a few minutes, clutch your stomachs, and race out to the peacefulness of New York City. You have stayed, and that warms my heart. Beatrice, my wife, predicted you would. I have long ago learned that she is always right . . . but I still doubted her.

"My paintings were born in the imagination of Dante Alighieri—images of fear and agony, of depthless suffering and eternal anguish. Images that have survived 700 years of human wondering, word pictures that have defined Western civilization's visions of Heaven, Hell, and Purgatory.

"Dante's quest was not to understand the afterlife. He was more interested in the here and now—*his* here and now, that is. But the plight of humanity in his time is not unfamiliar to our own age. How are we to live? How do you remain human in inhuman circumstances? I try to capture his answers in the faces I have drawn, in the complex compositions, in the countless struggles. The paintings of Hell project the how not. They are witness to unremitting moral deformity. Purgatory is far different. Those images are infused, or at least are meant to be infused, with the possibility of redemption—collectively they are a road map to redemption.

"But I have said more than I planned to. I just want to thank you for coming out on this rainy night, and for all your expressions of appreciation. They have warmed an old man's heart."

A woman in her middle thirties, wearing a simple black suit and holding a pad, called out, "Will you take some questions?"

"We hadn't planned to have a press conference," Sharon said. "We expected reporters to talk privately with Elias and me and other people who are interested in his art."

"I'd love to take some questions," Dante interrupted with alacrity.

The woman continued, "Do we need to be familiar with Dante Alighieri's poem to understand your art?"

Dante the Painter paused dramatically and looked at the questioner, a tender smile on his face. She did not smile. "I think the paintings speak for themselves, or at least that was my goal—each a complete emotional experience. But I do not know. The *Commedia* is so much a part of my life that everything I see is tinted by its verses; everything I read is read against its form, its content, its cadence. The more you know of the great poem, the more you will appreciate my work. Do you need the poem to guide you into the art, to hold your hand as you enter the frame and walk among the damned? I do not think so. Do you need to know the Bible to appreciate Titian or Michelangelo? Do you need to have mastered Greek mythology to see the beauty in a statue of Athena?"

"Do you think of yourself in terms of Titian and Michelangelo?" the woman asked, her eyes in wonderment.

"They are among my teachers," Dante answered, rubbing his beard.

A young man in an ill-fitting tuxedo put up his hand, but didn't wait to be recognized. "Do you believe in God?"

"You don't have to believe in God to appreciate descriptions of Heaven and Hell. Few of us know people who have gone there and reported back. All you need is to open your mind to other people's imaginations."

"That's not the question. I was just wondering if you believed in God."

"I don't think that is relevant," Dante said sweetly, again the professor answering a student.

The young man persisted. "It would tell us if you're a religious propagandist or just an illustrator of Dante."

"It wouldn't tell you anything of the kind," Dante shot

back. "I could believe in God and still not be a propagandist; I could be a non-believer and still be trying to sell you snake oil. My motives are not for review; my art is hanging here for your consideration. I hope you will find it good art."

"You're a great artist!" an older man shouted from the somewhere in the room. The gathering, which had grown uncomfortable with the young reporter's questions, began to clap.

When the applause died down, another reporter—a beautifully dressed young woman with long reddish hair—spoke in a quiet but assured voice. "We do appreciate your work, Professor Miller. You have mastered an enormous range of skills, from those of the Renaissance masters to those of the impressionists. I can't help but be overwhelmed. The paintings look like the work of multiple artists, each fully accomplished. I would like to write only about what I see, but I can't. My readers expect me to tell them about you, to get into your life and into your head. Whether or not you believe in the afterlife, in damnation and redemption, in heaven and God, has to be answered. We know that when Dante wrote *The Divine Comedy*, the Catholic Church was dominant and faith measured his life. He wrote what he believed. Have you painted these works because Dante has drawn you into his religious world, or did you decide on illustrating *The Divine Comedy* because you believe there is a growing market for contemporary religious paintings? Do you see a handsome market in the affluent religious right?"

Dante's face flushed and he began to look around for someone or something—Beatrice or Sharon or a large glass of wine.

My stomach knotted and I tried desperately to think of something to say to bring the questioning to an end.

"Is he prepared to handle this?" Paul whispered into my ear.

"I doubt it," I said, a little too loudly.

My mother, her trained voice in a stage whisper that could reach the back of the second balcony, took momentary command. "I didn't know the religious right collected art. I thought they only collected politicians."

A giggle ran through the audience. I wanted to turn around and hug her.

"Thank you," Dante said, and smiled at Janet, his eyes asking who she might be.

Sharon jumped in. "Perhaps we should hold the questions for later?" she said, her accent momentarily fading.

"No, no," Dante shouted. "I have to answer . . . but I could use a glass of wine."

"I'll get it," I called out without thinking, and eased myself toward the outer room where the serving staff was picking up. I took hold of a half-filled bottle of red wine and made my way to Dante. The crowd made a path for me.

"You don't have to do this," I whispered, handing Dante a filled glass.

"But I do," he answered. "What would I call dignity if I were silent?"

He emptied the glass and struggled to smile. "Don't you think it is rather presumptuous to assume what was in Dante's mind when he wrote the *Commedia*? He was at odds with the Pope. He felt sorrow for the Church. He believed that God's messengers had gone astray. They worshiped mammon. They lusted for power. That is in his poem. Do you think such beautiful words would enter a mind that was so blinded by faith that reason itself was outcast? Do you think the students at the universities in Bologna and Padua were mindless? Do you think my dear friend Giotto could have painted his frescoes without thought, without knowledge of the human condition?"

"Your friend Giotto?" the redheaded woman said, a hint of laughter in her voice.

Dante's eyes widened as he realized the impact of his words. "I slip now and then," he said in a low voice. "I've lived so long with the great poem. It has become part of me."

A fourth reporter, his dark brown beard almost as full as Dante's, his horn- rimmed glasses resting on the edge of his big nose, entered the exchange. In a remarkably judicious voice he asked, "Why did Dante write the *Comedy*? Wasn't it to instill fear of the afterworld into those who sinned? Wasn't he a soldier of the Church?"

For a moment, Dante looked perplexed, but then his expression warmed and he let out a rumbling laugh. "For twenty years, from the first raw envisioning to the completion of *Paradiso*, Dante struggled with the *Commedia*. If there ever was a single reason, it was lost in its creation, in the endless thoughts and visions that culminated in the poem. How many dreams do you have in twenty years? How many inspired spirits visit in the middle of the night or walk with you in the bright sun?"

Dante looked down at his hands and seemed surprised to see one rubbing the other. When he looked up again, he searched the assemblage for another question.

"Please go on," said the bearded man in a conversational tone. "It is most interesting."

"I'm afraid I'll bore you all to death if I keep talking about myself," Dante said, but there was more anxiety in his voice than sincerity.

Another reporter, her pearl-white evening gown fit for a bride, her notebook closed and the point of her pencil protruding through her short dark hair, moved closer to where Dante was standing. "Please, go on," she echoed in a sweet voice. "Please."

Dante turned around, much like an actor preparing to metamorphose from Jekyll to Hyde. He slowly poured the dark wine into his glass and took a sip. When he turned back to his audience, his face was relaxed, his eyes full of life.

Magritt took hold of my hand and squeezed it. "There is no way of protecting him, Larry," she whispered. "He has become the poet."

"Picture a man of forty—more than halfway through this mortal life—a tormented wanderer, empty of hope, dreamless and barren, longing desperately for the beauty of Florence, to walk its streets, to smell its cooking, to hear the sweet language of its people. A middle-aged man ever longing to hear the music of his native city, the sounds that had played in his ears since his birth. I leaked with anger. I burned for vengeance. I was frantic to get even, to torment my tormentors—cardinals and bishops, rulers and their sycophants. But how do you reap vengeance on the dominant? How do you undress the powerful? I had no faithful followers who could bang against the walls of the city until I was welcomed home. I had no army. I had no legion of wealthy who could pave with gold the road back to Florence. One possession I did have, one indestructible weapon, mightier than lightning and thunder: my poetry. How better to slaughter the small minds of Florence and Rome than to tower over them and reveal their shallowness? My goal was singular: to become greater than Virgil and Homer, to sing to the masses and to the ages in a voice stronger or more passionate than any heard before. I labored over the cantos of the *Inferno* year after year, writing in Italian, the language of the people, and not in Latin, the language of the Church. I spoke without fear. I called the contemporary Church the 'Harlot of Kings.' I prepared a seat in Hell for the living Pope. I carved a place for my beloved Beatrice in the Empyrean next to God. And throughout the nine circles of Hell, I sprinkled my enemies and the enemies of my family and damned them for all eternity."

You could have heard a pin drop. Not a breath, not a sigh, not a bored shuffling of a foot interrupted Dante's narrative. The reporters had put down their pens and stood mesmerized. Others, their mouths agape, stood motionless and gawked at the artist. Sharon was sitting behind the walnut table, holding her head up with her hands. DeCamp leaned against the wall behind Dante, playing with his braided ponytail, his face ashen.

Dante slowly lifted the half-filled glass to his mouth and drained it dry. He looked over his audience and read its faces, his eyes bright, his lips in a gentle smile, his skin glowing with pleasure. When he focused on Magritt and me, his smile broadened and he burst into thunderous laughter. He was having the time of his life.

"But that was the *Inferno*," Dante continued. "Most people never read beyond the *Inferno*. It is the most quoted portion of the *Commedia*. This has always saddened me— greatly—for I grew as a poet and as a man in the writing, and *Purgatorio* is much more sympathetic to sinners, more infused with humanity. I have tried in my paintings to give more life to the damned, but faithfulness to the poem kept me from going too far. When you look at my paintings of *Purgatorio*, I want you to see your face, to see your parents, to see your mayor and your president, to see your minister. For *Purgatorio* describes the world. It is located on the earth; it lies below the moon and the stars.

"My *Commedia* is the voyage of Everyman, not simply the

travels of Dante the Pilgrim. It depicts the trip all of us must make in life, journeying from the naïveté of Dante lost in the forest of midlife to the faith of Dante in *Paradiso*. In the *Inferno* I play second to Virgil; in *Purgatorio* I am the protagonist. In *Paradiso*, I become a man of infinite faith and love."

Someone to the side of the room must have said something funny, for a few people began to laugh. I watched Sharon study the crowd to discover the miscreant, her face filled with anger. In the back of the room, a male voice yelled out a woman's name and motioned with his fingers for her to join him.

Dante didn't notice the disruptions. He turned to pour more wine into his glass and then, facing his audience again, studied the uneasy congregation. "I've gone on much too long. I get carried away. But this night is about painting, not about poetry. If there are no more questions, I want to just thank you again for coming."

The woman in the simple black suit who had asked Dante if he were willing to take questions wasn't ready to have the evening end. "Please, Dante," she began in an ingratiating tone, "a few more questions. In your paintings, are you translating your poem into another language . . . or are you rewriting your earlier work?"

My God, I thought, imagining the articles that would appear in the next day's press. I was certain of only one thing: No reporter in this audience was going to concentrate on Elias Miller's art, on the imaginative beauty and horror of his work. That would be far too ordinary, too staid. In their frenzy to differentiate themselves from one another, fantasy would drive out journalism, and like members of every pack, the reporters and art critics would mimic each other in scripting amusing interviews with a long dead poet or smugly telling the tale of a mad painter who believes he is Dante Alighieri incarnate. Part of me laughed at the prospect, the part that detested Caleb and Harland and Sharon and DeCamp, the part of me that looked into their eyes and saw only dollar signs. But a larger part of me was frightened. Frightened by what this might do to Dante and Beatrice.

"Thank you, Professor Miller," I yelled out, "for being so free with your time. But we've already asked too much of you."

"Yes." Sharon jumped in, with her Italian accent intact. "The evening has grown late."

"No, no!" Dante shouted. "It is a very important question. I cannot let it go unanswered. I have not rewritten the *Commedia*; I have brought it back to the original. Before the words came the images, the slope of the landscape, the shape of the trees, the eyes of the leopard. I saw Medea floating over the City of Dis. I saw lust in the hearts of Francesca and Paolo. I looked upon Virgil's back as he led me out of the forbidding forest. The paintings preceded the poem. They are the first glimpses of the next world, visions untarnished by language."

Murmurs could be heard around the room. Nervous expressions exchanged by people who were struggling to discover if they were witnessing a charlatan or a madman, a stand-up comic or a mystic.

"And Heaven," the woman in the black suit continued, her voice as accepting and sweet as a disciple's. "Why have you not painted scenes of Paradise?"

"Or did they just not let you into Heaven?" a young man in a blue blazer chirped, a self-congratulatory tremor in his voice.

The young woman standing next to him gave out an appreciative laugh.

Dante's eyes darted from the reporter to the young man

and then back again. For a moment, he looked confused. Then a fearful shadow came over his face as the glory of the night twisted into calamity. He was naked before the heathen; he was the eccentric, the half-crazed bohemian, a marionette whose strings were being pulled by the soulless. He grabbed hold of his beard like a drowning man latching onto a rope and searched the faces of the crowd until he found Beatrice. He threw her a sweet but knowing smile, and, for a brief moment, I was hopeful that he would join the crowd and hug his beloved. Instead, he clenched his free hand, tightened his jaw, and fumbled for an answer.

"I tried to paint Heaven, but the paint dried and my brushes broke," he said in a weak voice.

A man standing in the back of the room laughed uncomfortably. Someone else nervously applauded.

Dante shook his head to clear his thinking. "My skills abandoned me. I could only illustrate the words of the poem. I could not recall the scenes. I did not remember the sights and sounds and smells of Heaven. *Paradiso* was written when the sun and planets moved around the earth, when the galaxy was fixed and all things had a purpose. Knowledge is different now."

"But that was also true for *Inferno* and *Purgatorio*. Everything that could be known was known in medieval thought," the young male reporter in the ill-fitting tuxedo snarled. "Are you saving pictures of Heaven in the hope of getting higher prices for them?"

Dante looked as if he had been hit across the bridge of his nose. His eyes widened; his bottom lip quivered. As he raised the glass to his mouth his hand trembled uncontrollably and red wine splattered over his yellowing white shirt. A nervous chuckle ran through the crowd.

"Beatrice," he yelled out. "Beatrice, are you here?"

CHAPTER TWENTY-TWO

AN OPPRESSIVE SILENCE filled the limousine on the ride back to the hotel. Dante sat next to the chauffeur like an archetype of sorrow, his shoulders rolled forward, his chin on his chest. Squeezed between Beatrice and Magritt in the back, I listened to the wipers brush the rain from the windshield, frantic to say something that would prevent our sinking further into melancholy. I mentioned the enthusiasm of the crowd, but no one picked up the theme. I talked about the quality of the paper and typography and cover of *Dante the Artist*, but Magritt placed her hand on my thigh and shook her head to quiet me.

When the black limousine pulled up to the hotel entrance, Magritt and I insisted on accompanying Dante and Beatrice up to the suite The DeCamp-Firenzie Gallery had provided for them. "Is mankind condemned to always be stupid, Laurence?" Dante asked, but didn't wait for an answer. He lurched into the bedroom and shut the door behind him.

"He's exhausted," Beatrice said feebly, as if her husband needed an excuse.

"He'll feel better in the morning," I said, unconvincingly.

"Perhaps," Beatrice whispered.

"If we can do anything," Magritt began, but Beatrice cut her short by echoing my words with even less conviction. "He will feel better in the morning. You will see."

THE INCESSANT RAIN had turned into a cold sprinkle by the time Magritt and I left the hotel. I clutched her elbow and together we made our way along the wet streets, our eyes on the pavement.

"They're the press. Did you expect them to act differently?" I remember saying.

"Dante and Beatrice deserve better than humiliation. How can you not bleed for them?"

"I do bleed for them, Magritt. Of course I bleed for them," I insisted, my voice loud, my words rapid.

Magritt didn't give any sign of hearing me. She turned away and strode briskly ahead of me. "We did nothing; we did nothing to protect them," she shouted toward the shadows in front of her. "All we did was watch their world fall apart. Voyeurs, that's what we were. Not friends, not companions. Just voyeurs."

"There was nothing we could do. Nothing," I argued.

Magritt stopped walking and turned to look me in the face. "Will they ever forgive us, Larry?" she asked, her voice full of tears.

At first she resisted as I pulled her body tight against mine, but then she let go and cried on my shoulder, her body pulsating against my chest.

Exhausted, we fell into bed partially dressed. I entered a light, dreamless sleep, but Magritt talked to herself in the blackness, uttering meaningless sentences and foreign sounds that brimmed with anger and menace. I slipped out of the bed and quietly left the room. Through the living room window, I stared at the dark shapes of the surrounding buildings, wishing that they would miraculously evaporate and allow me to see the world the way it looked from the lake in Gettysburg—the moon in the heavens, the stars piercing through a black sky, and the promise of a long, multicolored dawn. But the urban skyline narrowed the world and hid the horizon. I was filled with foreboding.

Without a sound, my lover appeared at my side. She leaned her head against my bicep.

"Is this a beginning or an end?" she asked, as if she had read my mind.

"Only birth and death offer such absolutes," I whispered, before kissing her hair.

"If only that were true," Magritt said.

MAGRITT CALLED THE HOTEL shortly after sunrise, but no one picked up the phone in Dante's room. I called after my second cup of coffee and was informed that the Millers had checked out.

"Could you please check again?" I asked the clerk, hoping she was wrong.

"They left their key on the front desk," she answered in a sweet voice. "I've already sent the cleaning crew."

"Please check again," I pleaded.

I listened to her put down the phone and dance her fingers over a computer keyboard.

"I'm sorry," the sweet voice said.

"So am I," I answered.

Toward evening, after leaving a message on Dante's

answering machine in Gettysburg, I called DeCamp-Firenzie. Robert, the braided ponytail, answered.

"A wild evening, wasn't it?" he said—after finally recognizing my name.

"That's one way of describing it. Is Sharon there?"

"Of course, busy as usual—but what a night. I can't wait to hear from the critics. I'm sure they got more than they expected."

"We all got more than we expected, and Dante got more than he deserved. Have you heard from him?"

"Not a peep. But I didn't expect to. Why do you ask?"

"I'd like to talk to Sharon."

Robert cupped the receiver with his hand, and I heard his muffled voice yell out, "Sharon, your playwright lover is on the phone. He sounds uptight."

The phrase "playwright lover" hit my head like a migraine. Had she no shame, no sense of dignity—playwright lover—why not bedroom conspirator, or just fucking idiot? My God, I thought, what have I done?

"Larry, what a delightful surprise. A great night, wasn't it?" Sharon said cheerfully. "I can picture every minute."

"Have you been drinking? A great night? I thought you'd be pulling your hair out. You certainly didn't predict . . ."

"Of course not. Who could have predicted we'd travel back to fourteenth century Italy? Does he do that often, Larry—flip out of reality? You've been working with him for months."

"He doesn't flip out of reality; he just brings a different consciousness to the present. There is a difference."

Sharon laughed at my interpretation of Dante's behavior. "There may be a difference between flipping out and bringing a different consciousness, but I doubt if many of my guests noticed it. They think he just went ape."

"Have you heard from him, Sharon?" I asked with an angry lilt in my voice.

"No. I expected him to call and say thank you. We did go out of our way to introduce him to the public."

"You made a fool out him, that's what you did. You embarrassed a wonderful human being. And you expect a thank you? For making him a clown?"

"For making him the talk of the town, that's what," she said, her accent intact. "After last night, they'll be lining up for his paintings."

"You must be smoking something, Sharon. The critics will broadcast his eccentricities and not his art."

"Eccentricities, is that what you call them? It's a little more than that, Mr. Sullivan," Sharon offered and let out a knowing laugh. "But the critics will declare him a mad genius, not simply an accomplished artist. Do you think Van Gogh would command the prices paid for his work if he had happily retired at forty-five and not gone mad and killed himself? Never. Elias Miller's stock doubled last night, my love. You can put money on that."

"And what's with Robert's, 'your playwright lover's on the phone' business? Did you two plot that as well?"

"You weren't part of the plot, Larry, although Robert and I did plan the promotion of Dante the Painter together. He's a little jealous, actually. I usually keep business and pleasure separate. You, however, were an appealing dalliance. It could have been more if you had half tried."

"A dalliance? My God, and you playing the celibate wife."

"Oh, that Caleb thing—it wasn't planned. You and Magritt just jumped to a conclusion about an old rich man with a young, money-hungry bride. How could I not go along? And it turned out to be useful as well as fun. You were very easy," Sharon said in a leisurely voice.

"So you're Patron, aren't you—you and Robert?"

"I was looking forward to having a chance to tell you in person, with a long drink in our hands. It's so impersonal when you confess your sins over the phone. It takes some of the fun out of it."

"Don't fuck me around, Sharon. You're enjoying the call. I can tell."

"You are being difficult, but I imagine we'll have to put off the drink. Let me tell you how it happened. Caleb dropped into the gallery one day, with one of Miller's paintings tucked under his arm. It was just a hit-or-miss thing. I had never met him and he had never heard of me. Caleb being Caleb wanted to know if Elias's painting had any commercial value. Very little, I told him, but after learning how many such paintings he owned and the other parts of the story, I convinced him that I could make Dante the Painter a celebrity and Caleb lots of money. He was dubious at first, but I worked him up. It didn't take long."

"I'm sure it didn't," I said snottily.

Sharon gave me an accented laugh. "Not that way, Larry. I have many convincing skills, but I guess I didn't give you a chance to learn that about me. A pity.

"Caleb likes to make money. He's greedy, just like me. So it was easy to get him to come along. Harland was a little more difficult, because of his wife, I suspect. You noticed she didn't come to the opening, and neither did her brother. Harland brought in the Truth Foundation, a useful coincidence, and the fact that Madeline had given Miller paintings to a number of rich friends put the icing on the cake. Elias Miller would become a celebrity. I could feel it in my bones. And The DeCamp-Firenzie Gallery was going to ride his wave. So there, the full story."

"And Dante? Did you ever think of what this might do to him?"

"Fame, if not fortune, is what I thought it would do. He no longer owned the paintings, but good things could come his way. How many artists can claim one foot in the contemporary world and the other in the Renaissance? And if I was right, and he decided to paint Paradise, he could become wealthy, too—selling through my gallery, of course."

"Of course. But you're wrong. There won't be a market. There won't be paintings of Heaven. There is just an unhappy painter whose life you ruined," I declared, and then added self-righteously, "Did you ever think that your sexual dalliance might hurt me?"

"Oh, Larry, how carried away you can get. Enough, though. I don't want to argue. Robert and I have potential buyers to bargain with. Give my best to Magritt, Larry," she concluded, artificial sweetness dripping from her voice.

"So, there you are," Magritt said from the far corner of the living room, looking pale and forlorn.

Her presence surprised me. I nervously tried to calculate when she might have come into the room and what she could have heard. I hid my discomfort as best I could, and said, "I don't know where we are, except that Sharon plays a much larger role in this charade than I expected. She is Patron, if anyone is. Can you imagine? Caleb's trophy wife—or so we thought—is the mastermind behind the elevation of Elias Miller. It makes me dizzy."

Magritt was expressionless, her eyes aimed at me but unfocused and vacant. I had become the father who had abandoned her by dying young, the horny boys who had slipped their hands under her bra, the men who'd never cared that she only offered sex. Take her into your arms, my body screamed. Beg forgiveness. Seek absolution. But I was afraid to take the risk, hoping upon hope that she hadn't magnified the words "playwright lover" or "dalliance," praying that she had not heard in my voice the sounds of an outraged ex-lover.

Magritt turned her back to me and walked slowly into the dining room. I followed quickly.

"I wouldn't put anything past Sharon. If she says she's Patron, she is Patron. Why not? Long legs don't lower your I.Q.," I continued, frantically filling my voice with innocence. "But why were we so off the mark thinking it was Harland, or Caleb?"

Magritt didn't answer. She walked into the bathroom and closed the door.

I wanted to shout: "You didn't hear what you thought you heard. I'm innocent of whatever you're thinking. We were never lovers. We were never even friends." But I froze in fear. Fear of sounding guilty. Fear of deepening the lie. Fear of an argument I couldn't endure to lose.

I stood outside the bathroom and talked through the door. "Sharon was happy with the evening. She was overjoyed by the way things went. She thinks Dante's slipping into the persona of the classical poet will only increase the interest in his art. 'Do you think Van Gogh's paintings would demand the prices they do if he had stayed sane and died a quiet death in his old age?' she said, or some such thing. Can you imagine? Tell the world Elias Miller is cracked and they'll beat a path to your gallery and make you lots of money. Mad artists demand higher prices than balanced ones, it seems."

Magritt turned on the faucet.

"I imagine she's right. It is an insane world," I continued.

"Most probably," Magritt said somberly, "she seems to

know her way around." Then she turned the spigot further and mumbled something inaudible.

"We should try to reach Dante again. They may not be picking up their messages," I said, trying to shift Magritt's thinking.

I sat on the couch, inwardly trembling, and waited for Magritt. When she finally came out, she picked up the phone and dialed Gettysburg. No one answered.

We avoided each other for most of the day. Magritt sat alone in the den thumbing through a copy of *Dante the Artist*. After watching some news broadcast, I left the apartment to buy a takeout Chinese dinner for us. On the way back, I bought a good bottle of white Burgundy and a dozen long-stemmed yellow roses.

Alcohol erased the tension, and we found ourselves laughing about the pretentiousness of the art opening and the glamour of a chauffeur-driven limousine. I volunteered to do the dishes, and Magritt, to my delight, slipped into the bedroom to put on a newly purchased, white, ruffle-bottomed silk chemise and a matching kimono-sleeve wrap. By the time I dried the last wine glass, a Bruce Springsteen recording from my mother's collection was playing, the volume turned down to protect the neighbors. I moved some furniture to make room and we danced on the living room rug.

Magritt reached for my hand and pressed it between her breasts, and then, pushing me away, slowly ran her tongue over her lips. "Do you think I'm as attractive as Sharon?" she asked, her forehead glistening with sweat.

"Much more so," I answered anxiously.

"I think so, too," she said. She put her arms around me and pressed me toward her.

We broke from Springsteen's driving tempo and did a slow foxtrot, my body pressed against Magritt's, my heart swollen by her presence, my flesh burning. Was this how she would dispose of Sharon—liquidating her with lingerie and sex? Was this how that chapter of my life was going to end? Or was that too much to ask for?

Magritt danced me into my bedroom, slipped slowly out of the kimono wrap, and turned off the light.

We made sex, but not love. Her body was distant, separate, controlled by private thoughts, by an impenetrable shield that imprisoned her and locked me out. "What's wrong?" I asked.

"Nothing," she said, and turned away from me.

When I awoke in the morning, Magritt was packing.

"What are you doing?" I cried while pulling the covers down.

"That's evident."

"This is ridiculous, Magritt. What's gotten into you?"

"Why couldn't you have told me the truth? It was weeks ago. Why couldn't you just say, 'I'm screwing Sharon'? Would it have killed you?"

"You were with Eric. I was alone. What does it matter now? I never saw her after you and I began making love."

"Did you think I was so shallow that you couldn't tell me the truth? Or did you want to get laid so much you didn't care what you told me?"

"She never meant anything to me. She was just a lay."

"And that's supposed to make me feel better?" Magritt hissed. "What else did you lie to me about?"

"Don't dump this shit on me," I protested. "If you want to get out, get out. Don't make it my fault. If you've had enough of me, just say so. But why did you put on that sexy nightgown; why the seduction?"

"So you'd remember what you threw away," she spit out defiantly. Then her face caved in and her voice became softer, almost tearful. "My body can't accept you, Larry. It doesn't want you anymore. My body knows the truth. I'm angry. I'm humiliated. I feel terribly used. It's just too much."

Her coat was on and she was clicking the lock on her suitcase. I was out of bed, pacing the floor of the bedroom, a blue sheet draped around my body. "Please, let's just sit for a while and talk. It's the whole thing that's got you upset— Dante and Beatrice, not knowing where they are, feeling we betrayed them. Just let's talk. We can't break apart like this. Not after all you've come to mean to me. I love you; can't you tell? I love you, Magritt. Doesn't that mean anything?"

"But I don't know if I love *you* anymore. And I have to know."

"You don't mean that," I said stupidly.

Magritt dropped the suitcase on the floor and sat down on the bed, her thin body twisted in pained introspection. "I hate Sharon; I hate Caleb and Harland. I'm afraid that I will begin to hate you. I need some space, Larry; I just need to get away for a while."

"But I can help you," I argued.

"Not anymore, Larry. Now I share you. I share you with someone I don't like. I see her red hair folding over your chest. I see her image in your eyes."

"And don't you think I can see you with Eric?"

"But I never lied to you about Eric."

"I thought you were out of reach when I was with Sharon."

"Don't lie to me, Larry, don't make it worse."

"It's not a lie."

"Then it's not a lie," Magritt said sarcastically. She rose quickly and lifted her suitcase. "I'll write and tell you where I am."

"You're being terribly unfair," I shouted at her back.

"I'm sorry," she whispered.

I listened as she closed the door behind her. I listened to her footsteps strike the tiled corridor floor. I listened to the elevator door close, my chest heavy with Magritt's misery. I flung myself into a chair and stared at the door she had just walked through, telling myself it was a brief romantic rupture, that it would be healed by a telephone call, a late-night dinner, a weekend of lovemaking near the lake at Gettysburg. I tried to convince myself that in a few minutes the elevator doors would open and her key would slip into the lock. That she would enter the apartment, her face in a deep frown, and in a grade school teacher's puffed-up voice say, "Taught you a lesson, didn't I? Let's not have any more Sharons. You can't afford to lose me." But the elevator didn't open; the lock remained fastened. I could feel the Devil's ice entomb me.

By afternoon, pride had vanished. I rang her apartment and explained to her mother that we had had a lover's quarrel.

"Magritt is not here," she told me.

Two hours later, I called again.

"Magritt is out," her mother told me coldly.

"When will she be back?"

"Not for a long time."

"Where did she go?"

"She told me not to tell you," her mother said. "But I don't know. She didn't tell me either. What happened between you? She was so happy."

I drove down to Gettysburg the next morning, fumbling with the radio receiver as stations came and faded away, trying to find broadcasts that would keep me from thinking too deeply, exhorting myself to keep my eyes on the road, to read the traffic, to speed ahead of my daydreams and fantasies. I imagined Magritt sitting next to me, her hand on my thigh. I thought of Dante in the backseat, talking about Giotto and Florence, of teaching in Padua, of scratching his quill over rutted paper as he dreamed of *Purgatorio*. I imagined finding all of them at the lake, Magritt and Beatrice and Dante, waiting for me, an uncorked bottle of wine in Dante's hand, a huge smile on Magritt's face. "What took you so long?" Magritt would ask. "I'm only twenty-nine, is that too long to find your love?" I would answer, and shyly smile. "I was only nine when I met Beatrice," Dante would announce, and he'd break out into a boisterous laugh.

No one appeared when I reached the lake. No one came to the door when I rang the Millers' bell. No one peeked through a window, or scurried along a wooden floor. I used my key to the guesthouse and carried my suitcase to the upstairs bedroom. I lay down on the gray blanket that covered the mattress and sunk into sadness. The next morning, I drove back to Manhattan.

Days passed before I told my mother that Magritt had moved out and she was free to come home.

"What stupid thing did you do?" she asked angrily.

"Why do you think it was me? Maybe it was Magritt who did something stupid. Maybe she just got tired of me."

"Then you wouldn't be inviting me to move in. You'd be thinking of a thousand ways to get her back," my mother said, without humor. "It will do you good to live alone, Larry. Maybe you'll learn the value of what you lost," she continued, the disappointment in her voice stabbing my ear.

She hung up quickly, without a goodbye, or a take care of yourself, or I love you.

CHAPTER TWENTY-THREE

PAUL KNOCKED ON the apartment door three hours after my mother had banged our telephone call to an end. An emissary from Janet, I thought, to offer me the empathy that she could not yet give herself.

He caught me on the edge of a drunk, my T-shirt spotted by spilled booze, an empty glass in my hand. A large-sized pizza was precariously balanced on his crooked right arm; his left hand squeezed the long neck of a single-malt Scotch. "You look worse than I thought you would," he declared before I could wave him in.

I grabbed the bottle of Scotch. Paul kept the pizza from falling to the floor.

"An odd menu," I suggested.

"Easy, easy," Paul said as I lurched back into the apartment, my balance more compromised than I had realized. "I didn't know what I'd find, a broken-hearted teenager in need of comfort food or an old man wanting to drink away his sorrows."

"An old man in need of another drink is the better description."

Paul laid the pizza on the table and took the bottle from me. He poured a single over ice for me and prepared himself a double neat. "Cheers," he said, and took a long fortifying swallow. When our eyes met over the tops of our glasses, he smiled nervously. Then he leaned his thin body against the refrigerator door and stared into the drink, his car coat unbuttoned, his maroon cashmere sweater looking thick and rich under the kitchen's fluorescent light.

"Did my mother put you up to this?"

"She is worried about you, but coming over was my idea. She thought you would want to be alone. I thought you would want to talk. You can prove her right by throwing me out."

"Oh, take your coat off and stay awhile. I could use some talk. But unless you're hungry, I'll save the pizza for breakfast."

"Actually, I wouldn't mind a slice. Your mother has me on a diet."

I laughed. How could I not? Paul ate like a starved football player and never gained an ounce.

My laughter woke me up. I realized how glad I was to see him.

It was a week since I had returned from Gettysburg. Nine days since Magritt had left—lost days, fogged by intemperate emotions, confused by conflicting and incendiary thoughts. At first, I tried to be nonchalant. I wrote in the morning. I caught an afternoon movie. I took in an off-Broadway show. But her absence grew heavy as the days passed. Alone and isolated, I began to drink in the mornings, outraged by the way she had treated me, her easy dismissal, her unrepentant unfairness. Shouldn't love be stronger than that, strong enough to withstand a partner's hiccup, an imperfection, a minor subterfuge? No, if there was any sham in our coupling, it was *her* duplicity, not mine. I was no more than Eric, no more than any man or boy who had rolled on her bed, who had tugged at her panties. In the afternoons, other thoughts would invade. Memories of the joy she brought, of the energy that filled me when she held my hand, when she whispered a nothing into my ear, when she laughed. By evening, I was inconsolable. I beat myself for not pleading for Magritt's mercy, for not telling her how much I needed her, how much I wanted her, believing—as only a playwright could—that protestations alone could mend the wound in her heart. We had known each other for only a short time, and yet, I felt that we had shared more of ourselves in those few months than Hilla and I had shared in five years. And dreamed many more dreams.

On the fifth day, I ransacked the apartment to exhume every trace of her. I scoured closets and cabinets and drawers. I crawled along the floor like a madman, searching under the couch, under the beds, under every chair and table, desperate to discover what she had left behind—a brush that still held remnants of her hair; pantyhose with a run down a leg, a comb, a sweater, the jeans that were a size too small. I stuffed them into a large black garbage bag, dropped it on the middle of the living room floor, and took another drink.

But what if she came back that night? What if she returned in the morning? How could I explain erasing every trace of her from my world? I panicked. I raided my drunken memory to recall where I had found each object. I struggled to return everything of hers to where it once had been. Then I rolled onto my bed and cried myself to sleep.

A week passed before I could admit to myself that Magritt was not coming back. Two more days had to pass before I could admit it to my mother.

Paul threw his coat over a kitchen chair and pulled down two large plates from a cherrywood cabinet, evidently more familiar with my mother's kitchen than I was. I put a large slice of the thin-crusted pizza on the plate he handed to me, thinking that, if nothing else, eating would allow me to drink more. We took the food and drink into the living room. Paul took his favorite chair and I sat on the couch, worried that he had prepared some syrupy musings about how I would get over it, or, "Don't worry, Magritt will come back," or, "I never thought the two of you were right for each other." In a strange way, I was almost looking forward to puerile advice, if only for the humor and impracticality of it all.

Paul was to deny me.

"When I first met your mother—how many years ago is it now, ten or eleven?—you were just going off to college, and she was playing a young beautiful widow in an Off-Broadway play that ran for only sixteen weeks. I was one of its overly expectant investors. The first of my forays into show business—but you know the story. Instantly, I knew that something unexpectedly precious had fallen into my life, something beautiful and irreplaceable. I worried that it would end as suddenly as it began, and as unpredictably. A younger lover would appear—someone handsome, with humor, with glamour—and I would find myself lost and bereft. That's how I felt when you introduced Magritt—not that she would find someone better, never that—but that someone precious had fallen into your life, someone unexpected. I was happy for you. So was your mother. But Janet worried that something would go wrong. I never expected that would happen."

"My mother is usually right," I said with a bit of irony.

"Not completely, Laurence. Janet feared that you wouldn't realize how rare and valuable Magritt was and would let her go. I knew otherwise. You reminded me of when I met your mother, the way you looked at Magritt, the way you took her hand at the most unlikely moments—walking in the living room, eating at the dining table. But I was over fifty when I met your mother and much older than she was. She didn't have to worry about me in the same way Magritt must have worried about you."

I tried to lighten the mood. "So you think I have to wait another twenty years, give or take a few, to find my Beatrice?"

"Beatrice?"

"I'm still reading Dante."

"Beatrice . . . of course," Paul chuckled.

"Can I fill your drink?" I asked, noticing his was empty.

"Please. Playing father-knows-best does not come to me easily."

"I don't know. You do a rather good job."

Paul's face reddened. He would make a terrible poker player, I thought. The color of his skin allowed no deception. It turned red with the slightest embarrassment, pink when he laughed, and pale white when he confronted a disturbing thought. That was why he was an honest businessman, I'd once decided. His physiology demanded it. I was wrong. It was the other way around. His face was a product of his being; it mirrored his nature.

When I returned to the living room, the glasses refilled, Paul was standing up and looking out a window.

"I wasn't saying you have another twenty years in which to find your Beatrice," he continued as if there had been no interruption in our conversation. He turned around and took his glass from me, raised it to his nose, and lowered it without drinking. "To Magritt," he said. And we clicked glasses.

"What were you trying to say, then—that I'll get over this and go on with my journey?"

"My grandfather used to say—"

"Your grandfather the tailor," I interrupted, worried he was about to tell me a fable I didn't want to hear.

"The wise tailor, the only grandfather I knew. He used

to say that there is only one purpose in life: to mend the hole in the world."

"Now there's a very heavy burden if ever I heard one."

"Indeed, Laurence, indeed, but the saving grace is that you don't have to do it alone. 'You can't mend the world alone, Paulie,' he would tell me, 'but neither can you abstain from doing the work.'"

"And I could have done it with Magritt; is that what you're telling me?"

He looked down at his shoes and fumbled for words. Someday I would have to tell him how much I loved him, but not as a father substitute—he had never been that—but as an older brother, as a dear friend, as a sensitive human being who had won my mother's heart and saved her from loneliness. He had taught Janet how to live comfortably in this world. Who could ask for more? Please don't die before my mother, I found myself thinking. What would she do without you? How would she find an anchor for her life? What a peculiar act, I immediately thought, to think of death at this moment. But that was what was in the room. With Magritt gone, with Beatrice and Dante disappeared, death was my companion. I felt as Dante must have when he found himself in that dark wood, that he had died before he had stopped living. He desperately needed a Virgil and a Beatrice—a philosopher and a lover—to lead him through the worlds to come so that he might glory in the world he had. Where were my Virgil and Beatrice? Had they abandoned me?

I turned away, afraid that Paul would read my mind, and retreated to the couch. Paul continued to stand, his eyes sad and his mouth tense. His skin was slowly losing its color.

"What was I trying to say? I don't know, really. I came over to see if I could comfort you, if you could use a little company to take your mind off things. Maybe that's what

I should tell you—that you'll get over her, that she was a growing experience, that you'll find someone more suitable. But that's not what I feel. I'd march down every street in the city to find Magritt; I'd rip up the sidewalk, I'd prowl the subways and crawl through the sewers, even if it took a hundred years."

"Or seven hundred," I said.

"Or seven hundred," Paul repeated, without knowing that I was thinking of Dante. "Although that's a very long time," he said with a laugh. "But she is worth it."

"Well, you clearly aren't making me feel better," I said.

"I'm sorry," he said. "But you wouldn't want me to be dishonest, would you?"

"A little bit might not hurt."

Paul burst into laughter and took a long drink.

CHAPTER TWENTY-FOUR

SHARON WAS RIGHT. Manhattan's small, insular art world found Dante and the exhibit fascinating. Lengthy reviews appeared in *The New York Times*, *The Village Voice*, and *Newsday*. A select photograph or two of his work topped the columns, and observations like "brilliant," "inspired," "the best new artist I have seen in a decade," and "an artist to be remembered," sprinkled the articles. But the laudatory observations of Elias Miller's art were stifled by descriptions of the opening night, with questions about the artist's drift into the persona of Dante Alighieri: Was it mental instability or creative salesmanship? Was it self-promotion or self-eradication?

The debate wasn't contained to daily newspapers. Critics who publish in the many magazines that cater to the art world piled on, each stringing together clichés and canards in an attempt to say something original about insanity and the creative spirit. The captions were more interesting than the commentaries: "The Crazed Aroma of Oil Paints," "The Purgatory of Creation," "The Hell of Madness," "The Charlatan of the Underworld." They made me laugh.

"There doesn't seem to be an end to it," I said to my

mother, a plate of half-finished scrambled eggs in front of me, a cup of black coffee near at hand. I had called Janet early in the morning, hoping finally to bridge the gulf that had developed between us when Magritt left. Sounding delighted with my invitation to breakfast, she innocently suggested a little café that Magritt and I had frequented. We met there an hour later, I in a sports coat and neatly pressed slacks, she in a prim and proper dark suit, her blonde hair recently coiffed, her make-up so skillfully applied that it was barely noticeable. She looked beautiful.

Janet picked up her cup and drank just enough coffee to wash down the bite of English muffin she was allowing herself. Then she said, "I haven't been following the articles on Dante very closely, although I've skimmed a few. Dante has certainly given them something to write about, and I'm not thinking of his art. His behavior made him a hot topic. If he was a self-promoter, he'd be a genius."

"It was quite a scene," I chuckled, unable to keep the exhibition's absurdity from tickling my mind. "It would make a wonderful one act play—Elias's transformation into Alighieri, the audience's disbelief. But Dante's anything but a self-promoter, Mom. His eccentricity is genuine. I have to admit that sometimes I thought he was more than a little odd, but he's not mad. He doesn't beat his wife. He hasn't cut off his ear. He serves red wine, he laughs, he makes you feel good about yourself. What they're writing about him is unfair. Their readers are forced to choose between gifted charlatan and mad genius. Dante's neither. He's an artist."

Janet put down the coffee cup and looked over her rimless glasses. "So, you know what to do," she said, her voice certain and insistent.

"And what's that?"

"Write an article of your own, or maybe two or three. You know Dante and his work better than any of his critics. Say something. Your silence only adds to their authority."

"Oh, the idea has crossed my mind more than once. I'd like to set the record straight. But I'm a playwright, not a critic."

"You have a pen and you have a mind. You have something to say. And your work with Magritt—that wasn't playwriting. Yes, I think you would enjoy writing an article about Dante, and it would get you doing something," my mother said insistently. Janet's mouth grew tense and her eyes saddened. She inhaled before continuing, a clear sign that she was getting ready to say something she had prepared in advance, something that transcended the idea of an article. "Or are you planning to forget about all this, to push Dante out of your life or to put him into a notebook as a potential character for a play? Is that where Magritt has ended up, as a potential character for one of your plays?"

"That's unfair. You know that's not true. How could I possibly forget about Magritt or Dante?"

"So do something. Look for them, Larry. Get out of the apartment and look for them."

"I wouldn't know where to begin."

"Hire a detective. Put ads in *The New York Times*. Contact missing persons. There has to be something you can do."

I didn't have an easy answer, so I ate more egg and drank more coffee to excuse my silence. And I pouted until my mother's face softened.

"Forgive me, Larry. I worry about you. I liked Hilla. I even convinced myself that she was a permanent fixture in your life, but deep down I knew she was just helping you to grow up. But with Magritt . . . you were so different, so happy, so at ease with life. Now I'm afraid you'll never find anyone. That you will never settle down. I wonder if you had had a father . . ."

"Stop it, Mom. You were more parent than any child deserves. I love Magritt. I want her back."

"So look for her."

"I want her to look for me."

Frustration covered Janet's face. Her mouth tightened, and she looked down at her empty plate. "So there we are," was all she could bring herself to say.

"I didn't mean that, Mom. I really didn't. It just jumped out. The old me, I guess."

I turned my face away and began to look around the café. I nodded to a waitress I remembered; I smiled at another. I tried to remember the table where Magritt and I had sat the last time we had shared a meal in this restaurant, and struggled to remember what we had eaten, what feelings had fueled our conversation. A chill surged through my body. I wanted Magritt to mysteriously appear, to lean over the table and give my mother a kiss, to throw me a wink.

"Magritt and I used to come to this restaurant—breakfast on some weekdays, brunch most Sundays. It was our neighborhood escape."

"I'm sorry, Larry. I didn't realize."

"Don't be sorry. I should have come here before. I don't want to forget Magritt; I want to remember her. I haven't given up hope, although it might look that way."

"You do seem to have, Larry."

"Magritt didn't run away because of my fling with Sharon, she ran away because my deception seemed consistent with what she believed about men—that they cannot be relied upon, that the more you loved them the more likely they were to disappoint. Her father died when she was twelve. She has never forgiven him. How could he have abandoned her when she needed him most, when she loved him so deeply? And with every subsequent boyfriend who disappeared or she drove away, the truth of her childhood experience was driven home—love and abandonment are partners."

"You've lost me, Larry. What does that mean? That you've given up on her?"

"A part of me is afraid of finding Magritt, Mom. I'm afraid I'll hurt her again, that I don't understand enough about myself to give her the certainty she seeks, that I need to find a moral structure, something firm and lasting in myself, before I find her. I need to assure myself that I am solid and permanent. If I were to find and fail her . . . I don't want to put her through that hell again. I don't want to go through it."

"There is always risk," she said quietly.

"I know."

I broke from my thoughts and watched my mother lift her cup to her lips, her face cheerless.

"And how do you plan to find this enduring moral code?" she eventually asked, a drop of cynicism in her voice.

"Through my writing, Mom. I only seem to learn when I hit the keyboard and watch words accumulate on the screen. I'll write the article first and then, maybe, a play."

"It will take time."

"I don't want to rush."

My mother gave me a mothers-are-always-needed smile and pushed her glasses further up her nose. "Write the article, Larry. Paul can help get it placed. He has friends in publishing; he knows investors who know investors in publishing. Just get it written."

"I will."

INSTANT FAME: DANTE THE PAINTER was born that morning. Five days later, it was finished, ten thousand well-chosen words about the Truth Foundation, about Madeline Brewster's enthusiasm and her husband's chicanery, about the DeCamp-Firenzie Gallery's misuse of artistic genius, about the endless need of art markets to find new adorations, about the commercialization of taste. It took Paul almost no time to place my full piece in a journal he supported, *Connoisseurs and Collectors*, a bi-monthly publication religiously read by devotees of all things rare and beautiful.

Multiple bets on Dante's growing celebrity had been placed before my article came out. Three dozen Dante paintings were sold directly from the DeCamp-Firenzie exhibition and others had attracted interest. With each sale, the gallery raised its prices.

After my article, the word on the street had it that sales of Miller's work stalled—at least for a while—and a few critics began to raise some doubt about his art and the future monetary value of his paintings. "Did the art world succumb to gloss?" one observer wrote, and answered with a resounding "yes." Another was more thoughtful, "We may have saluted Dante the Painter too rapidly, surrendering the time needed to properly reflect upon his accomplishments. Let us not recreate that act and dismiss him reflexively, simply because people conspired to make money on his talents."

I relished my publication. I frolicked in the idea that DeCamp and Firenzie's clients might be having second thoughts, that Sharon was forced to explain once again why Dante the Painter was worth collecting. That she might be twisting in the breeze.

If I had any second thoughts about the writing, they were buried deep in my subconscious until the night Magritt's image floated slowly to the foot of the bed we had once shared. She was swinging a rolled-up copy of *Connoisseurs and Collectors* like a battle-axe.

"Did you ever think of what this might do to Dante?" she chastised. "Didn't you realize that condemning the charlatans would also humiliate him; that readers might think him second-rate, an artist whose fame rested on imposture, on connivance? You didn't, did you? You didn't think at all. Or you didn't care. Is that it? You just don't care about Dante or Beatrice. Or me."

"I love you," I shouted and reached out to grab her.

"What does that have to do with it?"

"I was very careful, Magritt. I wrote about his talents; I said he would have achieved fame without DeCamp-Firenzie, without reporters, without interviews. I would never do anything that would hurt him."

"Words, words, that's all I hear. Vanity, that's what did it. You'd do anything to beat up Sharon, to get your name into print."

I jumped from my bed and began to approach her, proclaiming my innocence, protesting her injustice, but the space between us grew and grew until she faded away. "I love you," I whispered when she was gone.

I called Gettysburg the next day to apologize to Dante, to tell him I meant no harm, to say I should have showed the article to him before it was published and that I would have torn it up if he thought it destructive. No one answered. Not even an answering machine took my call.

Three weeks later, I heard from Magritt for the first time since she had fled Manhattan. An envelope addressed by her hand arrived from France. My heart soared as I turned it over. I ran my fingers over the white paper. I lifted it up and inhaled her familiar delicate perfume. Then I rummaged through my desk to find the thinnest paper cutter I had to avoid any unnecessary tear, fearful that I might rip through a paragraph or cut out a word. A black and white photograph of Auguste Rodin's *The Kiss* appeared on the note card's cover—a sculpture of unrelieved sexuality.

Nice job, Magritt wrote. *You impaled the bastards and anointed Dante. I hope he gets a chance to read it. Did you know that* The Kiss—*the sculpture is far better than its picture—was originally named* Paolo and Francesca? *Understandable, since it was designed as part of Rodin's* Gates of Hell, *a work inspired by the* Commedia. *Rodin, it seems, dropped it from his monumental sculpture at some early date. Unlike Dante, he didn't think something as pleasurable as a passionate kiss belonged in Hell. He was wrong. I wish I had known this tidbit about Rodin when we were writing. It would have made a great footnote.*

No return address appeared on the envelope or in the card.

I closed her note and studied the image on its cover. Francesca's breasts press against Paolo's muscled chest. His large hand rests comfortably on her naked hip. Their lips are united for eternity.

I left the card on top of my bedroom bureau as if I needed a reminder of what I had lost.

The first of Dante's letters arrived a week later.

My dear friend,

Magritt has shared your article with me. Beatrice discovered her sitting on the steps of the Uffizi Gallery, eating an almond biscotti and drinking coffee from a paper cup. "I knew you would find me, if I waited long enough," Magritt said. "And how long would that have been?" I asked Magritt after Beatrice brought her to our apartment for dinner. "Long enough," she said. "But how did you know where we were?" I pressed, thinking she would tell me she had a mystical dream or a spiritual visit. "Where else would you be other than in Florence, and where in Florence would I be most likely to find you?" Magritt answered and laughed. "It's a perfect place for an art historian to meet her friends, the steps to the Uffizi."

She told me she was staying somewhere near Paris, but that she would be moving on soon. To where, she wasn't certain. I asked her to keep in touch, but she only nodded and made no commitment. I cannot tell you how sorry I was to hear that you had broken apart. She didn't want to talk about it, but her eyes moistened when she mentioned your name. It broke our hearts. Whatever you did to her, she deserved better.

He signed the letter, *Elias Miller*, just in case I had forgotten. On the envelope, the return address read *Dante Alighieri, Florence, Italy.*

Why me? Why is it always the man who is blamed for uncaring acts? A humanist should know better. And what was he trying to tell me by providing so fanciful an address? That I shouldn't bother to write back because he didn't care to read it? I put his letter aside, angry and disappointed. He of all people should know better, I told myself.

But even the futility of addressing a letter to Dante Alighieri didn't prevent me from writing a response. I wrote about Magritt in a matter-of-fact way and tenderly accused him of assuming that the love he and Beatrice had built over a lifetime was the same love Magritt and I had shared. I felt compelled to explain my affair with Sharon, to inform him of Magritt's disappointment in me, to assure him of my sense of loss and abandonment. I wrote on my mother's powder blue stationery, addressed the envelope to the great poet and his beloved city, and prepared to send it—an act of finality— never expecting him to get it. Whoever heard of addressing a letter to Dante Alighieri, Florence, Italy? But before leaving the apartment house to send off my confession, I

opened my mother's mailbox. There was another letter from
Dante.

> *My dear friend,*
> *As to your article, it was fun to read, and I appreciate all the good*
> *words you anoint me with, particularly the undeserved ones. You are far*
> *too loyal a student, my dear friend. Harland, and Caleb, Sharon and*
> *DeCamp are not worthy of your odium. They don't warrant so large*
> *a portion of your penmanship. I spent too much ink on my enemies,*
> *too many bowel movements, too many diseased moments full of outrage,*
> *of contempt, of loathing. I should have written less about them and*
> *more about Beatrice. I should have described sunsets and told of my*
> *neighbor's house and the way he frowned at his lazy children. I should*
> *have written more about Giotto, and talked more to Virgil about* The
> Aeneid, *and more to Saint Augustine about* The Confessions. *Do*
> *not exhaust your energy on what you dislike; save most for what you*
> *love. Write about Magritt, Laurence, write about Gettysburg. Or was*
> *your love for them transitory, as Magritt seems to feel? I hope not.*
> *But enough of a lecture—on to other things. Beatrice is becoming*
> *Italian, speaking with her hands and swinging her hips. She is learning*
> *the language and has made friends with faculty from the university*
> *and curators at the Uffizi. She regularly invites them over to meet her*
> *husband, Elias Miller, but after a few glasses of red wine, they are*
> *talking to Alighieri—as you understand, I'm sure. It doesn't frighten*
> *them away. They are Italian, half-secular and twentieth century, half*
> *Renaissance, with a large portion of Roman mixed in.*
> *It is good to be back in Florence, even if I spend a good portion*
> *of my time dodging motor scooters. They sound awful and smell worse.*
> *But I miss Gettysburg and my soldiers, and, of course, Magritt. I*
> *expected that you would have married, or made some other lasting*
> *accommodation, and once I dreamed that she was pregnant, with twins.*
> *You would name the boy Dante and the girl Beatrice. Now I know*
> *differently, and it breaks my heart.*

Beatrice sends her love, although there is a scowl on her face.
By the way, if you care to write to me, or better yet, send a copy of
your latest work, just address it to Dante Alighieri, Florence, Italy. It
will get to me. Beatrice has befriended people at the postal service as well.

This time the letter was signed *Dante Alighieri.*
I reopened the blue envelope and added promises to my
letter. I would spend less time thinking of the harm that had
been done to him, to Beatrice, to me, and more time trying
to understand the good moments of the past year. I would
never forget Magritt. I would love her always.

Three weeks later, a manila envelope arrived from
Italy. Inside were three eight-by-twelve-inch pieces of paper
pulled from an artist's sketchbook. Two were drawings: one
of *Giotto's Magnificent Tower,* as Dante noted, the other of a
young beautiful girl selling flowers, *Within Sight of the Duomo,*
Dante titled it, referring, I knew, to the dome of the Cathedral
Santa Maria del Fiore that dominates the city of Florence.

On page three, a letter began.

My dear friend,
They call my poem La Divina Commedia. *I'd rather they just*
called it the Commedia *and read it. Few people do, I'm afraid, and*
then it's usually to please an elderly professor who believes the classics
can structure the mind. Students and their professors think of the
Commedia *solely as an imaginative journey to the other side. They*
cannot conceive of a time when people as wise as them searched the forest
where the three beasts of Hades blocked my path into the underworld.
They believe the past is full of strangers who used a different calculus to
understand the world. They do not believe a supernatural force makes
us walk upright, leads us to justice, and brings purpose to our lives.
Perhaps they are right, but I cannot believe it. They know only now.

And yet, I am not filled with sorrow. I am challenged anew to
understand all that I once was certain I knew. I am doing what I have

long put off, sketching visions of Heaven. I draw early in the morning and study my work in the afternoon. By the time the sun falls, my drawings fail my revelations, so I throw them away, only to wake the next morning to sketch again, often replicating the same scene I sketched the day before, sometimes creating something new. I find it frightening, this passion of mine to reinvent Paradiso. Beatrice thinks it is about time.

I hope you are back to your writing—splendid writing, of course. Beatrice and I await the arrival of your words. The world will be the poorer if you hide your pen, dear friend.

Dante Alighieri

The last paragraph of the letter kept me up that night. Just graciousness, I told myself more than once, but that was not what I truly thought, not what I wanted to believe. Dante Alighieri had asked to read my words, to hear my voice, to burrow into my mind.

I once again opened the *Commedia*, hoping that rereading it would stimulate my creativity and drive me to a mission. I raced through the *Inferno* and *Purgatorio*, but I spent days reading *Paradiso*, imagining now and again the paintings Alighieri's exquisite poetry might spawn. I saw Beatrice growing ever more beautiful as she and Dante ascend to the Empyrean. I imagined the Divine glory in the Circle of Jupiter, where souls spell out the Biblical injunction, "Love Justice, you who rule the earth." I dreamed of climbing the golden ladder, the traditional symbol of the contemplative life, that Dante discovers on Saturn.

But, once again, *Paradiso* proved beyond my knowledge of Christian theology and medieval imaginings. Too ethereal, I told myself, too removed from human experience to penetrate a secular mind. And yet, despite the opacity of his visions, the poet's mission thrilled me, to describe that which was hidden from the living, the essence of Heaven.

EARLY ONE AFTERNOON, Sharon called.

"An interesting article," she said, her voice pleasant but formal.

At first, I didn't know what she talking about. It had been months since *Instant Fame* had appeared in print.

"I thought you'd hate it," I finally said.

"I enjoyed reading it, Larry, two or three times. I even hand out copies. If you had condemned the art, that would have been different. But you praise Elias Miller's work. It's a great advertisement, particularly coming from someone who is so clearly critical of commerce. Oh, it will take time for the market to return, but when it does, prices will be higher than ever. If you had expected something else, I'm sorry."

"But not really."

She laughed lightly. It almost sounded spontaneous.

"Oh, I've had a few clients ask to return the paintings they bought. And I purchased them, full price. I'll hold them for a while, and then sell them for more. I'm certain of it. I even have evidence. That's why I'm calling. I have a client who is not just content with his purchase; he wants to commission Elias Miller to paint some scenes from Dante's *Paradise*. He's already selected the sections of the poem he's interested in. But I don't know how to get in touch with Elias. That's why I'm calling. Do you know how I can reach him? Robert has driven down to Gettysburg. They seem to have gone abroad, or somewhere."

"I doubt if it will be worth Dante's time."

"My client is willing to pay handsomely."

"Before or after you take your cut?"

"My God, you are a misanthropist. It will be a considerable amount, even after my cut. If Elias doesn't think it's enough, he can always turn it down."

"He's living in Florence," I said after considering not

telling her anything at all. It had to be Dante's choice. Why shouldn't he make out? He had paid for it. "You can address a letter to Dante Alighieri, Florence, Italy. It will get to him."

"You're pulling my leg, Larry. Really, do you want to deprive him of the money?"

"Just do as I say. He'll be polite enough to answer."

"Don't you have an e-mail address or a cell phone number? I hate to waste time."

I hung up, not expecting her to call again.

SHARON DIDN'T CALL, but Dante did. Startled awake by its shrill ring, I fumbled for the phone in the pitch-black bedroom, adrenalin fortifying me for something dreadful.

"I hear I've become famous," Dante shouted over the Atlantic, sounding as clear and firm as if he were standing three feet away—and not at all sober.

Relief, shock, and delight knocked the air out of me. Seconds passed before I could answer. "That's what I hear as well," I finally squeaked out.

"Then it must be true," he said, bursting with laughter.

"So word has gotten all the way to Florence."

"Just to me, Laurence. The Italians are still innocent of my fame. They think me an aging pensioner who sits on the banks of the Arno absorbing the glows and glories of life, a sketchpad on my lap, a pencil and a bottle of red wine within reach; an old man whose ever-faithful wife comes every evening to lead him home. But I'm not calling about me. Can you imagine, Laurence? Sharon called me—Sharon Firenzie. You do remember her, don't you?"

"It's a familiar name. Is she trying to seduce you?"

"She's desperate. But it won't work. Beatrice is not in a sharing mood."

"I expect not," I continued. "Women find it difficult to be generous."

Dante laughed so hard I thought he'd choke.

I continued. "You sound wonderful, just wonderful. It is so good to hear your voice. How are you and Beatrice—as perfect as ever?"

"We *are* wonderful, just wonderful, although we do miss our lake and you and Magritt. We are in touch, you know."

"You and Magritt?"

"She sends me a letter now and then. She sounds like she is marking time but not unhappily."

My adrenalin surged. "And her address?" I barked.

He paused, and I imagined his eyes closing, his fingers lost in his beard. "She moves around a lot. I don't know where to find her. It's a one-way conversation. But it's better than nothing. Does she do the same with you?"

"Only once, shortly after my article came out, and not long before you wrote."

"I'm sorry," Dante said.

"So am I, but that's not why you called. Sharon the siren is trying to seduce you; that's what you wanted to tell me."

Dante forced a constrained laugh. Being reminded of Magritt's absence had diluted his pleasure. I could think of no way to undo the damage.

"Sharon has had requests for paintings of *Paradiso*, commissioned pieces. She wanted to choose the scenes, but said she could be talked out of that. But it must come from *Paradiso*. People seem to be willing to pay a great deal for my work. What do you think?"

"You are good, Dante. We should have expected you'd

be sought after. And you wrote that you are working on *Paradiso*. The cards are falling in your favor."

"I'm not interested in the money. I have been painting my *Paradiso*, Laurence, translating sketches into vivid oil colors and complex forms. But I am frightened by what the world will think if I make the work public. Will I be thought a fake? Will it prove that I was just after a market and withheld work on *Paradiso* until the money was good?"

"Some will come to that conclusion. There is no way to prevent it. If you want to paint Heaven, paint."

Dante's laughter roared across the Atlantic at the speed of light. "It could do with a painting, my dear friend, a scrubbing, and a painting. Sharon's call affected me deeply. If my paintings satisfy, I will give them away to museums that promise not to hide them in their vaults, to universities that will hang them in their libraries, to hospitals and kindergarten classes. I'll give one to you."

I heard Dante take a long drink before he continued. A good Italian red wine, I knew. "I finally know what *Paradiso* looks like, Laurence. I can close my eyes and see it, as certain as when I feel the afternoon sun or hear the traffic on the *Via Faenza*. But I don't have to close my eyes, my friend. When they are open, I see it even more clearly. Are you laughing at me, Laurence? I may be drunk, but I'm still wise."

"I'm not laughing, Dante. I'm just listening."

"You'll tell me it's the acceptance of my art that has inspired me. Now that I know people appreciate my work, I'm ready to do more. But you would be wrong. It's not that people have voted for me with their money. It's that I know what I want to paint. I do."

"And what is it?"

"You will see. You will see."

"That's it? You get my interest up and tell me nothing?"

"And what are you writing about, ha? Tell me what you're up to."

"I'm writing about Heaven, that's what I'm doing."

Dante guffawed. When he caught his breath, he said, "Good. We will see which one of us is right. Would you like to say hello to Beatrice?"

How could I resist? "Your husband tells me he's illustrating *Paradiso*," I said after we had clumsily exchanged some pleasantries and begun to relax with one another.

"That's what he tells me. He wants me to pose in the nude. Can you imagine? In my best days, even my mother would not have seen me prancing in *Paradiso*. Where is Magritt when we need her?" she said.

My ear searched for a hint of blame, but all it heard was Beatrice's good cheer. "I wish I knew, Beatrice," I said sadly.

"I know you do," she answered.

SLEEP BECAME IMPOSSIBLE. Dante lurked in the room, his beard unruly, his gray hair uncombed. "So you plan to write about Heaven," he laughed. "What makes you think you know something about Heaven? Have you seen the Devil? Was your soul scrubbed in *Purgatorio*?"

I was too quarrelsome to let that pass. "I don't believe in them," I said with authority.

Dante didn't yield to my conviction. "Then how can you believe in Heaven?" he laughed.

"I don't need Hell to believe in Heaven," I argued.

Dante's eyes grew small, his lips tightened. "Prove it to me," he chided.

Dante followed me as I made my way out of bed and sleepily entered the den. He watched over my shoulder as

I turned on my computer and opened the word processor. And he let out a quiet laugh when I began to write this book and typed:

"You've got to admit it's more than a little nutty," my mother called from the kitchen. "You got a weirdo who masquerades as Dante, a mysterious multi-millionaire who wants to make your faux-Dante a celebrity artist, and a co-author you've never met with a peculiar first name. What was it, again?"

A message from Magritt arrived a few days later. Beatrice, I decided, had somehow convinced her to have a bit of mercy. It was written on notecard purchased at the Tate, on its face a facsimile of Dante Gabriel Rossetti's *Woman in Yellow*. She filled the blank page in a small meticulous hand, each letter finely crafted in calligraphic script. Her first line: "A great artist, but far from as great as our Dante."

I should write about a woman artist. Gwen John, perhaps? I could couple her with her brother Augustus, sibling rivalry and all that stuff. He was a celebrated artist by the age of twenty-five, while his sister was known almost exclusively for her love affair with Auguste Rodin, the French sculptor, a half-century her senior. (There must be something powerfully seductive about working with marble.) Time has turned the tables, and I don't mean that Augustus is now sleeping with Rodin, although Dante would know more about what is going on in the afterworld than I do. Gwen is, if belatedly, an internationally reputed artist while her brother's light has faded. It's a shame she's long dead; she would have enjoyed this, I suspect. I will highlight the feminist element—"Gwen John: Refutation and Redemption," I'll call it. How could my dissertation committee turn it down? They're all men and wouldn't have the nerve.

The following day the mail delivered a sketch by Dante of Michelangelo's *David*. It was a perfect representation except that David's penis was erect and large enough to satisfy a whale. I immediately recalled Magritt's comment about Rodin and thought she was right: There is something miraculous in marble.

"I don't think Beatrice would appreciate this," I wrote back.

"She laughed all the way to the post office," he replied a week later, under a quick sketch of Beatrice handing an envelope to a postman. "But I sent it to suggest the type of prop you might use in your next play."

Months later, another card from Magritt arrived, this one purchased at the National Gallery in London, an illustration of Francesco di Giorgio's *Saint Dorothy and the Infant Christ.* "Good, but I prefer our Dante," was how she began.

I need to fill you in, Larry. The Gwen John idea quickly bored. For the last few months, I've been writing about Lucian Freud—I love his work—but not with the stilted vocabulary of an art historian. I slip into the persona of his grandfather, Sigmund, and take a number of Lucian's major portraits—they're often bizarre images of overweight ugliness—lay them down on an old leather settee, and have Grandpapa analyze them like he would any patient. Elias Miller has clearly influenced me. What do you think my doctoral committee will think of that?

Be careful, Larry, you are closer to the villains of our drama than Dante or I. If they catch up to you, remember to duck. You've become important to me.

CHAPTER TWENTY-FIVE

WINTER CONTINUED. Short cold days, the sun disappearing early, the air filled with ice crystals. Words poured rapidly onto the computer screen, memories of Beatrice building a fire by the lake, of Dante breaking into infinite laughter, of Magritt rubbing a bar of soap between her breasts, dabbing perfume behind her ear, crushing the pillow in her lean muscular arms. Months filled with long nights, torturous and wonderful, full of sentences written and erased, words sought and lost, perfect expressions hiding from my fingertips, perfect descriptions eluding my imagination.

Spring came unbidden and unwanted, with dwindling nights and rainy days. The writing grew more difficult as fears of repetition and sophistry deadened my imagination. Then came summer, hot and humid, with songbirds and voices floating up from the city's streets. Early morning walks through Central Park were followed by hours at the computer. Late afternoons were spent slowly drinking coffee in an outdoor café and watching women in thin dresses rush back from work. At night, I would sit in a local bar, a half-drunk glass of beer on the counter, and read for the third or fourth time the pages I had just written.

When fall arrived, it was finished. Eight obsessive

months and the first draft of this book, *In the Shadow of Dante*, lay on the top of my desk; ninety thousand words calling for a second draft, and a third. But I put the unpolished manuscript in a large envelope and sent it to Italy.

"It's only a first draft," I wrote to Dante and Beatrice, "and can only benefit from your critical review. Don't hold back. I promise to forgive you." Then I waited impatiently to hear from them. Beatrice began to appear in my dreams to tell me that Dante was disappointed in my hagiography. "'He needs to be more critical,'" she quoted her husband as saying. "'I do not want fans, I want students. And, anyway, he should be writing more about the *Commedia*, about Florence, about God.'" I would become annoyed. "Why can't Dante speak for himself?" I'd say to Beatrice. She would answer, "He's too busy painting Heaven." Magritt, too, stole into my dreams, usually arriving at sunrise. She would sit on the edge of our bed, my writings on her lap, smiling now and then at some memory recalled, sometimes turning sad. "Good," she would whisper. "Good."

Dante's letter arrived toward the end of October.

My dear friend,

Beatrice has read your manuscript three times; I have read it only twice—but with great care. We had expected to see the script of a play, but you have put your trust in another form. The old professor in me popped out and your pages are covered with blue pencil. Beatrice's comments—she is far kinder than I am—are in red. But we are not going to send them to you. Not out of malice, Laurence, but out of deep respect. We both enjoyed the read and love the book. How could we not? It is about us. We are far from objective editors. But more important, it is your work, not ours. I have written of my travels—long ago—and now I tell my tale with paint and images. I do not want to taint your work with what I think you should be writing. Beatrice feels the same. But, Laurence, we do read your story differently. Beatrice thinks it a love poem to Magritt—women tend to be over-romantic. I think it is a travelogue, and although you have not ventured through Hell and Purgatory, you have peeked into Heaven. That is more than most men do.

> *Dante Alighieri*

A travelogue, a love letter to Magritt—I rolled their comments around in my mind to enjoy their resonance. Why not both? Isn't a love letter a travelogue, a journey followed, a beginning found?

"You sound unusually cheerful," my mother said over the telephone after inviting me to dine with her and Paul.

"I've been mulling over a letter from Dante. He thinks my novel is a travelogue. Beatrice thinks it a love letter to Magritt."

"So, why haven't you shared a copy with me? I can read, you know. And so can Paul."

"It's only a first draft, Mom. I'll be happy to have you read it."

"Humph," she said. "Well, I like the idea of a love letter to Magritt. That would be sweet."

"I wasn't trying to write something sweet."

"What are you writing about?"

"About life."

"That helps me a great deal," replied the skeptic. "I hope it's not one of those disguised memoirs about an unhappy childhood and a cruel, insensitive mother."

"I describe you as a most wonderful and beautiful mother."

"Humph," she murmured again.

IN THE MIDDLE of November, a sober Elias Miller called. It was 4:00 a.m. and I was fast asleep.

"Have you got plans for Thanksgiving?" he yelled out to make sure his voice crossed the Atlantic.

"What time is it there?" I asked, and shook myself awake.

"Early in the morning. The sun is up and the coffee made. What are you doing for Thanksgiving? Entertaining your mother?"

"Why, are you planning a feast?"

"Beatrice and I have been thinking about it, but only if we can convince you to come."

"Are you joking? Italy may be a long way off, but if you give me your address and I can find my passport, I'll be packed in an hour. I'll even bring the wine," I said excitedly.

"What a terrible thought. I'll choose the wine, Laurence, and Beatrice will stuff the bird. All you need to bring is your appetite."

"You're not pulling my leg, are you?" I said, fearful that I was in the middle of a dream that I frantically wanted to be true.

"Is this what happens to writers, their heads swell so large they can't bring themselves to accept a simple invitation? You sent me your rendition of Heaven. I want to show you mine. Brilliant paintings; you'll see."

"And where should I show up?"

"In Gettysburg."

"Gettysburg?"

"I think we have an echo. You do remember Gettysburg, don't you?"

I made a pot of coffee and sat in Paul's chair waiting for the sun to come up. Then I called my mother.

"Take the car. I've just put on snow tires," she said, after

I told her my plans for Thanksgiving had changed. "And fill it with flowers and candy. Tell Dante we love his art and we love him. Give him a kiss for me."

I kept to the passing lane, speeding by countless family-filled cars racing to the holiday. I played with the radio. I studied the dashboard clock. I cursed the long lines at the tollbooths. But now and then, when recollections of my friends overwhelmed me, I'd slow down to soak in the beauty of the snow-covered countryside. I longed for Magritt. I worried that my memories of the house and the lake would turn painful in her absence. And then I'd speed up again and tell myself that life is good.

Smoke was billowing out of the chimney when I arrived and the cold mountain air bit my face.

"My God, it is you!" Dante roared as he walked across the frozen snow, his head covered with a Russian-style fur hat, his aged sheepskin coat open. "And the flowers, did you leave any for anyone else?"

He wrapped his arms around me and squeezed the breath out of my lungs.

Beatrice stood in the open door. "Hurry," she yelled, "or we'll all freeze."

Dante's laugh rang like music as he took the suitcase from my trunk and the brown bag filled with boxes of candy.

Beatrice treated me like a prodigal son, hugging and kissing me, then hugging me again, acting as if I were the runaway son and she the prayerful mother waiting longingly at home for my return. She grabbed the flowers from my hand and pushed her nose into them.

"Enough, enough!" Dante shouted. "That's not something to do in front of your old husband, kiss someone else's flowers. Come, Laurence, come, you must see my art. Come into the living room. It is *Paradiso.*"

"Let him at least take off his coat," Beatrice argued while pushing me toward the living room with her flower-filled fists.

"He will have time to take off his coat later," Dante argued.

Paintings flooded the walls and leaned against the furniture. Large compositions, full of subtle velvety colors, and the brilliant indirect light normally saved for great landscapes, for paintings of Venice and Florence, for studies of the great harbors of London and Istanbul. But Dante's spaces were filled with faces: children playing, men drinking in outdoor cafés, Magritt and Beatrice wading in the lake at Gettysburg. Everyday scenes: boys kicking a ball, teenage lovers holding hands outside a theater, a couple dancing at their wedding—her gown a bouquet of white flowing satin, the tails of his jacket moving with the music. His face is filled with love and expectation; hers is sadder, a bit of doubt and fear etches the corners of her smile. In another painting, an old woman is sitting on a park bench feeding pigeons, her face deeply creased, blue veins pressing against the skin of her hands. On a nearby bench, a person whose gender is hidden by a dusty newspaper blanket sleeps. In yet another portrait, a young man waits for an unemployment check. And in another, a bearded, middle-aged man, wearing a tattered military uniform, sits in a wheelchair, a tin dish on his lap; a young boy drops in some coins.

"What do you think?" Dante said.

"Magnificent," I answered. "And totally unexpected. Where are the illustrations of the *Commedia*? Are they still packed?"

"You know they are not. Heaven is all over the room. Remember at the end of *Paradiso*, Laurence, Pilgrim has a flash of intuition—an epiphany he cannot translate into words despite the greatness of his poetic skill. God did not drive Adam and Eve from Eden. He left the Garden, bewildered that his creations did not realize they were in Heaven. That is the meaning of the *Commedia*, Laurence, the magnificence that cannot be revealed by words: Eden grows in our soil, it thrives in our forests, it is built along the edges of our coasts. Heaven and Earth are a partnership. If you believe in a loving God, you cannot deny this. Would a loving God demand endless worship and self-flagellation before granting us Heaven? Would He demand we enter the grave before we find happiness? Heaven lives in my paintings. Life lives throughout the great poem, in *Inferno*, in *Purgatorio*, and in *Paradiso*."

"Perhaps," I said, too overwhelmed at that moment by the power of his work to talk rationally of God and Heaven.

"'Perhaps,'" Dante repeated, and broke into a thunderous laugh. "I talk of a great epiphany and all you can say is 'perhaps?'"

I walked closer to the painting that hung over the fireplace. "Tell me about this one," I said. The image was riveting. A man and a woman, their backs to the viewer, look upwards toward the plethora of stars that fill the night sky. A cylinder of gossamer light surrounds them, its circumference narrowing as it reaches to the heavens, its radiance growing ever more brilliant and luminous.

"I thought you'd like that one," Beatrice answered. "Dante found the subject in an ancient Chassidic tale. Each person, it is believed, emits a light that travels all the way to Heaven. When two souls come together in a predestined unity, one light, ever more brilliant than the previous two combined, warms God's Heaven. It is a very romantic painting. *Beatrice and Dante* is its title."

But I didn't see Beatrice and Dante in the painting. It

was Magritt, and I standing next to her. I smelled her thick black hair. I felt her arm tucked under mine. I imagined the fog of our breaths uniting in the cold midnight air.

"What do you think? Is it not a glorious love poem?" Beatrice asked.

Before I could answer, Dante broke the mood. "Do you hear a car?" he asked, and grabbed hold of his fur hat.

"Good," Beatrice said, "I was getting worried."

Dante, suddenly made young, raced to the front door, and Beatrice, as animated as her husband, moved to the back of the living room to look out on the driveway. I followed her, astonished by their sudden excitement.

In the dim light of dusk, I watched Magritt ease herself out of her car and reach into the back seat for her coat.

"Beautiful, isn't she?" Beatrice whispered before breaking away from me and making her way to the front of the house.

I stayed in the living room bracing myself, wondering if I should shake Magritt's hand, if I should give her a kiss on the cheek . . . if I dared to take her into my arms.

I could hear Dante take her coat; I heard Beatrice say, "He came about an hour ago."

Then she was there, her arms folded across a thick white Irish-knit sweater, a delicate smile playing on her lips.

Months of loneliness gave way and the primal emotions I had held in retreat by writing this memoir erupted. "You are beautiful," I began to say, but the word beautiful caught in my swelling throat, and I found myself burying my face in her shoulder, desperately trying not to embarrass myself. It was too late. A torrent of tears poured out and my body trembled in her arms.

"Shush," she whispered, "They're going to think you're not happy to see me."